# Decimation

# The Girl Who Survived

# RICHARD T. BURKE

## *Other books in the same series:*

Termination: The Boy Who Died
Annihilation: Origins and Endings

## *Other standalone books by Richard T. Burke:*

The Rage
The Colour of the Soul
Assassin's Web

# Decimation:
## The Girl Who Survived

**Richard. T. Burke**

Updated: March 2021

First Printing: 2017
ISBN: 9781542931649

www.rjne.uk

## For Mum and Dad

Thanks for everything

Even though the future seems far away, it is actually beginning right now.

Mattie Stepanek

## Monday 3rd January 2033

She sensed the contraction approaching like a breaker bearing down on a beach, and then it hit, engulfing her, crashing through in an implosion of bone and muscle. It seemed as if every sinew and tendon in her body was being stretched to its limit.

"Just try to relax," the midwife said, her voice muffled by the white surgical mask that hid the lower part of her face.

"You've got to be bloody jok—"

"Breathe, Antimone," the girl's mother interrupted, her face also partially covered by a mask. She brushed a stray strand of hair from her daughter's cheek.

The girl fought through the pain and forced herself to exhale through gritted teeth. Just when she thought she could bear it no longer, the tension eased as if somebody had loosened a band around her stomach. The white material covering her nose and mouth felt damp as it clung to her skin.

The midwife glanced at her watch. "That was three minutes. I think we need to get her to the operating theatre." She strode across the small white room and through the open door.

Antimone turned her head to the right and met the anxious gaze of her father. He clasped her hand between his own, and she realised her fingernails had been digging deep into the flesh of his palm. She smiled gratefully at him, and he gave a gentle squeeze in return. The harsh ceiling lights reflected from a tear forming in the corner of his eye.

"Don't worry, Dad, it'll be alright," she said although she knew it wouldn't.

"It's just so damn unfair," he began, but before he could continue, the midwife returned to the bedside.

"The porters are coming now, and they'll take you to the operating theatre. I know we've been over this before, but you know what'll happen next?"

Antimone stared out of the window at the dark clouds scudding across the pale grey expanse of the winter sky. This would be her last glimpse of the world outside. Her eyes slid across to a poster on the opposite wall. In the picture, three remarkably healthy-looking patients in hospital beds surrounded a cartoon representation of a sneezing man who seemed far more unwell than any of them. 'Always Wear a Facemask' read the caption beneath, followed by the text 'Germs Kill'.

The midwife raised her voice. "Antimone, you know what's going to happen next?"

"Yeah, yeah," Antimone snapped. "You're going to put me to sleep, cut me open and take the baby out. Oh, and I'm never going to wake up. Is that about right?"

A flicker of irritation crossed the midwife's face before she forced a tight-lipped smile. "We'll try to make you as comfortable as possible."

"They're only trying to help," the girl's mother said.

"Okay, I know," Antimone said. "I'm sorry."

The midwife stepped outside the small room, leaving the father, mother and daughter together, each counting down the seconds until the inevitable conclusion.

"We'll look after the baby as if... well, as if it were you," her mother said.

"I know you will," Antimone replied. "Just don't let him get anyone pregnant."

Her father made a sound that started as a laugh but turned into a sob.

A metallic clanking noise drew their eyes to the door. Two porters dressed in pale green overalls entered the room pushing a narrow hospital trolley. The midwife followed a couple of paces behind.

The taller of the two consulted a clipboard. "Are you Antimone?" he asked, pronouncing it An-tee-moan.

"It's Antimone," her father replied. "Like the metal."

The man stared at him blankly.

"An-tim-oh-nee," her father repeated, stressing each syllable.

"Nice name. Okay Antimone, if you could just pop yourself off the bed and onto this trolley, please."

Antimone made no attempt to move. The man turned to his colleague in confusion. "Is she...?"

The midwife intervened before he blundered further into the minefield he was laying for himself. "She's paralysed from the waist down, so you're going to have to help her."

The man's face turned a bright crimson colour as he consulted the clipboard once again. "I'm s-s-sorry."

The smaller man took charge. "You're her parents, right?"

Antimone's mother and father responded in unison.

"We'll put a sheet underneath her, then slide her over."

He manoeuvred the trolley alongside the bed and applied the brakes. Meanwhile, the midwife unfolded a sheet and laid it out, adjusting the girl's position until she lay on top of it. In one swift movement, they transferred

Antimone across. The taller man, his cheeks still glowing with embarrassment, removed the brakes and raised the sides.

"Another one's coming," Antimone said.

"Okay, we'll wait here until it passes, and then we'll move you," the midwife said. "Don't fight it, just let it come."

Within seconds, another contraction enveloped her. Her teeth ground together as she tried to ride the wave, her head thrown back. She groaned in agony. It was as if she was trapped in a machine that was testing the breaking point of the human body. Just as she felt she was about to snap, the pressure lessened.

"Jesus," she muttered. "What a way to die."

The midwife consulted her watch. "That was less than three minutes. We need to get her to that operating theatre quickly." She led the way as the two porters wheeled the trolley along a corridor interspersed with numbered doors every few metres. Her parents hurried behind. They turned two corners before arriving at a room labelled 'Operating Theatre 3.'

The midwife addressed Antimone's parents. "I'm afraid you're going to have to wait outside during the procedure. It's time to say goodbye now."

Antimone's mother bent over and hugged her daughter. "I love you so much."

"I know, Mum."

Her mother could no longer hide her tears as her father embraced Antimone one last time. "You know we both love you. We couldn't have wished for a better daughter."

"I love you too, Dad."

"You can watch through the viewing window if you want," the midwife said, leading Antimone's distraught parents away.

Antimone brushed the tears from her eyes with the back of her hand. Despite the presence of the two porters, she had never felt more alone in her life. They pushed the trolley on which she lay through a set of double swing doors. A woman wearing a dark blue operating theatre gown, a light blue hairnet and a white surgical mask separated from the other two doctors and crossed the room. She consulted the clipboard and smiled down at Antimone.

"I'll be putting you to sleep. We just need to get you ready for the surgeon."

The porters turned away, the taller of the two giving Antimone a self-conscious wave.

The anaesthetist positioned the trolley beside a rectangular platform covered in a green sheet and applied the brake. The two men halted their conversation, one moving to Antimone's head, the other to her feet. On the count of three, they transferred her to the operating table.

The woman removed Antimone's surgical mask. In its place, she slipped on a black mask connected to a beige-coloured box by a snaking corrugated pipe.

"Let's just pop this on. We'll let you know before we turn on the gas."

Antimone inhaled the smell of rubber and strained her senses to detect any change in the air hissing through the tube. The woman raised Antimone's hospital gown, exposing her distended abdomen.

A door to her left opened, and a man dressed in blue surgical attire entered backwards, his gloved hands extended in front of his body. He stopped by the operating table and peered down at Antimone through a pair of large, plastic-framed glasses.

"The name's Martin," he said. "I'll be the lead surgeon today. In a second, we'll put you to sleep, and this will all be over."

A surge of adrenaline made Antimone's heart beat faster as the full implication of his words sank home: over, as in dead. Her life was moments away from ending. Despite coming to terms with her predicament, now that the time had arrived it was all happening far too quickly. When her mother had given birth, it had been a joyful experience. Now pregnancy was a death sentence.

A faint hissing sound joined the beeping and humming of the assorted machines. Antimone's eyes darted across the room in panic, attempting to identify the source. She sensed dampness on her face and stared up at several evenly spaced, white, circular plastic boxes on the ceiling, each of them emitting a fine mist into the room.

"Nothing to worry about, just anti-bacterial spray," the surgeon said. "We need to keep everything germ-free in here."

The woman who had fitted the black mask moved back into Antimone's line of vision. "Right, we're going to put you to sleep. Start counting aloud backwards from ten."

"Ten, nine…"

*This isn't happening. I'll wake up in a second, and it'll all be a bad dream.*

"Eight, seven, six…"

A sickly-sweet scent invaded her nostrils. She experienced a brief sensation of nausea as her vision greyed out.

"Five."

Antimone sensed the approach of another contraction but was unconscious before it took hold.

***

One of the assistant doctors painted yellow-brown liquid across the lower part of Antimone's stomach. The surgeon peered down at the stained skin and nodded his approval.

"Cauterising scalpel please," he said, holding out a hand expectantly.

Grasping the instrument like a pen, he made a confident incision horizontally across her abdomen. Like a well-oiled machine, the surgeon lifted his hand away as the doctor swabbed away the small quantity of blood that welled from the cut.

"Spread the incision," the surgeon said, using his left hand to open the wound from his side of the operating table. On the opposite side, the doctor used a metal instrument to pull back the layers of skin and muscle and expose her uterus. In his other hand, he held a suction tube that hissed and gurgled as he inserted it inside the cut.

"Making the incision," the surgeon announced. With a steady stroke, he drew the scalpel towards him in a straight line.

"Okay, we're in. Let's bring the nipper into the world."

Both men used their hands to ease the baby's head out. Within seconds, they grasped a slippery, screaming bundle of life and handed it to the doctor who had been waiting patiently at the side.

"A boy," the man announced, although none of those present in the room paid any attention.

The surgeon waited until his assistant had clamped the umbilical cord, then severed it. The third man cleaned the baby and placed him in an incubator.

The anaesthetist looked up from the readout on her machine. "She's flat-lined."

The surgeon glanced up at the wall clock. "I see no point in attempting resuscitation. Call it at two forty-eight. There's nothing more we can do for her." He began the job of suturing the open wound.

The row of stitches extended across a quarter of the incision when a repetitive chiming sound filled the room. The doctor closest to the flashing terminal strode towards it. "I'll get it." He swept a hand across the front of the screen.

The image of a woman's head occupied the display. "Mr Martin and Dr Carlson are wanted in operating theatre one as soon as they're free," she announced. "Emergency C-section."

"It sounds like we're needed elsewhere, Dr Carlson," said the surgeon, addressing the anaesthetist. He turned to face the two male doctors. "One of you can finish up in here. The other can assist me next door." He strode away without waiting to see who volunteered to join him.

The two men stared at each other. "I'll sew her up," said the doctor who had assisted Martin during the procedure, "but it all just seems a bit pointless when the pathologist is only going to open her up again."

"I know what you mean," the other said, "but the dragon will fire you if you don't follow procedure. In any case, the girl's parents may still be watching through that window."

"Good point," the doctor said turning back to the lifeless body. "See you later. Have fun."

***

The blue-gowned medical staff departed, leaving Antimone's body lying on the operating table. The doctor hurriedly completed the stitching job before rushing away to his next call. The faint hum of the machines was the only sound in the room. A thin film of moisture from the inactive atomisers in the ceiling coated every surface.

A cough and then a low groan broke the stillness. The fingers of Antimone's left hand twitched. Her head moved first to one side and then to the other. She sucked in a lungful of air but couldn't seem to satisfy her body's unconscious craving for oxygen until finally she was forced to exhale and draw in another deep breath. Sensations crowded in on her as she began the painful return to full consciousness. The reek of the anti-bacterial spray filled her nostrils and stung her throat as she inhaled. She ran the fingertips of her right hand down her arm, the skin feeling cold and clammy. Instinctively, she brushed her hand against the outline of the bump that had been a feature of her body for the past few months, but snatched it away as she sensed the rough edge of the stitches through the thin hospital gown.

Slowly her thought processes ground into gear. She moved her elbows back and tried to raise her head, but the excruciating pain as she tightened her stomach muscles forced her to lie back. Once again, she probed the edges of the incision. *The baby's gone. Why am I still alive?*

In a rising panic, she inspected her surroundings.

"Help! Someone, please help me!" she croaked, her throat muscles still sore from the exertions of the labour.

She lay back, trying to goad her oxygen-starved brain into action. Her eyes scanned the deserted operating theatre. *They think I'm dead. It could be hours until somebody comes. I've got to get help.*

Steeling herself, she shifted her elbows backwards for a second time and raised her torso. She almost passed out from the jagged shards of pain ripping through her abdomen, but eventually manoeuvred herself to a sitting position. Spots of blood appeared on the front of the hospital gown where it touched against the rushed stitches. Using one arm to support her upright posture, Antimone used the other to slide her left leg until it was dangling over the edge. She paused for breath, allowing the agony to subside before repeating the process with the right leg. With excruciating slowness, she shuffled her body forwards. It was over a metre to the floor, far higher than she would have attempted under normal circumstances.

"Here goes," she muttered as she edged her bottom over the rim of the operating table. Her toes touched the ground, but as she passed the point of

6

no return, she couldn't stop her momentum and pitched forward. She tried to break her fall but still smacked her head on the white, plastic-coated floor.

For several minutes, she lay motionless, dazed by the blow. Finally, she moved her right hand and probed her forehead, which had borne the brunt of the impact.

"Christ, that hurts," she whispered.

Using her arms, she dragged herself across the floor, centimetre by centimetre, with frequent pauses for rest, until she found herself up against the door. A thin smear of blood trailed behind her. She attempted to push the door open with one arm but couldn't budge the heavy mechanism. She had no more luck when she used both hands. Rather than achieving the desired effect, she found herself pushing her own body backwards. In frustration, she rolled onto her back and closed her eyes. Within seconds, exhaustion overcame her, and she was asleep.

A sudden bumping against her head awakened her. Her brain struggled to make sense of her surroundings before she recalled where she was. Somebody was entering the operating theatre.

"Hang on," she croaked, "I'm trying to get out of the way."

The door stopped moving, and the sound of low voices filtered through. She shuffled her body out of its arc.

"Okay, you can open it now," she called.

The door opened a few centimetres, and a head peered tentatively through the gap.

"Who the hell are you?" the man asked. His eyes tracked the smeared blood trailing from the operating table to where Antimone lay. "My God, you just had a baby, and you're alive? Nick, get in here and call Mrs Baxter. This one's alive."

A second man entered the room, pushing a trolley. "Yeah, right. Nice one."

The smile vanished from his face when he took in the girl lying at his feet and the patchy, red streaks across the floor. While the first man tended to Antimone, the other rushed to the wall-mounted terminal and swept his hand from right to left in front of it.

"Call Mrs Baxter," he said in a trembling voice.

After a few seconds, the irritated expression of a man in his mid-twenties with jet-black hair, and a narrow face filled the screen.

"I'm Nick Jenkins from the mortuary. I need to speak to Mrs Baxter urgently."

"Mrs Baxter is busy. What's it about? If it's something to do with overtime or working conditions, take it up with Personnel."

"No, it's nothing like that. Could you please inform her that the woman who just gave birth in operating theatre three is still alive?"

"Alive? Are you sure? If this is some sort of practical joke, there will be serious consequences."

"I'm telling the truth. She's talking to my colleague right now. We came in to pick up the body and found her on the floor."

"Wait right there. For Christ's sake, don't touch anything… In fact, don't move at all."

The display went blank.

# PART ONE: ORIGINATION

## 9 ½ months previously

*T*he woman lay back against the cold brickwork and closed her eyes. She was twenty years old but would have struggled to answer had she been asked her age. Her brown hair was straggly and greasy. She couldn't remember when she had last washed it, or any other part of her body for that matter. Her face might once have been described as pretty, but a life on the street had hollowed out her cheeks and etched dark shadows beneath her eyes. Her body was angular, all sharp corners and jutting bones, due in the main to the starvation diet she had endured for the last few weeks. She wore a grimy pair of blue jeans and a thick green woollen sweater that was several sizes too large. On her feet was a pair of tattered trainers, which she wore sockless.

Her home, if it could be called that, was the alley in which she currently sat. If the weather was good, as it was now, she occupied the space between the two large industrial waste bins. When it rained, she would often take shelter inside one of the brown plastic enclosures if the stench from the contents was not too much to bear.

The sole purpose of her life was to consume the next fix of 'Chill Black', a narcotic that, for a few brief moments, generated a sensation of immense pleasure and allowed her to ignore her woeful existence in the real world. She was prepared to do pretty much anything to obtain a supply of the small yellow pills. She had frequently sold her body although she drew the line at unprotected sex—even in her drug-addled state, she knew that one simple mistake could cost her life as it had her mother. Recently the flow of men willing to overlook her poor physical condition had dried up, and she was forced to resort to begging and stealing to feed her habit.

She opened her eyes and fingered the small pill, rolling it between a grubby forefinger and thumb. Placing it in her palm, she stared at it in hungry fascination. She savoured the moment, the build-up before she popped it in her mouth. Another user—it would be inaccurate to refer to her as a friend— had taught her that she could prolong the mind-blowing high by placing it beneath her tongue. She found it amazing that this small yellow capsule held the power to transport her to a place where nothing else mattered.

In the rare moments of clarity between the highs and the subsequent lows, she contemplated seeking help. She had led a relatively normal home life until her mother had fallen pregnant six years earlier and then, like every other expectant mother, had died in childbirth. Her father had lost his job soon afterwards and had been unwilling or unable to cope with looking after a new baby. He had offered the child up for adoption and in the following weeks had descended into an alcohol-fuelled depression. When his anger turned towards his remaining daughter, she had moved out. Initially, she had stayed with friends, but when she wore out her welcome, she turned to a life on the streets. From there it was a short and painful trip to where she now found herself. As a consequence, there was no parent to whom she could turn, and the authorities would only send her on a rehabilitation course, after which she would, more than likely, end up back in the same situation.

She delayed the moment of gratification, prolonging the anticipation ahead of the oncoming rush. She was about to lift the pill to her mouth when a shadow passed in front of her. Lifting her head, she saw a smiling man wearing a pair of blue overalls. The man was well-muscled, with blond hair and piercing blue eyes. For a moment she wondered whether this was part of the trip, but when she glanced down the pill was still in her hand.

"What do you want?" she asked in confusion.

"I'm here to help," he said, still smiling. Although his English was perfect, he spoke with a slight accent.

"I don't need any help," she said, her voice hardening.

"But I think you do, actually." The man took a pace forwards and held something up to her neck.

There was a short hiss, and she experienced a sharp stinging sensation. The man stepped backwards and studied her carefully. A feeling of light-headedness swept through her as she stared at him blankly. His blue eyes drew her in.

After thirty seconds had passed, he spoke again. "You want to come with me, don't you?"

The girl nodded, although it felt like somebody else was moving her body on her behalf. She rose shakily to her feet and took a tentative step towards him.

"My van's just over there," he said, gesturing vaguely behind him. "It's comfortable in the back. I think you should lie down there."

"Okay."

He led the way to a white van and unlocked the rear doors. On the floor were a pile of blue mats.

"There. Why don't you have a nice relaxing sleep? You're feeling a bit tired, aren't you?"

"Yes," said the girl, clambering into the back and lying down. She curled up into a foetal position and closed her eyes. Within seconds, she was unconscious and breathing heavily.

The man slammed the van doors and locked them. He returned to the driver's seat and pressed a button on the dashboard.

After a brief pause, a male voice crackled over the internal speakers. "Yes, what is it?"

"I've got one. I'll be back in about forty-five minutes."

"Okay, we'll be ready."

The man started the vehicle and inched his way out of the alley onto the main road.

On the ground, between the two bins, lay a small yellow pill.

## Sunday 4<sup>th</sup> April 2032

Antimone Lessing raised her right arm and extended it backwards behind her head. She repeated the exercise on the other arm, all the while the music booming in her ears. She wore her brown hair in a ponytail that draped over a bright yellow, long-sleeved training top. Her legs, dressed in a form-fitting black material, were bunched beneath her body in a kneeling position suspended above the lightweight frame of her racing wheelchair.

The only other girl in the group of athletes sat beside Antimone on the damp grass and leant forwards until her nose touched her outstretched leg. Erin Riley had little in common with Antimone other than their shared interest in athletics. Neither girl was popular, but for different reasons. Despite her athletic physique, Erin was not physically attractive with her thin fly-away hair and bland features. She tried to ingratiate herself with her fellow pupils by trading gossip but instead had earned a deserved reputation for being indiscrete.

Antimone, by contrast, owed her lack of popularity to being different from her peers. The wheelchair was one aspect of it, but the fact that her parents could barely afford to send her to Oakington Manor even on a scholarship didn't go unnoticed by her classmates. The majority came from privileged backgrounds and held a casual disregard for money. They intuitively identified Antimone as an outsider and maintained a distance.

Five metres away, a boy, a man really, was performing a similar set of warm-up exercises on his calf and thigh muscles. Max Perrin was a little over six feet tall, maybe six two, she estimated. His hair was a close-cropped golden brown. He wore a designer training top and a pair of baggy training pants. On his feet was a pair of high-end athletics shoes. Every few seconds, an illuminated pulse swept along the red stripe on the side of each shoe.

Three other boys warmed up a few paces away, flashing jealous glances at Max as he flirted with two attractive fifteen-year-old girls. The taller of the girls wore an expensive-looking, pale green T-shirt and a short, pink skirt. The skirt seemed to possess a life of its own, fluttering up and down in waves even though there was no wind. The control system carefully coordinated the movement to ensure that it preserved her modesty at all times. Antimone had heard about these so-called 'Marilyn' skirts but had never seen one in action.

Seeing the impact the billowing skirt was having on the group of boys, and not to be outdone, the second girl, who wore a similarly skimpy but conventional white skirt, tapped the nail of her little finger with her thumb. A gasp rose from the small group as a hole seemed to open up through her midriff and expand in size. The ragged edges exposed her internal organs and lent the image a gruesome reality. The girl flashed a smug smile now that she was the centre of attention and leant forward to whisper something in Max's ear.

Antimone rolled her eyes. Max Perrin was good-looking and from a wealthy family. He used those assets to his advantage when it came to the opposite sex. As far as athletics went, despite an over-confidence in his own abilities, he ranked only slightly better than average. That didn't stop most of the teenage girls at the school from lusting after him. *But two at the same time? Didn't they have any pride?*

Antimone's gaze meandered past another group of three boys and two girls perfecting their sprint starts and settled on a boy practising his run up for the javelin. He looked faintly ridiculous as he charged up to the white line identifying the end of the runway, simulated a throw and juddered to an abrupt halt.

A voice rose above the thrashing beat. "Antimone!"

Antimone glanced up at her coach and noticed his lips were moving. She realised everybody was staring at her. She tapped the fingernail of her right middle finger with her thumb, and the music ceased abruptly. "Sorry, Coach. What did you say?"

John Marshall was approaching retirement and had taught Physical Education at the school since its inception ten years earlier. He insisted the students addressed him as 'Coach' at training sessions. He was a no-nonsense teacher with a background in the military, but beneath the brash exterior he was conscientious and genuinely cared about the progress of his pupils. At this particular moment in time, however, he did not appear impressed.

"Look, when you're at the track I expect your undivided attention. I don't give up my afternoons so you can daydream during my sessions."

She opened her mouth to speak, but he interrupted before she could apologise. "Two hundred metres at three-quarters pace followed by two hundred metres warm down. Six reps, please. The same applies to all of you."

Antimone groaned inwardly. She loved the big occasions, the important races, the roar of the crowd, but training was just so boring—and often painful. *But six repetitions?* She must have really upset him. It was clear from the scowls on the faces of her fellow athletes that they blamed her for the harsh instructions.

Seeing her lack of enthusiasm, the man nodded towards the track. "Come on. Let's get going. You won't improve if you don't put the effort in. And turn on your logger, Antimone. I want to study the pattern of your push." He turned his focus to the two girls still flirting with Max. "I take it you ladies aren't training today. Maybe you could cheer on your champion from the stands."

Max smirked as the pair sauntered across the track, swaying their hips in an exaggerated manner, aware that every eye was upon them. The arrival of the sprinters down the home straight spoiled the effect, forcing the girls to hurry to avoid being trampled underfoot.

"Hey, fancy going out sometime?" Max asked, turning to Antimone.

"Um… maybe," Antimone replied in confusion, unsettled by the question. Despite her ambivalence, the thought of how it might improve her image to go on a date with him sprang to the forefront of her mind.

"Thought so. The problem is I don't fancy going out with you," he said with a sneering laugh. "The trike queen wants to go out with me," he announced, draping an arm around one of the other boys.

"I only said maybe," Antimone replied hotly, but nobody was paying any attention.

The coach clapped his hands and turned back to the group. "Come on, I haven't got all day. Is this a fashion show or a training session?"

Antimone propelled her wheelchair towards the white start line slashed across the ochre surface of the running track, her face still burning, and frustrated that she had let Max get the better of her. Tapping the nail of the little finger on her left hand, she navigated the menu structure with no need for the audio cues whispering in her ear. She selected the logging option, and a green light illuminated on a panel located just behind the front wheel. She fitted the helmet resting on her lap and pulled a pair of protective gloves from the pockets in her training top, then slipped them on.

At first glance, the racing wheelchair resembled a tricycle with a single wheel at the front and the back two wheels canted inwards, but it was hand- rather than pedal-powered and lacked the handlebars of a traditional cycle. The in-built sensors and data logger allowed her coach to analyse in detail the timing of her propulsive stroke and suggest ways to race faster whilst at the same time consuming less energy. At the level of competition she had attained, every millisecond counted and could make the difference between gold and silver medals.

Her talent was first identified when, as a skinny thirteen-year-old, barely a year after the car accident that had left her paralysed from the waist down, her father had taken her for a trial at a local athletics club that catered for disabled athletes. During a four hundred metre race, despite having no training and using an obsolete wheelchair, she had thrashed her more experienced opponents, leading from the start and winning by over ten metres. Within weeks of that race, the trustees of the prestigious private school, Oakington Manor, had offered her a sports scholarship. There was no way her parents would have been able to cover the extortionate fees without financial assistance, but the generous bursary covered tuition costs, leaving them only to find money for incidental expenses such as the school uniform—and the gear for wheelchair racing. Now, one month short of her sixteenth birthday, those in the know were touting her as a potential Paralympics medal winner in the eight hundred metres event.

Out of instinct, Antimone looked across to the stand. She knew her parents were not there, but it was an ingrained reflex. A group of six adults sat together at the front towards the centre, chatting and paying no attention to the training session. As her eyes swept along the rows of seats, her gaze came to rest on a man standing by himself at the far-right end. Besides being the only person on his feet, what struck her as odd about him was his black woollen hat. It seemed totally incongruous amongst the expensive attire of the other wealthy, well-dressed parents,

The coach's voice drew her attention back to the track. "Let's get going then."

She grabbed the circular metal bar that rimmed the wheel and propelled the chair forwards, accelerating with several powerful shoves. Settling quickly into a steady rhythm, she guided the vehicle between the stark white lines. She rounded the bend, and as she approached the end of the straight, she reduced the stroke rate, allowing the chair to coast down to a slower speed.

"Hey! Don't just slow down suddenly like that. I nearly ran into the back of you. You need brake lights on that bloody thing." Max jogged alongside, glaring angrily at her. Antimone maintained her focus on the track, doing her best to ignore him.

When they arrived back at the starting point, Max surged forwards and cut ahead of her, two of the others following a few paces behind. Antimone delayed her acceleration as she steered the chair into the third lane. Max glanced behind him, grinned and moved out to block her progress. Antimone swung out into the fourth lane and then the fifth, accelerating as she did so. Max and the other boys ended the bend in a line across the track, Antimone now out in the sixth lane.

By the end of the fifth lap, the rest of the group were tiring and had dropped back by twenty metres, leaving Antimone and Max leading the way. Perspiration trickled down her face, and her biceps felt like they were on fire as she moved into the curve. Max drew alongside and matched her pace even as she increased her push rate. As the straight ended, Antimone slackened the power of her strokes, and her speed slowly reduced. Rather than decelerating,

Max continued to maintain the same pace into the next bend until he was five metres ahead. He glanced over his shoulder.

"Not tired are you, trike queen?" he gasped between breaths, lengthening his stride.

Antimone knew that she shouldn't respond, but his smug expression goaded her on. Despite her aching arm muscles, she accelerated once more, maintaining the distance between them around the curve. As they reached the start of the straight, she allowed the chair to drift out into the second lane and applied the power to close the gap. The separation gradually reduced. Three metres... two metres... one metre. Ten metres short of the finish line they were neck and neck, both determined to cross first.

Antimone drew on her last reserves of strength and put everything into one final shove. As she did so, a droplet of sweat splashed onto the shiny metal ring, and her left hand lost a small amount of grip. The difference in torque between the two wheels was minimal, but it was enough for the chair to veer sideways and cross the line separating the lanes. Her left wheel caught the outside of Max's right foot.

The effect on the wheelchair was insignificant, but the contact sufficed to disrupt the boy's stride pattern. For a second it looked like he would keep his balance, but a couple of paces later, arms wind-milling, he pitched forward and crashed to the ground. Antimone shot across the line and quickly brought the chair to a halt. By the time she had turned around, Max was sitting on the floor cradling a gashed knee. Blood dripped from a long graze on his left arm.

"You stupid cow," he screamed. "You did that on purpose." He examined the shredded material of his training pants. "These cost over a grand. You're going to pay for a new pair."

"I'm sorry," she muttered. "It was an accident." She looked up to see the coach hurrying over.

"Are you okay?" he asked the prostrate boy.

"The stupid bitch tripped me deliberately."

"Max, watch your language. What were the pair of you thinking? That was supposed to be a warm down, not a damned race."

"Sorry, Coach," Antimone mumbled.

Erin sidled up beside her. "Nice one."

"I didn't—"

"Jack, go and get the first aid kit," Marshall said, addressing one of the boys who had formed a semi-circle around Max. The boy hurried away across the track.

"Antimone, come with me." He strode away from the group without looking to see whether she was following. When they were twenty metres away and out of earshot, he swivelled and thrust his face towards her.

"What the hell were you playing at? I know it was an accident, but Jesus, why can't you do what I ask? Anything like that happens again and you find yourself a new coach. Now I suggest you get out of here while I sort this out."

"Sorry, Coach," she said, but he had already turned away and was heading back to the group where Jack had returned carrying a green medical box.

Antimone slipped off her gloves, unclipped the helmet and placed it on her lap. She shivered as the perspiration on her arms and upper body cooled. For the second time that afternoon she was furious at herself for being drawn into a confrontation with an idiot like Max Perrin. Blowing out her cheeks, she steered the wheelchair towards the changing rooms, giving a wide berth to the small crowd clustered around the injured boy. The parents had all come down from the stand. Two of the women glared at her as she rolled past.

Keeping her eyes downcast, she propelled herself down the tunnel. She approached her locker and the conventional wheelchair a few paces away. She opened the door and flung the helmet and gloves inside. Grabbing her bag, she turned the key then banged the grey metal with the palm of her hand. "Damn!"

She tossed the bag onto the other wheelchair and undid the straps securing her to the racing chair.

A voice came from behind her. "Do you need any help?"

Antimone whipped her head around. The boy, who had been practising the javelin run-up, stood in the doorway, a wry smile on his lips.

"No, I can manage," she replied tersely.

"Jason Baxter," he said, extending a hand.

"Antimone," she replied, aware of the sweatiness of her palm.

"Good race," he said after a short pause, the smile remaining.

"If you say so. Coach didn't appreciate it, though. It wasn't supposed to be a race."

Jason laughed. "Always good to see Max Perrin being taken down a notch or two. So, did you intend to trip him?"

Antimone stared back in silence.

"Okay, a bit of a sore point, I see," Jason said, the smile fading. "I'll take that as a no then."

He watched as she used her powerful arms to transfer herself from one chair to the other.

When she had finished, Antimone looked up. "Do you still want to help?"

Jason nodded.

"In that case, could you put the racing chair in the storeroom for me, please?"

She followed as he wheeled it down the corridor. She didn't like asking for assistance, but it was difficult to move one wheelchair while seated in another.

He tried the door, then turned back to her. "It's locked."

"Oh, sorry." She fumbled inside the bag that now rested on her lap. She tossed the key to him and watched as he secured the racing machine.

"Here you go," he said, handing the key back.

"Thanks."

The only way to leave the stadium was to retrace their steps to the running track and depart via the main gate. Several metres short of the tunnel, a group of three people, silhouetted by the bright light from the archway, approached from the opposite direction.

"Look, it's the cripple," Max said, hobbling forwards, supported by a boy at each shoulder.

Antimone and Jason moved to one side to allow the three to pass, but Max shrugged off his two helpers, limped over and stood before them, blocking their path. "You really shouldn't have done that," he said with a sneer.

Jason stepped in front of Antimone and glared at Max. Face to face, Antimone realised that Jason was a few centimetres shorter than the other boy, but what he lacked in height, he made up for in upper body strength. "Big man, threatening the girl in the wheelchair. It looked like an accident from where I was standing."

"No, the bitch was sore that I didn't want to go out with her, and she was getting her own back."

Jason gave a snort of derision. "Frankly, I think she's got better taste than to go out with you. Now get out of the way."

Max made no attempt to move.

Jason turned to Antimone. "Come on, we're leaving," he said, barging past Max. The injured boy staggered and leant against the wall for support. Antimone followed a short distance behind as they emerged into the stadium.

"You're going to regret that," Max shouted to their backs.

They passed through the main gate without speaking.

"I can look after myself, you know," Antimone said eventually without looking at Jason.

"I'm sure you can," he replied, glancing down at her, "but it doesn't hurt to have a bit of support from time to time. Anyway, I wouldn't worry about him—he's all bark and no bite."

"I'm not worried."

They stopped opposite the pedestrian crossing that traversed the two-lane road. "Okay—um, where are you heading? Do you need a lift?"

"No, I've got my own transport, thanks." This wasn't true, but Antimone wasn't in the mood for conversation.

"Well, I'm just over there. Listen, I'm having a birthday party next week. I wondered if you'd like to come."

Antimone glanced up sharply. "You know I can't feel much down there, right?"

Despite his attempts to mask his surprise, an expression of shock flickered across Jason's face. "Okay, well thanks for the information, but I had kind of guessed that. It was only a party invite, not an offer of marriage. I'll see you around then."

She immediately regretted her harsh words. "God, I'm sorry. That came out all wrong. I'm just a bit shaken up by that whole Max thing. I'd like to come to your party."

"Good. Are you sure about the lift?"

Antimone relented. "Um… okay then, why not? Thanks. Are you going to be able to get the wheelchair in?"

"Yeah, no problem. It's one of my mum's company vehicles. Plenty of room."

"What does your mum do?"

"She runs Ilithyia Biotechnology, you know, on the edge of Northstowe. I think that's one of the reasons I'm not Max's favourite person. His dad works for my mum. Anyway, the car's just over there."

Without thinking, Antimone set off in the direction he was pointing. A bright flash accompanied the screech of brakes. Time seemed to stand still as she flinched before the impact that never came. She turned to her right to see a man mouthing insults at her through the windscreen of a small white car with a blue dome affixed to the roof. The car had stopped with under a metre to spare.

The man wound down the window. "What the hell do you think you're doing? I nearly had a bloody heart attack. You'll definitely be getting a fine for that, you fricking moron. Look where you're bloody going."

The car waited while Antimone completed the crossing to the central reservation, then moved off, the electric motors humming softly, the man still shaking his fist at her. Antimone raised two fingers in return.

Jason hurried across to the paved area at the centre of the road and stood beside her. "You certainly believe in living life dangerously, don't you?"

"I didn't see him."

"No, but luckily he saw you. I think he might be right about getting a fine, though—I saw the flash go off."

"No, I don't think so," she replied, a slight tremble in her voice. "It took my picture, but the database will tell them I'm disabled. They're pretty lenient with disabled people."

Despite her seemingly calm outward appearance, Antimone's heart was racing. Memories of the accident which had paralysed her flashed through her mind. The circumstances had been remarkably similar, walking out into the road without looking, not hearing the approach of the electric vehicle, the screech of brakes. The only difference, in this case, was the improved reaction time of the computer compared to that of the human driver. She clamped her hands onto the arms of the wheelchair so that Jason wouldn't notice the shaking.

Jason made a point of looking carefully to the left before stepping out to complete the crossing. When they reached the far side, he turned to face her.

"I have to say there's certainly never a dull moment when you're around."

## Monday 5th April 2032

The hubbub of conversation died down and was replaced by the scraping of chairs as the members of the cabinet rose to their feet to welcome the Prime Minister. Andrew Jacobs, or 'AJ' as his friends and colleagues knew him, was in his early forties and was a vigorous man who somehow found time every day to fit a thirty-minute jog into his busy schedule. His rapid advancement in politics was largely down to his attention to detail and his single-minded approach to any problem he encountered. He was also a consummate negotiator who more often than not got what he wanted through charm and a smile. His film-star good looks and witty repartee had led to a popularity rating far greater than that usually attained by a premier nearing the end of his second term.

He wore a tailor-made suit and a blue tie as he stood at the head of the table. "Please sit down," he said, waiting patiently until everyone else was seated. "I'd like to introduce you to Rosalind Baxter, the CEO of IBC, that's Ilithyia Biotechnology Company for those of you who don't know."

He nodded to an aide who opened one of the tall wooden doors to admit a smartly dressed woman, wearing a white blouse together with a matching green jacket and skirt. Her blonde hair was styled in a trendy bob and framed an attractive face. The bright red colour of her lips was in stark contrast to the paleness of her cheeks. She was two weeks short of her forty-sixth birthday but looked at least ten years younger. She exuded an air of confidence as she strode across the room to stand by the Prime Minister.

"I've asked Mrs Baxter, or should I say, Rosalind, to join us today to brief us on her company's progress towards finding a cure for this terrible virus. As I'm sure you're all aware, this disease is the most pressing crisis this country has ever faced. Rosalind, over to you."

"Thank you, Prime Minister. Before I start, I'd like to go over the background, just in case any of you are not up to date with the facts."

She clicked the button of a small device she held in her hand and a three-dimensional image of a blue sphere, with an array of protruding spikes, appeared, floating above the long wooden table.

"This is the Orestes virus, so-named after the character from Greek myth who killed his mother, Clytemnestra. The first case was sixteen years ago. Since then, we believe that it has infected every single person on the planet. We still don't know where it originated, but we have good information that it was probably somewhere in central Africa. As I'm sure you're aware, it has no discernible effect on either men or women—that is, until a woman gives birth. At that point, something triggers a change in the virus, causing it to suddenly become extremely aggressive and destructive, attacking the mother's brain and vital organs. For those of you who have not witnessed the effects first hand, the final stages can be particularly traumatic. For that reason, these days we generally anaesthetise the mother and perform a caesarean section to spare both her and the family any unnecessary suffering."

"Mrs Baxter, you're not telling us anything we don't already know." The speaker was the Secretary of State for Health, a grey-haired man in his mid-fifties, wearing the standard attire of dark suit and blue tie. "Please get to the point."

She picked up a glass of water and took a sip before continuing. "My company has analysed statistical data for the United Kingdom's population, and we have performed some projections on the way the numbers are likely to change over the coming years."

Another click, and a graph replaced the image of the virus.

"This graph shows the population of the United Kingdom for every year since the start of the century and the projected population from now until twenty fifty if no cure is found. As you can see there was a sharp dip around twenty seventeen when the virus first broke out. This was exacerbated by a sudden increase in drug-resistant bacteria at about the same time. Together, these two effects mean that our population is currently being decimated every six years, and I use the term in its literal meaning of one in ten. One of the biggest issues, however, is that even if we find a cure now, one that's a hundred percent effective, the population will continue to decline because the proportion of women of child-bearing age has shrunk drastically."

"Yes, Mrs Baxter, I think we're all aware of this," the Secretary of State for Health said. "What we want to know is what you're doing about it."

Rosalind Baxter smiled thinly. "I was just coming onto that. The Orestes virus is a very tricky customer. Just when we think we're getting close to a solution, it mutates. The rate of mutation is unprecedented compared to any other virus we've ever seen, and that's the main factor making the development of a treatment so difficult."

"So, what you're saying is that you're no closer to a cure than you were this time last year?" said the same man, drumming his fingers on the table.

"Well, I wouldn't say that," she replied. "We have a better understanding of the virus' mechanisms for reproduction, and we are developing several unique approaches to counteract it."

The Chancellor of the Exchequer, a dark-skinned woman of African-Caribbean descent, impeccably dressed in a black dress and wearing matching pearl earrings and necklace, spoke. "How much money did your company receive in government grants over the past year, Mrs Baxter? Actually, let me tell you. My figures indicate it was a fraction under one billion pounds. Does that sound about right?"

"The figure for the last financial year is nine hundred and eighty-three thousand. What is your question?"

"Practically all our scientific research budget is going towards finding a cure. So why, Prime Minister, are we pumping such huge sums into the coffers of this woman's company when there is little or no appreciable progress? Surely, she must demonstrate that this money is not being frittered away. There are several multi-national research efforts on which I believe these funds would be better spent."

Several sharp intakes of breath rose from around the table, followed by a number of whispered conversations.

Andrew Jacobs waited for the disturbance to settle down before he spoke. "I'd like you all to remember that Mrs Baxter is here as a guest today. The questions you raise deserve to be answered, and I expect Mrs Baxter to do so in due course, but that was not the purpose of today's discussion. I want to move the conversation on to ways in which we can counteract this dramatic reduction in population. Do you have any ideas, Mrs Baxter?"

Rosalind cleared her throat. "I understand from my colleagues in the medical community that considerable research effort is being expended on artificial wombs. All the papers I have read indicate there are several insurmountable problems, and a breakthrough is fifteen or twenty years away at the earliest. By then it may be too late. This country is going to need as many fertile women as possible in the future to rebuild the population. There are certain chemicals that can be put in the water supplies to skew the proportion of female to male conceptions in those women who do fall pregnant. Likewise, there are other chemicals that increase the likelihood of multiple births. If a woman is going to die anyway, she may as well give birth to triplets or quadruplets instead of a single infant. It's even better if all the children are female."

A stunned silence occupied the room before the Chancellor spoke again. "That's a pretty callous attitude. What's more, if the public discovered we were secretly putting drugs in the water supplies, we'd all be lynched. We have enough trouble with campaigners objecting to Fluoride in tap water. Voters would never agree to something that radical."

"Drastic times call for drastic measures," Rosalind Baxter replied, "and the voters don't necessarily need to know. There are no simple solutions to this crisis. It's scientifically possible and my company could assist with the implementation."

"I'm sure you could," the Secretary of State for Health said, "no doubt at huge expense to the taxpayer."

Once again, several whispered conversations broke out.

Andrew Jacobs rose to his feet. "Ladies and gentlemen, I'd like to thank Mrs Baxter for joining us today. We'll pause for some refreshments, and then we'll continue the debate. Thank you, Mrs Baxter, for sparing the time from your busy schedule."

He shook the woman's hand, then accompanied her to the tall wooden doors. He paused as he rested his hand on the ornate handle. "Thanks for coming in Rosalind. Some interesting ideas. I'll be in touch."

He opened the door and stood back to allow her to pass. Her heels clicked across the highly polished oak floor. Her aide, who had been waiting outside the cabinet room, hurried along beside her.

"How did it go, Mrs Baxter?" he asked.

"Pompous, arrogant pricks," she said as she stormed towards the guarded entrance.

*T*he girl opened her eyes. Her first observation was that she was no longer in the alley. Her mind immediately turned to the yellow pill. She had been holding it when... when... The memory refused to surface. She held up her hand to her face and blearily inspected it. No, the pill was definitely not there. She sat up quickly, realising that she was lying in a bed with crisp white sheets and a thin blue blanket. The acrid scent of body odour no longer filled her nostrils—somebody must have washed her. She was dressed in a loose white gown of some sort. A quick check confirmed she was not wearing any underwear.

She sprang from the bed and stripped the upper sheet back. She inspected the mattress, but there was no sign of the small capsule. She fell to her hands and knees and peered beneath the metal bed frame, hoping to pick out the yellow colour against the white plastic floor covering. Maybe she had swallowed it, but if that was true, she had no recollection. Maybe this was all part of the trip, but it didn't have that other-worldly haze that was a common facet of the experience.

"Shit," she muttered.

With the absence of the pill confirmed, she scrutinised her surroundings. As far as she could determine, she seemed to be in a windowless hospital room. The biggest clue was the pervasive antiseptic medicinal smell.

There were two closed doors leading off the room, both coloured white, one incorporating a narrow rectangular window at head height. She padded over towards the windowed door first and was unsurprised to find it locked. A red light shone out from a small white box affixed to the wall beside the doorframe. She peered through the glass pane onto a featureless white corridor containing another three identical-looking doors. Similar white boxes were mounted beside each door, electronic card readers she assumed. Beneath each window frame was a black three-digit number. They were numbered consecutively from 221 to 223.

She turned her attention to the second door. When she twisted the handle, this one opened to reveal a cramped windowless bathroom containing a sink, toilet and shower cubicle. She focused back on the main room. The bed appeared to be typical of those found in a medical institution, and the walls were a bright white colour. Beside the bed was a cream coloured, metallic bedside cabinet on wheels. A quick check of the interior proved it to be empty. The harsh ceiling light illuminated a space devoid of any decoration.

Where was she? How on earth had she arrived here? She cast her mind back. She remembered how she had scraped together enough cash to buy one of the yellow capsules from the scruffy, rat-like man who operated his business from an alley, not unlike her own. She recalled the sense of anticipation and the feel of the pill rolling between forefinger and thumb. But then what? Maybe it had been part of a bad batch, and that was causing her amnesia. Perhaps a passer-by had discovered her in the alley and called the emergency services. But in that case, why was she alone?

A thought occurred to her. Maybe somebody was monitoring her remotely. Her eyes swept the ceiling, but the glare of the light made it hard to detect the presence of a camera. She returned to the small window and banged on the door with the flat of her hand.

"Hey! Is anybody there?"

Silence.

"Hey! Open this bloody door!"

She continued to shout and hammer at the door until her voice was hoarse, and her hand ached. She shuffled back to the bed and sat down, staring around the room at the featureless walls. With rising frustration, she raised her legs from the ground and shoved them against the cabinet. A resounding crash filled the room as it toppled over. Encouraged by the sound, she rose to her feet, placed her hands along the sides of the frame, lifted it and tipped it onto its side. The noise was not quite as satisfying, the mattress absorbing much of the impact.

She surveyed her handiwork before once again returning to the door. The corridor was still empty. If somebody was watching her through a hidden camera, they weren't overly concerned by her demonstration of petulance. Dejectedly, she trudged back to the toppled bed, pulled the mattress away and laid it flat. She dropped onto it and curled up on her side, her arms around her knees.

An electronic beep disturbed her repose. She sat up and saw a balding man wearing a white medical coat and carrying a clipboard enter through the windowed door.

"Ah, I see you've rearranged the room," he said, a thin smile on his lips.

"Where am I? What am I doing here?"

"Both good questions. You're in a secure facility undergoing treatment for your addiction."

"I didn't ask for any help."

The man stared at her for a moment before continuing. "Well, technically we don't need your assent. You were discovered unconscious in an alley, suffering the after-effects of a bad batch of..." He consulted the clipboard.

"Ah yes—I believe the street name is Chill Black. Under the terms of the Misuse of Substances Act, twenty thirty-one, we can hold you here indefinitely for your own good."

"You can't just keep me locked up in this fricking shithole."

"Ironic that you should call this place a shithole after the alley in which you were found, but the truth of the matter is that we can keep you under our care until we determine you're well enough to leave."

"How long will that be?"

"Well, young lady, that depends on how cooperative you are, but I would estimate several weeks at least in your current state. Why? Do you have any pressing engagements?"

The girl folded her arms but remained silent.

"Do you want a hand sorting out the bed?" he asked.

"No. I haven't slept in a bed for over three years. Why the hell would I start now?"

"Do what you like. We're only trying to help you get better. Please note that we are monitoring you, and we will restrain you if we believe that you may be a danger to yourself."

The girl glowered at him.

"Somebody will bring you food in a few minutes," he added, strolling towards the door.

He halted at the entrance and turned back to her. "Enjoy your stay."

## Saturday 10th April 2032

Antimone took a sip from her drink as her eyes roamed the room. The house was beginning to fill up as people arrived. Jason had invited eighty-five guests to his birthday party, although he had admitted that some were there at his mother's request, including Max Perrin. Apparently, she did not wish to risk alienating important contacts by excluding their children from this celebration.

As Antimone had predicted, no threatening letter had arrived as a consequence of the near miss with the car a week earlier. She had been more worried about her parents finding out than by any prospect of a fine. Following the accident which had placed her in a wheelchair, they had been overly protective, and she was glad to have avoided what would have been a difficult conversation.

She had done her best to avoid Max since the fateful training session, although that was not always possible given that they attended some classes together. There had been no major confrontations, but there had been a number of low-level incidents, which she attributed to him. One morning she had attempted to open her locker only to discover that the keyhole was filled with glue. Another morning, the outline of a huge penis had been drawn on her locker door. The most sinister was a drawing that had appeared on the wall of the female toilets, depicting a girl in a wheelchair with a noose around her neck. As the only wheelchair student at the school, it was fairly obvious to whom the graffiti referred. That last episode had drawn the attention of the school authorities. Following a brief and inconclusive investigation, there had been no further problems.

Since arriving she had chatted briefly with Erin Riley, but the other girl soon lost interest and wandered over to another group to collect the gossip around which her life revolved.

Antimone sensed a presence behind her, accompanied by a whiff of expensive perfume. She spun her wheelchair around to discover Jason's mother, elegantly dressed in a fashionable green dress with a black belt cinched around her narrow waist. Her assistant, a slight, narrow-faced man with thinning black hair and wearing a dark suit, stood a pace back.

"It's Antimone, isn't it?" the woman said, extending a hand. "It's a pleasure to finally meet you."

Antimone took the delicately manicured fingers in her own and was surprised at their coolness. "It's nice to meet you too, Mrs Baxter."

"This is my assistant, Julian Stefano."

Antimone shook hands with the man. By contrast, his handshake was warm and sweaty. She wanted to wipe her palm on her cream coloured trousers but resisted the temptation.

"I've followed your athletics career with great interest," the woman said. "It's fantastic that the school has offered a bursary to an up-and-coming Paralympian such as yourself. In fact, I'm sure you're aware that my company is a major contributor to the scholarship fund."

"Yes, Mrs Baxter. I'm very grateful for the opportunity."

"Oh, please call me Rosalind."

"Okay. Well, thanks very much… um, Rosalind."

"Can I get you a refill?"

Before she could reply, the assistant spoke. "I'm sorry, Mrs Baxter, but I've got Dr Perrin on the line."

"I'll catch up with you later, Antimone," Rosalind Baxter said as she strode away, her offer to replenish Antimone's glass already forgotten.

Antimone turned back to face the window and tapped a fingernail to start her favourite album playing in her ears. Soon the driving beat had her nodding her head in unison. She stared vacantly out at the carefully manicured gardens as she allowed the music to wash over her.

The reappearance of Rosalind Baxter on the stone-paved area by the back door drew her attention. The assistant was nowhere to be seen, but she was deep in conversation with a scruffy looking, bearded man wearing a black woollen hat. Antimone paused the playback as the man pointed a forefinger at Jason's mother and shouted something at her. There was something familiar about the man, but at first, she couldn't place him. She racked her brains trying to jog loose the recalcitrant memory. Then it came to her—she had seen somebody wearing similar headgear in the stand at the athletics stadium just before the training session last week. Was it the same man? He didn't look like a parent, but there was always the possibility that one of the pupils had an eccentric father. And what was the argument about?

At that moment, two muscular men dressed in matching grey suits emerged from the house and took up positions, one on either side of Jason's mother. The man jutted a finger at her, but then took a hurried step backwards as the two men advanced towards him. Rosalind swivelled on her heel and re-entered the house, her face a mask of fury. The two grey-suited men hustled the third, bearded man through the gate that led to the front of the house.

Antimone was jolted from the drama by a bang on the back of her wheelchair. She spun around to see Jason staring down at her, a grin on his face.

"Something exciting going on out there?" he asked.

"Um, no, not really," she replied after a moment's hesitation.

"Why don't you come over and join us?"

"Sure," Antimone said, smiling.

Jason studied her, pondering his next statement. "I guess it's hard joining in a conversation at a party when everybody else is standing up."

The comment caught her by surprise. The observation was correct, but she hadn't expected Jason to be so perceptive. "Yeah, I suppose."

"Tell you what, why don't we go over to the sofa? At least then we'll be at the same eye level."

"Okay."

Jason led the way across the room and through the doorway into a lounge that was big enough to accommodate the whole of the ground floor of Antimone's house. He clapped a couple of boys on the back and accompanied them, and the girls they were chatting with, to a huge red L-shaped sofa arrangement in the corner.

When everybody else was seated, Jason said, "I'll just get something to drink. Back in a sec."

Antimone sat in silence as the other four resumed their previous discussion. She was relieved when Jason reappeared carrying a large glass bowl containing a red-coloured liquid and a ladle. "Fruit punch? Strictly non-alcoholic. The alcohol only comes out when my Mum's disappeared."

Antimone smiled and watched as Jason topped up her glass. After serving the others, Jason refilled his own glass, dipping it directly into the bowl.

"To the next sixteen years," he said, standing up. The rest of the group echoed the toast, and the conversation flourished as Jason played the part of the perfect host, ensuring that everybody joined in. Antimone began to relax and was soon engaged in good-natured banter as Jason gently teased one of the other boys who fancied himself as a good footballer.

"I'm just going to get a refill," Jason said, getting to his feet and retreating with the empty bowl. This time, Antimone joined in with the exchanges in his absence. He returned carrying the topped-up container. He quickly replenished his guests' glasses and sank back onto the sofa.

Antimone took a sip of the second batch. It tasted slightly different to the first, but she put it down to the contents being mixed in different proportions. After a couple more mouthfuls, she felt dizzy. "Zu haven't putz alclol zin tish, has zu?" she asked. Her tongue felt too big for her mouth. Jason shook his head, but he too seemed to be struggling to speak.

Antimone closed her eyes, only dimly aware that all conversation in their corner of the room had ceased.

*** 

"Wow! Somebody must have spiked the drink."

Antimone groaned and opened an eye. Max Perrin was standing a few paces away, staring down at her.

"It's probably your first taste of alcohol, eh, trike queen?"

"Piss off, Max," she replied, running a hand across her face. A headache was pounding behind her eyes, and she felt bile rising in her stomach. She belched. The sweet scent of the fruit punch repeated on her, and she immediately felt better. The others, including Jason, were sitting where she had last seen them, all still unconscious. She glanced at her watch. She had been asleep for just under an hour.

Ignoring Max, who stood with a half-smile on his lips, she wheeled herself across the room and through the doorway. The body of the party seemed to have gravitated to the garden, judging by the raucous laughter and music coming through the back door. She was at the bathroom door when she heard the sound of breaking glass. Antimone stopped and cocked her head. At first, she thought somebody must have dropped their drink. The throbbing beat continued from outside, but the sounds of merriment had died down.

A shout accompanied the tinkle of more falling shards. She pushed through the door into the garden. A large group of people were staring towards the side of the house.

A man's voice rose above the music. "Hey! Stop!"

One of the two grey-suited men she had seen earlier with Jason's mother clambered through what she could now see was a shattered ground-floor window and set off at a sprint across the lawn. He headed towards a wooden gate embedded in the well-tended hedge, leading into the adjoining field. The man barrelled through the partially open gate, leaving it swinging on its hinges.

Several people ambled in the direction the man had taken and craned their necks to peer over the hedge. A couple tentatively approached the gateway. Somebody had turned off the music.

"What happened?" Antimone asked a girl, standing a few paces away.

The girl dragged her attention away from the unfolding scene and glanced down. "Well, a chair crashed through the window, and this man sort of climbed out and started running towards the gate. Then these other two, they came out of the window after him and shouted for him to stop. They all ran into the field."

"Who was the man, the first one I mean?"

"Dunno. I've never seen him before. He had a beard and this funny black woolly hat. I think the other two were security or something. I saw them when I arrived."

Before Antimone could ask any more questions, a woman's voice rose above the hubbub. "I'm sorry about that, everybody," Rosalind Baxter said. "There was an intruder, but my people are dealing with it. Please carry on and enjoy yourselves. I'll get somebody to sweep up the broken glass."

The buzz of conversation increased, and the music restarted although at a lower level than previously. Antimone turned to thank the girl, but she had already wandered off to join a larger group. Antimone resumed her trip to the bathroom but bumped into Jason as she entered the house.

"What's going on out there?" he asked.

She ignored the question and asked one of her own. "Did you spike the drink?"

He appeared shocked. "No, I'd never do that."

"So, if you didn't, who the hell did?"

Without waiting for an answer, Antimone made her way across the hall. When she reached the bathroom door, she turned back to Jason.

"I'm calling my parents, and then I'm going home."

## Monday 12th April 2032

"Damn. Well, thanks for letting me know, Nigel."

Rosalind Baxter put the phone down. Another test failure. She allowed herself the luxury of staring out of the huge plate-glass window onto the well-manicured gardens surrounding the Ilithyia facility. A gardener was digging in one of the flower beds filled with a colourful array of spring flowers. The man glanced up, perhaps sensing that someone was watching him. Rosalind turned back to her computer monitor, even though she knew there was no way he could see her.

She swept her hand across the screen, manipulating a column of figures. A pulsing red dialogue box disturbed her concentration. It seemed to hang in mid-air a few centimetres in front of the display. The text indicated her secretary wanted to talk to her, so probably an incoming call. She sighed. This was the part of being in charge of a company that she hated the most. There was never enough time to concentrate on anything without being disturbed.

She snatched up the telephone handset. "Yes," she snapped.

"I have the Prime Minister's office."

"Okay. Put him through."

There was the faintest of clicks. "Hello, this is Rosalind Baxter. How are you Prime Minister?"

A female voice that was clearly not that of the leader of the country replied. "Please hold for the Prime Minister."

Rosalind rolled her eyes. This overt display of one-upmanship irritated her, the implication that his time was more important than her own. *I earn at least twenty times his paltry salary*, she thought. For a moment she considered putting the handset down. *Then he would have to wait for me for once.*

She was still toying with the idea when the familiar, well-cultured voice of Andrew Jacobs came on the line. "Sorry to keep you waiting, Rosalind."

"No problem, Prime Minister." *It's not as if I've got anything better to do.*

"So how are you, Rosalind? And please call me AJ."

"I'm fine. And yourself?" *Not that either of us really cares about the health of the other.*

"Fine, fine. Thanks for coming in last week."

"It was my pleasure." *As if I had a choice.*

"About that. I'm under a lot of pressure to reduce the funding your company receives. Certain members of the cabinet believe we might get better value for money by diverting it to our American friends."

*That bitch, the Chancellor of the Exchequer.* "You know as well as I do AJ, that of all the biotech companies in the world, we are the closest to finding a cure. We've already done it once, which is more than anybody else has achieved. No other organisation has even come close."

Fifteen years ago, Ilithyia Biotechnology had still been a small business on the Cambridge Science Park when the development of a prototype treatment had catapulted the company into the limelight. During the next three months, the value of the company's stock rose by several thousand percent, making the shareholders, including Rosalind Baxter, hugely wealthy. The company had relocated twice since then, finally settling in a purpose-built facility at the edge of the new town of Northstowe. Even after the virus mutated and the drug lost its effectiveness, the flow of research grants had continued and now accounted for a sizeable proportion of its revenue.

"Be that as it may, Rosalind, we can't keep pumping money in with no sign of progress."

"Look, Prime Minister. We're close to having an answer, one that works for more than a month or two. If you cut our funding, you'll be jeopardising the world's best chance at a solution to this problem." *And you'll cripple Ilithyia's stock value.*

"I hear you, Rosalind, but there's a limit to how much cash we can provide without any concrete results."

"So, what are you saying?"

"I know this sort of work takes years, and I'm happy to fight your corner—at least for the time being—but I need evidence that these funds are being put to good use. There are those in the cabinet who still support you, and I can hold the doubters off for nine months, maybe a year, but after that, I'm going to struggle to finance your company without positive results."

*Good to know the money I transfer to those accounts in the British Virgin Islands every month isn't totally wasted then.* "I appreciate your support AJ. I'm confident we'll have something by then."

"I hope so, Rosalind. Do keep in touch. And good luck."

"Thank you, AJ, I…" Rosalind trailed off as she realised she was talking to a dial tone.

*T*he electronic lock beeped, drawing the girl's attention to the door. As it swung open, she jumped to her feet and took a pace towards the balding doctor. He still hadn't told her his name.

"Hey! Why haven't you brought me any food?"

"I'm sorry," replied the man. "I should have told you sooner. We did some tests on the blood we took when you arrived, and we need to perform a minor operation. Unfortunately, you can't eat for several hours before a general anaesthetic."

The anger on the girl's face changed to concern. "What operation? What's wrong with me?"

"Like I said, it's a minor operation. We just want to take some more samples to confirm that your treatment's going according to plan. The procedure can be a bit painful, so it'll be less unpleasant for you if we do it while you're asleep. It'll all be over in half an hour or so, and then you'll be able to eat."

"What are you going to do to me?"

"We're going to insert a probe inside you and extract a small sample of material."

"Are you going to cut me open?"

"No, nothing like that."

"So where exactly are you going to insert the probe? Down my throat or up my arse?"

"Um, the second of those," said the doctor, looking slightly uncomfortable.

"Great. So, you cop another good look at my fanny."

"Look, I see naked bodies every day of the week. It's just part of the job. You're no different—I've seen it all many times before."

"Not mine, you haven't." The hint of a smile touched the girl's lips. "But I bet you wouldn't mind having my undivided attention for an evening with both of us naked." The smile turned more lascivious. "If you let me out of here, I would do anything you wanted. I can be quite… um… accommodating when I put my mind to it."

The arrival of two orderlies wheeling a hospital trolley spared the doctor a response. "Just pop yourself on there and lie down."

The girl ambled sullenly to the trolley and lay down as instructed. As soon as she was on her back, each of the orderlies grabbed an arm and fastened it to the frame with a strap. She struggled briefly against her bonds. "Hey! Why are you tying me down?"

"Just a precaution in case you get any ideas about making a run for it."

Once they had secured her arms, the two men turned their attention to her ankles. When they had securely restrained her, they raised the sides and wheeled her through the door, the doctor following a couple of paces behind. As they travelled down the featureless white corridor, she swung her head from side to side, trying to garner any clues as to where they were holding her. In the week she had been here, this was the first time she had been outside her room. Was that a face at the small window of one of the numbered doors? She couldn't be sure in the short time before one of the men obstructed her view.

They turned a corner and approached a door labelled 'Operating Theatre S1'. The girl passed through the swing doors into a brightly lit room where a woman wearing a blue medical gown, hairnet and white surgical mask stood beside a machine covered in indicators and dials. "I'm just going to slip this over your nose," she said, placing a black mask linked to the machine via a corrugated tube on the girl's face. "Start counting backwards from ten for me."

Almost immediately, a sickly-sweet smell filled her nostrils. She fought the encroaching darkness for a second or two, but was soon unconscious.

The doctor, who had by now also donned a hairnet and mask, entered the room pushing a wheeled cabinet on which rested a syringe connected to a long rounded barrel. He raised the girl's gown up until he had clear access to the lower part of her body, then carefully inserted the plastic tube and slowly depressed the plunger.

"Nice fanny," he muttered under his breath.

## Sunday 25th April 2032

"I want to practice sprinting this afternoon," John Marshall said, addressing the group of five. Antimone was the only girl—Erin was suffering from a cold—and also the only wheelchair athlete. "Let's do eight reps of one hundred metres sprint pace followed by one hundred metres jog. I want to see some effort today. Let's see you really push it around those bends."

Max had still not returned to training, even though it was over three weeks since his fall. There had been no further incidents following the party, and she was hopeful he had finally put the accident at the track out of his mind. He had even been moderately polite on a couple of occasions in the past week, acknowledging her and calling her by her real name when they crossed paths.

In contrast, it seemed that John Marshall had still not entirely forgotten the episode. While there was no major change in his behaviour, he was far more distant and business-like in his dealings with Antimone. He had discussed the results of the analysis taken from the data logger with her, but it felt like he was doing it more out of duty than through goodwill. She had tried to follow his instructions to the letter, but she had the distinct impression that there was a lot more work to do to restore her good standing with him.

She glanced over towards the javelin runway. There was no sign of Jason. She had questioned him the day after the party about the spiked drink, but he remained adamant he had not been responsible. She had kept her ears open, hoping to hear rumours of who the instigator was. Surprisingly, the school grapevine was quiet on the subject. In any case, she didn't need the distraction of any romantic involvement, what with both exams and trials for the British Paralympic team coming up in the next few months.

A wave of nausea swept over her as she placed the helmet on her head, tightened the strap, then slipped on her gloves. She had not been feeling well all day and put it down to the onset of the cold that was doing the rounds. She directed the wheelchair to the start line, waiting for a nod from the coach to begin. When it came, she surged ahead, rapidly accelerating as she entered the bend. At the end of the curve, she allowed the chair to coast down and tried to recover her breath. Within a few short seconds she reached the start of the next bend and once again propelled herself forwards.

By the time she had completed the second lap, she had built up a lead of over fifty metres over her fellow athletes, but the queasiness had increased to the extent that she had to stop and pull over onto the grassed oval at the centre of the track. She leant forwards and retched. A thin stream of mucus dribbled from her mouth, and she spat on the grass to try to remove the aftertaste.

"Not working you too hard, am I, Antimone?" Marshall said, strolling over.

"No, I'll be okay in a sec, Coach," she replied, spitting again.

"If it's not hurting, it's not doing any good."

"Yeah, I know." She glanced over to see that the rest of the group had nearly caught her up.

"Come on. Halfway. Two more laps," he shouted as the four boys approached. "Let's see you really put some work into those sprints."

As soon as they had passed, Antimone edged out onto the track and accelerated. She finished the bend in the fourth lane, five metres behind the pack, pulling wide to avoid any recurrence of the collision with Max. The last two laps were sheer agony as she pushed her body despite the bouts of nausea that seemed to creep up on her as she coasted between sprints.

Finally, she joined the rest of the group, all of whom lay on the ground, panting for breath. Once again, her stomach heaved, and she spat out a mouthful of foul-tasting vomit. This appeared to set off a chain reaction as two of the other boys copied her example.

The coach sauntered towards the athletes, a faint smile on his lips. "Good session ladies—at least so far. There's nothing to be ashamed of with a bit of puking. Just make sure you stay warm. We don't want any strained muscles. We've worked on your stamina, so we're going to do some weight pulling next to improve your power."

The two boys who had retained their stomach contents rose to their feet, grinning down at their vomiting training partners.

"I think they must be suffering from morning sickness, coach," one of them said.

"Nah," laughed the other, "not possible. I reckon they're all virgins."

## Thursday 20th May 2032

Antimone unlocked the blue front door and propelled herself into the hall of the small detached house. It occupied a plot at the end of a cul-de-sac in a modern housing development at the edge of the town of Northstowe. Her parents had bought the property shortly after the award of the scholarship at Oakington Manor. The house was a short bus ride from the school, but her father's commute to his place of work at an engineering company on the south eastern side of Cambridge had increased by half an hour compared to their previous residence.

Her mother, who had trained as a primary school teacher, had already lost her job prior to the move due to the drastic decline in pupil numbers resulting from the Orestes virus. She was now retraining as a nurse at Addenbrooke's Hospital to the south of Cambridge city centre. Both parents left for work long before she caught the school bus, but they had taken the afternoon off so that they could be at home to greet her when she returned home on her sixteenth birthday.

The sound of whispered voices came from the lounge. As Antimone pushed open the door, an out of tune rendition of "Happy Birthday" burst out. Her mother proudly held a cake topped by a forest of lit candles. Halfway through the song, the candle flames merged together, and her mother had to put the cake down to avoid singeing her hair. The melody petered out as her father hurriedly knelt down to blow out the blazing mass.

"I told you to place them further apart," he said to his wife when they were finally extinguished.

"My hero," she replied. "I've always wanted a big, strong fireman to look after me."

Laughter rang around the room as Dominic and Helen Lessing bent down to hug their only daughter.

"I thought I was supposed to blow out the candles," Antimone said.

"I can relight them if you want," her mother replied, "but we should probably call the fire brigade first."

"On second thoughts, maybe not."

"Who'd have thought it?" her father said. "My little girl, sixteen years old and all grown up."

"Let's sit down," her mother said. "We've got some presents for you."

A pile of brightly coloured parcels on the coffee table drew Antimone's gaze. She followed her parents as they crossed the room and settled onto the blue-coloured sofa.

"Here's one that I think you'll like," her mother said, picking up a small bright green package wrapped in a red ribbon.

Antimone undid the ribbon and tore the paper off. She lifted the lid of a blue, hinged box to reveal a pair of earrings in the shape of the five Olympic rings.

"They'll go well with the gold medal around your neck in September," her mother said, leaning over to hug her daughter.

"I've got to be selected for the British team first, Mum," Antimone replied.

"Yeah, but you'll breeze the final selection race," her father added. "You've only got to finish in the top three to guarantee your place and your times this year are faster than anybody else in the country by several seconds."

"Thanks for the support, Dad, but I've still got to do it on the day."

"I've every confidence in you."

"Oh, that reminds me," her mother said. "I was talking to one of the doctors today—"

"Not a handsome one, I hope," her father interrupted.

"As I was saying, I was talking to one of the doctors who's a specialist in spinal injuries. He said that there have been some exciting breakthroughs in repairing spine damage, with stem cells and the like. It's all a bit experimental, but he said that he might be able to get you into one of their programmes if you want."

The smile disappeared from Antimone's face. "So, one minute you're talking about me racing at the Paralympics and the next about me walking again."

"But you can do both," her mother replied. "After that court case last year where the man received treatment and regained the use of his legs, he was allowed to continue competing in the Paralympic wheelchair races."

Antimone sighed. "Yeah, but none of the other athletes want anything to do with him. What is it they call him? A Fake-Olympian? He may have won the court case, but once you start letting able-bodied people take part, there'll be loads of people giving it a go. Before you know it, the genuinely disabled won't get a look in."

Her mother's face dropped. "I thought you'd want to walk again, but if you're happy to stay in that contraption…"

"Helen, let's change the subject," her father said. His expression brightened as he picked up a shiny red package and handed it to Antimone. "This one's from both of us."

Antimone removed the paper, uncovering a rectangular shaped plastic box.

"Go on then, open it," her mother said, the earlier conversation seemingly forgotten.

Antimone inspected the contents and pulled out a wristwatch with a large black dial.

"It's the latest in health watches," her father said excitedly. "It measures pulse rate, blood sugar levels, time of the month, if you know what I mean, and so on. It even tells the time. Try it on."

Antimone slipped the gadget over her wrist and tightened the strap. The black face illuminated to display a clock face reading five thirty-two and a 'Calibrating' message at the centre of the dial in green text. After four or five seconds, a heart icon appeared in the top left corner with the number fifty-two to the right of it. A yellow exclamation mark flashed in the top right.

"Look, your heart rate's fifty-two beats per minute," her father said. "That's pretty low, but you are a well-trained athlete after all. I don't know what the yellow symbol means, though." He picked up the box and removed the instruction card.

"Why do they always have to make the text so small?" he complained, squinting at the tiny letters. "Ah, here we go. Press the button in the bottom right quadrant."

Antimone did as he suggested and depressed the sliver of black plastic that protruded from the body of the watch. She stared at the message displayed in the centre but remained silent.

"What does it say then?" her mother asked.

"Um—it—it can't be right. It says I'm pregnant."

"What?" her father said, jumping to his feet. "Let's have a look at that."

"You haven't…" began her mother before tailing off.

Antimone rubbed the back of her neck. "Oh, don't be ridiculous. Of course not."

"It must be faulty then," her mother said. "I'll take it back tomorrow and get a replacement."

"Bloody cheap crap," her father added before realising what he'd said. "Actually, bloody expensive crap. Look, we can exchange it for something else if you want."

"No, it's okay, Dad," Antimone said, chewing a fingernail.

"Why don't I try it on?" suggested her mother. "It might give us a clue as to whether it's faulty or not."

Antimone slipped the watch off her wrist and handed it over.

Helen Lessing tightened the strap and inspected the dial. "Heart rate eighty-five but no exclamation mark."

"That's a bit fast," her husband replied.

"Well, I'm a bit bloody stressed," she snapped. She clicked the same button that Antimone had pressed, but the only things to be displayed were her blood sugar level and a green tick. A quick consultation of the manual revealed that the tick was an indication she was not in her fertile window.

The room descended into silence, the unopened presents forgotten on the table.

## Friday 21st May 2032

The following morning, Helen Lessing was ready to leave the house before seven o'clock. It was too early to phone in sick, but she had every intention of letting her employers know she was feeling too unwell to work as soon as the reception staff arrived. She had persuaded Antimone to accompany her on the trip to Cambridge city centre, where she had originally bought the watch. The plan was to depart early enough to beat the morning rush hour and be there by the time the electrical goods store opened at nine o'clock.

The previous evening, she had grilled her daughter about her sexual activities despite the vociferous protests. It was only when Antimone screamed at the top of her voice that she had not even kissed anybody in the last six months, let alone had sexual intercourse, that her mother finally relented. "It must be faulty, then," she had stated as if announcing a court verdict, reluctantly accepting that her daughter was telling the truth.

"Call me when you know anything," Dominic Lessing said as the two women departed the house into the dull grey morning. Helen helped Antimone enter the small red autonomous car, collapsing the wheelchair and placing it in the boot. She selected their destination on the central navigation screen and waited while the onboard computers performed their start-up checks. After a few seconds, the vehicle exited the short driveway and smoothly edged onto the quiet residential street. They sat in silence, each lost in their own thoughts as it navigated itself along the already busy roads towards the Grafton Centre car park.

"Let's have breakfast at one of those coffee bars while we're waiting for the shop to open," Helen suggested when the car announced it had reached its destination.

"I'm not hungry," Antimone said, but her mother insisted she needed to eat something. They found an empty table at a Coffee Station restaurant and ordered a hot drink and a croissant each.

"It's got to be faulty. There's no other explanation," Helen said, grasping her daughter's hand across the table.

"Yeah, I know, but I'm still allowed to worry, aren't I?"

45

Time dragged as they watched the minute hand slowly edge around the clock face. At ten to nine, they left the coffee shop and began the short journey to the Gadget Gangsta store where Helen had bought the watch the previous week. As they arrived, a man dressed in matching red trousers and shirt was busy raising the security shutters.

"We'll just be another minute or two if you'd like to wait," he stated cheerily. He completed the task, then held the door open for them, smiling brightly. "How can I help you?"

The man seemed puzzled as Helen explained their problem. "I have to say these watches are pretty reliable," he said, "but if you want to try another one, I'll just go and fetch one."

He hurried away to the stock room and returned a minute later carrying a box identical to the one that rested on the counter. "Here, put this on."

Antimone slipped the chunky black watch over her wrist and adjusted the strap. The dial displayed the calibration message. This time, the heart rate read ninety-two. Her eyes homed in on the top right corner where the exclamation mark had appeared. Nothing. She exhaled loudly and turned the watch face so her mother could see. Helen's pallor turned an ashen white as her eyes met her daughter's. In confusion, Antimone glanced down a second time and spotted the flashing yellow icon.

"Oh Christ," she said in a low whisper.

The man's gaze flitted between mother and daughter. "Um, on rare occasions I have heard of... um... inaccuracies with this type of technology. You could always go to the chemist for a more reliable test. So, do you want to return it, keep that one or take the original?"

He had barely finished speaking when Helen said, "We'll keep it," snatched up the empty box and hurried towards the door, pushing her daughter's wheelchair from behind. Under normal circumstances, Antimone would have objected violently to being pushed, but her mind seemed to have turned to mush, and she allowed her mother to propel her forwards.

"Okay, well have a—" The man stopped when he realised he was talking to a closing door.

Helen hurried along the concourse past the brightly coloured shop fronts until she spotted a familiar green cross. Several customers and staff watched in interest as mother and daughter raced down the aisles. Finally, they came across a shelf stacked with five different brands of pregnancy test kit.

Helen grabbed one of each, dropping them on Antimone's lap and rushed towards the checkout. She quickly retrieved the boxes, placed them in the scanning area, then waved her card at the machine, not even bothering to check the amount. No sooner was the transaction confirmed than she tossed the selection of kits back to her daughter and swept out of the store.

"Mum, wait," shouted Antimone. Her mother stopped pushing, her breathing coming fast and ragged. "Just calm down. We need the loos. They contain little sticks that I need to wee on. Look there are some toilets over there." She indicated a corridor with a large sign above it. "And by the way, I can push myself."

"Okay, sorry. Shall I carry some of those?"

"No, I'm fine. Just make sure I don't drop any."

Antimone guided the wheelchair into the ladies toilet area. She found a stall reserved for the disabled, and both she and her mother hustled inside. As she transferred herself to the seat, her mother opened one of the boxes with fumbling fingers and handed a tester to her daughter.

After losing bladder control as a consequence of her injury, the surgeons had fitted Antimone with an implant that warned her when she needed to urinate and controlled the flow using fingernail sensors. She tapped out the correct combination and held a strip in the stream.

"It'll say on the display," her mother said, her face a mask of tension.

Both mother and daughter studied the indicator at the end of the short white stick. Within five seconds, the word 'Pregnant' was clearly visible.

***

The small vehicle pulled into the staff car park at Addenbrooke's Hospital. They had tried another pregnancy kit, just to be sure, but the result was the same. Helen Lessing had contacted a work colleague and arranged to visit her employer's maternity department to get a final confirmation and an estimate of how long since conception. She was still struggling to come to terms with the fact that her daughter had no inkling how she had become pregnant.

"But you must have some idea," she said in exasperation.

Antimone sighed. "Mum, if I knew, don't you think I'd tell you? It's not the sort of thing I'd be likely to forget, is it?"

"When we know how far along you are, that might give us a clue. Let's just pray it's less than four weeks."

Silence fell between them as they hurried down the brightly lit corridor. No sooner had they entered the maternity reception area, than a woman in her early fifties with greying hair tied back in a ponytail and wearing a blue nurse's uniform rushed over to greet them. Her face was etched with concern.

"Thanks for doing this, Angie," Helen said.

"No problem." She stared down, but Antimone avoided her gaze. "I just hope… Anyway, follow me, and we'll start the tests. So, you have no idea how this happened?"

Antimone shook her head. The nurse glanced towards her mother for confirmation.

Helen shrugged her shoulders. "Apparently not."

"We'll need to take a urine sample. I'll take a blood sample too, just in case. We should have the results in about half an hour if I rush them through."

The nurse led them to an examination room containing a single hospital bed. A door opened into a cramped bathroom. "I just need you to wee in here," she said handing a small plastic container to Antimone. "Just screw the lid on when you've finished."

"Do you need any help?" Helen asked.

"Jesus, Mum. I think I can pee in a jar."

When Antimone returned to the room, she handed the specimen bottle over. The nurse wrote on the label, then asked her to roll up her sleeve. She fitted a rubber tourniquet just above the elbow, then inserted a needle and withdrew a vial of blood. Once again, she recorded the details.

"That's it," she announced brightly. "I'll take you back to the waiting room, and we'll have the results shortly."

\*\*\*

Antimone glanced at her wrist before remembering she was no longer wearing a watch, having removed it to try on the one given to her for her birthday. Instead, she turned her attention to the large clock dial on the wall. It was now forty minutes since they had left the examination room. Her eyes roamed across the room. Only two of the seats were occupied. On one of them sat a woman with long dark hair who appeared to be in her mid-thirties and was clearly pregnant. She was engrossed in the display of her phone, her fingers performing intricate manoeuvres above the screen. The other seated a woman with mousy shoulder length hair, leaning forward, her head in her hands. It wasn't clear from her outline whether she was pregnant, but her demeanour told another story.

Antimone and her mother both looked up sharply as the sound of footsteps signalled the nurse's return. Her face gave nothing away.

"Sorry, that took a bit longer than expected. Let's go back to the examination room."

Antimone's heart hammered in her chest, and her breath came in short bursts as she propelled herself along the corridor beside her mother. This must be how a prisoner felt before learning whether the judge was about to pass a death sentence.

The nurse closed the door and turned to face mother and daughter. Helen rested an arm on Antimone's shoulder.

"I'm sorry to say, but you're definitely pregnant. Unfortunately, the tests indicate that you're six weeks along, which means it's too late to consider a termination. I'm really sorry."

Antimone gasped. A rushing sound seemed to fill her head. Her ears burned, and her face felt flushed. She had only nine months left before she died—no, less than that—seven and a half months.

48

"Are you absolutely sure?" Helen asked, her voice quivering. "Can you run the test again?"

"I already ran it twice, which is why it took longer than I said it would. Do you need some time alone? I can arrange counselling if you'd like."

"No," Antimone said. "I want to go home."

## Friday 21st May 2032

The policewoman peered sceptically at the father, mother and daughter who sat before her on the other side of her desk. Karen Atkins, or Kat as her friends and colleagues knew her, was a senior investigator for the Maternity Crimes Unit, more commonly referred to by its abbreviation, MCU. The division was established to investigate allegations of rape and to put a stop to the activities of the backstreet abortionists who offered their services when the government-appointed health professionals announced that a pregnancy was too far advanced to operate. Kat professed a particular hatred for the charlatans and criminals, who in practically every case, ended up terminating the pregnancy but also killing the patient at the same time.

The unit had been formed eleven years earlier, and she had been appointed to her position following a successful career in the Metropolitan Police Service. After more than a decade of seeing the depravity wreaked upon women by men, many of whom still professed to love their partners, Kat thought she had seen it all, but encountering a victim who had no recollection of the crime was a new one for her.

She wore her straight brown hair just over her ears, although at the age of fifty-one, its uniform colour owed much to the contents of a bottle. The room was a couple of degrees too warm, which caused the collar of her white shirt to chafe at her neck and the black skirt to feel sweaty around the waistband. She adjusted her position on the chair and resumed her questioning.

"So, let's go back to the beginning again. You're six weeks pregnant, but you've no idea who's responsible?"

Antimone shook her head. "No."

"And you can't remember how it happened?"

"No, but I think it must have been when I was at a friend's party."

"When was the party?"

"It was the tenth of April, just under six weeks ago."

"And whose party was it?"

"Jason Baxter invited me. He's the son of Rosalind Baxter. She's the owner or something of this big biotechnology company."

Kat made a mental note. She knew exactly who Rosalind Baxter was. Rich and powerful people generally wanted to protect their privacy in situations such as this and were often prepared to flex political or financial muscle to ensure it happened. This case would have to be handled sensitively.

"So, what makes you think you got pregnant at the party?"

Antimone paused before replying. "Well, um… a group of us were sitting in the corner—I mean I was in the wheelchair, but the others were sitting on the sofa. Jason went to get a refill for the fruit punch and shortly after that… um, I couldn't get my words out, and then I fell asleep."

"So, you think the drink was spiked?"

"Yeah, it looks like it."

"You never mentioned that before," Dominic Lessing interjected.

"Please let her continue," Kat said. "Do you know if it had any alcohol in to start with?"

"No, I don't think so, but after he came back, it tasted slightly different."

"In what way?"

Antimone thought for a second. "It's difficult to describe, but there was a bit of a funny taste to it."

"Was anybody else drinking alcohol?"

"No, I don't think so. Jason made a joke about only getting the alcohol out when his Mum wasn't around."

"So, his mother was at the party?"

"Well, I saw her when I arrived, but then she received a telephone call and left the room."

"And afterwards?"

"I eventually woke up about an hour later. All the others were still asleep on the sofa. I think it must have happened while I was unconscious."

"Why are you only telling us this now?" interrupted her father angrily.

"Sorry Dad," Antimone replied, "I didn't think it was important—well at least not until I found out I was pregnant."

Kat raised her hands. "Mr Lessing, please let your daughter tell me what happened."

"Well, I was feeling a bit sick and wanted to splash water on my face so I started heading towards the bathroom. Then I heard a shout outside, so I went into the garden and saw one of Mrs Baxter's security guards jump out of a broken window and chase after a man who was running away."

"Did you see the man: the one being chased?"

"No, but somebody told me he had a beard and was wearing a woollen hat of some sort. I think I saw him arguing with Mrs Baxter earlier."

Kat scribbled on the pad in front of her, preferring the old-fashioned pen and paper method of taking notes. "And you don't know who this man was?"

"No… although I think I may have seen him at the athletics track."

Antimone continued to explain about the training session and how she thought she had seen the same bearded man in the stand.

"What happened next at the party?" Kat asked.

"I phoned my Mum, and she came to collect me, then took me home."

"Okay. Well, we'll need an official statement, and I'm going to talk to Mrs Baxter and her son. We'll also take a blood sample so that we can do some paternity tests. I know it's not much of a consolation, but we're going to find the person who did this to you."

Kat walked around the desk and shook hands with Antimone and her parents. "I've got your details. I'll be in touch in the next day or two. Thanks for coming in."

She waited for the door to close, then returned to her chair. She picked up the phone and dialled a number. After a few seconds, somebody answered.

"I've got an interesting one here."

# 13

*T*he girl winced as the needle slipped into a vein on the inside of her elbow. She had been scared of needles since the age of four when a staphylococcal infection had resulted in her being hospitalised and hooked up to a drip containing powerful anti-bacterial drugs. Even now she could remember her childhood terror when the doctor first inserted the shiny needle. What had helped to sear the memory in her mind was the trauma of the nurse ripping off the anaesthetic patches afterwards, two from each arm. Ironically, they had been put in place to numb the area where the needle would be inserted but had been left on for so long that each one came away attached to a rectangle of skin.

The balding doctor filled two vials with blood, then positioned a small wad of cotton wool over the puncture wound and told her to press down on it. He placed the two small tubes on the bedside cabinet and affixed a piece of surgical tape to hold the cotton wool in position.

"That wasn't so bad, was it?" he said, not looking at the girl as he wrote on the labels.

"What do you need it for?" she asked.

The man waited until he had finished writing, then turned to face her. "You know we took that sample a few weeks ago? Well, we're just checking up on something. How are you feeling anyway?"

"Actually…" The girl paused for a second, deciding how to answer. "I've been feeling a bit sick the last few days."

The doctor frowned and sat down on the bed. "About that. There's something I need to tell you. I'm sorry, but I've got some bad news."

The girl looked up sharply. "What? What's wrong with me?"

"We think you're pregnant. This blood test will help to confirm how far along you are, but it's at least seven weeks."

"How could I be? Seven weeks? I've been here for—what?—five. You're saying I was pregnant when you brought me here? I haven't had sex with a man, proper sex that is, for months and even then, he wore protection."

"Look, I don't know how it happened, but I suspect it was while you were out of it on one of your trips."

"That's impossible. I'm never so far gone that I don't know what's going on in the real world. The drug heightens reality—it doesn't replace it. You're lying."

"I wish for your sake I was, but unfortunately, it's true. I don't know how you got pregnant. All I know is that we went back over the blood tests, and it had already happened by the time you arrived here."

"If I'm pregnant, why have you only discovered that now? I've been here for ages."

"I'm really sorry. We were concentrating on treating your drug dependence. We didn't realise you were pregnant, and you didn't tell us."

"How the hell could I tell you?" she screamed. "I didn't bloody know."

"I'm sorry, it's very unfortunate."

"Unfortunate? You tell me I'm going to die in a few months, and it's fricking unfortunate? Christ, you people. So, it's too late for an abortion?"

"I'm afraid so. After four weeks, the chances of survival are practically zero, and you've already been in our care for five. I know it's not good news, but you're in a place where we can give you the best treatment throughout the pregnancy."

"I still don't know where this place is. Have you forgotten to tell me that too?"

"You're in a state-of-the-art hospital. We have excellent facilities, and we'll make you as comfortable as we can."

"I don't give a toss where I am or what facilities you have. Just get out and leave me alone."

The doctor rose to his feet. "Once again, I'm really sorry to bring you this bad news. I'll be back later to check on you again." He crossed the room to the door, swiped his card at the reader and let himself out.

The girl clambered off the mattress and screamed at the top of her voice. Then, for the second time during her stay, she lifted the bed and hurled it onto its side.

## Monday 24th May 2032

None of the Lessing family had left the house that morning. Dominic and Helen had phoned their places of work and Antimone her school, all claiming to be unwell. The weekend had passed in a haze as they tried to come to terms with the shocking news they had received the previous Friday. Antimone had gone over in her mind the events at Jason's party, but the only rational explanation was that somebody had raped her when she was unconscious. How could that have happened at a busy gathering? Surely somebody would have noticed?

"I'm making a pot of tea," Helen said, rising to her feet. "Does anyone else want one?"

"Yes, please," Dominic replied.

"Antimone?"

Antimone shook her head. "No, thanks." She had already consumed one cup of coffee and two of tea that morning, and it still wasn't yet ten o'clock.

The doorbell chime echoed through the house.

"I'll get it," came a call from the kitchen. The sound of footsteps preceded the scrape of the heavy wooden door opening.

"Who is it?" Dominic called.

His question was answered when Helen led Karen Atkins into the lounge.

"Can I take your coat?" Helen asked.

Kat shrugged out of the lightweight brown overcoat and handed it over. She wore a black skirt and a matching jacket over a white shirt. "Thanks"

"I'm just making a cup of tea. Do you want one?" Helen asked.

"Yes, please," Kat replied, taking a seat on one of the two green armchairs. "White, no sugar."

"Have you got any news?" Dominic asked.

"Yes, but let's wait until your wife returns. How are you, Antimone?"

"Alright, I suppose," Antimone said. "None of it seems real yet."

"Yeah, a lot of people in your situation say that."

The room descended into an awkward silence as they waited for the tea to arrive. Eventually, Helen bustled into the room carrying a tray on which sat three mugs and a plate of chocolate biscuits. Kat accepted the mug but declined a biscuit, conscious of the tightness of her waistband. When she had handed out all the drinks, Helen took a seat on the opposite end of the sofa to her husband, her hands resting on her lap.

"Well, we've made quite a bit of progress," Kat began. "I spoke at length to both Mrs Baxter and her son and several other guests. I haven't told any of them that you're pregnant yet, Antimone, just that you think you were sexually assaulted."

"And what have you found out?" Antimone's father said, leaning forwards.

"Well, we know the identity of the man who was arguing with Mrs Baxter and who was later seen fleeing through a broken window. His name is Daniel Floyd. He's a convicted murderer who was released from prison three months ago after serving a nominal life sentence."

"What was he doing at Mrs Baxter's house?" Helen asked, concern etched across her face.

"I'm just coming onto that. He was arrested after his wife went missing. The police discovered traces of her blood in the boot of his car, and he was convicted of her murder even though her body was never found. He claimed he had nothing to do with it. The wife used to work as a researcher for Mrs Baxter's company, and he apparently thinks she withheld vital information that could have helped clear him. Of course, she denies it, but it seems he still holds a grudge against her. Floyd and Mrs Baxter also have a bit of history together before he met his wife. By all accounts, they went out for a while just after they both left college, but then split up."

"So, what's this got to do with Antimone's rape?" Dominic asked.

"We have several eyewitnesses who spotted him at the house, including Antimone herself. We still have blood samples on record from the original investigation and from when he was in prison. We ran tests on the blood we took from Antimone last Friday, and we were able to create a genetic fingerprint for the baby. The analysis isn't as accurate as it would have been had we taken material directly from the foetus, but at this stage of the pregnancy that's far too risky. In any case, it's good enough to identify the father with a high degree of probability."

"And..."

"It appears that Mr Floyd is the rapist. There is a very strong correlation between his genetic material and that of the baby."

Antimone gasped and held a hand to her mouth.

"But why would he rape Antimone?" Helen asked.

"We don't know that, but we intend to ask him when we catch him."

"So, you haven't caught him yet?"

"The results only came in this morning, but a warrant has been issued for his arrest. It shouldn't be too hard to track him down because his address is registered as part of his parole conditions. I'm expecting the call any minute."

"So, what's going to happen to him?" Dominic asked.

"Well, obviously he'll be put back in prison, and then he'll be charged with rape. On the basis that there were no witnesses to the act itself, we'll need to rely on the genetic evidence to convict him. And that brings me onto a bit of a sensitive point. I'm assuming that you plan to carry the baby to term Antimone?"

"Why wouldn't she?" her mother asked, a hint of hope in her voice. "The doctors said it was too late for a termination."

"I know," Kat replied. "This situation doesn't happen very often because most women are aware that they've been raped and have the abortion within the first four weeks. There have been a few rare instances like your own when too much time has passed for the mother to survive a termination. Some of those women have the termination anyway."

"What, and die?" Dominic asked in horror.

"I'm afraid so. Some just can't bear to have the rapist's seed growing inside them. Not that I'm suggesting for one minute that Antimone should do that."

"I'm keeping it," Antimone announced firmly. "It's not the baby's fault, and I'm not ready to die yet either."

Kat appeared relieved. "Good. The only thing is, the Crown Prosecution Service will probably want to wait until after the baby is born before they open the case."

"Why can't they prosecute him now?" Helen asked.

"They'll want to take blood directly from the baby to prove paternity, and even then, it often takes six months to a year for the prosecution to build the case. He'll be kept in prison during that time, though."

"I just want to see him suffer," Dominic said vehemently.

"I can assure you, he won't have a pleasant experience in jail. Rapists generally get a very rough ride from both the guards and the other inmates."

"I hope they kick the shit out of him."

"Hmm," Kat said, getting to her feet. "Anyway, I'll let you know as soon as we have him in custody. Thanks for the tea."

Antimone remained in the lounge while her parents saw the policewoman out. They returned to find her reading the screen of her phone.

"What are you looking at?" her father asked.

"Just the details of the original court case."

Dominic peered over his daughter's shoulder at a photograph of an attractive woman, smiling brightly into the camera. It had obviously been cropped from a group picture because a man's arm was clearly visible in the bottom right corner. The image appeared dated, but that was probably due to the fact that it was recorded in two dimensions compared to the more common three.

"She was a beautiful woman," he said.

Antimone didn't respond but scrolled down to read the story. "It says she worked at Ilithyia Biotechnology. In those days it was only a small company on the Cambridge Science Park. He was a physicist working at a research laboratory. Apparently, he phoned the police to say she hadn't come home from work, and he was worried about her. When they checked his car, they found a pool of blood in the boot."

"Does it say anything about why he did it?" Dominic asked.

"No. He used to go out with Mrs Baxter and the police had a theory he still loved her and wanted to get rid of his wife so they could get back together. But it says here that when he was sentenced, he tried to get out of the dock and attack her."

"And they never found the body?"

"A witness said they'd seen his car parked by the river. They used divers and dredged it, but they didn't find anything. He claimed he was at home at the time, sick in bed."

Antimone scrolled down further until she came across a photograph of the killer. In the image, he had short brown hair with a parting to the left and was smartly dressed in a white shirt with a blue tie. His smile seemed unnatural and forced. She attempted to reconcile the picture with her memory of the bearded man she had seen through the window but could not detect any similarities. She shuddered slightly as she focused on his hazel eyes.

"I hope the bastard rots in hell," her father said.

## Saturday 5th June 2032

Antimone heard the sound of a car door shutting and pulled the curtain back to look out of the window. A slightly built man wearing a dark suit walked around the back of a silver-coloured car and opened the door on the opposite side. *Rosalind Baxter's personal assistant. But what the hell was his name?* His boss' immaculately coiffured head appeared above the roof of the vehicle. She glanced once in Antimone's direction, then murmured a few words to the man. He nodded and got back in using the same door.

The elegantly dressed woman approached the ramp leading up to the front door. A second or two later the doorbell rang. Both parents were out. Her mother was doing the weekly shopping, and her father was at work making up for some of the time he had lost during the past fortnight. Antimone debated for a moment whether to pretend she wasn't in but then propelled herself along the hall.

A concerned expression occupied Rosalind's face as Antimone pulled the door open. "Hello, Antimone. I was so sorry to hear the bad news. Are your parents at home?"

A waft of expensive perfume drifted into the house. Antimone shook her head.

"Um… do you mind if I come in for a second?"

Antimone thought it would be rude to refuse. "Okay."

Rosalind closed the door behind her and followed Antimone into the lounge. "May I sit down?"

Antimone nodded.

Rosalind perched on the edge of her chair and stared at Antimone for a moment before speaking. "I just wanted to let you know how sorry I am that you were um… assaulted… at Jason's party. I feel really bad about it—not that I could have anticipated…" Her voice tailed off.

Antimone had a sudden urge to challenge this woman. "I saw you arguing with him before I was drugged."

Rosalind seemed surprised at the boldness of the statement. "I'm afraid the man's totally delusional. I assume you know his wife used to work for me.

He thought I kept back evidence that would have proved he was innocent of her murder, but it's all total nonsense. I told him if he didn't leave, I'd call the police, and I thought that was the end of it. I had no idea he would come back and... well, attack you."

"I read that you used to go out with him."

Rosalind frowned. "That was a very long time ago, and I very quickly corrected my mistake. It's not something I really like to discuss."

Antimone realised that she had overstepped the mark and changed tack. "So, do you know if they've caught him yet? The police said they would tell us when he was arrested, but we still haven't heard anything."

"No, they haven't told me anything either. It seems that he hasn't been back to the address he registered with his parole officer. I just hope they find him soon." Rosalind sat back a fraction. "There was another thing I wanted to talk to you about, but maybe I should wait until your parents are here." She hesitated, glanced at her watch, then seemed to come to a decision. "If I tell you my proposal now, perhaps you can discuss it with your mother and father and let me know your thoughts."

"Um, okay."

"As I'm sure you know, my company has a large facility very close to here. We're working hard to find a cure for this awful disease. I know it can never make up for what's happened to you, but I'd like to offer the use of our facilities when the time comes. There's a hospital on site equipped with all the latest machines. Of course, you'd have a private room and some of the best medical care in the world. If you like, I'd also be happy to include you in one of our experimental research programmes. I certainly can't promise anything, but we're making progress all the time."

Antimone had to admit that the proposal was unexpected. On the face of it, it was a generous offer, but a cynical part of her wondered whether this was all a ploy to prevent legal action, not that they had ever discussed the idea as a family. The real carrot was the hint of a cure.

"Um... Thanks."

"So, you'll discuss it with your parents when they return? Here's a card with my private number on it. Call me anytime."

Antimone took the rectangular card and placed it on the coffee table.

Rosalind stood up, brushing down her grey skirt and smiled. "I've enjoyed our little chat. Don't worry, I can let myself out." She crossed the room and strode along the corridor without looking back, her heels clacking on the wooden planks. Antimone followed a short distance behind.

Rosalind opened the front door, turned briefly and raised a hand in farewell before pulling it shut after her. She descended the ramp and hurried across to the car. Her assistant was still only halfway out of the door by the time she slid in beside him.

"Am I not paying you enough to open doors for me?" she snapped.

Julian Stefano mumbled an apology. He had been taking a call and hadn't noticed her leaving the house until it was too late, but he knew better than to make excuses.

When she had finished instructing the navigation system to take her home, she turned to him with a smug expression on her face. "So, are you going to ask me what happened?"

"Okay. How did it go?" he asked dutifully.

"Impertinent little bitch. Her parents weren't there, but I don't think she'll be a problem."

## Monday 21st June 2032

The pregnancy wasn't showing yet, but even so Antimone deliberately wore loose, baggy clothing. She waited with her mother and father outside the head teacher's office. Her 'I Level' examinations were due to start the following Tuesday. Part of her had considered leaving school and skipping these tests—she was sixteen years old, after all—but her parents had persuaded her to continue with her studies. As it turned out the hours of revision had been a welcome distraction from her predicament.

Normality was what Antimone craved the most. The initial shock had abated to the extent that it was now little more than a foreboding thought lurking in the back of her mind. Every so often it would creep to the forefront. When that happened, she would descend once again into a dark pit of despair. It was the mundane activities of home life and school work that helped her to maintain an even keel. She worried that if she didn't keep herself occupied, she would give up and descend into a spiral of depression.

She had not attended athletics training since she had discovered she was pregnant. Thoughts of the Paralympics were now a distant dream. By the time October came around, she would be six months pregnant and in no state to compete. She didn't think she could even tolerate watching coverage on the television. It would be a painful reminder of what could have been. Her coach, John Marshall, seemed the most disappointed. It was clear he knew nothing about her condition. Shortly after her return to school, he had cornered her in the corridor and asked what was going on. She had spun out some story about commitments to examinations getting in the way, but her explanation had sounded unbelievable even to her own ears.

The solid wooden door opened and the figure of a tall man, wearing a dark suit and red tie, emerged. Two patches of grey hair, one on either side of his head, framed a bald patch on top. He wore a pair of frameless, rectangular-shaped glasses, the strong lenses exaggerating the size of his eyes. The slightest hint of body odour wafted through the open doorway.

"Mr and Mrs Lessing, Antimone," he said. "Sorry to keep you waiting. Please come in."

Dominic and Helen Lessing rose from the low-slung, red armchairs and followed their daughter across the deep pile of the blue carpet.

Two wooden chairs with black leather seats occupied positions in front of the large oak desk, the surface of which was empty apart from a black computer display and matching keyboard perched on the left side. Framed certificates ringed the walls and sunlight streamed in through the wide, floor to ceiling windows.

"I'm John Weaver," he said, shaking hands with each of them in turn. He had to stoop to shake Antimone's hand. "I think we've met a couple of times before. Do take a seat."

He rounded the desk, sank into the high-backed swivel chair, then leant forwards, his elbows resting on the polished surface. "I wanted to start by saying what a wonderful student Antimone has been but… um… I was shocked and saddened to hear about what happened. I understand they're still looking for the man responsible."

"Thanks," Dominic mumbled. "He seems to have disappeared off the face of the planet, but the police are still searching for him."

"Well, I hope they find him soon. Anyway, there's something else I need to discuss with you today. I know Antimone's scholarship was established to cover the fees until the end of her secondary education, but it is the duty of the trustees to ensure that the funds are used effectively. Given Antimone's condition, I imagine she won't be pursuing her athletics career, and that was one of the major factors in deciding to offer the scholarship in the first place. It also seems unlikely she'll be able to complete the academic side of her education. I feel the other students will find it unsettling to have Antimone sharing the classroom with them in her current condition so it's with regret that I have to inform you the trustees and I have decided we will be withdrawing Antimone's place at this school with immediate effect."

Dominic turned to Helen, who reflected his own shocked expression, then back to the tall man seated opposite. "What? So, you're expelling her? I don't believe this. There are only six weeks of term to go."

Weaver appeared flustered. Antimone noticed that his left hand was trembling until he clamped his right on top. "I wouldn't call it an expulsion, but we do have to consider the welfare of our other students."

"You mean your other *fee-paying* students," Dominic spat. "My daughter is sexually assaulted, gets pregnant through no fault of her own and now you want to kick her out of school a week before she takes her exams in case it upsets your other students. What about upsetting us?"

"Look, I'm sorry, but the board's decision is final. Also, I'm sure I don't have to remind you about the non-disclosure agreement you signed when we offered Antimone the scholarship."

"What, because I might want to tell the press about the despicable actions of this school?"

"Dad, just leave it," Antimone interrupted. "It's not worth it. It's not as if the qualifications will be any use to me, anyway."

"That's not the point," her father said.

"My hands are tied," the head teacher said. "Regretful though it is, there's nothing I can do. Of course, all fees are covered to date."

"Well, that's good to hear," Dominic said, his voice dripping with sarcasm. "I wouldn't put it past you and your friends on the board to send us a bill." He rose to his feet. "Come on, we're leaving."

Weaver came around the desk. "Once again, I'm really sorry. Our thoughts will be with you."

"Yeah, right," Dominic said, turning his back on the man. He strode towards the door, followed by his wife and daughter.

When they had left, Weaver turned the key in the lock and exhaled deeply. He returned to his desk, withdrew a phone from his jacket pocket and selected a number. The call was answered after a couple of rings.

"Hello, it's John Weaver. Can you let Mrs Baxter know that I've told them?"

## Monday 2nd August 2032

A ntimone's phone rang. She didn't recognise the number, but she could tell from the code that it was another mobile. "Identify," she murmured on the off chance that some public database held the details. Two seconds later, the screen displayed a 'not found' message.

"Oh, what the hell," she muttered and pressed the answer button. "Yes?"

"Antimone?" a male voice said.

Her finger hovered over the disconnect button. "Yeah, who's this?"

"It's Jason, Jason Baxter. You're quite hard to track down."

Antimone didn't respond.

"Are you still there?" he asked.

"Yes, I'm here."

"So, how are you? I didn't get a chance to say goodbye when you left school."

Antimone wasn't sure whether Jason was aware of the pregnancy. She figured it was likely that he was because the police had interviewed him, and his mother certainly knew.

"Alright I suppose," she answered tentatively.

"Erin Riley said you'd been expelled."

"Yeah, well, you know what she's like. Let's just say they decided I wasn't worth the cost of the scholarship any longer."

"Bastards. I'll have a chat with my Mum. She's on the board of governors."

"Don't bother. I'm not sure I'd want to go back anyway."

"Look, I'm so sorry about what happened at the party. I had nothing to do with it, but I still feel partly responsible. If you hadn't sat with me and the other guys…"

*So, he did know.* "It's okay, Jason. I don't blame you if that's what you want to hear." She immediately regretted her harsh words. "I'm sorry. I appreciate the call."

Jason sounded relieved. "So, what are you up to?"

"Oh, you know. Watching vids, listening to music, reading. Nothing much, really. What about you?"

"Much the same. Hey, look. Mum's said I can take one of the cars this afternoon. I was thinking of going to the seaside. Maybe Hunstanton. Do you want to come?"

"Just you and me?"

"Unless you think you need a chaperone."

"It's a little late for that, I think."

Jason laughed nervously. "I'm glad you've still got your sense of humour."

"So, when? Now?" Antimone asked, glancing at her watch. It was already twelve thirty.

"Yeah. I can be round in ten minutes."

Antimone hesitated. She didn't really feel like socialising, but the more she contemplated Jason's offer, the more the idea of getting out of the house grew on her. Both her parents were at work, and she was starting to get bored being on her own. She might not be able to feel the sand between her toes anymore, but the seaside always brought back happy memories. "Go on then, why not? But make it twenty minutes. I need to grab a bite to eat before we go."

"Great. I'll be there around one. Get your beachwear on."

\*\*\*

The journey took nearly two hours, but Antimone hardly noticed. The car was a far more expensive model than the one owned by her parents and was equipped with a state-of-the-art entertainment system. They spent the first half an hour playing with the various controls as the onboard computers navigated them through the Cambridgeshire and Norfolk countryside. Jason was a witty and entertaining companion, and he soon had her laughing at the outrageous stories of what he had witnessed at his mother's parties.

Eventually, the conversation moved on to parents.

"So, do you see your Dad?" Antimone asked.

Jason suddenly became serious. "I was adopted as a baby. I don't remember my biological mother, and my father apparently died from cancer before I was born. Mum's never really told me much about them. I've always wanted to find out more, but every time I ask, she changes the subject. Either she doesn't know or she doesn't want to tell me."

Antimone was silent for a moment. "I hope you don't mind me saying this, but your Mum doesn't seem like the type to adopt a child."

Jason laughed. "Well you know my Mum. She's so busy she wouldn't have found time for a pregnancy, so getting a readymade baby was probably the ideal solution for her."

"So, what's she like? I've only met her a couple of times, but she seems very... um... serious."

"Mum? If there's one word to describe her it would be driven. For the first ten years of my life, I was closer to the nannies she brought in to look after me. She began to show more interest once I could hold an intelligent conversation with her, but even then, the business always seemed to come first. That's just the way she is. Sometimes I think she's more attached to that little toad, Julian Stefano."

Antimone giggled. "Yeah, he's got a really slimy handshake. It felt like shaking hands with a slug. I wanted to wash my hands afterwards."

"I know exactly what you mean. He's like her poodle. If he had a tail, it'd be wagging every time she spoke to him."

Antimone did an impression of a dog barking as they both descended into fits of laughter.

***

The car navigated itself to a parking spot a hundred metres from the seafront. Jason slipped on his sunglasses, retrieved Antimone's wheelchair from the boot and helped her into it. He was wearing a multicoloured T-shirt that would have looked out-of-place anywhere but the seaside and a baggy pair of beach shorts.

"Let's head towards the promenade," Antimone suggested, the wind tugging a wisp of hair across her face. She wore a tight pink T-shirt and blue jeans but felt slightly drab compared to Jason's garish attire.

"Good idea."

They navigated their way across several roads, following the brown tourist signs that pointed to the south promenade. When they reached their destination, Jason ran on ahead, dodging between the tourists who strolled along the pedestrianised road adjacent to the shore.

"I thought you were supposed to be a wheelchair athlete," he called over his shoulder.

Antimone laughed as she steered around the pedestrians. "I could wup your ass anytime in a straight race, spear boy."

At a point where the beach was at the same level as the road, Jason slowed and allowed her to catch up. "How about here?" he asked.

"Yeah, why not?" She propelled herself onto the soft sand until the wheels sank deep enough that she could no longer move forwards.

"I think the lady's got a problem," he smiled. "Do you want to stay in that contraption of yours or sit on the sand?"

"Could you assist me to the ground, sir knight?"

"Yes, my lady." Jason picked her up, surprised at how little she weighed, and deposited her on the sand. He flopped down beside her. They both stared out in silence towards where the cloudless blue sky met the darker shade of the sea. The tide was on its way out, revealing the wooden groynes that seemed to pen in the holidaymakers like sheep in a field.

After a while, Antimone turned to Jason. "Thanks for bringing me here. I was starting to go a bit crazy stuck at home."

"You're welcome." He placed his hand on top of hers. When she didn't remove it, he leant sideways and kissed her gently on the cheek. She turned her head sideways, and their lips met.

After a few seconds, Antimone pulled back. "I really like you, Jason, but are you sure you want to do this? I'm not going to be around for much longer. We both know how this ends."

Jason took her face between his hands and kissed her again. "I really like you too. I know this can never be a long-term relationship, but I want to get to know you better in whatever time is left. I'm a good listener, and I'm here for you if you need me. So how are you bearing up?"

"Well, it's like... um... it still hasn't sunk in yet. I know I'm going to die in five months or so, but it still seems a long way off. I feel like I'm in a car hurtling towards a cliff, and I know the brakes don't work. It's like I'm still far enough away that I don't need them yet. But when I do... well, I don't know how I'm going to feel."

"I wish there was something I could do."

"Your mother did put me on one of her experimental programmes. One of her doctors gave me some pills, but he wouldn't say what they were. He did warn they might be a placebo, and even if they weren't, the chances of success were extremely small."

"Well, they've certainly got good facilities there. She's always moaning about how much the equipment costs."

"Yeah, it was also part of the deal that I went to her hospital for the birth."

"I'm sure they'll look after you well."

"Anyway, I don't want to talk about that anymore," Antimone said, brightening. "What sort of music do you like? Not that crap you had in the car I hope?"

Jason laughed and dropped a handful of sand on Antimone's lap. "You better be nice to me. Just remember you need me to get home."

"Yeah, that crap music was *really* great," she replied, returning the gesture.

***

The sun was getting lower in the sky. Antimone glanced at her watch. It was just before five o'clock. "We need to think about getting back. I haven't told my parents where I am."

Jason turned to face her. "Do you tell them everything you do?"

"Ever since the accident, they've been a bit over-protective. Anyway, I'll give them a call so it's not a problem."

"Time for an ice-cream before we go?"

"Why not? It wouldn't be the seaside without one."

Antimone brushed the sand off her jeans, and Jason helped her back into the wheelchair. He pushed the chair back onto the firm surface of the road.

"I can manage now," she said sharply.

"Um... I guess you don't like people pushing you."

"Not really. It's like... I don't know... like somebody playing with your hair or something... or prodding you in the back when you're walking to make you go faster."

Jason raised his hands. "Sorry, I didn't know."

Antimone silently cursed herself. She seemed to have developed this habit of pushing people away when they were only trying to be helpful. "Don't worry about it. Look, there's an ice-cream van just there."

"I'll get them. What's it to be? A cone?"

"Yeah, thanks, with one of those chocolate flakes in it if they've got one."

The white van was parked to the side of the pedestrianised road. Jason ran ahead and joined the queue of holidaymakers. Antimone turned her wheelchair to face the sea. At this spot, the promenade was two metres above the beach with stone steps leading down to the sand. She watched as families packed up their belongings in preparation for the journey home.

Her observations were distracted by somebody grabbing the wheelchair handles. "Jesus, Jason. I told you I don't like that."

"It's not your boyfriend, you little whore," said a voice deeper than Jason's. "If you scream, I'll push you over the edge. Come to think of it, I might just do that anyway."

Antimone jerked her head around. A man wearing a pair of large aviators and dressed in a navy-blue T-shirt stood behind her. Even without the beard, she recognised his face instantly as that of Daniel Floyd, the rapist.

"What do you want?" Antimone asked, her voice quivering with fright.

"What I want is for you to tell me why you set me up."

"Set you up? What're you talking about?"

"Give it a rest, alright. Was it that harpy, Rosalind Baxter? Was it her idea?"

"I'm sorry. I don't know what you mean."

"Oh, come on. You can't keep your bleeding legs together, get pregnant and then blame me. Haven't you heard of bloody contraception? It was that boyfriend of yours, wasn't it? I should have known the apple wouldn't fall far from the tree."

Antimone finally understood. "You think Jason raped me?"

"Raped?" the man said angrily. "It didn't look like that to me. I saw him come out of that bedroom looking as if he didn't have a care in the world. You followed him a minute or two later, and you certainly didn't seem distressed."

"What bedroom?"

"Oh, for Christ's sake, I *saw* you. How did you convince the police it was me? They must have done blood tests. Who did you bribe, or was it that witch, Baxter?"

"I—I didn't bribe anyone. I don't remember any of it, I was drugged."

"Drugged? That old excuse. You expect me to—" A shout came from the other side of the road. "You better watch your back," the man growled before he turned and ran.

"Who was that?" a breathless Jason asked. He held a cone in each hand, but one of them had lost the scoop of ice-cream and chocolate flake. "Are you alright?"

Antimone shivered and folded her arms across her chest even though it wasn't cold. "Daniel Floyd," she whispered.

"Daniel Floyd? What, the rapist?"

She nodded mutely.

"Christ, we better call the police."

Jason grabbed his phone from a pocket in his shorts and dialled. "Yes, it's an emergency. Police, please."

As he described what had happened, Antimone spoke in a dull voice. "He said he didn't do it."

"Hang on a sec," Jason said into the phone, then pulled it away from his ear. "What did you just say?"

"He said he didn't do it."

***

Antimone arrived home just after ten o'clock. The curtains twitched, and a face briefly appeared at the window before the front door swung open to reveal her anxious parents. "Let's get you inside," her mother said. Her father strode in the opposite direction to talk to the policeman who had helped Antimone out of the car.

When Jason had made the call, the emergency operator, determining that they were in no imminent danger, had instructed them to wait where they were until assistance arrived. By the time an officer located them half an hour later, Floyd was probably miles away. They had been driven to Hunstanton police station and were questioned separately. Antimone had repeated several times everything she could remember about the man's appearance and what he had said. The police had circulated Floyd's description but admitted they had little hope of catching him with the town packed with holidaymakers. Afterwards, when the sergeant had asked if she wanted to travel home with Jason, Floyd's words echoed through her head. *I saw him come out of that bedroom looking as if he didn't have a care in the world.* Sensing her discomfort, the man had offered to give her a lift, and she had gratefully accepted.

Several times during the journey, Antimone's mobile had rung. Other than a brief exchange with her parents when she told them the police were driving her home, the remainder were from Jason. Until she got her thoughts straight in her head, she didn't want to talk to him and so had rejected his calls. Now the phone rang again and Jason's number appeared on the screen. Reluctantly, she pressed the answer button.

"Thank God. Are you alright?" he asked, the worry in his voice sounding genuine.

"I'm okay," she replied.

"They said they were giving you a lift home."

"Yeah, I've just got back."

"So... um... Why didn't you come back with me? You didn't believe what that bastard said, did you?"

"He said he saw you come out of the bedroom, and that I followed you moments later. Why would he say that?"

"He's just messing with your head," Jason said.

"I don't know. I just need some time to think things through."

"Look, I promise you I had nothing to do with it. You believe me, don't you?"

Antimone ended the call without answering.

## Tuesday 3rd August 2032

Mother and daughter waited in the interview room at Parkside Police Station in Cambridge. Two cardboard cups of cold tea rested on the industrial grey table. Antimone had allowed hers to cool without touching it and now nervously tapped her finger on the metal surface. She glanced up at the video camera in the corner of the ceiling and idly wondered whether anybody was watching them.

The sound of footsteps echoed down the corridor, and a moment later Karen Atkins bustled into the room, carrying a file under her arm. "Good morning, Antimone, Helen. Thanks for coming in." She opened the file and read for a few seconds before raising her eyes. "It seems you had a bit of excitement yesterday, Antimone."

"Yeah, you could say that."

"I've got your statement here, but I'd like you to go over what happened one more time."

Antimone recounted the events of the previous evening.

Kat interrupted a couple of times to clarify Antimone's words but mostly listened in silence.

"I'd say you were lucky that Jason came back when he did," Kat said when Antimone had finished.

"I suppose."

"Have they caught him yet?" Helen asked.

"No, I'm sorry. At this time of year, the town's extremely busy. He could be anywhere by now, but obviously we'll keep looking."

"Do you think he'll try again?"

"I think that's unlikely, but I'd recommend you take some precautions. Keep the doors and windows of your house locked and make sure you've got a phone handy at all times."

"He said he saw Jason and me coming out of the bedroom. What if he's not the rapist?" Antimone asked.

Kat considered her response before speaking. "The blood tests have been checked. There's definitely no mistake there. He *is* the father of your child.

Sometimes rapists blame the victim. You've got to remember this man's a convicted murderer. You can't judge his behaviour by the norms of society."

"He just seemed so—I don't know—angry, I suppose. He accused me of framing him."

"Well, he has got a history of doing that. He claimed he was framed for his wife's murder too. You'd be surprised how many prison inmates protest their innocence despite conclusive proof to the contrary."

"So, you're still convinced he's the murderer?"

"You mean rapist, right?" Kat asked.

"Yeah. Isn't that what I just said?"

Helen put an arm around her daughter.

Kat's gaze alternated between the two. "Yes, I'm still totally convinced he's the rapist."

## Saturday 25th December 2032

Antimone stared at the pulsating patterns of the lights on the Christmas tree. Her parents had spared no expense to ensure that their last Christmas together as a family was special, but the atmosphere in the house was still sombre. In some ways they were trying too hard. The enforced joviality was wearing thin. The basketball-sized bump sitting on her stomach worsened her mood. The size and shape meant she had been struggling to get comfortable at night.

The last few months seemed to have rushed past. Daniel Floyd was still on the run, and there had been no sightings since the day at the seaside. She suspected that the police had scaled back the hunt for the rapist but had heard nothing officially. Karen Atkins visited once a month to reassure them the search was continuing and that they would catch their man. No doubt the birth of the baby would stimulate a fresh burst of activity, but by then it would be too late for Antimone.

Things hadn't been the same with Jason following the incident at Hunstanton. It was clear he still felt aggrieved about Antimone travelling home without him and her failure to acknowledge his assertion of innocence. He had called twice since, but the conversations had been awkward and stilted, and eventually he stopped calling altogether.

She had struggled to make friends at Oakington Manor, so there had been little contact from her other classmates. The only person who might have fallen in that category, Erin Riley, had also called once. She had started by appearing sympathetic, but Antimone had hung up when she asked what the sex was like.

True to her word, Jason's mother, Rosalind Baxter, had arranged for her to give birth in the private hospital at Ilithyia Biotechnology. The midwife had warned them the contractions could start at any time, and Antimone's father had prepared a holdall so they wouldn't need to waste time packing when that happened. Once a month, Antimone attended the Ilithyia clinic for an examination and to pick up the next batch of pills. Her parents still clung to the hope that she might survive the birth, but she was realistic enough to understand that the odds were infinitesimally small.

"Right," Helen said brightly. She picked up a red, book-shaped parcel, tied with a turquoise–coloured ribbon, from beneath the tree. She read the label aloud, although she already knew what it said. "To Antimone, with all our love, from Mum and Dad."

Antimone accepted the package and ripped off the garishly coloured paper to reveal a book. She turned it over to examine the title: 'The 2032 Delhi Olympics and Paralympics: A Review'.

"We know you couldn't compete," her father said, "but we thought you might find it interesting to look at the pictures."

"Thanks, Mum, Dad." The gift was a reminder of a past life, one that no longer held much interest for her, but she knew they meant well. She had deliberately tried to avoid all contact with the Olympics but had relented when it came to her own event, the eight hundred metres women's T54 wheelchair final. The British girl, whom she had beaten in their last two races, finished just outside the medals in fourth place.

The present giving continued until a single brightly wrapped parcel lay beneath the tree. Most of the gifts Antimone received were frivolous and jokey. *After all, what do you give a girl with less than two weeks left to live?* she thought.

Helen picked up the blue-wrapped package and searched for a label. "It doesn't have a name on it," she said.

"I know, Mum. It's from me to the baby. By the way, I want to call him Paul."

"Oh… um… well, should we open it now?"

"Yes, please. I want you to see it too."

Antimone's mother removed the wrapping and held up a large book with a multi-coloured, patterned cover.

"Look inside," she said.

Helen placed the book on the coffee table and carefully turned over the jacket. Antimone's father sat beside her, staring at the open page. Inscribed in neat calligraphic script were the words, 'To Paul Lessing. Everything you need to know about your mother.' Beneath the writing was a photograph of a smiling Antimone, proudly holding up a gold medal.

"It's a scrapbook. That's what I've been spending my time doing the last few months. Turn to the next page."

Her mother did as instructed. An envelope was taped to the paper. Handwritten on it was the text, 'To Paul, on your first birthday.'

"I've written letters to him for every one of his first eighteen birthdays and one for his wedding day. You're going to have to read the first ones to him until he's old enough to read for himself. Make sure he doesn't open them ahead of time. I've also included a whole load of other stuff, what music I like, the books I've read and masses of photos. I know a lot of it's online, but this sort of tells a story."

Antimone watched as her parents slowly turned over each page. Tears streamed down both their faces.

"Hey, I don't want you getting it wet," she said, smiling.

"What a wonderful idea," Helen murmured, staring at her daughter.

Then she rose to her feet and hurried out of the room, her face in her hands, no longer able to hide the violent sobs wracking her body.

# PART TWO: EVALUATION

## Monday 3rd January 2033

Rosalind Baxter held the handset against her ear as she hurried along the corridor. "So which patient are we talking about?"

She listened impatiently to the reply. "What? You're sure? The sixteen-year-old girl in the wheelchair?"

The other person responded affirmatively.

"Well, get her down to the basement emergency ward immediately and the baby too, but keep them apart. And Julian, get Grolby to make sure those two goons from the mortuary don't talk about this."

Anders Grolby was Ilithyia's Head of Security. He was a blond-haired Swede who had been with the company for the past eighteen years. He had been discharged from the Swedish army in his mid-thirties after an incident in Iraq when a family of four locals had been shot dead. Fortunately for Grolby, despite the overwhelming circumstantial evidence, there had been no solid witnesses, and he had escaped prosecution.

She stabbed the end call button and waved a key-card at the reader on the wall by a door labelled 'Biohazard—authorised personnel only'. The light on the box turned green, and the electronic lock opened. She barged through and strode down a passageway towards a lift bearing an identical sign. She jabbed the call button, pacing backwards and forwards while she waited for the doors to open. When they did, she hurried inside and stared into the red glare of an iris scanner. A display panel illuminated, and she stabbed a finger at the on-screen 'B' icon.

The floor sank down beneath her feet and a second or two later pressed up again as the lift decelerated. She stepped out into a brightly lit, white corridor. The clacking of her heels echoed as she bustled towards her destination. One of the numbered doors opened ahead of her, and a white-coated doctor wearing a surgical mask emerged. She immediately altered direction to intercept the man.

"Find Dr Perrin and tell him to go to the emergency ward."

"But I was just about to—"

"I don't give a damn what you were about to do. If you still want to be employed at this hospital tomorrow then locate Dr Perrin and get him to the emergency ward in the next two minutes."

The man said something, but she had already turned her back and resumed her journey. She took a left turn, then a right and reached a set of wide elevator doors just as they opened. Two men wearing pale green overalls manoeuvred a trolley through the gap.

On the trolley lay a girl with a white sheet drawn up to her chin. Wisps of damp hair framed an attractive but exhausted-looking face. A bruise was forming on the girl's forehead. Her eyes alighted on Rosalind. "Mrs Baxter," she croaked, then broke into a cough.

Rosalind ignored the girl and picked up the clipboard at the foot of the trolley. Her eyes scanned down the text, then she replaced it.

"Mrs Baxter," the girl repeated.

"Just lie back, Antimone. You're in good hands. We're taking you to an emergency room to make sure you're okay."

"My baby."

"Your baby's fine. We're just checking it over." Rosalind didn't know whether her statement was true or not, but she figured it was better to keep the patient calm.

"Can we..." interrupted one of the men.

Rosalind waved a hand impatiently. "Yeah, get on with it." She trailed behind the two men as they wheeled their cargo down the corridor, then turned right through a set of swing doors. She followed them into a room containing four beds, only two of which held patients. An array of machines sat next to the head of each bed. A nurse who had been sitting at a desk making notes rose to her feet.

"Mask," Rosalind snapped, holding out a hand. The nurse hurried to a dispenser and handed her a surgical mask. "Get them out of here," she said, sweeping a hand towards the occupied beds.

"But these—"

"Why the hell do I always have to repeat myself in this place?" Rosalind snarled. "I said get them out of here. I don't care where you put them." She turned to the two porters. "Get this patient into that bed there."

The two men positioned the trolley beside the empty bed, removed the sheet covering Antimone, then slid her across using the under-sheet upon which she lay. She grimaced at the sudden movement.

The arrival of a bald-headed man wearing a white coat and surgical mask saved the men from Rosalind's wrath.

"Nigel, about time," she said.

"What's going on?" he asked, his gaze following the nurse who was busy disconnecting machines from one of the patients.

"Let's get these other people out of here, and then we'll talk about it."

"Rosalind, these women are seriously ill. If you move them now, they might die."

"Look," Rosalind hissed, "You see that girl on the bed over there? She just gave birth and survived. Now tell me which patient is more important. I don't want any risk that she might get infected."

"My God. You're serious?" His eyes bored into hers, his brain already whirring. Seeing no change in her humourless expression, he whipped around. "You two. Get this one to room two oh eight and the other to two ten. When you've done that, come back and take the machines with you."

He pointed at the nurse who was busy disconnecting equipment from the second patient. "She'll tell you which ones they need."

The nurse completed her task and stood up. "Dr Perrin, what's going on here?"

"I want you to reconnect those two and keep an eye on them. This girl is a high priority, and we can't run the risk of cross-infection. I want you to call Personnel right now and get more nursing staff down so there's cover twenty-four hours a day. They must have the highest level of security clearance, at least an eight but preferably a nine."

"But what's so special—?"

"Samantha," Perrin interrupted, "Please just do as I ask. This is really important."

The nurse smiled tightly. "Of course, Dr Perrin. I'll get right on it."

While the other members of staff busied themselves with their allotted tasks, the doctor strolled over to Antimone's bed and picked up the clipboard which had been transferred from the trolley.

"Hello, Antimone," he said, staring down at the girl. "How are you feeling?" He held her wrist, measuring her pulse rate.

"Like crap," she replied. "Where's my baby?"

Perrin glanced towards Rosalind, who shook her head. "We're looking after your baby, but it's going to be a while until we can bring it to you."

"Why? Is something wrong?"

"No, just routine tests."

"And by the way, *he's* called Paul."

"Of course. I see you've had a Caesarean. I just want to look at the stitches."

Perrin rolled back the sheet and carefully lifted the blood-spotted hospital gown. Rosalind edged closer to inspect the wound herself.

"Hmm," Perrin said, studying the hasty stitching. "One or two of these stitches have popped. We're going to have to do some repair work. We'll give you a local. You won't feel a thing."

"Where are my parents?"

"There's too high a risk of infection at the moment," Rosalind said. "You'll be able to see them in a day or two."

Antimone tried to sit up, then flopped back, her face a mask of agony. "Can't I talk to them? Do they even know I'm alive?"

"Antimone, you need to relax. You've been through a traumatic experience. We'll let your parents know you're okay. Maybe a mild sedative, Dr Perrin?"

Perrin nodded, then strode to a set of cabinets beside the nurse's station. A few seconds later he returned carrying an injection gun, a small glass vial of clear liquid protruding from the top. He held the barrel against Antimone's arm and depressed the trigger. The drug entered her bloodstream accompanied by a short hiss. "This'll help you relax."

Antimone's eyes grew heavy-lidded. "I want my baby," she murmured, but within seconds she was asleep. By now, Rosalind and Perrin had the room to themselves.

"You know what this means, Nigel? Do you have any idea of this girl's value? If we can work out what makes her special, we can finally develop a cure. This company will be worth billions, maybe even tens or hundreds of billions."

"We'll have to get blood from both mother and child and test for the presence of the virus. We'll also need to sequence their genomes. I'll get the tests started right away."

"This has to remain tightly controlled, only the highest level of security clearance. We can't afford for anybody to find out she survived. Not even her parents can know."

"What do we tell them?"

Rosalind pondered a moment. "Well, they already think she's dead, so let's keep it that way. Tell them the child died too, some bacterial infection so dangerous that we had to cremate both bodies immediately. Get one of the doctors who works down here to sign the death certificates. If we give the parents some ashes, they won't know any better."

"She's not going to stop asking to see them, though. That might become a problem."

"What's she going to do? Yes, she'll be pissed off, but she can't get out of here. I'll get Grolby to arrange for an armed guard to be stationed outside her room."

"I'll get a gynaecologist to look her over, somebody we can trust."

"Who did the C-section?" Rosalind asked.

Perrin consulted the chart. "John Martin."

"That old fart. But at least he needs the money. He's an eight, right? We need to keep the circle of people who know about this as small as possible."

"But that stitching was a disgrace. If he did that, I don't want him anywhere near her."

"He might not be the most dynamic character in the world, but as far as I know he's conscientious," Rosalind said. "Find out who did this work then sack them. If it wasn't Martin, get him down here. If it was, find someone else."

"I'll get on it right away, Rosalind. By the way, what are we going to do about the child?"

"Until we've done the tests, keep them separated. I want round-the-clock care. Nobody needs to know what's special about the boy."

"She's definitely not going to like that," Perrin said.

"I suggest we use it as leverage. Threaten to keep them apart unless she behaves."

"Good idea. That should work."

"Let me know as soon as you find out anything. You know, Nigel, this is going to make Ilithyia the biggest company in the world." For the first time that day, Rosalind Baxter smiled.

## Tuesday 4th January 2033

ominic Lessing wandered from room to room, more than anything to give him something to do. There were reminders of Antimone everywhere: the colourful snake draught excluder she had given them for Christmas last year, the cushion she liked to lean against when she was sitting on the sofa, the stair-lift that enabled her to go upstairs.

The image of his daughter's stomach being cut open before they removed the baby would be seared in his mind for the rest of his life. He had wanted to rush in and stop the operation, but he knew it was beyond his control. He had read about the agonies endured by women after they delivered their children naturally, the way the virus turned the body on itself, basically turning their internal organs and brains to mush. He couldn't bear to think of that happening to his own daughter and just prayed that she hadn't suffered.

The doctor had held the boy up to the observation window so they could see their grandson. To Dominic he had looked like any new-born child: a scrunched-up face, eyes that couldn't focus yet, fine wisps of hair, mouth open as he exercised his lungs in a high-pitched wail. That first glimpse had been all too short as the baby was whisked away and placed in an incubator.

A counsellor had guided them away before the surgeons had stitched up the incision. The only real consolation the woman could offer was that their daughter's death had resulted in a new life. In many ways, Dominic relished the prospect of the sleepless nights and the endless routine of feeding and changing as a way of distracting him from darker thoughts. Before any of that could begin, though, they had to wait for the hospital to call. The child seat was already installed, the formula milk was piled up in the cupboard, and the crib was assembled in the spare room.

Dominic glanced at his watch once again. Half-past eleven. The midwife had assured them that the baby would be ready to go home sometime this morning.

"Dominic, will you please stop pacing?" His wife sat on the sofa, cradling her fifth cup of tea of the day. "You're driving me mad."

"Sorry, but I can't sit down. Why don't we drive there now? They've got our mobile numbers."

"I think I'd rather wait here than in a hospital waiting room. It's only ten minutes away."

The trilling of the phone interrupted the conversation. Dominic took two swift paces and snatched the handset from its cradle. Helen's gaze followed him expectantly.

"Yes, this is Dominic Lessing. Can we come over now?"

"Problem? What problem?"

Dominic's mouth opened, and his face turned an ashen colour. He seemed to be struggling to breathe. With a moan of anguish, he sank to his knees.

Helen rose to her feet in consternation. "What is it? What's happened?"

Dominic dropped the phone and pitched forwards onto all fours. His shoulders heaved, and he vomited on the carpet.

An expression of terror occupied Helen's face. "Are you alright? What the hell's wrong?"

Dominic raised his eyes slowly to meet his wife's panicked stare. Even without speaking, the depth of his evident despair told her everything she needed to know.

"No. Not the baby?"

The slightest nod of the head. She bent down and picked up the phone, almost as if somebody else was controlling her body. "This is Helen Lessing. Who is this?"

"It's Jennifer Anderson, the counsellor at Ilithyia. We met briefly yesterday. I'm so sorry, Mrs Lessing. The baby's—Paul's—condition deteriorated overnight, a bacterial infection. The doctors did everything they could, but unfortunately, he didn't respond to the drugs. He passed away at just after ten o'clock this morning."

"He's dead?"

"I'm afraid so. On behalf of everybody at Ilithyia, I'd like to offer our condolences on the loss of your grandson."

"But… but he seemed healthy when he was born."

"I'm sorry, I don't have all the details, but I understand the infection began to develop during the night and didn't respond to the drugs."

"But…"

"I know you must be in shock. I'm going to drop by this afternoon, but I felt you needed to hear this terrible news as soon as possible rather than finding out when you phoned the switchboard."

"Um…"

"There is one other thing I need to tell you. Well—ah—because of the nature of the infection we were left with no option but to cremate the bodies of your daughter and your grandson. I'll bring the ashes with me this afternoon. I'm really sorry for your loss. Our thoughts are with you."

"Th-thanks."

Helen ended the call. She walked as if in a trance to the telephone cradle and deliberately placed the handset in the slot.

She turned and stared down at her husband. He lay on the carpet in the foetal position, his face in his hands.

# 22

*T*he girl lay on the bed. The bump on her stomach was so large that whichever way she turned she could not get comfortable. Even though she knew that giving birth would kill her, in some ways it would be a relief. When she had asked the doctors when it would be, they had been non-committal, telling her that it could happen anytime in the next few weeks. After almost nine months cooped up in this room, she felt like a prisoner on death row.

She knew they were planning something for her. No food had arrived that morning. She wondered whether they intended to perform the Caesarean on her that evening. It would be just like them not to inform her. Her fears were confirmed when the door opened, and the balding, white-coated doctor entered the room accompanied by two orderlies, dressed in pale green overalls.

"Is it time?" she asked, her voice quivering with anxiety.

"No, not quite yet," the doctor said. "We just need to do an examination to see how the baby's doing."

"Why can't you do that here?"

"We're going to use a scanner, and we need you to be completely still, so we're going to give you a general anaesthetic."

"Is something wrong with the baby?"

"No, we don't think so, but given your history of drug abuse, we just want to be absolutely sure. Do you need a hand getting on the trolley?"

"No, I can manage."

She shifted her body around until her legs dangled over the edge of the bed, then shuffled forwards. She sighed when her feet touched the floor, then waddled towards the waiting trolley. The two men helped her up and when she was lying down again, strapped her arms and legs to the frame and raised the sides.

"Is it really necessary to tie me down? It's not as if I'm going to be able to run far, is it?"

"It's just a precaution," the doctor replied, smiling.

One man stood on each side, and they manoeuvred the trolley down the white corridor. This was only the second time she had been outside her room since arriving. Her brain soaked everything in: the doors containing the small windows, the recessed lighting, the smoke detectors on the ceiling, all of it a welcome distraction from the monotony of the same four walls for months on end.

They passed the sign for the first operating theatre. She was just about to ask where they were taking her when they pushed through a set of swing doors labelled 'Operating Theatre S2'. The arrangement of the room was identical to the one she had been to previously. A woman wearing a blue medical gown, hairnet and white surgical mask awaited her. The girl couldn't be sure, but she thought it was the same woman who had administered the anaesthetic the last time.

No sooner had the trolley stopped moving than the woman slipped a black mask over the girl's face. "Hello again," she said. "It's just like before. Start counting backwards from ten."

***

The girl opened one eye. Her gaze tracked along the white floor to the featureless white walls. For a moment her sluggish mind refused to function, and a sense of disorientation engulfed her. Her head felt like it was full of sand. She blinked open the other eye and, as her brain engaged, she concluded she was back in her room, lying on her side in bed. Instinctively, her hand moved to her stomach. For a brief second or two, hope flared that the baby had been born and she was still alive, but the presence of the bump indicated otherwise.

"Don't try to move," a voice said from behind her.

She ignored the instruction and tried to face the speaker, but her legs wouldn't respond. With a rising panic, she realised she had no sensation at all below the waist. She lowered her hand and brushed against warm skin, but the touch of her fingers didn't register at all. It was as if she had placed her hand on somebody else's body.

Her heart rate increased, and she felt the baby kick. Her breathing came in ragged bursts, a rushing sound in her ears. Her mouth was suddenly dry.

"What the hell have you done to me?" she gasped, trying to locate the man.

A chair creaked and soft footsteps came around the bed. The bald-headed doctor entered her field of vision.

"Just try to remain still and relax."

"I asked what you've done to me. I can't feel my bloody legs."

"Yes, I'm afraid there was a complication."

"You told me I was going for a scan. How the hell can a scan go wrong?"

"During the scan, we discovered a growth on your spine. While you were under the anaesthetic, we decided to deal with it there and then."

"So now I'm paralysed from the waist down, you bastard," she screamed.

"We hoped that we'd be able to remove the tumour without any side effects, but unfortunately it was so close to your spine that it didn't prove possible."

"You lying sack of shit. I don't believe a word you're telling me. You've lied to me since the day I arrived."

"We only have you and the baby's best interests at heart. Now you need to calm down."

The girl stared at him for a moment, then opened her mouth and screamed. The doctor winced. He fumbled in his pocket and withdrew a small injection gun. He adjusted the settings and stood just out of reach of the hysterical girl.

"I was hoping it wasn't going to come to this," he said.

She drew breath and screamed again. She tried to bat his hand away as he lunged towards her and pressed the barrel against the top of her arm, but he was too quick. He depressed the trigger and sprang back.

The girl's eyes rolled up in her head, and within seconds she was once again unconscious.

## Thursday 6th January 2033

Rosalind Baxter and Nigel Perrin entered the large CEO's office on the second storey. Rosalind shut the door, then took the chair behind the heavy black wooden desk facing the floor to ceiling plate-glass window. Perrin sat opposite, clutching a sheaf of papers, silhouetted by a beam of sunlight that broke through a gap in the slate-grey clouds. He seemed ill at ease.

"Too hot in here for you, Nigel?"

"No, I'm fine."

"Still, it's a little too bright for me."

Rosalind pressed a button on her keyboard. "Darken," she said. The light streaming into the room decreased until the glare no longer bothered her. "Stop," she commanded.

"So," she said, addressing Perrin, "what have we got?"

"Well, to start with they're both doing well. We're keeping them separated for the time being, but she's starting to get difficult, demanding to talk to her parents and see the child."

"Keep stalling her for the moment. What about the test results?"

He consulted the reports he held on his lap and placed them one by one on the table. "We've taken blood from both mother and child, cheek swabs, urine and faeces samples. We've also done full body scans." A small mound of documents rested on the black surface of the desk. Several sheets of paper remained on his knee.

"You don't expect me to read all that, do you? What are the highlights?"

"Okay, Rosalind. The virus is still active in both their blood samples. For whatever reason, it hasn't entered the destructive phase in the mother. Urine and faeces don't show anything unusual. We've sequenced the DNA from the cheek swabs on the child, and there's nothing obvious there. I've asked them to repeat the mother's cheek swab. It looks like somebody mixed up the samples."

"I take it you know who that was?"

Perrin nodded.

"Well fire them. If there's one thing I won't tolerate in this organisation, it's incompetence. We pay well above the going rate, and I expect the best."

"Um… okay Rosalind, but it's not easy to find good technicians. She's never made a mistake before."

"I don't care, Nigel. Get rid of her. If you don't want to do it personally, phone somebody in Personnel."

"No, I'll do it," he said in a resigned voice.

"What about the body scans?"

"Nothing unusual in the child's. As you know the mother has a fracture between the T-eleven and T-twelve vertebrae."

"You don't think that's got anything to do with her surviving, do you?"

"I already thought of that, Rosalind. It seems unlikely, but I have instigated an experiment."

"Good. The mother was being treated here before the birth. What did you prescribe her?"

Perrin glanced up sharply. "I did as you asked and gave her the placebo."

"And you're sure none of the technicians mixed up the pills?"

Perrin sighed. "No, Rosalind, I can't be a hundred percent, but the chances are extremely small. In any case, as you know, we always conduct trials on a number of patients, and so far, none of the others has survived." He shifted his weight on the chair.

"Something's bothering you, Nigel. What is it?"

Perrin hesitated. "I told you we discounted the DNA test on the mother, but there was something of note about the baby."

Rosalind leant forwards. "You just said there was nothing unusual in the child's DNA. Make up your mind. What did you find?"

"I meant nothing to explain why the mother survived. What I didn't mention was that we also used it to determine paternity."

"Oh, for crying out loud, Nigel, get to the point."

Perrin placed the remaining sheets of paper on the table. "When we ran the sequencer and analysed the results, I immediately recognised the signature, even though it was many years ago."

"Yeah, that arsehole Daniel Floyd. I have to admit, for all his faults, I never took him for a rapist. He was probably just trying to get back at me, but even so. He wasn't happy when I got the security guards to throw him out."

Perrin stared at her without speaking.

"Stop playing games, Nigel. I haven't got time for this."

Perrin inhaled deeply, then slowly released his breath.

"He's not the one I'm talking about. Daniel Floyd isn't the child's father."

## Thursday 6th January 2033

Anders Grolby waited at the side of the road, although all of his attention was focused on the screen of the head-up display inside his helmet. A map displayed the stretch of the A14 road where he sat stationary astride his electric motorbike, his feet keeping the lightweight machine upright. A green dot drifted slowly from right to left, approaching the blue icon of a car at the centre that signified his own position. A red dot trailed the green one by a centimetre, travelling in the same direction.

Grolby muttered a series of instructions and studied the scrolling text to confirm the system had interpreted them correctly. Over the course of the next few seconds, the distance between the green and red dots halved. Satisfied that everything was going to plan, he extended his gaze to the grey ribbon of tarmac. The traffic was quieter than usual at this time of day. The schools weren't back yet, and people were probably extending their Christmas break until the end of the week. He had no qualms about causing collateral damage, but the fewer witnesses who were present, the better.

For what he planned, human observers were less of a worry than the electronic eyes of the cameras fitted to all modern vehicles. The bike he rode was a popular model, indistinguishable from the thousands of others, at least to the untrained eye. He had upgraded the motor and battery systems to provide far greater power and range than the unmodified version. The mirrored visor meant that nobody would get a look at his face. He had also disconnected a wire from the vehicle's transponder. If the police stopped him, it would appear as if a damaged connector was the culprit, but the chances of them being vigilant enough to spot the absence of the signal were extremely slim. Even if a camera picked him up, they would have a hard job identifying him.

Grolby consulted the map once again. The green dot overlaid the blue car symbol. He had fitted a tracker the previous evening, attaching the small magnetised disc to the underside of the body where it was parked on the road. They should be visible by now. He surveyed the passing traffic, seeking out the target. There it was, a small, silver autonomous vehicle, two passengers. He had a good idea where they were going. He had tracked them from their house to the local supermarket, and now they were returning home—or so they thought. He pulled out into the traffic and slotted into a gap two cars behind them. If he was correct, they would take the next exit.

This type of work was different to what he had done before joining the company. When he was in Iraq, the rules of engagement had been a major source of frustration. Anybody could tell that half the population would happily kill the infidel invaders given the chance. He could see it in their eyes. They tried to hide it with their lowered heads and subservient body posture, but it was all just a mask for their true intentions.

Whilst on patrol, his contingent had come under attack from a group of insurgents. One of his team had died, and another had taken a bullet to the thigh. As soon as the soldiers returned fire, the attackers melted away. Grolby had recognised one of them as a local shopkeeper. He notified his commander, but after interviewing the suspect, the decision had been made to set him free. Grolby trailed him along the bustling streets to the scruffy house where he lived with his wife and two sons.

When Grolby burst through the door, the man was embracing his wife. The boys, aged ten and twelve, looked up at the blond westerner who had invaded their home. The man turned around and screamed in Arabic at the interloper, gesticulating wildly as he attempted to usher him out. Grolby smiled once then emptied his entire clip leaving the devastated bodies of the father, mother and two boys lying in an expanding pool of blood. The way he figured it, if he killed only the man, the surviving members of the family would have all the motivation they needed to become insurgents themselves. Best to deal with the issue before it became a problem.

During the court martial he had denied ever being at the man's house, and there was no proof other than a couple of eye-witnesses who described having seen a tall, blond, white man fleeing through the dusty alley. In light of Grolby's initial accusation and the sighting of a man matching his description immediately after the incident, the circumstantial evidence was overwhelming. However, his lawyer had argued that the description matched half of the unit and the whole group knew the murdered man's identity. In the end, Grolby received a dishonourable discharge from the army but served no time in jail.

Working for Ilithyia had been tedious at first, but as time went by, Grolby had grown into the role. He had ample budget to put in place the security measures he wanted and was allowed to recruit his own team of like-minded men. Jobs like this one made him nostalgic for the old days in the military. Yes, he could have commanded one of his subordinates to undertake the task, but there was nothing quite like doing it oneself. Now that he was closing in on the target, the jolt of adrenaline and the racing heartbeat brought a smile to his lips.

The silver car indicated left a good two hundred metres before the junction. Grolby twisted the throttle and surged ahead of the vehicle before veering off at the exit. Once again, he muttered instructions into the microphone located inside his helmet. He raced down the slip road and arrived at the roundabout at the bottom of the slight incline just as the traffic lights were turning amber. He accelerated, hugging the inside of the traffic island and leaning into the curve. He reached the opposite side, just over one hundred metres away, as the target drew to a halt at the lights. Turning off the bike, he dismounted and propped it on its stand.

He gave the final set of commands. The distance between the green and red dots on the display narrowed to a couple of millimetres. He glanced up expectantly and grinned as a massive yellow driverless truck appeared at the top of the ramp and began the descent downhill. The sound of the goods vehicle changing gear reached his ears, but instead of slowing down, it increased velocity down the gentle incline.

The traffic lights changed to green, and the small silver car pulled away but not fast enough. By now the truck had achieved a speed in excess of seventy miles an hour as it gained momentum from the downward slope and the straining engine. The blunt nose of the cabin smashed into the slow-moving car, instantly crushing the vehicle to half its original size. For a second or two, the concertinaed body of the car was shunted forwards before the front wheels of the articulated truck lifted off the road, dragging what remained beneath it.

The truck careened across the lanes of the roundabout and towards its centre. For a moment, Grolby thought it was coming straight for him, but the front wheels dug into the soft earth causing it to jack-knife. He felt the tremor through his legs as the goods vehicle toppled onto its side, churning up huge piles of earth and vegetation. The screech of tortured metal accompanied a subsonic rumble, the energy of the sounds creating a deep vibration in his chest and setting his teeth on edge. Chunks of soil and fragments of metal pattered down around him. He dropped to the ground as a wheel from the car flew past like a bouncing bomb, centimetres from his head.

A metallic clang made him flinch. He glanced behind and was relieved to see no discernible damage to the motorbike. If something took it out of action, he would have a serious problem.

After what seemed an age, silence returned to the scene of devastation. Grolby stood up and brushed dirt and shredded vegetation off his black leathers. The truck lay on its side, a great gouge of broken earth trailing behind it. One of its wheels continued to rotate. Amidst all the bent metal, nothing was recognisable as the remains of the car.

He strolled to the cab of the heavy goods vehicle and placed a small, black plastic box on the radiator grill. A metallic ticking sound emanated from somewhere inside the engine as it cooled. He retreated from the wreckage. When he had reached a distance of fifty paces, he withdrew a second unit from inside his leather jacket. A solitary red button was the only feature to break the smooth black surface, and he stabbed it with a gloved finger. Nothing visible happened to the truck, but his head up display flickered for a second or two. The electromagnetic pulse generated by the first box would wipe the memory of all the electronic devices on the vehicle, leaving no evidence of the software he had inserted allowing him to control it. He hurried back to retrieve his equipment before returning to the motorbike.

He mounted the bike and glanced back once more at the twisted metal.

"Jesus Christ!" Grolby muttered to himself. "Now that's what I call a crash."

## Thursday 6th January 2033

"When are you going to let me out of here?" Antimone asked.

The nurse looked up from the computer screen, then rose to her feet. "That's up to Dr Perrin."

"You can't keep me locked up like this without my permission."

The nurse approached the bed, lifted her surgical mask and stared down at Antimone. "I don't think you're in any condition to be going anywhere, young lady."

"That's a point. When can I have my wheelchair back?"

The woman tutted. "You're not getting out of that bed until the stitches are taken out."

"When's that going to be?"

"They have to be left in for at least five days, so maybe another forty-eight hours."

Antimone sighed. "I want to see my baby and talk to my parents. Do they even know I'm alive?"

"That's—"

"Let me guess," interrupted Antimone. "That's up to Dr Perrin."

The nurse smiled humourlessly. "Yes. You're learning fast."

"Anyway, why can't I see my baby? And don't tell me I have to ask Dr Perrin."

"We don't want either of you giving the other an infection. It's a miracle you survived, and we don't want to risk the health of you or your child."

"I thought breast milk was supposed to help strengthen a baby's immune system. These," she indicated her nipples, "are really sore and they keep dribbling. They're not going to like, burst or anything?"

The woman laughed. "No, I wouldn't worry about that. You'll stop lactating in a day or two. The baby's being fed on artificial milk, but it's every bit as good as the real thing, if not better."

Antimone remained silent for a moment. "Do they know why I survived yet?"

"They're still working on it. That's why you've been having all these tests. I'm sure Dr Perrin will let you know when they find anything out."

"Yeah, I feel like a pin cushion, all the blood they've taken the last day or two. I'm surprised there's any left."

"I know it's uncomfortable, but they only take a small amount—"

"They took quite a lot actually, at least five or six of those little tubes last time."

"Your body soon makes more," the nurse said. "Is there anything you need?"

"Just to get out of here."

"Apart from that."

"Nah. Although a book or some music would be good. When are they going to give back my ear implants?"

"You can't keep those in when you're in the scanner. You'll—"

"… have to ask Dr Perrin," Antimone said, completing the sentence. She blew out her cheeks. Her eyes drifted across the room and settled on the telephone handset resting on the nurse's desk.

The nurse tracked her gaze. "You can't dial out from down here—even mobile signals are blocked, so I wouldn't even think about it."

"So, when is Dr Perrin coming back?"

"Whenever he's ready," the nurse replied. She was on her way to the desk when the swing doors opened, and a middle-aged woman, whom Antimone hadn't seen before, swept into the room. Her hair was tied back in a severe bun, and she could have been attractive were it not for the permanent expression of distaste on her face. She wore a white coat and flat shoes.

The newcomer strode up to Antimone's bed. "They need to repeat a test."

Antimone groaned. "Not more blood."

"Not this time." The faintest glimmer of a smile. "Just a cheek swab. Open your mouth, please."

"What if I don't?"

"We sedate you and take it anyway," the woman said, her face returning to its original disdainfulness.

Antimone reluctantly opened her mouth and allowed the woman to run the tip of the white plastic rod across the inner surface of her cheek. The medic removed the stopper from a transparent tube, dropped the sample inside, then resealed it.

Seconds later she had departed, leaving the doors swinging in her wake.

## Thursday 6th January 2033

Jason took the stairs two at a time. He rarely came to his mother's place of work, but Julian Stefano, the little toad, had called and said his mother urgently wanted to see him. He could have taken the lift to the second floor, but after the Christmas and New Year break, he decided he could use the exercise. Her personal assistant wouldn't say what it was about, just that his mother needed to speak to him face-to-face. A car had been sent to pick him up and dropped him off outside the front entrance.

He strode along the plushly furnished corridor, past the original oil paintings hanging on the wall, his feet swishing against the deep pile carpet. The place seemed quiet, but it was a quarter to one, so people were probably still on their lunch breaks. He reached the door bearing his mother's name and thought about knocking. He decided against it. His mother's secretary occupied the outer office and would let her know he had arrived.

He pushed the door open and stuck his head in the gap. The secretary's desk was empty. Presumably, she was on her break. The inner office door was partially ajar, and he detected the sound of muffled voices. He crossed the floor, the heavy carpet masking the approach of his footsteps. He raised his hand to knock but halted as he recognised the familiar voice of his mother.

"Where is the little bastard, Julian?"

"He should be here by now. Do you want me to find out if the car's here yet, Mrs Baxter?"

Jason took a step back. His face flushed, and his ears burned. *Was he the subject of the conversation?*

"Yes, and if the little prick has arrived, get Grolby to locate him and bring him up here."

A rapid sequence of beeps signalled the start of a telephone call.

"Yes Anders, it's Julian. Check whether Mrs Baxter's son is here, and if he is, please escort him up."

*So, they were talking about him.*

Several seconds passed while Stefano listened to the Head of Security.

"What? You've tracked him down? Excellent news. Where is he?"

Jason's heart sank. *They knew he was here.*

More silence.

"I don't know Bedford that well. What, near the railway station?"

*They were obviously discussing somebody else, but who?*

"Okay. Don't do anything for now. I'll discuss it with Mrs Baxter and get back to you. And like I said, bring the boy up here when you find him. Bye."

"What was that about?" his mother said.

"Grolby's managed to track Floyd down. He's hiding out in a derelict building in Bedford. What do you want to do about it?"

"Good question. Well, we know he's not the rapist, but he'd still make an excellent scapegoat. I assume the police don't know his whereabouts yet?"

"No. We could just make an anonymous call and tip them off."

"Hmm. I want to think this through. I'll talk to my son first, then let you know."

"Do you want me to go and look for him, Mrs Baxter?"

"Go on then, Julian. He must be here by now."

Jason thought about slipping away, but part of him wanted to find out what this was all about. In any case, Anders Grolby would know by now that he had arrived and would be looking for him. He ran back to the door, pulled it open, then spun around as if he had just come in.

Stefano appeared shocked to see him there. "Your mother's waiting for you."

Jason strode towards his mother's inner office, aware of the man's gaze on his back. He didn't bother to knock and entered, shutting the door behind him.

His mother looked up sharply. "Jason, about time."

When he showed no sign of taking a seat, his mother stood up. "Sit," she said, pointing at the chair.

Jason reluctantly settled into the visitor's chair. "What's this about, Mum?"

Rosalind paused, gathering her thoughts. She remained standing and leant forwards, her hands resting on the surface of the desk. "Do you know how much this company is worth, Jason? The nearest billion will do."

"I don't know. Four, five billion?"

"Close enough. And what do you think would happen if it became known that the CEO's son was a rapist?"

Jason's mouth opened, but no sound came out.

His mother's face flushed apart from two white patches on her cheeks. "After everything I've given you," she screeched, "what the blazes do you think you're doing raping that girl?"

"I... I," stammered Jason.

"What? Did you think the police would just forget about it when the baby was born? How could you be so bloody stupid?"

"But..."

"She was in a wheelchair, for Christ's sake. What the hell were you thinking?"

"But I..."

"Jesus. I can't believe you would do this to me."

"But I didn't."

"Don't lie to me. You've done enough damage as it is. I have a good mind to turn you in myself and see you rot in prison for the next fifteen or twenty years."

"Mum, I didn't do it."

"DO-NOT-LIE-TO-ME. There's no doubt. I double checked the results. You're definitely the father of that child."

"But there's a warrant out for Daniel Floyd."

"They're incompetent tossers. I just hope they don't study the baby's blood samples too carefully."

"Seriously Mum. If I did it, I don't remember anything about it."

Rosalind's glare pinned him like a butterfly to a board. "How can you not remember raping a girl?"

"Somebody spiked the drink. I woke up on the sofa an hour later. I swear to you, I know nothing about it."

"If you're lying to me, I'll drag you down to the police station myself."

"Honestly, Mum. You must know I'm not like that."

"I don't know a thing about you anymore." Rosalind finally sat down. "What a bloody mess."

"So, the baby's been born? Antimone's dead?"

"Yes."

"Shit."

Jason hung his head. Several moments of silence passed while they each considered the implications of what they had learned. "I'll turn myself in," he said.

"You'll do no such thing."

"But you just said I'm definitely the father."

"You are, but that doesn't necessarily mean you're to blame."

"I don't understand."

"Think about it. That bastard, Daniel Floyd, has been plotting his revenge for years from that prison cell. What better way of discrediting me than by making my son look like a rapist?"

"But I don't see how he could have done it. How could a stranger wander through a party without anybody noticing him?"

"I don't know. But he was definitely in the house."

Jason took a sharp intake of breath. "Unless..." He ran the theory through his head. The more he thought about it, the more plausible it became. "I think I know who might be behind this."

He explained his suspicions to his mother.

When he had finished, she stared out of the window, deep in her own thoughts. "I suppose it's possible, but we have to keep this between us until we have proof."

Rosalind turned back to Jason. "I need you to go downstairs and get some tests done."

"I don't understand. What tests?"

"Just do as I say, Jason. Go to the Medical Diagnostics department and wait there. Somebody will come and get you."

Jason stood up to leave.

Rosalind waited until he had left the room, then picked up the phone. She explained what she had learned. "I think he's telling the truth. He was drugged when it happened. He's on his way down to Medical Diagnostics. I want full blood, DNA, body scan—in fact, the same as the girl and the child. Maybe there's something there to explain how she survived, and we need all the facts. He doesn't know they're alive, so keep it that way."

"Oh, one more thing, Nigel. There's something else I want to talk to you about. Come up to my office once the tests are underway."

## Thursday 6th January 2033

Nigel Perrin paced in front of the desk. Every few seconds he glanced at his watch. In his hand, he held a ballpoint pen, which he clicked in and out several times a second.

Rosalind Baxter stared at the column of figures but found it impossible to concentrate. "For Christ's sake, Nigel, sit down. And stop that damned clicking. You're driving me nuts. He'll be here in a minute."

Perrin returned the pen to his jacket pocket and lowered himself onto the leather-bound chair. He leant forwards and tapped his hands on his knees. Rosalind sighed. The tapping was almost as distracting as the clicking and the pacing.

"Oh, sorry," he said. Rising to his feet again, he crossed to the window. His eyes roamed the barren flowerbeds, slashes of black against a background of green. He put his face against the glass, straining to get a glimpse of the path leading to the entrance, but the angle was against him.

A knock at the door broke the silence.

"Come," Rosalind said.

Perrin spun around expectantly but seemed to deflate when Julian Stefano's bespectacled head appeared in the gap.

"Do you have a moment, Mrs Baxter?" He held up some pieces of paper. "I just need some signatures."

Rosalind beckoned him in and snatched up a pen. "What are these for?"

"Letters of condolence," he replied. "The first one's for the Lessing family."

Rosalind signed the letter without bothering to read the content.

"This one's for Nick Jenkins, the guy from the mortuary. He and his wife were killed two days ago when an out-of-control lorry ran into the back of them. A terrible shame. The letter's to his parents."

Rosalind scrawled an illegible mark above her printed name. "Most unfortunate," she said, without a hint of irony. "Is there another one?"

"Um, no. Were you expecting something else to sign?"

"No, that's okay, thanks, Julian. Is there anything else?"

"No, Mrs Baxter. Let me know if you need me for anything."

The slightly built man left the room, closing the door behind him.

"I know you like him, but he gives me the creeps," Perrin said, turning back from the window.

"I don't *like* him," Rosalind replied, "but he is very efficient. I know what you mean, though." A thin smile crossed her lips. "He is a bit creepy."

Perrin returned his attention to the glowering winter sky, lost in his thoughts.

A second knock at the door, this one more tentative.

"Where's my bloody secretary?" Rosalind muttered. "Come," she said in a louder voice.

Max Perrin shuffled into the room, his face a mask of trepidation. He seemed shocked to see his father glaring at him from beside the floor to ceiling glass.

"You asked to see me?" Gone was the cocky confidence.

"The Lessing girl," Rosalind said.

The colour drained from Max's face.

"You didn't have anything to do with her getting pregnant, did you?"

The boy glanced towards his father. The older man frowned and provided no offer of support. Max turned back to Rosalind and swallowed hard. "Er…" He remained mute, acutely aware of the two pairs of eyes boring into him.

"For God's sake, it's a simple question," Perrin senior yelled, although the boy's delay was all the answer he needed.

"Um… I…"

"Tell us what happened, Max," Rosalind said.

"I didn't mean for her to get pregnant," he gabbled. "She deliberately tripped me. I was injured for weeks. I was just trying to get even."

"Go on," his father said in a menacingly low voice. "What did you do?"

"You'd talked about those drugs that make you, like, do things that other people say. I was in your office, and I saw this sort of little bottle. I looked it up on the Internet and realised it was some of that stuff."

"I've told you before, Nigel, dangerous drugs like those need to be kept locked up," Rosalind said.

"Go on, Max," his father said, ignoring the admonition.

"I put it in my pocket and took it home. It was a few days before Jason's birthday. At the party, I poured it into the fruit punch just before he picked it up. I didn't expect it to do anything."

"So, what happened?"

"Well, I followed him back to the group of them sitting on the sofa. They all seemed, like, spaced out. I didn't know whether it was the drug so I told one of the boys to kiss the other, and he just, like, did it, snogged him right on the lips."

"And…"

"So, I told her to follow me to the bedroom, the one on the ground floor, and she pushes herself along behind me. I told her to take her top off, and she does it, just like that. Then I said to take everything off, but she couldn't do it in the wheelchair, so I put her on the bed. Next thing I know, she's lying there naked. I took some pictures."

"Where are they?" Rosalind snapped.

"They're still on my phone," Max replied.

"Did you show them to anyone?"

The boy shook his head.

"Nigel, when we finish in here, get Grolby to delete them permanently." She turned back to Max. "What did you do then?"

"Um…"

"You didn't…" his father began.

Max lowered his head.

"You raped her?"

He nodded.

"Jesus Christ," Perrin senior bellowed. "What the hell were you thinking? I raised you better than that."

"His brain wasn't doing the thinking," Rosalind said drily. "Did you wear protection?"

"What do you mean, like a condom? Yeah."

"So, let me guess. After that, you went back to the group and got Jason to have sex with her too?"

"Yes."

"What did you tell him?"

"I dunno. I think I just told him to shag her, or something like that."

"What, while you watched?"

"Yes."

"I don't fricking believe this," his father said.

"But he didn't have a condom?" Rosalind asked.

Max shook his head. "I didn't think she'd get pregnant, what with her being in a wheelchair and all that."

"So afterwards, you tell them to get dressed and forget everything that's happened?"

"Yeah. Jason went back first. It took her a bit longer to put her clothes back on, and then I had to put her back in the wheelchair. I waited until they'd gone, then waited a few minutes and followed them back into the room. When they woke up, I pretended I'd been affected too."

"Unbelievable," his father muttered.

"Well, that explains a lot," Rosalind said.

Several seconds of silence passed.

"So, what happens now?" Max asked.

"You go down to Medical Diagnostics and get some tests done while your father and I discuss what to do with you."

"Medical Diagnostics? I don't understand."

"Just do as you're bloody told," Perrin senior bellowed.

"Okay, I'm going."

"We haven't finished talking about this. Now get the hell out of here."

"What about my phone? You said about deleting the photos."

"Give it to me now."

"It's biometrically locked, though."

"We know where to find you if we can't unlock it."

After his son had departed, Perrin retrieved his own phone from his shirt pocket. He made a couple of calls, then turned back to Rosalind. "I'm really sorry about all this. I had no idea. I remember the vial going missing from my office. I thought Grolby had taken it."

"Hmm. Your son does seem to have a problem understanding the concept of proportionate response. Well on the bright side, if none of this had happened, we would've missed this opportunity."

Perrin removed the pen from his pocket and began clicking the tip in and out again. "So, what do we do now?" he asked.

## Thursday 6th January 2033

Jason emerged from the MRI scanner changing room, still trying to come to terms with what he had learned that day. Somehow, he had been manipulated into raping Antimone and making her pregnant. Now both mother and child were dead. Maybe Antimone had subconsciously identified him as the rapist, and that's why she had pushed him away. A heavy dread enveloped him. Even though he knew he was a victim too, a deep sense of guilt pressed down on him. Whether intentional or not, his actions had caused Antimone's death.

Surely the police would eventually identify him as the child's father. But why were they still chasing after Daniel Floyd? It didn't make any sense unless they really were as incompetent as his mother had suggested. There had been one obvious suspect, and they seemed to have latched onto him without considering the alternatives. As far as he could remember, the police had never requested a DNA sample from him. How would he be able to prove his innocence if they ever did test him? Any evidence was long since gone.

If his hunch was correct, all of this stemmed from the incident at the track. He found it hard to believe that Max Perrin would go to such lengths just to get even for what was obviously an accident. The guy was a bully and would have interpreted Antimone's actions as a direct challenge to his perceived status. But to rape and effectively murder her? Maybe he was wrong after all, and Floyd was somehow behind it.

As Jason passed an open doorway, a flashing red light at floor level caught his attention. He retraced a couple of steps and stared down. A man sat with legs extended, his face and body obscured by the angle of the walls. On the man's feet was a pair of blue trainers with a familiar illuminated logo. If they were originals, they were hugely expensive, and there was only one person he knew who could afford such an item. Jason read the nameplate above the door: 'Medical Diagnostics—blood tests.' Less than an hour ago he himself had waited in this same room to have a blood sample taken.

He stuck his head around the door and confirmed the person's identity. That could mean only one thing. His suspicions had been correct. The likelihood of Max Perrin undergoing the same test on the same day by coincidence was tiny. Jason felt his ears burning, and his breathing quickened. With no thought as to what he was going to do, he strode through the doorway and stood in front of the seated boy.

Max raised his eyes and a flash of fear crossed his face. In that moment, Jason knew with certainty that Max was responsible for administering the drug and everything that followed. He reached forwards and grabbed his surprised classmate by the lapels of his designer jacket. He hauled him to his feet and shoved him backwards.

Max crashed into the wall. The chair he had been sitting on skittered across the floor.

"You bastard," Jason growled. He shot out his hand and dragged the other boy upright. His fist drove into Max's stomach. Max doubled over, gasping for breath.

Jason seethed with pent-up rage and frustration. "You're a fricking murderer."

Another blow slammed into Max's face. Two more followed in quick succession as Max attempted in vain to fend off his attacker.

Jason was unaware of the shocked expressions of the other patients or the running feet behind him. He launched a vicious kick that connected with Max's midriff, but before he could strike again, strong arms wrapped around him and hauled him away.

"Call security," a voice from behind shouted as Jason struggled to free himself.

"Alright, alright, I'm stopping." Jason allowed his muscles to relax and sensed a corresponding loosening of the grip on his arms. Without hesitation, he once again hurled himself at the other boy. His foot smashed into Max's nose with a satisfying crunch of cartilage.

This time, the two men who had been caught by surprise wrestled him to the ground. Seconds later they wrenched his arms behind his back and bound them together with a plastic restraint.

A tall man in a brown uniform stood over Jason.

"I'll take him to the security office. You better sort the other one out."

# Friday 7th January 2033

Antimone inspected her new surroundings—monotonous white walls, a cream-coloured floor and no pictures or decorations of any kind. The only window in the small room was a small rectangle at the top of the door leading onto the corridor. Another door led into a cramped bathroom containing a toilet, sink, and shower. A white plastic chair with metal legs occupied the shower stall. The facilities were a definite improvement on the emergency ward where she had to be helped with even the most basic bodily functions.

Earlier that morning, an orderly had turned up with a battered wheelchair and despite her protests, had insisted on pushing her to her new quarters. They had passed along a featureless corridor with sequentially numbered doors, all of them starting with a two. The wheelchair was a clunky, old model, nothing like the lightweight one she had arrived at the hospital in, but at least she had regained her mobility.

They had even returned her ear implants and music player to her. It was the loud song booming in her ears that prevented her from hearing the door open. The first she knew about it was when a nurse entered her field of view carrying a tightly wrapped bundle. Antimone stopped the thrashing beat and focused all her attention on the object in the nurse's arms.

"Is that…"

"Yes, Antimone, it's your baby."

Antimone reached out to accept her son. Clasping him to her chest, she stared down at his tiny face. He stirred slightly, one eyelid opening a fraction then shutting again. He pursed his lips before settling back into an expression of contentment. *I never thought I'd meet him. He's perfect.*

She glanced up at the nurse, tears of gratitude in her eyes. "Thank you."

"I'll leave him here for a couple of hours. I've brought this in case he needs feeding." The nurse pointed to a pushbutton on the side of a plastic bottle filled with a white liquid. "Press that button there, and when the green light comes on, it's warm enough. Is there anything else you need?"

"No, I think I'll be alright."

"Well if there is anything, just shout or wave your arms. I'll be keeping an eye on you." She gestured towards a small black circle in the ceiling, obviously a camera and microphone. "I'll be back in a second with a cot."

The woman strode to the door and waved her access card at it. Antimone's eyes remained focused on her child, but out of the corner of her eye, just before the door closed, she picked up the outline of a uniformed man sitting in a chair in the corridor. Evidently, she was still a prisoner.

She studied the baby's face, the wispy, light brown hair, the button nose and the delicate eyelashes, imprinting the features on her mind. She raised a finger and gently touched an ear. The size of her hand seemed to dwarf the diminutive head. Her fingertips caressed the scalp, marvelling at the warmth and the softness. Strange to think this tiny, defenceless creature would turn into an adult one day. She watched in fascination as the child's fists clenched and unclenched. A sensation akin to déjà-vu swept over her, a sudden revelation that she was studying an extension of her own body as if she and her son were one entity.

The return of the nurse pushing a wheeled crib disturbed her moment of reflection. This time, the woman left the door open.

"If you need to put him down, slide the side down like this, place him inside then raise it again. Got that?"

Antimone nodded.

"Right I'll leave you to it."

The doorway revealed a better view of the guard. He wore a brown uniform and sat impassively, facing away from the entrance.

"What's he doing there?" Antimone asked.

The woman glanced behind her, then faced the girl once again. "Him? Oh, just a precaution."

"What? To keep me in or to keep somebody else out?"

The nurse smiled but didn't answer the question. "I'll see you in a couple of hours." She was halfway across the room when a muffled scream originated from the direction of the corridor. The baby tensed suddenly, flinging both arms out sideways.

The woman quickened her step and closed the door.

Antimone glanced down to see a pair of unfocused eyes staring upwards, the pale blue irises contrasting against the black dots of the pupils.

Seconds later, the baby's mouth opened, and a high-pitched wailing sound erupted.

*N*igel Perrin stood outside the girl's room, peering through the small window. "Have the contractions started?" he asked.

The midwife took her turn at the glass. "No, I don't think so. She's just hysterical. Since the operation, we've had to keep her restrained. Even though she has no use of her legs, she pushed herself off the bed a couple of times. We had to tie her down for her own safety."

"So, you've no idea what started this latest episode?"

The woman paused for a second. "I think it's just a culmination of things— being stuck in the same room for nine months, losing her mobility, being heavily pregnant. I think the kindest thing to do would be to do the C-section now. The baby's about due in any case. You don't honestly think severing the spinal cord is the answer, do you?"

"We won't know for sure until she gives birth—but no, I don't. If it was that simple, hundreds would've survived. As you know, there've been no verified accounts of a woman living through childbirth for over fifteen years."

"Still, it seems cruel abducting these women and making them pregnant."

Perrin turned sharply to the midwife. "You're not getting cold feet are you, Rose? We only take subjects with a low life expectancy in the first place, drug addicts and prostitutes. Think of all the women leading constructive lives and contributing to society who die in childbirth. The ones we take are just throwing their lives away. If we want to find a cure, we have to do this sort of work. If somebody doesn't come up with a solution and quickly, the whole of the human race is finished. At least this way, they're being productive."

"Yes, you're right, Dr Perrin. I just wish it wasn't necessary. So, what're we going to do about her?"

"I agree with your suggestion, Rose. I'll sedate her now. While I'm doing that, can you organise a surgeon to do the caesarean?"

The doctor opened the door and entered the room. The woman strapped to the bed craned her neck to identify the intruder. "Are you going to untie me, you bastard?"

"No. I'm sorry, but it's time."

She struggled against her bonds, pulling first one way then the other, her breath coming in frantic gasps. "No, no, no. Leave me alone."

Her eyes followed the doctor as he moved to the head of the bed. "No-no-no," the syllables blending into each other.

As he approached, she opened her mouth, filled her lungs and screamed. The cords in her neck stretched taut like ropes. Her wide-eyed gaze tracked him as he pulled out the injection gun. A deep intake of breath. Another shriek. The short hiss of the instrument. A final "No," almost a whisper, then silence.

The tension vanished from the woman's muscles. Her body seemed to sag back on itself.

"Sleep well," the doctor muttered.

***

Nigel Perrin coughed as the stench of the anti-bacterial spray filled his nostrils. It was like standing in a thin, drizzly, chemical rain.

John Martin drew the electronic blade of the cauterising scalpel towards him. "Spread the incision." He raised his eyes, frowning. "I said spread the incision."

"I'm sorry," Perrin said from the opposite side of the operating table. "It's a while since I've assisted during surgery. Twenty years at least, I reckon."

"Use that instrument to pull the wound apart so I can get to the uterus," the surgeon snapped.

"Oh, right." Perrin fumbled with the metal instrument.

"No, the other way," Martin said in mounting frustration.

The doctor adjusted his grip and used the tool to separate the edges of the cut.

"Good. Keep it like that."

Another smooth stroke and the wall of the woman's uterus parted.

"Okay, we're in."

Martin reached inside the deep gash in the patient's belly and eased the baby's head out. Using his other hand, he grasped the body and guided it into the harsh light of the operating theatre. The midwife stepped forwards to accept the child, and within seconds the boy was exercising his lungs in a reedy wail. She severed the umbilical cord, clamped it and placed the infant in an incubator.

"I'll sew her up," the surgeon said. "If there's any chance she might survive, we better do a good job."

Perrin ignored the implied insult, although he was happy to allow Martin to complete the work. "Check her pupillary response," he said to the midwife.

The woman raised an eyelid and shone a bright handheld torch at the exposed pupil. "Very little dilation," she reported.

The anaesthetist, a man in his early thirties, peered closely at the readouts of his instruments. "Heart rate erratic," he called. "She's crashing... That's it, she's flat-lined."

The surgeon glanced up from his work. "It doesn't look like this one's going to survive Dr Perrin. Do you want me to attempt resuscitation?"

"No, don't bother. It was always a long shot." Perrin focused on the anaesthetist. "But I need you to stay with her for at least an hour, just in case."

The man groaned. "Whatever you say, Dr Perrin."

"And check her core temperature before you record the time of death, just to be absolutely sure."

The room fell silent.

"Right, I've finished here," the surgeon said.

Perrin inspected the neat row of stitches. "Thanks, John."

He turned back to the anaesthetist.

"Just remember, we thought the girl who survived was dead as well."

## Friday 7th January 2033

Karen Atkins sat impatiently in the reception area at Ilithyia Biotechnology, studying the contents of the beige folder. Glancing at her watch, she noted that she had already been waiting for twenty minutes, and there was still no sign of the Chief Scientist, Nigel Perrin. She was about to approach the receptionist for the second time when a bald man wearing a white lab coat burst through a set of doors marked private. He halted and surveyed the room before his gaze alighted on Kat. He navigated the rows of chairs and stuck out a hand.

She rose to her feet. "Are you the Chief Scientist?"

"Yes, I'm Dr Perrin. What can I do for you, Ms…?"

"Atkins, Karen Atkins, but everybody calls me Kat. I'm an Inspector at the Maternity Crimes Unit. Is there somewhere we could talk in private?"

"What's this about?"

"Oh, I'm just checking up on some results from a woman and her baby who died here recently, an Antimone Lessing."

"Do you know how long this will take? Only we're very busy at the moment."

"Well, that depends to a certain extent on the answers to my questions but probably no more than a few minutes."

"Right. Well, follow me."

The man retraced his footsteps and upon reaching the door held up a card to the electronic reader. A short beep and the red light turned to green. He pushed through the door, holding it open for her. "Just down here."

He marched down the corridor, Kat following two paces behind and struggling to keep up. He entered a room on the left, the lights automatically ramping up in brightness as he crossed to a chair facing the doorway. He gestured to a seat on the opposite side of the polished oak table, then sat down.

"Nice facilities you have here," Kat said, studying the framed prints and expensive looking furniture.

The doctor removed a ballpoint pen from his pocket and began clicking the tip in and out. "Yes, well you've got to set a good first impression in business. So, what can I do for you?"

"Could you start by telling me a little about the work you do here?"

"Like I said earlier, I'm very busy just at the moment so I'll keep it brief. We have a research centre and a private hospital at this site. Most of what we do is targeted at creating drugs to treat the Orestes virus, and the majority of our patients are pregnant. I'm sure you're aware that we developed a cure a few years ago, but then the virus mutated, making it ineffective."

"So, how's the research going? Are you close to finding another cure?"

The doctor returned the pen to his jacket pocket and stared across the table. "I can refer you to our PR department if you need background information on the company, but you'll find pretty much all of it on our website."

"Okay, maybe I'll take a look when I get back to my office. So, do you run experiments on pregnant women?"

Perrin frowned. "The patients who come here do so of their own accord. We make no promises, but we do offer them experimental treatments that aren't available elsewhere. As you know, getting pregnant these days is a death sentence if it isn't terminated within the first four weeks. We're doing our best to make sure all that changes in the future. Anyway, as I just said, you can download all this information. You mentioned a specific patient. What did you want to know about her?"

"Yes, Antimone Lessing and her son Paul. I understand you treated them here."

"We treat thousands of patients a year. I certainly don't remember them all."

"Well, this girl was sixteen years old and in a wheelchair. The reason my department became involved was because she claimed she'd been raped."

Perrin scratched his head. "Yes, I do remember her. As I recall, the baby died of a bacterial infection."

"Yes, very sad. I met the girl and her parents several times, a nice family." Kat withdrew a couple of pieces of paper from the folder. "We requested that your company provide a blood sample from the child, mainly so we could identify the rapist."

"Was there a problem with the sample? I'm sorry, there's nothing much I can do about that. Both mother and child were cremated."

"So, you do remember them."

"Well... yes, as a matter of fact, I do."

Kat raised her eyes from the printed sheet. "There was an oddity. Our analysis shows no evidence of any infection. Don't you find that strange? From what I understand, the child died within twenty-four hours of being born."

"Do you mind if I look at that?" the doctor asked, extending a hand.

Kat passed the report over and studied him as his eyes ran down the page.

He handed the sheets of paper back and met her gaze. "It's not that unusual, really. New-born babies are at risk of all sorts of infections. The blood sample would've been taken soon after birth, so there's a good chance either the child hadn't yet been infected, or the bacteria levels were too low to detect."

"But it doesn't reflect well on your hospital if he picked up the infection here, or you failed to spot that he was already infected."

The doctor's eyes narrowed. "We go to great lengths to prevent infections. For example, this company made a large investment in anti-bacterial mist systems in all our operating theatres two years ago. You wouldn't find that in the majority of National Health Service hospitals. You must know that a lot of these bugs have resistance to anti-bacterial drugs. Sometimes there's just nothing we can do."

"But still, to go from no evidence of infection to death within what, just over twelve hours, you've got to admit it's strange."

"Like I said, infections can take hold really quickly, particularly in babies where the immune system isn't fully developed."

"I asked our expert, and he said the same thing, except that he thought the timescale was extremely short."

"What can I say? He's right, but all cases are different."

Kat rose to her feet. "Okay, well thanks for clearing that up. I'll let you get back to your work."

Perrin shepherded her out of the room and back towards the main entrance.

"Thanks for your time," she said, shaking hands.

He watched until she had left the building, then withdrew his phone from his pocket. He dialled a number and waited. The ring tone repeated six times.

"Yes."

"Hello, Rosalind. I've just had a chat with the police about the blood samples we provided for the child. It seems they might not be quite so incompetent after all."

## Friday 7th January 2033

Jason Baxter drew back the curtain and stared out of the window. The car headlights dazzled him, but a second or two later the curving drive returned to an inky blackness. As his eyes accustomed themselves to the dark, the vehicle's interior light came on, and he recognised the silhouette of his mother. He watched as she got out, reached in to grab an attaché case, then slammed the door behind her.

She hadn't returned home the previous two nights and had refused to accept his calls. His heart rate increased as he anticipated the forthcoming encounter. The key turned in the lock, and he picked up the lightweight virtual reality glasses, slipping them onto his face. The clicking of her high heels approached but didn't stop. He knew that the light beneath the door revealed his presence, but she had chosen not to talk to him. Not a good sign.

He heard the kitchen door open and the click of the light switch. For a moment he contemplated going out to greet her but thought better of it. He was still wearing the glasses when the footsteps returned along the hall, and the door opened. His mother stepped into the room clutching a glass of red wine.

"Hello, Jason."

"Hello, Mum."

Rosalind took a sip and stared at her son. "Have you eaten?"

"Yeah, I did a frozen pizza in the oven. What about you?"

"I'm going to make a salad—after I've had another of these." She lifted her glass. "You can't beat a Chateau Margaux. It's not a seventeen eighty-seven, but it's not bad. What are you doing?"

Jason removed the glasses. "Oh, you know, just watching a film." He tracked his mother's gaze to the headset, noted the absence of a green light and realised she had caught him in a lie. She drained her glass, turned on her heel and headed back through the open door without speaking. Jason fidgeted on the sofa, wondering whether he should follow her.

Several minutes later, she reappeared carrying a tray containing a plateful of salad and a half-empty wine glass. She crossed to an armchair, sat down and ate her meal, perching the tray on her knee.

Jason waited patiently until she had finished. "Everything okay at work?"

Rosalind nodded. "Really busy. Never a quiet moment. I should have called to let you know I wasn't coming home. I slept at the office the last two nights. Sorry about that."

Jason shrugged. There was nothing unusual about his mother staying at work overnight, but it was unlike her not to call. Rosalind rose, placed the tray holding the empty plate on the coffee table, then returned to her seat, clutching the glass to her chest. The silence built between them like an invisible barrier.

Jason leant forwards. If she wouldn't speak, he would. "So, you heard about the... um... incident at the hospital?"

His mother stared down as she swirled the contents of the glass, then raised her eyes. "I assume you're referring to the thing with Max. Yes. I can't say I blame you."

"What about Max?"

"He'll survive."

"That's not what I meant. What's going to happen to him?"

"Nothing. Unfortunately, there's no evidence. If we go to the police, they'll discover you're the child's father and... well, like I said, there's no proof you were drugged."

"So, he's just going to get away with it?"

Rosalind didn't reply. She drained the glass, then stood up. "I'm going to get a refill."

Jason sat back on the sofa, his mind whirling. She knew about the assault, but why had they been testing Max? It must mean their parents believed that both boys had something to do with Antimone getting pregnant. What puzzled him was the reason for the tests. Why the interest in the blood and DNA samples and why the scan? Something else was going on that she wasn't telling him.

Rosalind returned to her chair with a full glass.

"So, what will happen about Daniel Floyd?" he asked.

His mother's eyes were slow to find him. He realised that she must have been drinking before she came home.

"He's a convicted murderer. If the police catch him, he's only getting what he deserves."

"So, you're not going to let them know they're after the wrong man?"

Rosalind glanced up sharply, spilling a drop of wine on her dark skirt. "No," she said, brushing the liquid off. "If I knew where he was, I'd tell them."

*But you do know,* Jason thought.

"I'm off to bed," his mother said, rising to her feet. More wine sloshed from the glass onto the carpet. "I'll see you in the morning."

"Are you working tomorrow?" he asked.

"I'm not planning to," she said, but both of them knew that meant very little.

"Good night, Mum."

"Good night, Jason."

## Saturday 8th January 2033

Antimone stared at the face reflected back in the mirror. The previous evening a technician had unscrewed the fixture from the wall and lowered it to the correct height for somebody in a wheelchair. Beneath each grey-blue eye was a crescent-shaped dark shadow. She hadn't slept well since she had arrived. In the darkness, a sense of claustrophobia built up inside, the featureless white walls seeming to close in on her. Her breathing became tight and the thudding of her heart echoed in her ears. Only when she turned on the lights did the panic subside. During the last two nights she had slept with them on but had woken up every few hours, disturbed by the unfamiliar illumination cast by the ceiling panels.

Her gaze moved down her face. The faint tendrils of broken blood vessels adorned the top of each cheekbone, the after-effects of the contractions. A prominent blackhead occupied a position just above her left nostril. She applied her fingernails and forced out the small black dot. Instinctively she reached out a hand to grab the antiseptic face cleanser she always kept by the sink at home, only to find it wasn't there. Old-fashioned soap would have to do on this occasion. Another item to ask for when the nurse came.

She washed and dried her face. Leaning forwards, she ran a finger over her cracked lips. The atmosphere down here was warm and dry. Every morning she woke up with a raging thirst. She added lip balm to her mental wish list.

Her dark hair was tied back in a ponytail. She brushed a stray strand behind her ear, her eyes drawn to a small vein pulsating at her temple. She pressed it in then released it, studying the way it fluttered briefly before resuming the rhythmic pulsing. Her heart beating, something she hadn't expected to be the case a few short days ago. In the months before the birth, she had often wondered what it would be like to be dead. No sense of feeling, no thoughts, just like being asleep except with no prospect of ever waking up. The hardest thing to come to terms with was the idea of the world carrying on without her. In a sudden epiphany, she understood the urge to reproduce and have children. It was about part of a person continuing after they died. Without that, death would be a permanent ending.

The beep of the electronic lock disturbed her moment of reflection. She swivelled the chair around and headed into the main room. A nurse shuffled in carrying a tray containing Antimone's breakfast, a breezy smile on her face.

"How are we today?"

She had only uttered four words, but already she had annoyed Antimone.

"*I'm* okay," Antimone replied, glancing behind her to emphasise the point. "I don't see anybody else here, though."

"Somebody's in a bad mood this morning, aren't they? Didn't you sleep well?"

Antimone wanted to snatch the tray out of this smug woman's hands and fling it against the wall, but the smell of bacon and hot coffee was making her hungry. "I think you might be bad tempered too if you were stuck in one room, twenty-four hours a day with no sunlight."

"These lights provide the same spectrum as the sun," said the nurse, setting the tray down on the bed.

"You don't get it, do you? It's driving me mad being cooped up in here."

"But you do get to see your baby, don't you?"

"Yeah, but it's boring as hell the rest of the time."

"I wish I had the time to sit around and do nothing. You've got your music and reading material. What else would you be doing?"

"Jesus Christ," Antimone muttered, shaking her head. "You really think it's okay to keep somebody locked up in a tiny room as long as you bring them food and books and let them listen to music?"

"Well, um…"

"You must lead a really boring life if you think this is fun."

The nurse flushed and folded her arms. "I'm doing my best to help you, but if you'd rather I didn't."

Antimone's lips twitched with a slight smile. "I appreciate what you've done for me, but I'd just prefer to be elsewhere."

The nurse seemed mollified. "By the way, my name's Rose. Is there anything else I can get you?"

"Um… Thanks, Rose. Actually, is there any chance you could get some face cleanser and maybe some lip balm?"

"I'll see what I can do. Any chemicals, medicines or things like that, I need to get Dr Perrin to sign off first."

Antimone shrugged. She glanced towards the open door, spotting the legs of the guard seated in the corridor. "Has he been there all night?" she asked.

The nurse looked perplexed for a second, then turned around to see what Antimone was looking at. "Oh, him. Yes, I think so, or at least one of his friends."

"You never answered me last time. Why is he there?"

The nurse hesitated. "You'd have to ask Dr Perrin or Mrs Baxter. They don't tell me that sort of thing. That reminds me. Mrs Baxter said she'd be popping in to see you later."

"Oh, right."

"Well, I best be off. I'll bring Paul round in half an hour or so. He's a pretty baby. I'm sure he'll break a few hearts when he's older."

"If he ever gets out of here," Antimone muttered.

## Saturday 8th January 2033

Jason yawned and examined the dial of his alarm clock. Nine thirty. He flung the sheets back and slipped his feet into a pair of brown moccasin slippers. There was a silence about the house that suggested he had it to himself. His mother had said she was not planning to go to work today, but that meant nothing. Over the past fortnight, she had seemed more distant, spending less time than usual in the house, almost as if she was avoiding him. He still couldn't get the overheard conversation out of his head. What had she called him? A little bastard and a prick.

She was certainly not the most affectionate of people. As a young child, she had kept him at arm's length, relying on nannies and au pairs to look after him. Apart from a perfunctory kiss at bedtime, she had demonstrated very little warmth towards him. He could still recall his abiding childhood wish to be hugged by her, but it rarely, if ever, happened. When he turned thirteen, she explained that she had adopted him. She was reticent in providing details about his birth-mother. She told him his father had succumbed to cancer, leaving his pregnant mother to fend for herself. When his mother died in childbirth, Rosalind had agreed to adopt Jason. Over the years, Jason had pressed her to describe his biological mother, but she always replied that she hadn't known the woman well. She had even refused to let him know her name, saying she would tell him when he was older.

Over the last year or two, he felt they were becoming closer. He sensed that he still came second after the company, but at least they had shared some interesting conversations. She had even discussed some key business decisions with him and seemed pleased when he offered his opinion. During the past week, the longest discourse they had exchanged was in her office. By the time he woke up, she had long since departed for work. On the occasions when she had returned home at night, such as the previous evening, it was usually late and mostly, she was uncommunicative.

Jason wondered whether she still blamed him for getting Antimone pregnant. For the past two nights he had lain awake until the early hours, worrying about the future. It was clear that someone had drugged him, but where was the evidence? The only person who truly knew what had happened was Max, and he wasn't about to confess. The big question was what to do about it. He could go to the police and tell them the whole story, but Max would only deny it. And if his mother wasn't speaking to him now, he could only guess at what her reaction would be if he handed himself in.

One thing was clear, though: she intended to let Daniel Floyd take the blame. The man had certainly been in the house and had at the very least been trespassing. Why was he there? Apparently, nothing had been stolen, but he didn't trust his mother to be truthful if something had gone missing. On top of that, he was a convicted murderer, so did it matter if he took the rap for another death? The more he thought about it, the more it gnawed at his conscience. It was hard to feel sympathy for somebody who had slaughtered his own wife, but the man was innocent of Antimone's rape. But what could Jason do about it?

As he rolled that question around in his head, probing it like a sore tooth, an idea came to him. He didn't know whether his mother had revealed Floyd's location to the police yet, but if she hadn't, he could warn the man to expect a visit. It wasn't a complete solution, but it would at least give Floyd a fighting chance of evading capture and help to salve his feeling of guilt.

But how to contact Floyd? Ideally, he wanted to remain anonymous, but that was impractical. He knew the approximate location, a derelict building close to the railway station in Bedford. He could travel there by train, find Floyd and alert him. How the man would react was anybody's guess, but he relegated that concern to the back of his mind. Maybe he could get some answers of his own, perhaps find out what Floyd was doing in the house and what he was searching for.

There was obviously some prior history with his mother, but she had always been reticent on the subject. He had read about Floyd's court case on the Internet and discovered that his mother and Floyd had studied the same course at Cambridge University. According to the report, they had even been boyfriend and girlfriend for a while. His mother never talked about that phase of her life and deflected any questions on the matter.

Jason padded along the hall to his mother's room. He pushed the door open and was greeted by a waft of expensive perfume. "Mum," he called, sticking his head in the gap. The curtains were drawn and the king-sized bed was made. Feeling like an intruder, he crossed the scarlet-coloured carpet to the en-suite bathroom. He rapped his knuckles on the solid wood and called her name again. No reply. He edged into the fully tiled wet-room. The scent of perfumed soap and shampoo assaulted his nostrils, but it was empty. He closed the doors behind him and retreated back to the hall.

He descended the stairs and was unsurprised to find the kitchen deserted. As expected, there was no sign of a note. He opened the dishwasher and inspected the contents: a plate flecked with toast crumbs, a coffee cup and a knife still smeared with butter. It seemed that his mother had eaten her customary breakfast and returned to work. For a moment he toyed with the idea of phoning the hospital to be sure but decided against it. After all, where else would she be?

He poured himself a bowl of cereal and sat at the island in the centre of the kitchen. What should he do? What would Antimone want him to do? The right thing was to hand himself in to the police and tell them the whole story, but he wasn't quite ready to take that step yet.

"Damn it," he said, dropping the spoon into the bowl. His mind decided, he hurried upstairs and got dressed.

## Saturday 8th January 2033

Antimone glanced up as the door opened. Rosalind Baxter entered the room, wearing a matching pale blue jacket and skirt. Antimone switched off the music, her gaze following the woman as she strolled across the floor.

"Hello, Antimone. How are you feeling today?"

"Bored," Antimone muttered. "When are you going to let me out of here?"

"We still need to run some more tests, make sure you and the baby are okay."

"He's called Paul."

"Yes, I know. I have a question for you, Antimone. Do you know how many women have survived childbirth in the past fifteen years or so?"

"I'm guessing none."

"That's right. In all that time, not one single woman has given birth and lived. Do you know how special that makes you?"

"Yeah, but I don't feel very special at the moment. Why are you keeping me a prisoner in here?"

Rosalind smiled, but it didn't reach her eyes. "You're not a prisoner. You're here so we can look after you."

"So why is there a guard outside my door?"

"This is a classified area. We need to make sure no unauthorised people are wandering around."

"Okay, but why is he sitting outside *my* door?"

"It's just a convenient spot. He can see the whole corridor from there."

"Hmm." The tone of Antimone's voice indicated her scepticism. "So why can't I speak to my parents?"

"We've told them you're doing well, but we can't risk any possibility of infection."

"That doesn't mean I can't talk to them, though."

"I'm sure it's been explained to you. The work we do down here is very commercially sensitive. For that reason, we don't allow calls to outside lines. Mobile phone signals are also blocked. You'll be able to see them in a few more days."

Antimone folded her arms. "Well, that's a load of crap. Are you telling me you can't arrange a telephone call?"

Rosalind's expression hardened. "You should've checked the contract you and your parents signed. We agreed to give you the best care available, but in exchange you gave us exclusive rights to your genetic makeup. You also gave us permission to choose the treatment we felt most suitable for your condition. What we have decided upon is to keep you in total isolation."

"But I didn't expect to survive."

"We didn't expect you to survive either, but that doesn't change anything. It's our decision as to how we treat you."

"So how long is this going to last?"

"Until we're ready to discharge you, and we still have a huge amount to learn, so I'm not going to put a timescale on it."

Antimone frowned. "You're saying you can keep me here as long as you want?"

"Yes."

"But I have human rights. We studied that in Ethics at school. You can't just lock me up against my will."

Rosalind sighed. "Look, Antimone. Do you know how many women have died since this virus first started? Let me tell you. Across the globe, it's tens if not hundreds of millions. And amongst all those millions, you are unique. Do you have any idea how important you are?"

Antimone shrugged. Rosalind fixed her with her blue-grey eyes and continued. "Unless we find a solution in the next five or ten years, mankind is doomed. Already the birth rate has declined to something like a twentieth of what it once was. There aren't enough children being born to maintain the species. But *you* contain the answer. Somehow *you* survived. Think about the lives you can save. It's no exaggeration to say that you could be the person who saves the human race. Isn't that worth a few days of your time?"

"I still don't see why I can't talk to my parents."

"Look. We can do this the easy way or the hard way. At the moment we've provided a wheelchair, we allow you to see your son several times a day even though it's extra work for the nurses, you have music to listen to and books to read. Now imagine life stuck in this room with none of those things. Think what that would be like."

"So now you're threatening me?"

"No. I'm just saying how things could be. I hope you realise how important it is that we determine why you survived and agree to cooperate. For whatever reason, you've been given a remarkable gift. Don't you think it's right to share it with the rest of the planet?"

"Okay, I'll tell you what. Let me speak to my parents, and I'll let you do what you like without complaining or anything."

The two females stared at each other in silence.

"Well?" Antimone asked.

The ring of her mobile phone spared Rosalind from having to answer. She withdrew the device from a pocket inside her jacket and held it to her ear.

"Yes, Nigel. What is it? I'm a little busy at the moment."

She listened while the voice on the other end of the line spoke.

"You've what?"

Antimone heard the tinny voice say something else but could not distinguish the words.

"Excellent news. I'll be with you right away."

Rosalind clicked off the phone and put it away.

Antimone glared at her. "I thought you said mobile phones don't work down here."

"My phone is different," Rosalind said, turning around and heading for the door.

## Saturday 8th January 2033

Jason stepped from the train onto the platform at Bedford station. A handful of people hurried towards the exit. He followed the general flow and waved his phone over the reader to open the barrier. A cold wind infiltrated his blue winter jacket as he descended the steps outside. He looked both ways, attempting to identify any buildings that gave the appearance of being derelict. A row of trees obscured his line of sight. The only structure of which he had an unobstructed view was a nine-storey block of flats. Faded text extended along the brickwork above the ground-floor windows, but the lettering was no longer decipherable. Whilst it seemed a little run-down, the curtains in the windows and the furniture on the balconies indicated that people still lived there.

He passed a taxi rank of autonomous vehicles as he crossed the car park. A residential road led straight ahead, but all the properties seemed to be in a good state of repair. He debated with himself whether to knock on one of the doors and ask if the resident knew of any abandoned properties in the immediate vicinity. Instead, he decided to investigate further before approaching the locals. Glancing to his right, he spotted a green and yellow sign, just over a hundred metres away and headed in that direction. As he drew closer, his eyes picked out the words, 'Service, Tyres and Batteries'. Maybe the owners would be able to give him some hints as to where to look.

The reception area ran parallel to the pavement, but when he pushed against the door, it was locked. Glancing down at the notice above the handle, he read that the business was closed on Saturdays.

"Damn," he muttered under his breath.

Ahead, the straight road ended in a roundabout. He strode along the pavement as the cold winter wind ruffled his hair. On his right, he passed another local business. A sign painted in a variety of pastel shades read 'Low-Cost Printing', but the lack of internal lighting indicated that it too was closed.

On the opposite side of the road, an elderly man traipsed along behind his dog. The man shuffled forwards, his face barely visible between a black woollen hat, a thick, slate-coloured scarf and the upturned collar of his coat.

The dog, a small, brown animal with pointed ears, ranged ahead at the full extent of the lead, vigorously sniffing the wall of the adjoining property.

Jason waited for a gap in the traffic, then hurried across and approached the man. "Excuse me."

The dog gave a high-pitched growl, then sensing that the stranger was not a threat, lifted a leg and urinated before resuming its analysis of the wall. The man took a step backwards, dragging the dog away from a particularly interesting scent. "I'm sorry, I don't have any change."

"Right. I don't need change."

A pair of rheumy eyes inspected Jason. "Well, what do you want, young man?"

"Well... um... I was wondering if you know whether there are any derelict buildings near here."

The man scratched his left ear. "Derelict buildings?"

"Yeah."

"You're not one of those squatter types, are you?" the man asked, looking Jason up and down. "You don't look old enough."

"No. I'm trying to find a... friend."

"So, your friend's a squatter then?"

"Look, it's a long story. This friend of mine moved recently, but he didn't leave a forwarding address. I remember him saying that his new house was near a derelict building close to the railway station."

"No new houses here, you know."

"No, it wasn't a new house. It was an old house, just new for him."

"The railway station's over there," the man said, pointing.

"Yeah, I know. I just came from there."

"What's your friend called?"

"Um... Daniel. Why does that matter?"

"I don't know anybody called Daniel," the man replied.

Jason shook his head. "Never mind. Thanks for your help." He had taken a couple of steps when the man mumbled something from behind his back. Jason turned to face him. "I'm sorry, I didn't catch that."

"The old sorting office is derelict."

"Sorting office?"

"That's what I said. It must be what, five years ago, no... nearer ten I should think. They moved it all to Milton Keynes, been empty since then. No call for letters anymore. It's all this new email rubbish. Can't use a computer to save my life."

The dog approached Jason and sniffed his shoe. Jason bent down to stroke it but hastily removed his hand when it growled.

"Oh, don't mind Billie," the man said. "He's all bark and no bite. Thinks he's a Rottweiler."

"Um… okay. How would I get to the sorting office?"

The man pointed. "Just the other side of that road, but it's all locked up. I don't know where your friend might be living unless it's somewhere along here."

"Thanks," Jason said. "I'll try that."

"You must want to find him badly. Owes you money, does he?" The old man cackled, his laugh turning into a hacking cough. He raised a gloved hand and waved to Jason before resuming his shuffle along the road.

"Have fun and good luck," he called.

## Saturday 8th January 2033

Rosalind strode down the brightly lit corridor, her heels clicking on the white linoleum floor. She reached a door labelled 'Chief Scientist' and turned the handle without knocking. Behind a large wooden desk sat Nigel Perrin. A frown creased his forehead, and his fingers clasped a pen that he clicked in and out in a rhythmic pattern. "Couldn't you knock for once? You nearly give me a heart attack every time you do that."

A smile twitched on Rosalind's lips. "I've got to keep you on your toes, Nigel. So, what's the big news?"

"Come and have a look at this." He returned the pen to his pocket, jumped to his feet and rounded the desk. Grabbing one of the visitor chairs, he dragged it with him, placed it next to his own swivel chair and invited Rosalind to sit.

She crossed the room, her eyes sweeping over the framed certificates and photographs that lined the walls. She and Perrin featured on the majority of the images, smiling alongside a selection of politicians and celebrities. She had never understood the need to display the trappings of fame like this, an unspoken statement that the well-known personalities were somehow more important than the people who did the real work. It occurred to her that she could probably afford to buy most of these people ten times over. Unfortunately, the Public Relations people insisted that famous faces had to be present at the big occasions.

The doctor moved his seat to the side and angled the monitor to direct it towards the visitor's chair. "Can you see that okay?" he asked as Rosalind sat down.

She nodded, her eyes drawn to the three-dimensional display. "What am I looking at?"

Perrin could barely contain his excitement. "You know we had to re-run one of the tests?"

"Yes. As I recall, a technician mixed up the samples, and you fired her."

"Well, it seems that we sacked her unfairly."

Rosalind turned her head sharply to the doctor. "That's not going to be an issue is it?"

"No, no. She received a generous pay-off, and I gave her a good reference. She won't be a problem."

"Okay, you better explain then."

Perrin turned his attention back to the screen. "Right. Well, as you know, we took blood samples and a buccal swab from the inside of her cheek. We ran both samples through the DNA analyser. So, this is the blood sample." He jabbed a finger and a three-dimensional graph floated a few centimetres in front of the monitor.

"So, what am I looking at?"

"There's nothing particularly special about this. But here..." He gestured to the display as if beckoning the data to come out. "Here we have the sample from the cheek cells."

The original graph reduced in height, and a second one appeared just below it.

Rosalind squinted and leant forwards. "Are these supposed to be the same? They look totally different. Are you sure they didn't mix up the samples again?"

The doctor grinned. "Not possible. I personally took another blood sample and cheek swab just to be absolutely sure. There's no mistake. They're both from the girl."

Rosalind frowned. "That doesn't make sense. How can one person have two different...? Oh, hang on. She's not a—what do you call it? You know, a —"

"Yes," Perrin interrupted. "She's a chimera, and what's even more interesting is that the DNA from the cheek cells is male."

"What? So, the blood cells have different DNA to the cheek cells?"

"We need to do more analysis, but here's what I think happened. When her mother got pregnant, two eggs were fertilised, making one male and one female foetus. As they developed, something went wrong, and somehow the two foetuses fused together. Basically, the female foetus absorbed the male one, but some of the male cells remained and were incorporated into the female."

"But what about rejection? Wouldn't the female's immune system attack the male's cells?"

"Apparently not. You've got to remember that they share the same parents, so they're likely to be genetically close in the first place. It also depends on when the merge took place. If it was early enough, the immune system wouldn't have had time to develop yet and would recognise both sets of cells as the body's own."

"So how rare is this?"

"I did some reading. There were a couple of well-reported cases twenty or thirty years ago. In one of them, a woman offered to donate a kidney to her sick son. When they did a compatibility match by taking a cheek swab, they told her she wasn't the mother. As you can imagine, that came as quite a shock. It had been a home birth, so there was no chance that the child had been mixed up with another at the hospital. They confirmed it by testing her other sons, none of whom matched the DNA taken from her cheek either. When they ran the blood, they found a different set of markers that were a match for all the sons."

"So, she was a chimera?"

"That's right."

"But how rare are they?"

"From what I've read, male-female chimeras are incredibly rare. It's difficult to know what proportion of the population are chimeras because they don't tend to display any overt sign of their condition. Apparently, it's quite common in fraternal twins when they share the same portion of the placenta. Each twin can incorporate the other's blood marrow cells, so they can even end up with two different blood types. If I had to hazard a guess, I'd say for the male-female variety, maybe one in eight hundred million or more."

Rosalind pulled an earlobe, deep in thought. "Okay, so let's say she's a chimera. How come she survived?"

"Well that's a different question, but it's got to be more than a coincidence. I'm guessing that something in the foreign cells prevented the virus' normal reaction to the changes that take place in the mother after childbirth."

"Could be. I don't need to tell you how important this is, Nigel. If we can work out what those cells are doing, we can create a cure."

"I know, I know," Perrin said, shifting on his seat. "I'm well aware of the implications. The first thing we'll have to do is identify the disposition of the different cell types. That's going to mean taking a lot of samples. It's going to be pretty uncomfortable for her."

Rosalind stared at the doctor. "And? What's one girl's discomfort compared to saving the human race?"

"Yeah, I know, but one of the nurses was saying that she's becoming less cooperative, wants to talk to her parents."

"Not a chance. If they find out she's alive, we won't be able to hold onto her. There'd be all sorts of awkward questions to answer. I spoke to her earlier today, threatened to remove access to her son and to withdraw things like the wheelchair and the music. I don't really care if she likes it or not. We're going to do what's necessary to develop this treatment."

"Of course, Rosalind. It's just easier if she cooperates."

"Oh, I think she will. By the way, how are we going to discover whether the boy had anything to do with her survival?"

The doctor scratched his bald head. "Good question. Maybe we make her pregnant again, this time by a different father."

"Hmm. I don't like the idea of waiting another nine months."

"We could always deliver the child early, say at six months. In fact, if you don't care about it surviving, any time after about six weeks would be fine to test the hypothesis."

"Good point, Nigel. Let's wait until we know more, but that's not a bad idea."

"We're going to require more test subjects. I better tell Grolby to find some."

"Yes, do that. One other thing, Nigel," Rosalind said. "I want you to keep all of this to yourself. Make sure that all samples are destroyed. I don't want any of the workforce knowing what's going on."

"Um… okay, but that's going to slow things down a bit. All the ones who work down here are on the highest security clearance. Don't you trust them?"

"Look, Nigel, it's all about degrees of trust. Would you leave ten or a hundred billion pounds lying around, just waiting for somebody to walk off with it? If one of our researchers were to learn about a cure, the temptation might be too great, especially given what it would be worth. Grolby's got the security pretty tight around here, but this takes it to a whole new level. I'd rather delay things if it means that we reduce the risk of losing out to a competitor. You can use other staff to help you, just ensure they don't get too much of the overall picture."

"Fair enough," Perrin replied. "I'll get on it right away. Have you decided what to do about the boys? Max hasn't been sleeping, worrying about what you might do. Jason gave him quite a going over, although from what he told us I think it was justified."

"Tell him not to worry. I'm not going to jeopardise the future of this company just to save a low-life like Floyd. Tell Max to keep his mouth shut. I'll get Grolby to give the police an anonymous tip-off. Do you see any problem with that?"

"No, no problem at all."

## Saturday 8th January 2033

Jason walked in the direction the man had indicated. At the roundabout, a tunnel led beneath a flyover to a locked gate. A sign on the gate read 'Bedford Network Rail'. He hurried across the road and peered through the bars. Railway tracks cut through an area of open ground. Patchy grass and weeds poked up through the industrial landscape. A large, red brick building emblazoned with the text 'Bedford Depot' dominated the scene. Twisting his head to the left, he could just about make out a four-storey structure, although at this distance it was impossible to determine whether it was derelict or not.

Jason followed the pavement in the general direction of the building, his view blocked by the elevated roadway. After fifty metres, the ramp had descended, and he obtained the first glimpse of his target. A Royal Mail icon still adorned the beige-coloured structure. A high fence surrounded it, but the broken windows suggested that there was a way past, at least for the local vandals. This could well be the location that Grolby had mentioned. It certainly met the vague description he had overheard. The problem was how to get in. Whilst the surrounding fence was scalable, he could hardly do so in front of the steady stream of traffic rolling along the main road.

As Jason strolled past the tired-looking facade, he spotted a narrow alleyway running down the side of the structure alongside the barrier. He waited for a gap in the flow of vehicles, then crossed the busy highway. The alley provided access to the rear of a row of terraced houses. Backyards and garages, many of them with paint flaking off the woodwork, backed onto the narrow strip of concrete. More fencing blocked off the end, but alongside it stood a low storage shed with white doors. A paved footway switched back on itself and led to the back gate of one of the properties. A metal handrail divided the two opposing directions of the path.

Jason ambled down the alley, his head down. When he reached the shed, he glanced around and confirmed nobody was paying him any attention. If he could get on the roof, he could drop down into the fenced off area. There was no certainty that Floyd was even hiding here, and for a moment he questioned the sanity of the decision to warn the man.

"Ah, sod it," he muttered.

He placed one foot on the handrail and pushed himself up. On the first attempt, he lost his balance and dropped down. He repeated the process and this time maintained enough stability to jump the short distance to the shed roof. His stomach bore the brunt of the impact as he landed on the sharp corner.

"Shit."

The flat roof creaked ominously but held his weight. He pulled his legs up, crawled forwards then lowered himself down inside the delivery office compound. Feeling exposed standing by the railing, Jason sprinted across the open space to the side of the building. Most of the windows were broken, but heavy metal bars blocked the frames, making it impossible to gain entry. He followed the wall away from the main road and came across a door. He twisted the handle, but it refused to budge. A second door was also locked. He rounded the corner and crept along the end of the structure. Glancing up, he spotted an empty window frame, just above head height, that did not appear to be protected by bars. Jagged shards of glass rimmed the aperture. He would cut himself to ribbons if he tried to get through. If there was no other way of getting in, it might be worth reconsidering.

He turned the next corner, his hands brushing against the dusty brickwork. Seeing no means of entry through the windows, he proceeded to another door. That was locked too. He was about to resume his search when an area of freshly splintered wood around the lock caught his attention. This one had been recently forced open. There was no handle, so he dug his fingertips in between the door and frame where the material had been prised loose. A splinter embedded itself beneath his fingernail.

"Damn." He snatched his hand away and delicately withdrew the thin sliver. A small spot of blood welled up, and he placed the injured digit in his mouth. More gingerly, this time, he applied both hands and attempted to lever the door open. No movement at all. Somebody had definitely come through here in the recent past judging by the fresh state of the exposed timber, but they had obviously used a tool to crowbar their way in.

Jason lowered his eyes to the ground and searched for a suitable implement. His gaze settled on a rock about the size of his hand. He bent down and picked it up, but when he held it to the frame, he realised that it was too big. He dropped it and sighed in frustration. As he surveyed the wall, he spotted a corroded metal sign, the lettering long since eroded away. Four rusty screws secured it. He retrieved the stone and banged it down on one of the protruding screw-heads. The sharp thud sounded incredibly loud over the swish of passing traffic, and he scanned the surrounding fence for observers before studying his handiwork. The end of the screw was bent at an angle. Another blow and it dropped loose with a metallic tinkle.

He repeated the process on the second screw-head and after three strikes had reduced it to the same state as the first. One side of the sign now sat slightly proud, held only by the two remaining fasteners. He levered the plate backwards until it separated from the brickwork in a shower of dust.

He returned to the door frame and slipped the flat piece of metal in the spot where somebody had gouged the wood away. He pressed against the lever. The base of the door made a scraping sound, but there was no perceptible movement. He flung himself at the improvised tool, and this time, a crack opened up. Three more shoves and the space between door and frame was large enough to obtain a grip. He inserted both hands through the gap and pulled, but the timber had warped and resisted his efforts. With increasing frustration, he placed a foot against the wall and heaved backwards. Finally, the door surrendered and screeched open.

A damp, mouldy smell assaulted his nostrils. He slipped through the opening and yanked the handle towards him. The door closed most of the way, but a thin sliver of light remained around the frame. He tossed the faded sign on the floor. A loud clang reverberated through the cavernous space. If there was somebody here, Jason had certainly announced his arrival.

He surveyed the hangar-like building in the dim illumination that leeched through the narrow, barred windows. Grey tiling extended outwards in a zig-zagging pattern. Dark shadows indicated where machinery or shelving had stood. In several spots, dampness had lifted the tiles, spoiling the symmetry of the lines. Rows of fluorescent tubes hung by chains from the high ceiling every few metres, but they had probably remained unused for years. Even without the aid of artificial illumination, he could see that the entire space was empty.

Jason waited for his heart rate to slow, then strolled across the tiled flooring, his footsteps echoing in the vast room. There was no evidence of anybody living here and no place to hide. Maybe Floyd was hanging out in the multi-storey building at the front of the structure. Set in the grubby beige wall at the far end were two green doors. The first was locked, but when he pulled the second, it opened. Glass fronted offices lines both sides of a corridor that led towards another green door. Jason crossed the grey linoleum, glancing into the empty interiors as he passed. Still no sign of habitation.

He reached the door and turned the handle. It moved a few centimetres before sticking. He applied his shoulder, and it juddered open the rest of the way. He found himself in what was once a large open-plan office. The carpet was a tatty dark-grey colour, the indentations of furniture still visible in places. Once again it was deserted. He inspected the glass-fronted offices that ran around the edge of the room, but all were empty. A short corridor led to male and female toilets. A quick search showed no sign of recent activity.

He retraced his steps and passed through a set of double doors into what must have been the reception area. The curved desk bearing the Royal Mail logo still occupied its place in the centre of the tiled floor. Two sealed lifts and another pair of swing doors were set in the wall adjacent to the wide staircase that led up. Jason pushed through the doors. He emerged into what was a carbon copy of the first office area, but a quick survey proved this to be equally empty.

He was beginning to suspect that he had made a wasted trip when a muffled scraping sound reached his ears from above. Maybe somebody was here after all. His heart thudded in his chest as he returned to reception and headed up the stairs. The staircase turned back on itself and led to a space with a lift on one side and toilets on the other. An archway opened into an even larger room with individual offices extending along each of the side walls. The same dark grey-coloured carpet covered the floor.

Jason figured the time for stealth was long since over. "Um, Mr Floyd?" he called, a slight tremble to his voice. A cloud of steam rose from his mouth in the frigid air. If Floyd was here, he must be hiding in one of the offices. "Mr Floyd?" he called again, louder this time.

He held his breath and strained his ears. No reply. A sharp bang and the sound of something rolling across a hard surface broke the silence. He spun around. His eyes darted around the dilapidated interior. Nothing moved.

He headed to his left and pushed open the first office door. Empty. He worked his way along the row. All of them were deserted. Maybe it was just a rat he had heard. The thought of their scaly tails made him shudder. A sudden movement at the periphery of his vision caught his attention. The cord for a raised blind shifted in the air entering through a shattered window.

He tried to calm his frayed nerves and traversed the room. He tried the first door on the other side. A half-full black plastic bin bag occupied a spot in the far corner. Jason widened the top and peered inside. The rancid stench of rotting food wafted out. He wrinkled his nose and turned away. There was no way to know how long the rubbish had been there, but judging by the condition of the banana skin he had spotted, it couldn't have been more than a few days.

Jason pulled the door handle towards him, eager now to inspect the adjoining offices. The door slammed into his midriff, knocking him to the ground and winding him. Before he could recover, a figure barged into the room and knelt on his chest.

The man clamped his left hand on Jason's throat. His right grasped a long-bladed knife. The tip quivered less than an inch from Jason's eye. "What are you doing here?" he growled.

Jason wrenched his gaze from the knife and towards the man's face. "I…"

The blade touched Jason's cheek. "How the hell do you know my name?" The man paused and frowned. "Shit, it's you. The Baxter bitch's son."

Jason made a choking sound. He raised a hand, trying to loosen the stranglehold. "I can't…"

Floyd's grip slackened slightly, but the razor-sharp edge remained in place. "How did you know I was here? Spit it out or I'll start cutting."

Jason drew a deep breath and coughed. "My mother's Head of Security found you."

"How did he do that?"

"I've no idea. I overheard them talking on the phone."

"So, I'm going to ask you again. What are you doing here?"

"I… I came to warn you."

"Warn me? Warn me about what?"

"The police are coming."

An expression of incredulity crossed the man's face. "You came here to warn me that the police know where I am?"

Jason tried to nod, then thought better of it. "Yes," he rasped. "Look I can't breathe properly. Can I at least sit up? I'm not going to run away. If I wanted to turn you in, I would've already done so."

"Okay, empty your pockets. You're not carrying any sort of weapon, are you?"

Jason shook his head. He withdrew his house keys, wallet and phone and placed them on the floor.

"Lean against that wall," Floyd said, releasing his grip. Jason shuffled backwards until he felt the hard surface against his back. He rubbed his throat.

"Don't try anything. I don't want to redecorate the place with your blood. Am I clear?"

Floyd picked up Jason's belongings. He flipped open the wallet, inspected the contents, then tossed it back on the ground.

"Okay, so you discovered where I was hiding, and you decided to warn me. You haven't told me why."

Jason stared up at the bearded face, the black woollen hat, the grimy skin. "I know you didn't rape the girl."

Floyd fixed him with a glare. "Go on."

"My mother was going to let you get arrested for it."

"So why should you care?"

"Well… um, I don't know. It's just not right."

"Yeah, life's not fair, and I should know. So, do you know who the rapist really is?"

Jason hesitated. "Um… no, I don't."

"But you know it's not me?"

"Yes."

Floyd scratched his chin. "I don't believe you, but we'll come back to that. When are the police coming?"

"I've no idea. I found out two or three days ago. All I know is that my mother knows you're here."

"You say you want to help me, and yet you waited all that time before warning me? I could be banged up in a prison cell by now. Why did you leave it so long?"

"I'm not sure. I had a lot on my mind."

Floyd looked down at the busy main road, then turned back to Jason. "Do you have any idea how long it took me to discover this place? And now you want me to move on your say so?"

"Look, do what you like. All I'm telling you is that they know where you are. Why does my mother hate you so much, anyway?"

"Your mother and I go back a long way. I don't think the vindictive cow has ever forgiven me for dumping her. Not that I owe you any answers."

Silence settled on the small room. Floyd stared at the winter sky, deep in thought. Suddenly he tensed. "Shit, it looks like the filth have arrived." He whirled to face Jason. "I knew I shouldn't have trusted you. You've brought them right here."

Jason shuffled sideways to increase the distance between them. "I already told you—if I wanted to turn you in, I wouldn't have bothered talking to you. I'd just have told them where to find you."

"Maybe." He turned back to the window. "Well they're here now, and they've come in force."

Jason rose to his feet and stood beside Floyd, surveying the empty car park and the road beyond. Three white vehicles were parked in front of the entrance gates. As he watched, people emerged from the cars. One of the men approached the gates holding a large pair of bolt-cutters.

Floyd hurried out of the room and into the adjoining office. Seconds later he emerged carrying two bulging plastic bin bags. "If you don't want to get arrested, I suggest you follow me." Without waiting for a response, he rushed towards the staircase. Jason needed no second invitation. He snatched up his own belongings and trailed the other man down the stairs. When they reached the ground floor, Floyd retraced Jason's route into the huge hangar-like building. However, instead of going to the door Jason had used to gain entry, he headed to one at the far end. He drew back the bolts, pulled it open and darted out into the overcast afternoon.

He sprinted ahead to a gap between two buildings, apparently towards a dead-end. The area ended in a low single storey structure. He tossed the two bags onto the roof, then shimmied up a drainpipe after them. Keeping his head lowered, he ran up the shallow incline and then down the other side. Jason followed a short distance behind. The pair dropped down beside some adjoining shrubs.

Floyd stuck his head around the corner of the building. Satisfied that nobody was there, he turned to Jason. "Thanks for the tip-off. Give my regards to your mother… actually, on second thoughts, don't bother." He took two paces, then hesitated. He spun around and studied Jason's face for a moment before coming to a decision.

"Have you still got your phone?"

Jason nodded.

Floyd held out his hand. "Unlock it and give it to me."

Jason held the lozenge-shaped device up to his eye and stared into the camera. When it beeped, he handed it over.

"I'm adding my number," Floyd said, tapping at the keys. "If you have any more tip-offs, call me. It's under the name F."

He tossed the phone back.

Jason opened the contacts list and found the entry as Floyd had indicated. When he looked up again, the man had disappeared.

## Saturday 8th January 2033

Karen Atkins surveyed the dingy grey carpet and shivered in the frigid atmosphere.

"Jesus, I wouldn't want to live here," she muttered.

The uniformed policeman who was carrying a black bin bag of rubbish towards the stairs looked at her questioningly. "Eh?" he said.

"Oh, nothing," Kat said. "Where's your sergeant?"

The man pointed in the direction of one of the abandoned offices. Kat thanked him and strolled to the door he had indicated. She stepped inside to find a tall man in a dark blue uniform staring out of the window with his back to her. The man whirled around at the sound of footsteps behind him.

"Ah, you must be Karen Atkins," he said, taking a step forwards. "Mike Knowles." He extended a meaty hand and crushed hers in a powerful grip.

"Hi Mike," she said, subconsciously rubbing her knuckles. "Everybody calls me Kat. So, what have you got?"

The man frowned. His hair was brown but flecked with grey and receding at the temples. A thin layer of stubble ran from cheek to cheek. It was a large face, but all the elements were in proportion. A typical policeman's face, thought Kat. "Well, somebody was certainly here recently. There was a bag of rubbish, a couple of books, a comb."

"Yeah, I just saw one of your men carrying an evidence bag out."

"We'll check everything for fingerprints. We should be able to confirm pretty quickly whether it's your man or not."

"So, you don't know yet if he was living here by himself or not?"

"Like I said, the fingerprints should tell us that, but all the signs are that he was alone."

Kat paused for a second. "I take it you've searched the entire building?"

The sergeant held her gaze before replying. "We may only be the local police, but we do know what we're doing."

"Um… sorry," Kat replied. "I wasn't trying to imply…"

"Right," the man said, relaxing slightly. "As luck would have it, we did have a drone up this afternoon. Unfortunately, it was quite high to cover the whole of the town—the cuts, you know. I'm having one of my men examine the footage now."

"So, you'll be able to see when he left and where he went?"

"Yeah, but the resolution probably won't be good enough to identify him."

"Okay. Can you let me know as soon as you hear anything? How did you know to look here?"

"Anonymous tip-off," the policeman said. "The caller knew Floyd's name and described the location perfectly, which is why we took it seriously. It came from an unregistered mobile, but we do know it originated from somewhere around Cambridge."

Kat stared out of the window, deep in thought, before turning back to the sergeant. "Isn't that a bit strange? If the call came from Cambridge, the person must have been hanging onto the information for a while. It's not as if the informant spotted our man and called it in straight away."

"Yeah, it is weird, but I'm not sure what it means. Maybe they thought about it before calling us."

"Have you tried to trace the phone?"

"I've got one of my men looking into it now, but I don't hold out much hope. If whoever it is doesn't want to be identified and is savvy enough to use an unregistered phone, they're unlikely to leave it turned on."

"But if that's the case, it doesn't sound like your average law-abiding citizen, does it? I mean, who's going to buy a mobile and then throw it away after one call?"

The policeman ran a hand across his stubble. "Let's see what the trace turns up, but it's a good point."

"Do you mind if I have a look around?" Kat asked.

"Sure, do what you like, but I'm sure I don't have to remind you not to touch anything."

It was Kat's turn to roll her eyes. "Don't worry, Mike, I may not be the local police, but I do know how to treat a crime scene."

"Touché," the policeman said, grinning.

Kat returned the smile, turned around and left the office. She walked a few metres and stuck her head inside the next door. Another policeman was photographing something on the floor in the far corner of the room.

He glanced behind him. "Can I help you?"

"Karen Atkins, Maternity Crimes Unit. What have you got?"

"Hi. It's a comb. It may belong to the suspect. I'm just about to bag it."

"Yeah, your sergeant mentioned it. Anything else?"

The man shook his head. Kat thanked him and returned to the large open-plan area. She looked inside each of the rows of offices but discovered nothing out of the ordinary. She had just about decided that there was nothing further to see when the sergeant strode across the room towards her.

"Kat, glad you haven't left yet. You'll want to hear this. I've just heard back from the drone unit. They saw two people leave the premises shortly after we arrived."

"Two people? Are you sure?" Kat asked.

"Yeah, they used one of the doors out of the old sorting room."

"Sorry, where's that?"

He pointed in the direction of the staircase. "You know, the big long building tacked onto the back of this one. They came out together and climbed over the roof of one of the outbuildings. Then they split up."

"Do you know where they went?"

"One of them headed back towards the station."

"Do you know which train he caught?"

"It's difficult to say. The main entrance is under cover, so he disappeared from view when he went in. If we check the footage carefully, we may be able to work out which platform he came out on and from that, the time of the train, but it's going to take a while. Remember what I said about the drone being high up."

"Damn. Isn't there CCTV in the station?"

"Hmm. There should be, but from past experience, it's often on the blink."

"What about the other man?"

"Unfortunately, he headed away from the city centre and out of the drone's camera range."

Kat scratched an ear. "Any cameras on the ground along his route?"

"Maybe, but in the current climate, there's not been much investment in that sort of thing. We'll check it out, but don't expect anything quickly."

"He's a slippery bastard, this one, but it looks like he's not working alone."

"Yeah, it's galling to get so close and let him slip away again."

Kat sighed in frustration. Suddenly she shot out a hand and grasped the sergeant's arm. "Hang on. You said one of the two people went to the train station. Isn't it possible that he arrived by train too? If he did, you could backtrack his movements and work out what train he travelled on."

"The drone's only up for three or four hours at a time. They generally don't fly at night, but if he got here in the last couple of hours, we'd be able to tell when and where he came from. I'll get my team on it right away."

"Thanks," Kat said. "You've got my number."

## Saturday 8th January 2033

Jason opened the door and entered his mother's outer office. The lights came on as he crossed the threshold. Her secretary was not at the desk, but that was hardly surprising on a Saturday evening. He approached the door leading to her inner sanctum and knocked. No answer. He stuck his head inside the room and saw that it was empty. Typical. He pulled his phone from his pocket and double checked the message.

*Fancy going out for a meal tonight? Meet me at the hospital at 6pm. Mum.*

He tapped out a reply.

*I'm here. Where r u?*

His mother was probably in a meeting. He typed out a second message.

*I'll wait at hospital reception.*

Jason strolled along the corridor towards the stairs. Despite the exertions of that afternoon, he would still have felt guilty if he had taken the elevator. He trotted down the staircase taking two steps at a time and emerged into the reception area. Even at this hour on a weekend, medical staff bustled to and fro, like worker ants around sugar.

A solitary receptionist wearing a headset pressed a button on the screen in front of her. "Just putting you through." She turned her attention to Jason and smiled brightly. "Hello, sir. What can I do for you?"

"Um… I'm here to meet my mother, Mrs Baxter."

The smile dropped a notch. "Right. I'll try her office."

Jason opened his mouth to explain that she wasn't there, but the woman had already placed the call.

"There's no reply. Do you want me to page her?"

"No, don't bother. I just wondered if you knew where she was. I'm supposed to meet her at six."

The receptionist glanced up at the large illuminated display above the entrance. 18:10. "I'm sorry, I don't have your mother's schedule, but if you'd like to take a seat, I'm sure she'll be along shortly."

"Thanks." Jason turned and ambled towards a row of blue-coloured armchairs. As he did so, he spotted a middle-aged woman in a blue nurse's uniform staring at him from a few feet away.

She took a pace forwards. "Did I just hear you say you're Mrs Baxter's son?"

Jason nodded.

"Oh hello. It's nice to meet you." She extended a hand. "My name's Rose."

The skin of the woman's palm felt rough and dry.

"I've just seen your mother with Dr Perrin," she said. "They're in the basement lab. I can take you down there if you want."

"Um… sure, thanks," Jason replied.

"Okay, follow me," the woman said, heading in the direction of a set of double doors labelled private. She waved a card at a box on the wall and barged through. She led the way down a corridor to another door carrying a large yellow warning sign. 'Biohazard—authorised personnel only.' Once again, she used the card to gain access and pressed the lift call button.

"Is it safe down there?" Jason asked, a worried expression occupying his face.

The woman looked puzzled for a second until she realised what had drawn Jason's attention. "Oh, yes," she laughed. "Don't worry about that. You'll be perfectly alright."

A ping announced the lift's arrival, and they stepped inside. Rose stared into the red light of the iris scanner and selected the basement level.

"I never even knew this was here," Jason said as the floor sank away.

"Yes, this is where a lot of the sensitive work takes place," Rose said. "All very hush-hush, but then again, you are the boss's son."

The doors slid apart to reveal a featureless white corridor. The illumination cast by the diffuse ceiling lights was so bright that Jason had to shade his eyes.

"Yes, it is a bit dazzling, isn't it?" Rose said as she guided them past several numbered doors. They turned a corner and encountered a guard wearing a brown uniform sitting outside one of the rooms. "Hi Tony," she called. "Just taking Mrs Baxter's son to see her."

The man waved a hand but didn't reply.

"It's just at the end," Rose said, pointing.

"Um, Rose," Jason said, slowing down. "Is there a loo nearby?"

"There's a Gents just there. I'll wait for you here."

A strong perfumed scent hit Jason's nostrils as he entered, in stark contrast to the medicinal smell in the corridor outside. He relieved himself at the urinal, then stood by the white marble sink and examined his reflection in the mirror. The cold winter air had coloured his cheeks a rosy hue. His hair looked like he had just got out of bed, several patches sticking out at odd angles. He rinsed his hands under the tap and smoothed down the stray tufts. He used the dryer, then pulled the door towards him.

As he exited into the corridor, a movement to the right drew his eye. The end of a hospital trolley emerged from the room outside which the guard was sitting. A body lay on top, covered by a sheet. Jason half expected the head to be covered too, but it wasn't. He only gained the briefest of glimpses, but he instantly recognised the face of the patient. *It couldn't be. She was dead. His mother had told him so.* Yet her eyes were open, staring at the ceiling.

Two orderlies wearing green outfits followed the trolley out, partially obscuring his view. An arm moved. The person lying on the stretcher was definitely alive. The two men turned the corner and disappeared from sight, pushing their cargo before them.

Jason stood slack-jawed, staring after the departed trolley. The nurse's voice dragged him back to the real world. "It's this way. We don't want to keep your mother waiting."

Jason stumbled towards her as if in a trance.

"Are you okay?" she asked. "You don't look well."

"I'm fine," he replied, but his face felt flushed, and his ears were burning.

Rose resumed her route, a worried frown creasing her forehead. Reaching the door labelled 'Chief Scientist', she knocked loudly.

A voice inside shouted, "Come."

She turned the handle and held the door open for Jason. "Your son was waiting in reception, Mrs Baxter. I thought I'd do you a favour and bring him down."

Even as she said the words, she realised from the shocked expressions on the two people's faces that she had made a terrible mistake.

## Saturday 8th January 2033

The pen tip clicked in and out at an alarming rate. "Jesus Christ, Rose. What were you thinking? You know about the security precautions. We have them for a purpose."

The nurse's chin quivered. She looked like she was about to burst into tears at any second. "Sorry Dr Perrin. I… I thought—"

"That's exactly the problem. You didn't think."

"But he's her son. I thought it would be alright to bring him down here. I was only trying to be helpful."

"Look," Perrin said, attempting to control his temper. "We have several women being held down here against their will. What do you think would happen if he discovered what we were doing? The boy's sixteen, for heaven's sake. Would you tell your teenage son something like that?"

"I haven't got a—"

The doctor slammed the pen down. "Jesus, Rose. Are you winding me up deliberately?" He glared at her across the desk. Now, she did start crying. She pulled a handkerchief from a pocket in her uniform and dabbed at her eyes. A series of mewling whimpers emerged from beneath the square of cotton.

Rosalind and Jason Baxter had departed a few minutes earlier. Perrin knew from the paleness of the CEO's face and the vivid red spots on her cheeks that she was struggling to maintain her composure. He had been unfortunate enough to witness several meltdowns over the years and had offered to handle this situation, knowing that if left to Rosalind, the nurse would be unemployed by morning and also probably on Grolby's to-do list. He debated with himself what action to take. The easy option would be to fire Rose on the spot. She had committed a grossly irresponsible breach of security and could have no complaints if they sacked her. In her favour, she was actually a good worker and would be hard to replace. That, and the fact that she knew too much. What she said next would help him to decide.

"So, did he see anything he shouldn't have?"

Rose lowered the handkerchief and sniffed loudly. "Um, like what?"

Perrin frowned. "Are you being deliberately obtuse, Rose? Do I have to spell it out? Did the boy see anything he wasn't supposed to?"

"Oh, you mean like one of the patients?"

"Yes, that's exactly what I mean."

The nurse hesitated for a moment. "No, I don't think so. We were only in the corridor for a second or two."

Perrin's eyes bored into her. "You do realise that the sixteen-year-old girl, Antimone, was his girlfriend?"

The colour fled from her face. "His girlfriend?"

"Look, Rose, you're really stretching my patience. Antimone Lessing was Jason Baxter's girlfriend. You just led him right past her room. Now did he or did he not see anything?"

"N–n–no," she stammered. She met the doctor's gaze for a second, then stared down at her feet.

"You better not be lying, Rose. Are you sure?"

A quick glance up. "No, he definitely didn't see anything."

The doctor relaxed slightly. "Good."

Another sniff from the nurse. "So, is Mrs Baxter going to fire me?"

"I'll have a chat with her in the morning. Just make sure you stay out of her way. Are you working tomorrow?"

She nodded.

"Okay. You're going to take a couple of days off, starting immediately, as holiday of course. There's been a breakthrough in developing a cure, so hopefully she'll be in a good mood over the next week or so. I can't make any promises, but I think I can persuade her not to do anything too drastic."

Rose buried her face in the handkerchief again. "Thanks, Dr Perrin. I really appreciate it. I was only trying to be helpful."

"Yes, I know, Rose. Now I suggest you go home. Have a good break, and when you come back, for heaven's sake, do as I said and keep out of Mrs Baxter's way."

Perrin watched as the nurse got to her feet and shuffled towards the door, her body language a picture of dejection. He waited until he had the room to himself, then walked around the desk and made sure that she was not standing outside. He returned to his seat and stared at the phone for a second or two. Placing the handset to his ear, he spoke Grolby's name. A click and three rapid beeps. The sound of a ring tone. Another click as somebody answered.

"Grolby here."

Perrin remained silent, wrestling with his thoughts.

Grolby's voice again. "Is anybody there?"

"Sorry, Anders. It's Nigel. It's nothing. I dialled your number by mistake."

## Saturday 8th January 2033

Aburst of raucous laughter erupted from the corner of the restaurant. Three suited men and their expensively dressed partners were sharing a table and by the sound of it, several bottles of wine. La Cordonnerie was one of the most expensive places to eat in Cambridge, but in spite of this, always had a long waiting list. However, when Rosalind Baxter's personal assistant had called about a reservation, a table for two miraculously became available.

Jason sat across from his mother, studying her as her eyes ran down the menu. The journey had passed mostly in silence. Throughout the drive, she had remained engrossed in the screen of her mobile phone, but he could tell by her uneven breathing and the slight tremble in her fingers that she was still seething with anger. As they neared their destination, she had finally emerged from her fugue-like state and had asked him about his day. He had been deliberately vague, implying that he had not left the house.

The aroma of French cooking made his stomach rumble, overlaid though it was with the scent of his mother's perfume. Rosalind dropped the folded menu on the tablecloth, and within seconds the waiter was standing beside them, pen and pad at the ready. Neither of them ordered a starter, Jason choosing the pan-fried duck and his mother a tuna salad.

Rosalind ran a finger down the wine list. "Ah, a Chateau Margaux, twenty twenty-five. Not a bad vintage. I'll have a bottle of that, please. Do you want a drink?"

Jason shrugged. "Water's fine, thanks."

"I thought we should go out to celebrate," she said. "I know I haven't been home much recently, but we've made an exciting breakthrough. We might finally be on the path to a cure."

"Good," Jason replied. "Is that what happens in the basement?"

Rosalind frowned. "The work that goes on down there is top secret. I know that nurse meant well, but she should know better than to bring unauthorised people down there, even if you are my son."

"Anyway," she said, brightening, "Back to school on Monday. Any more thoughts about what you might want to do for a career?"

"Well, obviously something related to science with the subjects I'm studying, but I'm not really sure yet."

The arrival of the waiter holding a bottle of wine interrupted the conversation. He presented the label to Rosalind. She nodded her approval, and he withdrew a corkscrew from a pocket in his jacket before removing the cork. He poured a small amount into Rosalind's glass and waited while she took a sip.

"That's fine," she said, putting it down.

The man half-filled the glass with ruby-coloured liquid. He turned to Jason. "Would Monsieur care for some wine?" he asked.

"You're sixteen now," his mother replied on his behalf. "I think you're old enough for a glass."

Jason was not unaccustomed to the taste of alcohol, but on the few occasions he had tried it, he couldn't really see what all the fuss was about. At his age, it was more a case of conforming with his peers, but he wasn't about to go into that with his mother. "Yeah, okay," he said.

The waiter smiled and poured the wine, barely covering the bottom of the glass. He placed the bottle in the centre of the table and draped a napkin around the neck.

"Now, where were we?" Rosalind asked once the man had departed.

Jason stared at his mother for a moment before replying. "I know she's alive. I saw Antimone this evening."

Rosalind froze, the wineglass halfway to her lips. Slowly, she returned it to the table. The tinkle of cutlery and the muffled conversations of the other diners seemed to increase in volume to fill the silence.

Finally, she spoke, her voice a low whisper. "Jason, you don't know what's going on."

Jason leant forwards. "But you told me she was dead. You lied to me."

A flush rose from Rosalind's neck. "I did it to protect you."

"So, she's the breakthrough that you mentioned?"

The pinkness had extended to her cheeks. "The less you know about this, the better."

"But you're not denying that she's alive?"

The silence stretched longer this time. "Yes, she survived the birth, and she's being cared for at Ilithyia."

"But she's my friend. Jesus, I'm the father. You let me think I was responsible for her death. Did the baby survive too?"

An expression of anger flashed across Rosalind's face. "Keep your voice down," she hissed. "You might be the child's father but, as we both know, you're not culpable when it comes to the pregnancy. Unfortunately, the child died."

"What happened?"

"A bacterial infection is what happened. Now I don't want to talk about this here."

It was Jason's turn to display his anger. "So, when are we going to discuss it? You hardly ever come home these days."

Red blotches formed in the centre of her cheeks. "I don't answer to you."

"Would you rather I discussed it with the police?"

Rosalind pushed the table back and stood up, wine sloshing from her glass and staining the tablecloth. The sudden movement drew glances from the other diners. "Right, we're leaving." She strode towards the bar at the entrance and entered into a low conversation with a man in a bowtie standing by the till. She withdrew her phone from her purse and waved it at the reader, then stormed out onto the pavement without checking whether Jason was following. Her fingers jabbed at the screen of the phone and within a few seconds their driverless car drew up alongside. Almost before the vehicle had stopped moving, she extended a hand and yanked the door open. She climbed in and slammed it closed behind her.

For a moment, Jason thought she was going to drive off without him, but the car remained stationary. He crossed to the far side, opened the door and clambered in. He buckled himself into the seat on the opposite side from his mother. She stared straight ahead, a vein throbbing prominently at her temple.

Finally, she turned to face him and spoke, ice dripping from every word. "You do not talk to me like that... ever. Am I clear?"

Jason remained silent, his heart thudding in his chest. He had never pushed her this hard before.

"Am I clear?" she repeated, raising her voice.

Jason met her eyes, nodded, then looked away.

"There is more going on here than you can possibly imagine," she said. "Yes, Antimone survived the birth against all expectations. It was nothing to do with any treatment that we gave her. It seems that she has some natural immunity to the virus. Now, think about it for a minute. Millions of women have died since this virus first emerged. Your friend, Antimone, holds the key. Think of the lives that could be saved. Now, knowing all that, do you think she could just saunter out of the hospital and resume her life? Of course not. Apart from being hounded by the press, she'd be a target for every religious nutcase and lunatic who thinks it's a punishment from God. What's more, she'd be top of the kidnap list of every foreign power trying to develop a cure of their own.

"Keeping her survival quiet is the best thing that could happen to her. When we've found a way to treat this disease, she'll no longer be such a big story. She'll just be one of many women who have survived giving birth. But that means we have to keep the fact that she's alive a secret. If news gets out, she'll be in danger, and the chances of finding a cure will be reduced. You can see that, can't you?"

Jason hung his head, then glanced at his mother. She fixed him with her gaze. "I suppose."

"Good. I'm glad you understand, but you mustn't mention this to a soul. As far as you're concerned, she's gone. Just forget about her."

"I assume her parents know she's still alive though?" he asked.

Rosalind hesitated for a moment. "At the moment, no. I don't think that's something they'd be able to hide, so it's best for Antimone if we keep things that way for the time being."

"So, you're just letting them think their daughter's dead when she's actually alive and well?"

Rosalind sighed. "Like I said, until we work out a treatment, it's the best thing for her. That's all we're thinking about."

"Did she ask about me at all? Does she know I was the one who made her pregnant?"

Rosalind's tone hardened. "Look, Jason, didn't I just say that you have to forget about her. She still thinks it was Floyd who raped her and no, she hasn't asked about you. She's still grieving for the loss of her baby."

"Alright, I'll keep it to myself, but I want to talk to her," he said, a note of belligerence entering his voice.

Rosalind folded her arms and fixed him with an angry stare. "Haven't you listened to a word I've just said? You have to put her out of your mind. Pretend she never existed. It's for her good and your own—and the future of the human race. Now I don't want to hear any more about it."

"But Mum."

"Enough."

Jason wanted to argue with his mother. Even though he had been under the influence of mind-altering drugs at the time, he still felt partially responsible for Antimone's death. Learning that she was alive had lifted a huge weight off his mind, and the fact of the matter was that he enjoyed her company. He still hadn't come to terms with his feelings concerning the baby's death. Technically the child was his son, but there was no real emotional attachment. Now that he knew Antimone had survived, he desperately needed to see her, but it was obvious that his mother had no intention of allowing that to happen. There was nothing to be gained by prolonging the argument, but he was already planning how to circumvent her mandate.

"Alright then," he said. "I'll do what you say."

## Sunday 9th January 2033

Antimone coughed. Sharp, shooting pains sparked through her body. "I didn't see him," she mumbled through cracked lips. In her mind she heard the squeal of brakes, the car still hurtling towards her. A quick sideways glance, the shocked face of the elderly male driver, everything happening in slow motion. The force of the impact, limbs tangled together, the surface of the road rushing up to greet her, then darkness. Then the sudden inrush of agonising pain, unable to draw breath, the panic as her muscles refused to obey her commands.

"I can't move. No!" Her head thrashed from side to side, the sheet clenched between her fingers. She tried to open her eyes, but they felt gritty, the eyelids gummed shut. Hysteria bubbled up inside her before first one, then the other blinked open. Her gaze traversed the white ceiling, the featureless white walls and the door with the small window. The realisation grew that she was in the hospital room, lying on the bed.

She felt like a herd of elephants had trampled her. The slightest movement sent a cascade of agony rippling outwards. Her head throbbed, and her throat felt as if she had swallowed a set of nail files. Her lethargic brain attempted to make sense of the excruciating sensations. Slowly it came back to her. They had told her they were going to perform a series of tests, but the after-effects were way beyond anything she had expected.

With slow, microscopic movements, she raised her right arm and stared at it blearily. A white dressing was affixed to her wrist, another on her forearm. A grid of brown plasters covered the limb at regular intervals. She lifted her left arm. It was a carbon copy of the right. With trembling fingers, she picked at the edge of one of the plasters and peeled it back to reveal a small circular incision. A scab had started to form, surrounded by a circle of inflammation.

She touched her face, feeling the outlines of at least six more plasters. A tight sensation drew her fingers to her scalp. Her fingertip brushed over bare skin, then the surface of another plaster. Her delicate probing revealed a regular pattern of sample points across her skull. All her hair had been shaved off, leaving her totally bald.

Whilst the plaster-covered wounds felt tender and there were more of them, the dressings were the main source of the throbbing pain enveloping her body. She picked at the surgical tape securing one of the white squares. She winced as she slowly lifted the gauze material.

The electronic beep of the door lock interrupted her efforts. A nurse entered and strode towards the bed. She gently took hold of Antimone's wrist and placed it back on the sheets.

"Glad to see you're finally awake," she said, "but that's not a good idea. Those dressings need to be kept on for a few days. If you take them off now, you'll be risking infection."

The woman had greying hair tied back in a ponytail. She wore a pale blue top that extended to just below her ample waist, and dark blue trousers. Her face was round and ruddy coloured. Her chin blended into her neck.

"What the hell have you done to me?" Antimone asked, her voice coming out barely more than a whisper.

"I'm sure they told you what they were going to do beforehand, but you probably weren't paying attention. They've taken a series of skin biopsies. That's where the plasters are. The white dressings cover the sites where they took bone marrow samples. They shaved your head to prevent hair getting in the wounds."

"They said they were going to do some tests," Antimone rasped, "but they never said anything about drilling holes all over my body and shaving my hair off."

"I can give you some painkillers. That should help. You'll feel a lot better in the morning."

Antimone groaned and closed her eyes.

"I'll be back in a sec." The nurse bustled out of the room, closing the door behind her as she went.

As soon as she was alone, Antimone picked at the dressing again. She lifted the edge to reveal an angry looking circular wound, several millimetres across. If what the woman had said was correct, and there was no reason to think otherwise, they had drilled through the skin into the centre of the bone to extract a sample of the marrow—and not just once, but all over her body. No wonder the pain was so intense. For the first time in her life, she was thankful she had no sensation in her legs. Gingerly, she pressed the surgical tape back into place.

She glanced up as the nurse re-entered the room, carrying a bottle of pills.

The nurse crossed to the small shower room and returned a few seconds later with a glass of water. She shook out two tablets and passed them to Antimone. "Here, you'll feel a lot better after a couple of these but no fiddling with the dressings. After all you've been through, we don't want you succumbing to a bacterial infection, do we? You're far too valuable for that."

Antimone accepted the pills, placed them in her mouth and washed them down. She drained the glass and handed it back. "Can you get me a refill?"

The woman retraced her steps and watched as Antimone drank a second glassful. "Okay now?"

Antimone nodded. "Thanks."

"Is there anything else I can get you?"

"No." Antimone sank back onto the pillow with a groan. The sharply focused stinging sensation on her back told her they had taken samples from there too.

"You've been through a major procedure. I suggest you try to get some sleep. If you need anything, just shout. I'll be keeping an eye on you through the monitor."

Antimone closed her eyes and remained immobile, waiting for the pain to subside. As she did so, something the nurse had said kept repeating in her head. *You're far too valuable for that.* In a burst of insight, she realised that was how they saw her—a commodity to be bought and sold. They weren't interested in her wellbeing or that of her son. It was even possible they had no interest in preventing countless thousands of women from dying in childbirth. It was a business. Everything was geared to making money. They could have asked for her help, and she would willingly have offered it, but instead they had kept her a prisoner and performed experiments without her permission. They had refused to allow her to speak to her family and then threatened to withdraw her few remaining privileges if she didn't cooperate.

As the thoughts spun through her head, another realisation came to her. Nobody other than the hospital staff knew she was here. If they had lied to her about the medical procedures, could she trust them to inform her parents that she was still alive? Surely her mother and father would have insisted on visiting her by now or, at the very least, talking to her on the phone. If nobody knew she had survived, they could keep her here and perform whatever experiments they wanted until they had all the answers. And once they had their answers, what then?

Her scalp prickled with anxiety as the implications of her situation hit home.

How far would they go? What would they do with her when she was surplus to requirements?

## Wednesday 12th January 2033

Jason stared out of the window of the coffee shop as two nurses walked past on their way home. Neither of them was the one he was looking for. It was just after six o'clock in the evening. He had been sitting here for three hours and was beginning to question the wisdom of his plan.

The last few days had passed in a blur. He should have been excited about returning to school and meeting his friends after the Christmas break, but he couldn't get the conversation with his mother out of his head. He had told her that he would forget about Antimone, but he had no intention of doing so. Several of the teachers had commented on his distracted state of mind, mistaking it for a lack of enthusiasm following the holidays.

He had pondered his options but kept coming back to the same conclusion. He desperately wanted to talk to Antimone but didn't want to alienate his mother. There was no way he could sneak past the security measures designed to keep people out of the basement laboratory a second time. Even if he did manage to get down there, a guard was stationed outside her room. The chances of being detected were too high, so where did that leave him?

The only plan he could conjure up was to ask the nurse who had escorted him there previously to take a phone to Antimone so that they could at least have a conversation, even if it wasn't face-to-face. He had therefore bought two cheap phones and had programmed into each of them the number of the other. If one of them was discovered in Antimone's room, he didn't want to make it easy for his mother to discover who she had been talking to by leaving his own number in the phone's contact list.

The plan had several flaws, not the least of which was how he would persuade the nurse to smuggle the mobile in. She seemed to be a decent person, and he hoped that he could convince her to help without coercing her. He wasn't sure how far he was prepared to go if she chose not to assist, but he decided to worry about that if and when the time came. In the meantime, his biggest concern was locating her and putting forward his proposition.

This was his third consecutive evening spent in the coffee shop. He only knew the nurse's first name, Rose, and he had no idea at what time she started or finished work. He could have asked at reception, but there was a good chance he would be recognised. It would be doubly suspicious if he asked about the working patterns of a woman whose surname he couldn't supply. He resolved to take that risk if he struck out for the third night in succession.

Jason took a sip of his coffee, his second of the evening. The brown liquid was cold, and he gave a shiver of distaste before putting the cardboard cup down. His eyes followed a tall, balding man heading outside. The man paused to chat to somebody entering the building carrying an open umbrella. As the person retracted the umbrella, Jason recognised the outline of the nurse. Finally.

In his haste to get up, Jason knocked over the cup, spilling coffee across the surface. He snatched a paper napkin from the holder in the centre of the table and dropped it on the expanding puddle. It quickly absorbed the liquid, turning a pale brown colour. Cursing his clumsiness, he trotted towards the door and burst into the foyer. The woman was still chatting to the man, but a couple of seconds later the man waved his hand and pushed through the revolving door. The woman shook her umbrella and glanced up as Jason approached.

"Oh, hi Rose," Jason said, trying to sound nonchalant.

"I've got to start work in a few minutes," Rose said, her face a mask of alarm. "I haven't got time to talk."

"Maybe we could have a chat when you finish your shift or maybe another day." He hadn't considered the practicality of his suggestion before the words came out.

"I don't think that's a good idea." Rose tried to edge past him.

"I know Antimone's alive."

Rose's head jerked upwards as her eyes fixed on Jason's. "You didn't tell your mother, did you?" she asked, a tremble in her voice.

Jason hesitated before replying. "Um, not yet. Could you just spare a minute for a quick chat?" he asked, gesturing towards the coffee shop.

Rose glanced at her watch and seemed to make a mental calculation. "Okay, but I haven't got long. My shift starts soon."

Jason re-entered the shop and took a seat at a table close to the door. Rose sat down opposite. "What's this about?"

"I know she survived. She's a friend of mine, and I wondered if you could do me a favour."

Rose placed her hands on the table. "I don't know. What sort of favour?"

Jason pulled one of the phones from his pocket and positioned it in front of him. "I was hoping you might be able to give her this. I've programmed my number into it."

Rose's face paled. "You've got to be joking. I'd be fired in the blink of an eye if they caught me taking a phone in. In any case, it wouldn't work."

"What do you mean? Why not?" Jason leant forwards.

"The basement is shielded from electromagnetic radiation," she replied. "Mobiles just don't work down there. Senior management have specially modified ones, but they're custom-built."

"There must be phones there. How do the medical staff talk to other people in the company?"

"They have land lines, but they're carefully controlled and monitored, apart from which they can only call other numbers in the building. All outside calls are blocked."

Jason sat back. "So, there's no way I can speak to her?"

"Not a chance. Didn't you see the guard sitting by her room?"

"So, what's that all about?"

"Keep her in and everybody else out," said the nurse. "Look, I can't help you. In any case, I'll probably get fired if your mother even sees me after what happened on Saturday night."

"Yeah, sorry about that."

"It was my own fault. No good deed goes unpunished." Rose's lips twitched in a half-smile. She got up to leave.

"If I gave you a message, could you get it to her?"

A look of trepidation flashed across the nurse's face. "What sort of message?"

"I don't know." Jason's gaze alighted on the stack of napkins in the centre of the table. He grabbed one of them. "What if I wrote something on this?"

She sat down. "Um, that's not a good idea. I'm already on the brink of being fired."

"Look, what's the harm in passing her a bit of paper? I already know she's alive although my mother doesn't know that I know." He paused and met her gaze. "Yet."

Rose looked down at the floor. She held the position for a moment before raising her head. "Okay, but just the once. I'm planning to find a new job soon, anyway. It's just a lot easier to do that with a decent reference."

"Thanks, Rose. Do you have a pen on you?"

The nurse delved in her handbag, pulled out a cheap biro and handed it over.

Jason scribbled a few sentences on the napkin, then folded it into a triangular shape. "I really appreciate this," he said, giving her both items.

"Right, well I better get to work." She rose to her feet again.

"How will I get her answer?" asked Jason, also standing.

"It's a twelve-hour shift so I won't finish until six fifteen in the morning. I'll meet you tomorrow afternoon at five o'clock by the entrance to the main car park. I've got a red Ford Calypso."

"See you tomorrow, then." Jason sat down and watched Rose's back as she crossed to the door and joined the flow of people in the foyer.

For the first time in three days, he smiled.

## Wednesday 12th January 2033

Rose strode down the corridor towards the nurse's station. She had slipped the napkin that Jason had given her beneath her bra, and now she glanced down to make sure it wasn't visible through her uniform. Nothing was discernible, but the paper felt uncomfortable against her skin. She still hadn't decided what to do about it. She was within a whisker of being fired. If she encountered Rosalind Baxter, there was no guarantee she would keep her job whatever she did. There was no way she could avoid the woman indefinitely, but she hoped that Doctor Perrin had made a good enough case to convince the CEO to retain her services.

One thing was for sure, she planned to look for different employment as soon as possible. Yes, the pay was far higher here than she could earn elsewhere, but the way they took those young women off the street and experimented on them made her extremely uneasy. Even if they were prostitutes and drug addicts with low life expectancy, it was still hard to justify what was done to them. She knew that sacrifices had to be made to find a cure, the loss of a few lives would save countless millions more and so on, but surely there were other ways. If Mrs Baxter did choose to sack her, maybe she could use her knowledge as leverage.

The question still remained. What to do about the note from Jason? One redeeming factor was that Mrs Baxter didn't know that her son had seen Antimone. The boy had said that he hadn't told his mother… yet. There was definitely an implied threat, but if she was honest with herself, she wouldn't even be contemplating the idea without some form of coercion. Would he carry through with it if she refused to do as he asked? Probably not, she thought, but what was the downside? The girl would more than likely want to write a reply. If it ended there, that wouldn't be too much of a problem, but Jason didn't seem like the type to give up. The safest thing to do was to keep the note to herself and tell him that she had abandoned the plan.

Her mind made up, she pushed through the door. A woman wearing a nurse's uniform sat at the solitary desk. She looked up at the new arrival, then glanced at her watch. "You're late."

"Sorry," said Rose. "A doctor wanted to speak to me."

The woman humphed. She was in her mid-fifties, grey hair tied back in a ponytail and carrying four or five stone of excess weight. "Oh, that's alright then. I don't mind working unpaid overtime just so you can chat up one of the doctors."

Rose knew better than to argue. "How are the patients?"

The woman gestured towards the screen before her. "It's all written down in the log." After a brief pause, she relented. "They're all okay apart from the sixteen-year-old girl. She's not in a good shape at all. They took biopsy samples a few days ago, and she's been in a lot of pain. I gave her oxycodone a couple of hours back, but she can barely move."

"Biopsy samples? That shouldn't be too bad. I don't understand."

The older woman pressed her lips together. "I think you should see for yourself. When I say they took biopsy samples, they took them from everywhere, and bone marrow too."

"Right. I'll pay her a visit."

The other nurse stood up, groaning from the exertion as she did so. "See you, then."

Rose watched as the woman waddled to the door. Her eyes slid across the row of wall-mounted monitors until they rested on the one displaying Antimone's room. She approached the screen and peered intently at the image. The girl lay on the bed with her eyes closed, her scalp totally devoid of hair. A regular pattern of dark brown patches dotted her skin, interspersed with larger white areas. It was unusual for her to be in bed at this time rather than in the wheelchair. "What have they done to you?" Rose muttered.

She settled herself in the chair behind the desk, the seat still warm from the previous occupant. She signed into the computer, selected the log and waved her hand in front of the monitor to scroll down the entries. She went straight to Antimone's data. The last recorded item was the prescription of the painkillers just over two hours ago. As her gaze ran down the list, she noted that the same drugs had been administered almost every four hours over the past three days. It was also apparent that she had eaten practically nothing over that time period.

Rose logged off and headed out into the corridor. She turned the corner and strode towards the man in the brown uniform sitting outside the door. He hurriedly returned the mobile device he had been playing with to a pocket inside his jacket.

Rose didn't recognise the man. The napkin seemed to press into her breast. She made a conscious effort not to glance down. "Hi, I'm Rose," she said.

"John," the man replied. "I assume you've just started your shift. I've got another two hours to go and then I'm off."

"Twelve more for me," she said, flashing a nervous smile. She held her identity card to the reader and pushed the door open. The first thing to affect her senses was the smell of urine.

"Hi Antimone, it's Rose. How are you?"

A groan was the only response.

Rose approached the bed. She took a sharp intake of breath as her eyes took in the prostrate girl.

Antimone lay on her back, the white sheet pushed down to her waist. Small brown plasters were spaced in an even grid pattern across her exposed skin, one every two or three inches. The grid extended to her face and scalp. One or two had fallen off, leaving small circular scabs surrounded by an area of pink inflammation. A line of larger, evenly spaced, white dressings held down with surgical tape ran up both arms. The one on her left wrist hung loose, exposing an angry looking, dark-red disc at its centre.

The girl lying before her was a shadow of the feisty teenager Rose knew from before. Beneath each eye was a purple-coloured, half-crescent hollow. Her complexion was pale, the skin a pasty colour. Rose was staggered by the decline in her appearance.

"Um, Antimone, can you look at me?"

The girl opened her right eye and stared blearily at the nurse. "How's my son?" she mumbled.

"Oh... he's fine. When was the last time he was here?"

"Dunno. Two, three days ago. Before they did this to me. I've not been well enough to look after him."

"Look, I'm really sorry. I'll see if we can get him brought down here so you can at least see him. I'll give you a hand with him. Why don't we get you to the bathroom and get you cleaned up first?"

"Can't move," Antimone whispered, closing the open eye.

"I'll give you a hand. I think you've had a bit of an accident, and we need to sort you out." She withdrew the sheet and winced at the scabs covering her legs where the plasters had fallen off. The smell of urine was almost overpowering.

With excruciating slowness, Rose manoeuvred the girl off the bed. On several occasions, Antimone cried out in pain as pressure was applied to one of the sample sites. Finally, she was seated in the wheelchair.

Rose propelled the chair forward into the cramped bathroom. She found it telling that Antimone didn't complain about being pushed. "Why don't you brush your teeth while I sort out the bed? When I've done that, I'll come back and help you wash." She grabbed the toothbrush from beside the sink, applied some toothpaste and handed it over.

While Antimone brushed, Rose returned to the main part of the room and stripped off the sheets. The dried yellow stains indicated that it had happened several hours ago. "Couldn't be bothered to get off your fat arse, you lazy cow," she muttered under her breath. Anger seethed through her. She knew this girl was important in finding a cure, but what they had done to her amounted to torture. If she was undecided about what to do before, what she had seen in this room had made up her mind. The least she could do was hand over the note. She needed to be careful, though. Cameras recorded everything, but they didn't extend to the bathroom.

Rose wiped down the plastic under sheet and remade the bed. She glanced surreptitiously at the camera, then headed back to rejoin Antimone. The girl sat in the wheelchair staring blankly into the mirror, still holding the toothbrush. Rose gently took it out of her hand. She turned on the taps and crouched down so her eyes were at the same level as Antimone's.

"Antimone, I need you to listen to me."

Antimone's gaze rose listlessly to meet the nurse's.

"Before I tell you this, you have to understand that it's vital you don't discuss it with another soul. If anybody finds out, we'll both be in a lot of trouble."

"What are you talking about?" Antimone rasped.

Rose hesitated for a second. "I've got a note from Jason. He asked me to give it to you." She placed a hand beneath her uniform and withdrew the folded napkin.

Antimone unfolded the paper with quivering hands.

GLAD YOU'RE ALIVE. ARE YOU OK? LOVE JASON

She raised her eyes. "He knows I'm alive?"

"Yes. He was down here three days ago, and he saw you as they took you to the operating theatre."

The girl became animated for the first time since the nurse had arrived. "Can you get a message back to him?"

"Yes. Write it on here." Rose took a pen from her front pocket and handed it to Antimone.

Antimone clutched the pen in her right hand, pondered for a moment, then wrote below Jason's words with slow, deliberate strokes. When she had finished, she folded the napkin and passed it back.

"Do you mind if I read it?"

Antimone shook her head. "Go ahead."

Rose unfolded the paper and stared at the message.

YOU HAVE TO GET US OUT OF HERE. ANTIMONE.

## Thursday 13th January 2033

Karen Atkins shifted her chair sideways to allow the skinny technician to sit beside her. They said that it was a sign of getting old when policemen started to look young, but this man looked like he should still be in school. He was not technically a policeman but a civilian who worked as an analyst for the police. He had a pallid complexion and several large, angry looking spots across his forehead. His black hair was greasy and parted to the side. He wore jeans and a faded T-shirt bearing the slogan 'Even duct tape can't fix stupid, but it can muffle the sound.'

Despite his appearance and the inappropriate T-shirt, he was good at his job. That entailed poring over video footage and analysing it to obtain nuggets of useful information.

"May I?" he asked, sliding his chair in front of the monitor. He tapped on a keyboard that seemed to float in mid-air and brought up a list of files. He selected the first, set the time bar to a point just over halfway through and hit the play icon. "Right, this is footage from the drone. The quality's not great, but you can see our man entering the post office compound here. Now, if we run the footage backwards, we see him talk to this man walking his dog. He's an elderly local, and we got one of the uniforms to have a chat with him. According to the officer, the old geezer wasn't quite all there, but he was adamant that the person he talked to was a boy of fifteen or sixteen."

"That's strange. Go on."

"Let's go back further. We see him walking along the road, and here he is emerging from the train station. Look at the time stamp. Nine minutes past one in the afternoon. The drone hasn't got an angle onto the platforms so it can't tell us which train he arrived on." The man paused.

"So that's it then?"

"No, not at all." The technician smiled, displaying his bad teeth. "There was one working camera near the entrance. Unfortunately, it's facing outwards so all we can see is his back." He opened a second file and froze the picture showing a figure dressed in a dark blue winter jacket exiting from the station. Once again, he hesitated.

"I'm guessing there's more," Kat said, sighing in exasperation.

"Yes, there is. Two trains arrived at around this time. One was from Leicester and the other from Saint Pancras. We managed to pick him up on the cameras at Saint Pancras."

"So, if he came from London, he could have started his journey just about anywhere, then?" Kat asked.

The man seemed to deflate. "Yeah, sorry. We went through the footage from Saint Pancras, and we spotted our suspect getting on the train, but it would take too long to work out where he came from." He selected another file, and the monitor displayed a grainy picture of what appeared to be a teenage boy wearing a blue jacket, his head angled downwards.

Kat leant forwards in her chair. "Is this the best you can get?"

"I haven't finished yet. So, we saw him arrive, but we also know he returned to Bedford train station when he left."

The technician opened the next file. The view changed back to an aerial shot. "Here we see him walk along the road and enter the station at…" He paused the video and pointed at the time stamp in the top right corner. "Three twenty-one."

"And this time, you should get a clear look at his face as he enters the station," Kat said excitedly.

The man grinned. "Exactly." He selected the final file in the list.

"At last," Kat muttered under her breath,

"And there we have him." The monitor displayed a figure wearing jeans and a dark blue winter jacket. This time, the face was clearly visible.

"I don't believe it," Kat said, sitting back.

A confused expression worked its way across the technician's face. "I take it you recognise him, then? Not who you expected?"

"I didn't know who to expect, but yes, I do recognise him. That's Jason Baxter, Rosalind Baxter's son, you know, the head of Ilithyia Biotechnology. But what the hell is he doing helping Daniel Floyd?"

***

Kat drummed her fingers on the desktop. "Yes, I'll hold." Before her lay several printed sheets relating to the investigation into Antimone Lessing's rape. Whilst all the records were computerised, she still liked to feel them in her hands and scribble notes on them. Her eyes roamed over the page. Jason Baxter and Daniel Floyd working together? She would never have guessed it in a million years, but the evidence was on the screen. Jason Baxter had broken into the old sorting office and had left at the same time as Floyd. She had asked the technician to go over the footage of the pair leaving the building one more time. The two men had clearly shared a conversation before going their separate ways, but it was impossible to detect facial expressions or read body language from the drone's vantage point. How did they even know each other? There was a link between Rosalind Baxter and Daniel Floyd, but how did Jason come into it?

Several witnesses had seen Floyd at Rosalind Baxter's house, and he had been sent on his way by the security men before later returning. But what had made him return? Was he meeting with Jason? Was Jason somehow involved in the rape? One thing was for sure, though—she intended to ask the boy.

A click on the line preceded the imperious voice of Rosalind Baxter. "Hello, Ms Atkins. What can I do for you?"

Now that it came to it, Kat hadn't really thought through what she was going to say. "Um, thanks for talking to me, Mrs Baxter. I'm calling about the Antimone Lessing case."

"Yes, poor girl. Have you found Floyd yet?"

"Actually, that's why I called. Floyd's still on the run, but I came across some surprising surveillance video, and I was wondering if you might be able to shed some light on it."

"Okay," Rosalind said.

"Well I—um, I don't really know how to put this. We discovered footage of Jason meeting with Daniel Floyd."

The line went silent.

"Mrs Baxter, are you still there?"

More silence then a more subdued voice. "Yes, I'm here. When was this?"

"Last Saturday afternoon in Bedford. Do you have any idea why they might talk to each other?"

"No. As you know I have some… ah… previous history with Mr Floyd, but I wasn't aware that my son had any interaction with him."

"Where is your son at the moment, Mrs Baxter?"

"Well, he's at school. They went back this week after the holidays."

"Okay. I'd like to have a chat and ask him why he met with Floyd. Your son's still under seventeen, isn't he? That means he needs to have a guardian present while we question him."

"You're not arresting him, are you?"

"No. I just want to have a talk with him for the time being."

The threat that it might turn into something more hung between them.

"Right," Rosalind said. "I'm really busy today."

"It doesn't have to be you."

"No, I want to sit in on this. Could you come here?"

"I assume here means Ilithyia," Kat said. "I could manage that."

"I can leave a message and get him to come to the hospital after he finishes school, say around five thirty or six o'clock."

"Okay, let's make it six. I'll see you later. Goodbye, Mrs Baxter."

There was a click on the line, and Kat replaced the handset in its cradle.

"This should be interesting," she muttered to herself.

167

No sooner had she ended the call than Rosalind Baxter placed another one. A voice responded before she even heard the ring tone.

"Hello, Mrs Baxter. What can I do for you?" The unctuous tones of Julian Stefano.

"Julian, I need the lawyers here in my office at six o'clock. No, make that five thirty. I want to have a chat with them first."

"May I ask what this is about, Mrs Baxter?"

"No, you may not. I pay you to do what I ask, not ask what I do."

"Um, sorry Mrs Baxter, I wasn't prying, I just wanted to know which particular lawyers you need."

"Right, Julian. The ones you contact before you talk to the police. Is that clear enough?"

"Yes, perfectly, Mrs Baxter. I'll sort that out. Is there anything else?"

Rosalind ended the call without speaking again. She stared out of the window at the glowering winter sky, but her mind was elsewhere. What the hell had the ungrateful imbecile done now? How did he even know Floyd? It must have been a coincidence, or the police had made a mistake, but the boy hadn't mentioned it to her. Surely, he would have told her about an accidental meeting, but maybe not. Over the last week or so, the distance between them seemed to have grown greater. She knew that she didn't spend enough time at home, but Jason was more than capable of looking after himself. After all, he was practically an adult now.

She wondered if it had anything to do with the girl. Maybe he still resented her for telling him to forget her, but if what the policewoman had said was correct, Jason had rendezvoused with Floyd before the night at the restaurant. Try as she might, she couldn't see any link that would lead Jason to deliberately seek out Floyd. The only way to find out was by speaking to her son, and preferably in advance of the police arriving. She retrieved her mobile from her handbag and signed in by holding the inbuilt camera up to her eye. She dictated a message and tapped the send button.

That left one last thing to do. She once again grabbed hold of the desk phone and spoke into the handset. This time, there were three repetitions of the ring tone before somebody answered.

"Hello, Grolby here."

"Anders, I've got another little job for you. I need you to get a man to follow my son, Jason."

"Your son, Mrs Baxter? Why do you want him followed? Are you worried about somebody attempting a kidnapping?"

"No, it's nothing like that Anders. I just had a call from the police saying that Jason met Floyd last Saturday."

"Floyd? I don't understand. Why would your son meet with him?"

"I don't understand either, which is why I want you to put a man on following him. He's at school at the moment. I don't want Jason to know he's being followed, though."

"Okay, I'll get right on it. I'll let you know if my man sees anything unusual."

"Thanks, Anders."

## Thursday 13th January 2033

Jason leant against the stone gatepost outside the imposing school gates, deep in thought. All his friends had left for the day, and he had delayed his own departure with meaningless tasks that could have waited until the following day. He retrieved the phone from his pocket and read the message again. Just three words:

*'Call me. Mum.'*

Had she found out that he had tried to contact Antimone? Did the brusque request indicate she was angry about something? There was only one way to find out, and that was by calling her. His heart hammered in his chest as he spoke her name into the handset. He felt out of breath, inhaling in gulps as though he had been running hard.

A ring tone. Another. A click, then his mother's voice. "Jason?"

"Yes, Mum. You said to call you."

A pause at the other end. The cold, quiet voice. "The police called me this afternoon."

Jason's heart rate increased. "The police?"

"Yes, the police. They wanted to know why you went to see Daniel Floyd."

A roaring sound in his ears. He opened his mouth, but no words came out.

"I take it by your silence that you know what I'm talking about. I'd like to know as well."

"I... uh—"

"I said I want to know what you were doing meeting Daniel Floyd," she screamed.

Jason held the phone away from his ear. "It's a long story," he muttered.

"Well, I want you in my office at five thirty to explain it. Is that clear? There's a policewoman coming to talk to you at six. If they somehow manage to get hold of you before then, you say precisely nothing until one of my lawyers is present. Got it? After everything I've done for you, this is the reward I get?"

"Okay. I'll be at your office by five-thirty," Jason said. He hesitated, then spoke again, "I'm sorry, Mum," but the line was already dead.

He returned the mobile to his pocket and blew out his cheeks. Somehow the police knew he had met Floyd. Did they know he had warned him about the raid? Did that mean they had captured Floyd? But if that was the case, what had Floyd told them? Jason cast his mind back. He had informed the man that somebody else was responsible for making Antimone pregnant. It wouldn't take a huge leap of logic to deduce the true identity of the child's father.

At least he had time to rendezvous with the nurse and get the message from Antimone before he had to meet his mother.

## Thursday 13th January 2033

Jason glanced at his watch. Five past five. The nurse had said she would be there at five, but no red cars had passed by in the last few minutes. He had even used the Internet to look up details of the type of car she drove to make sure he would recognise it. He couldn't afford to wait too much longer or he would be late for the meeting with his mother. The icy wind gnawed at the exposed skin of his face and pawed at his hair. He shuffled anxiously from one foot to the other.

A small red vehicle turned off the main road and merged into the steady stream of traffic heading to his mother's company. As the car drew closer, he identified the model as the one he was waiting for. It slowed as it came alongside, and the window lowered. With a sigh of relief, he recognised Rose's anxious face. The driver behind tooted his horn.

"I'll see you in D1," she called, then accelerated to close the gap to the car in front.

For a moment Jason didn't understand what she meant. Was she referring to a section of the hospital? After a moment's thought, it came to him. She was talking about the car park, of course. Cursing his stupidity, he studied the direction sign and jogged towards the area she had identified. A couple of minutes later, he spotted the entrance to car park D. Four blue signs with white text towered above the rows of parked cars, labelled from D1 to D4. D1 was at the near end, and his eyes ran down the lines, looking for the red car. The blip of an alarm being armed drew his attention. He caught sight of Rose as she strode along the footpath to the building entrance. Jason hurried to catch up with her.

"Did you give her the message?" he asked.

She stopped and turned to face him. "Yes, I gave it to her as agreed."

"Was there a reply?"

The nurse swivelled her head, inspecting the surrounding area for anybody showing an undue interest. Nobody seemed to be paying them any attention. She delved a hand into her coat pocket and pulled out a folded piece of white paper. Jason recognised the shape of a napkin, like the one he had written on the previous night.

"Before I give you this," Rose said, "you have to promise me that you're not going to involve me anymore. This is it. You're on your own from now on. I've got to think about myself too. If they catch me, I'll be without a job, and I won't be able to get a reference."

Jason nodded. "Okay. Can I see the note please?"

Rose handed the napkin over. Jason unfolded it and read Antimone's message scrawled beneath his own.

He took a sharp intake of breath. "You have to get us out of here?" His eyes locked onto the nurse's. "How is she? Is she alright?"

Rose grimaced. "She's in a bit of pain at the moment. She's recovering from some tests." She resumed her progress towards the entrance. "That's all I'm going to say."

Jason placed a hand on her shoulder.

Rose whirled around angrily. "This is exactly what I knew would happen. I should have just thrown the damn thing away. Now you need to leave me alone."

Jason raised his hands apologetically. "I'm sorry, but how am I going to get her out of there without help?"

"That's your problem. I suggest you start by talking to your mother. She's the one who's in charge."

"I don't think she's going to change her mind," Jason mumbled.

Rose turned away. "I can't help you anymore. Sorry."

"Thanks anyway," Jason called to her departing back. He watched as she pushed through the rotating doors and entered the glass and steel building beneath the logo of a new-born child. He pulled back his sleeve and glanced at his watch. Five thirteen. Just over fifteen minutes until the scheduled meeting with his mother and three-quarters of an hour before he had to explain himself to the police.

He took a step towards the entrance, then halted. He turned a full circle, deep in thought. "What the hell am I going to do?" he muttered to himself. His hand slipped into his pocket and emerged holding the phone. Almost subconsciously he unlocked the screen and scrolled through the list of contacts until he reached the names beginning with F.

For a long time, he stared at the display. Once, then twice, his finger moved to the connect button and hesitated.

"Ah, damn it," he said as he finally placed the call.

## Thursday 13th January 2033

Jason stared down at the wooden surface of the table. On the opposite side sat his mother, a glower on her face. They occupied one of the meeting rooms on the executive floor of Ilithyia Biotechnology. The lawyers waited next door.

"What the hell were you thinking about?" Rosalind spat. "I want to hear it all. Why you visited Floyd, how you knew where to go, what happened when you got there."

"Well, I woke up that morning, the Saturday, and you'd already left for work. I was just sorting out my breakfast when my mobile rang. I didn't recognise the caller, but I answered anyway. It was Floyd."

"How did he get your number?"

"I'm not sure. He never told me."

"Go on then."

"Okay, so he starts by asking if I know who it is. I say no, and then he tells me, you know, that it's him. Floyd. I'm about to hang up when he says he has some information I might be interested in, but it's going to cost me."

"What information?"

"He wasn't specific, but he said it was about Antimone."

"Antimone? What could he possibly know about her?"

"Well, he wouldn't say on the phone. He said if I wanted to hear what he had to say, I had to bring him supplies. Food and stuff."

"Why couldn't he just get it himself?"

"He was in hiding," Jason said. "He didn't want to go out in case somebody recognised him."

"So, what happened next?"

"He tells me where to go, the old sorting office in Bedford. He says to go inside and he'll find me. He warns me not to tell the police, or he'll break into the house and hurt us."

"Hurt us?" Rosalind snorted. "What the hell does that mean?"

"He mentioned arson or something like that. Anyway, I didn't call the police. I caught a train to Bedford and bought the stuff he asked for."

"Right. And then what?"

174

"I found the building. It's surrounded by a fence, so I had to climb over it. I managed to get one of the doors open. There was no sign of Floyd on the ground floor, so I went up to the first floor. I go into one of the offices, and he jumps out, holds a knife to my throat. He makes me sit down while he goes through the supplies. When he's checked them, he says he's ready to give me the information."

"Go on then, spit it out," Rosalind said. "What's so amazing that it's worth risking your life for?"

"He says he knows that Antimone is alive."

"What?" Rosalind leant forwards sharply. "How the hell did he know that?"

"He refused to say. All he would say was that she survived the birth."

"Did he know where she was being held?"

"Like I said, if he did know, he didn't tell me," Jason said.

"So, it's just pure coincidence that you saw her later that night when that stupid moron brought you down to the basement?"

"Yeah, that's right. I didn't believe him. I thought he was winding me up."

"What happened next?"

"The police arrived. I thought he was going to kill me, but I managed to convince him that I hadn't called them. Anyway, he led me out, and we escaped just before they searched the building."

"And then you caught the train back home?"

"Yeah, from Bedford back to London Saint Pancras, on the underground to Liverpool Street and from there up to Northstowe."

"And have you heard from him since?"

"No," Jason replied.

"Have you got your phone on you?"

"Um, yes." Jason withdrew it from his pocket.

"Unlock it and give it to me." Rosalind stuck out a hand.

Jason held the camera up to his eye, then handed over the pebble-shaped block. His mother reached across the table to grab it. Her fingers danced in front of the screen. Her brow furrowed in concentration.

Finally, she looked up. "There's no record of an incoming call on that Sunday."

The accusation lay heavy in the air between them.

"He told me to delete the call record. He watched while I did it."

"Okay, that's convenient." Rosalind shook her head. "We aren't finished discussing this yet, but we need to get the story straight for the police. You tell them everything you've just told me, but emphasise that you didn't believe what Floyd said about Antimone being alive. I'm going to keep the phone. If they ask for it, just say you haven't got it. It's at home or something."

"But it's got all my contacts on it," Jason protested.

175

"That's the least of your worries right now. In any case, you won't be needing your contacts if you end up in jail. I'm going to have a chat with the lawyers now. Don't answer any questions unless they indicate that you can. I'll get one of them to nod if it's okay. When you answer, just state the bare minimum. Don't elaborate. If you're unsure about something, it's fine to say you don't know. Got that?"

Jason nodded in acquiescence and watched his mother stride across the room, leaving him sitting by himself.

"What the hell have I started?" he muttered.

## Thursday 13th January 2033

Rosalind Baxter stared out at the deepening twilight gloom and scratched an earlobe.

"So, he's been talking to that damned nurse again?" she asked, turning to face Anders Grolby.

"That's what my man says, and I think the evidence is pretty conclusive." He waved a hand at the snapshots arrayed across Rosalind's desk.

"What's that in this shot?" She pointed to a photograph showing Rose handing a white object to Jason.

"It looks like she's passing over a note," Grolby said, shrugging.

"I don't suppose we can tell what's written on it, can we?"

"Not a chance. It might have been possible with a state-of-the-art camera and a telephoto lens, but not with the equipment my man's using. Anyway, that stuff would be far too big to carry around on a job, most of the time."

"Damn. I told Nigel to fire her. The bloody woman's a total liability. There's only one subject those two could be discussing, and that's the girl. You're going to have to deal with her, Anders."

"Are you sure, Mrs Baxter? If too many employees have accidents, the police might start to get suspicious."

"I know it's a risk, but the stupid cow is jeopardising everything, especially now that we're so close to developing a cure. Make it look like a suicide."

"Okay. What do you want me to do about your son?"

"That's a trickier one. Keep your man on him. We need to make sure he's not going anywhere near the girl—or Floyd, for that matter. I can't believe the little sod actually met with Floyd."

Rosalind had briefed Grolby on how Jason had paid a visit to Floyd at the old sorting office in Bedford, and how the police had questioned him half an hour earlier. The policewoman, Karen Atkins, had clearly been unhappy to see the lawyers present during the interview. Rosalind had asked the woman whether her son was under arrest, and when it became clear that he was not, she had emphasised she was only allowing the interview to take place as a courtesy. A smile twitched at her lips as she recalled the look of indignation on the woman's face when she had been informed that the interview was over.

"I want you to go through Jason's phone records," Rosalind said. "He told me that Floyd phoned him on the morning he went to Bedford, but there was no indication of an incoming call on his mobile. Apparently, Floyd made sure the record was deleted. Still, something doesn't ring true. For example, how did Floyd get hold of Jason's number? Check the outgoing calls as well."

"I'll look into it, Mrs Baxter. Is there anything else?"

"Yes," Rosalind said, thoughtfully. "How come Floyd knew that the girl survived? You don't think we have a leak, do you?"

Grolby ran his hand over the blond-grey stubble of his hair. "I don't know how he found out, but I'll be sure to ask him if I ever get my hands on him. If you can let me know who had access to that information, I can look more closely at their communications."

"I'll get a list to you. There are a couple of other things I need you to do too."

"Yes, Mrs Baxter."

"I think we should double the security on the girl's room. My son's still sniffing around, and Floyd knows that she survived the birth. I just want to make sure nothing untoward happens. That girl's worth billions. I'm sure we can afford the cost of another guard to safeguard our investment."

"I'll sort that out. And the other thing, Mrs Baxter?"

"Yes. I want you to find Floyd again and this time, no tip-offs to the police. He knows too much. When you find him, I want you to deal with him yourself."

"That would be my pleasure," Grolby said, smiling coldly.

## Friday 14th January 2033

Antimone ate her breakfast without enthusiasm. The nurse had told her it was morning, but there was no visual indication it was true. For all she knew, it could have been the middle of the night. Despite feeling stronger, she had slept little, spending several restless hours twisting and turning, trying to get comfortable. A thin layer of stubble now covered her scalp. The sites where the biopsy samples had been taken were beginning to heal, but they were incredibly itchy, and it took all her willpower to resist scratching at the scabs.

She dropped her spoon into the empty cereal bowl. It ricocheted off the side with a metallic clang and bounced onto the floor. She looked over the edge of the bed and saw it just beneath the metal frame, a few inches away. For a moment, she debated whether to make the effort to pick it up. She could almost hear her mother's voice telling her not to be lazy, to clean up after herself, but after everything they had done to her, she was in no mood to cooperate. They were holding her prisoner, keeping her locked up against her will with no access to the outside world. Despite the vital nature of the work, it didn't give them the right to treat her like a lab rat, performing tests and experiments without her permission. And still the nagging doubt persisted. What they would do when they had the answers?

She wondered briefly whether Jason had received her note. Even if he had, what could he do? He could hardly come down here and demand that she be released. She had to assume the worst. No help was coming. She was on her own. With that thought, a weight seemed to lift off her shoulders. She needed to take action, to fight back. She didn't want to hurt anybody, but after the latest experiment and their callous indifference to her welfare, she was prepared to compromise on that objective.

The big question was how? A guard sat outside the room, and her every movement was monitored by the camera in the corner of the ceiling. The bathroom, however, had no surveillance measures, at least that's what Rose had told her. How could she use that to her advantage? If she could lure the nurse inside and disable her, she could take the key card and unlock the door into the corridor. She would still need to find a way past the guard and somehow get out of the basement.

Her thoughts came crashing down with the realisation that even if she did escape, her son, Paul, would still be held captive. She had no idea where they were keeping him, but she assumed it was in some other part of the building. A vision of Paul as an adult, locked up in a room like this, flashed through her brain. She couldn't allow that to happen, but even if she escaped from this room, the odds of finding him and freeing him were remote. Only one option remained. Once she was out of here, she would have to rely on the police to locate and release him.

If the attempt went wrong, they would undoubtedly use her son to punish her. That was a risk she would have to take. She couldn't afford to wait any longer. The first problem was how to incapacitate the nurse.

Antimone picked up the tray. It wasn't heavy enough to do any damage. She would have to find something else. Her eyes swept the room. Nothing obvious came to mind. She manoeuvred her legs over the side of the bed, eased herself into the wheelchair and propelled herself to the bathroom. Once inside, she closed the door behind her. Her gaze immediately settled on the shower chair, a white plastic construction with aluminium legs. She reached out an arm and pulled the device towards her. The legs were screwed on, and she tried to twist one. At first, it didn't move, but as she applied more pressure, the metallic tube turned with a screech. She detached it and swung it experimentally through the air: a little light, but adequate for the job.

Next, her mind turned to the guard. From the brief glimpses she had obtained when the nurse entered, he sat facing away from the door. The door opened into the room, so the chances were he would see her before she had the opportunity to hit him with the chair leg. She was confident that she could outpace him over a short distance but probably not for long enough to discover a way out. She needed a way to slow him down. Her first thought was the cutlery they provided with her food. A knife or a fork stabbed into the leg would more than likely have the desired effect. The main issue was that the nurse invariably took an inventory of the eating utensils after each meal and ensured that all were accounted for.

Her eyes slid across to the mirror above the sink. If she broke it, she could use one of the shards as a weapon. She would need to make a handle by wrapping the glass in some material. Toilet paper would do the trick if she used enough.

With a plan in place, the only remaining question was when to implement it. The nurse would arrive shortly to collect the breakfast tray. Antimone was glad that it was the older woman and not Rose. She would have felt bad about hurting Rose, but this nurse was both bad-tempered and insensitive, and she felt no such qualms about her.

"No time like the present," Antimone muttered. She made sure the door was firmly closed, then swung the metal tube at the mirror. A star-shaped depression formed at the point of impact, and a solitary crack ran from top to bottom, but no fragments split away. She drew back her arm and smashed the chair leg into the glass with more force. This time, several shards fell loose, some landing on the floor, others in the sink. She selected a jagged piece approximately six inches long from where it lay on the white tiles and carefully picked it up. Resting it on her lap, she propelled the wheelchair forwards, the wheels crunching as they rolled over the slivers of broken mirror.

She grabbed the end of the roll and kept pulling until she had detached the entire length. Next, she held the tip of the dagger-shaped piece of glass between two fingers of her left hand and wrapped the tissue paper around it with the right. Within a minute, she had transformed the fragment of mirror into a wicked-looking blade with a white handle. Antimone picked up the weapon and slashed it through the air experimentally. She opened the bathroom door a crack and waited for the nurse to return.

***

Fifteen minutes later, the electronic lock beeped. Antimone moved the wheelchair back so the door could open just over halfway before hitting the wheels. In her hand, she grasped the metal tube. The makeshift knife lay down the side of her seat.

"I'm in here," she called. "Um, I've had a bit of an accident." Her heart pounded in her chest, and her breath came in short gasps.

"What's that?" the nurse asked, moving closer.

Antimone said nothing, but raised the rod above her head. The door moved, scraping against the fragments of glass that lay scattered across the floor.

"What the hell's going on here?" The nurse pushed the door open, her gaze focused downwards. The door bumped into the rubber tyre.

A head appeared in Antimone's line of sight. "What—"

The question went unfinished as the metal tube swished through the air and smacked into the woman's skull with a dull thud. Her eyes rolled up as she toppled backwards like a felled tree. She remained unmoving, her skirt hitched up exposing her white underwear.

Antimone scooted forwards, bending down to pull one of the nurse's legs away before shutting the bathroom door. She was relieved to observe that the woman was still breathing, her chest rising and falling in slow, steady movements. She rummaged in the left pocket of the woman's uniform. Empty. She tried the right. Her fingers grasped the key card and slipped it free.

Antimone reversed and pulled the door back. The nurse's prostrate form would be visible to the camera if anybody was watching, but she didn't have the strength to drag the woman out of the way. She would just have to hope that nobody was paying close attention to the image. She edged past the woman's legs and re-entered the main part of the room, dragging the door closed behind her.

Forcing herself not to glance up at the camera, Antimone approached the door leading out. She placed the card against the reader, grabbed the handle and eased it towards her. A crack opened onto the corridor beyond. She reached down the side of the wheelchair and closed her fingers around the improvised dagger.

"All done then?" a male voice asked as the door swung open.

Antimone surged forwards and plunged the mirror fragment into the seated man's leg. The guard screamed and clutched at the shard protruding from his thigh. Antimone accelerated away. From behind came a groan of agony followed by the tinkle of falling glass. A second or two later the crackle of a radio and a man's urgent voice echoed down the corridor, the words unintelligible as they rolled into each other.

Antimone rounded the corner and spotted the elevator doors ten metres ahead. Powerful strokes sent her racing forwards before she slammed her hands down on the wheels to bring the wheelchair to a juddering halt. The heat from the friction stung her palms, but she forced the pain out of her mind. She stabbed a finger at the call button, and the doors slid apart.

The sound of multiple running feet bore down on her. Antimone jerked forwards. The footsteps were louder, closer. A shout. "She's in the lift."

A bright red light emanated from a control panel on the wall. "Where are the buttons?" Antimone smacked her hand against the metal. "Come on, damn you. Move."

The floor vibrated. Antimone whirled around. A green coated doctor stood beside her clutching an injection gun. Several more people crowded in behind him. He took a step forward and stretched towards her. She tried to bat his hand away, but he avoided the attempt with ease. A short hiss, a sting on the side of her neck.

"No," she said. "I can't go back to…"

## Friday 14th January 2033

Jason's mother had departed half an hour earlier. True to her word, over the course of the previous evening, she had grilled him once again. She had made him promise that he would report any attempt by Floyd to make contact. That was one promise he was about to break less than twelve hours later.

Jason turned on the computer and started up the web browser. He navigated to the YouTube website and entered the text 'Deathly Daze' in the search window. He selected the topmost result, the video for a song of the same name. Within seconds, a thrashing beat emanated from the speakers. He muted the sound and scrolled down to the comments.

"I can't believe people listen to this shit," he muttered.

He reached out a finger and flicked the screen up several times before stopping.

"Here we go," he said to himself. "Running Man 1234."

Beneath the username, a string of nine digits preceded the words, 'Just because you're paranoid it doesn't mean they're not out to get you.' More digits followed the note.

Jason smiled. The message didn't seem to relate to the content in any way, but judging by most of the other comments, that wasn't unusual. He grabbed a pen from the desk and wrote down the two sets of numbers that surrounded the comment. Next, he created a new username and left his own message in reply. 'Keep wearing the tin hat. 1523129132220.'

When he had talked to Floyd by phone the previous day, they had settled upon this method to exchange information. The last three numbers of the first sequence in the original message were the identity of a left luggage box at Northstowe railway station. The first six provided the unlock code in reverse order. The second set of digits also in reverse order was the number to Floyd's new mobile. Floyd had not been best pleased when he had been forced to dispose of his old phone, knowing that the police would be able to backtrack the call made by Jason. Jason had mentioned that he already possessed a pair of new unregistered phones. His reply provided Floyd with the number of one of those phones, once again with the digits reversed. Floyd had instructed him to make contact only in case of emergency.

He glanced at his watch. Seven thirty in the morning. Plenty of time to get to the station before school started. He didn't know what was in the locker, but it had to be related to the deal he had struck with Floyd. At first, the man had been incredulous when Jason informed him that Antimone was still alive. After Jason had eventually convinced him that he was telling the truth, he had agreed to help Jason get Antimone out of the hospital if Jason did a favour in return. The locker contents were part of the price. Floyd had described in general terms what he intended to do and had told him that detailed instructions would be provided when he picked up the package. He had reassured Jason that nobody would get hurt as a result of his actions.

Jason consumed a hasty breakfast and hurried out of the house. He didn't notice the man watching from the silver vehicle parked at the side of the road.

***

Jason entered the bustling station. He couldn't help but gaze up as he did every time he came here. The domed, latticed ceiling made the building look like the interior of a Zeppelin. A row of spotlights ran down the centre of the roof, lending it an otherworldly appearance. Northstowe station was a highlight of the new town and was highly regarded by architects the world over.

Jason forced his eyes down. People streamed through the entrance, most of them heading to the platform for the Cambridge train. The buzz of the crowds echoed around the vast interior. Several passengers bumped into him as he read the signs, trying to identify where to go. After a few seconds of searching, he eventually spotted a wall covered in a grid pattern of metal doors of varying sizes. He retrieved the piece of paper from his coat. The lockers were ordered numerically, and it didn't take Jason long to locate the one he required. It was at waist level and big enough to accommodate a small suitcase. Once again, he consulted his notes and tapped out the remaining six digits on the small keypad.

The door beeped, and a red light illuminated. Jason frowned and studied the string of numbers. He cursed as he realised that he had forgotten to reverse the digits. He tried again. This time, a green light showed. The door swung open to reveal a padded, brown envelope propped up against the side. He grabbed the package and thrust it into his rucksack. This was not the time or the place to inspect the contents. He hurried across the busy concourse and exited into the frigid January air. After the noise and activity of the station, it seemed oddly quiet outside.

Hitching the rucksack higher on his back, Jason set off along the pavement in the direction of his school. A man in a black overcoat hurried after him.

## Friday 14th January 2033

R ose Griffin yawned and stretched out her arms. She hated the dark, dreary days of winter. She had always promised herself that one day she would move to warmer climes. Maybe that time was now. She had handed in her notice at the end of her shift at six o'clock that morning. In a month's time, she would be free of Ilithyia Biotechnology and ready to start a new life. Maybe they'd even let her leave earlier. It seemed that Rosalind Baxter would be all too glad to see the back of her.

Australia sounded attractive. She had overheard some of the other nurses talking about it. There was a shortage of trained medical staff, and the climate was vastly superior to that of grey, old England. She resolved to give the month's notice on the small flat she rented in a two-storey block on the outskirts of Northstowe. Over a third of her monthly earnings went towards the rent. That was another thing about Australia—the cost of living was apparently far lower.

She peered blearily at the bedside clock. Just after eleven o'clock. No wonder she felt tired. Normally after a night shift she wouldn't wake until at least two o'clock in the afternoon. Something rustled in the corner. She hadn't forgotten to close the window, had she? The climate control maintained a steady temperature, but she liked to let some fresh air into the room for a minute or two before turning in. She wouldn't be able to sleep if the curtains were flapping in the breeze.

With a groan and eyes still half closed, she flung back the covers and slipped her feet into a pair of fluffy slippers. She inhaled through her nose. A musty tang tickled the edge of her senses. She sniffed again, trying to identify the incongruous scent. It reminded her of tomcat urine, but just the faintest trace. She wondered whether it was just the remnants of a dream playing with her sense of smell. Frowning, she glanced at the curtains. Not the slightest ripple of movement.

A figure burst from the other side of the bed. Before she had time to react, a hand clamped over her mouth. She tried to scream, but the strong fingers blocked her airflow. A hiss. A cold sensation running rapidly down from her neck. Dizziness clouding her mind. The man's voice.

185

"You're not going to call for help, are you?"

Rose shook her head. Terror enveloped her, but it was as if somebody else had occupied her body.

"You're going to get dressed now." The tone was calm, persuasive.

She switched on the light, closing her eyes briefly against the sudden brightness. As they adjusted, her gaze settled on the man who had by now moved to block the door. He seemed familiar, but her addled mind struggled to place him. A burst of clarity. Grolby, the Head of Security at Ilithyia.

"Hurry up, we're going out," he said, maintaining the same resonant timbre.

She stretched out robotically, grabbed the blue uniform she had discarded on the chest of drawers earlier that morning and pulled it on over her T-shirt.

"Put some shoes on," the man said.

Rose slipped her feet into the flat-soled black shoes she wore for work.

"Before we go out, you're going to tell me what you gave the boy when you met in the car park."

"A note."

"Who was the note from?"

"The girl in the basement."

"What did it say?"

A look of anguish crossed Rose's face. "I can't remember the exact words."

"Don't worry about that," the man said soothingly. "Just give me the general gist of it."

"She asked him to get her out."

"Good. Did you tell anybody else?"

"No."

"Right, here's what you're going to do." He spoke to her in a low voice, explaining what he wanted and emphasising several points. Rose's breathing came ragged and harsh until he told her to breathe more slowly. Outwardly she appeared to be calm, but a vein throbbed rapidly at her temple.

"Do you understand all that?" he asked.

Rose nodded, her eyes darting frantically around the room.

"Okay, I want you to go now. You're going to follow my instructions, aren't you?"

"Yes," she said, a quaver in her voice.

She descended the stairs and undid the lock. Grolby looked on from the top step. She pulled the door open and stepped out without closing it behind her. She began walking, wearing no coat, only her thin nurse's uniform.

By the time she arrived at the railway station, her skin was turning blue from the cold. She was shivering uncontrollably, and several passengers threw her worried glances. One man asked whether she was alright, but Rose ignored him. She held her phone to the reader as she proceeded through the gates and onto the platform. She walked until she reached the end of the concrete strip, then turned and advanced until her feet straddled the yellow line a metre from the edge.

A high-pitched screeching sound preceded the rattle of an approaching train. Rose took a step forwards, her whole body trembling. The twin lights of the locomotive rounded the bend. Rose's head shook rapidly from side to side. The driver was now clearly visible through the windshield.

A second or two before it reached her, Rose stepped directly into the path of the incoming train.

## Friday 14th January 2033

Karen Atkins glanced up as the technician entered her office. It was the same guy who had captured Jason Baxter on the station camera. "I take it you've got something," she said.

The man smiled. "Well, um, not much really. The first problem was how to get hold of Jason Baxter's number. Luckily he had registered his mobile so that wasn't too hard."

Kat tapped her fingers on the desk. "Okay. You wouldn't be here if you didn't have something to tell me. I don't want to hear how clever you are, just give me the facts."

"Patience is a virtue," the man said. "So, I called in a favour and managed to get the phone company to release his records despite not having a warrant."

"If you've broken the law, keep it to yourself. Just cut to the chase."

"You told me he claimed to have received a call on the Saturday morning, the eighth of January, right?"

Kat nodded. "Go on."

"Well, the phone company have no record of that, so, in a nutshell, he was lying."

"That doesn't surprise me. There's something going on here that we don't know about. Did you check the rest of his phone records?"

"Yeah. There are some outgoing calls to numbers he's called several times before, but I'm pretty sure they must belong to his friends. He's also received a few incoming calls from his mother's office. I hear she's a real piece of work."

"You could say that," said Kat, grinning. "I guess you don't get to be head of a big company like that without a certain amount of attitude. So, nothing on the calls, then?"

"Well, there was one that may be of interest. A single call to a mobile he hasn't called before, unregistered of course, at seventeen sixteen yesterday afternoon. It's probably nothing."

"Hmm. That would have been just before our meeting. The other number was unregistered, you say? It might be worth putting a trace on it."

The technician grimaced. "I'd need a warrant for that, and given that we shouldn't have his call records in the first place, that's going to be difficult."

"Alright, let's leave it for now. We know the boy lied to us. We know he met with Floyd, but we don't know who told him to go there. The reason he gave for the meeting with Floyd is pure fiction. A girl surviving childbirth? He's got to be having a laugh. On top of all that, the drone pictures don't show him carrying any supplies. Basically, everything he told us is untrue.

"However, we do have him trespassing in the old post office. I think the time for playing games is over. I'm going to threaten to charge him with breaking and entering. We'll probably have to settle for a caution, but we might learn something while we're talking to him. I wouldn't mind seeing the look on that arrogant cow's face when we inform her that her precious son is facing charges."

"Sounds like a plan," the man said. "Anything else I can help you with?"

Kat frowned and remained silent for a second. "You know when the girl was raped at the Baxter house?"

"You mean the one in the wheelchair?"

"Yeah. Did we take DNA from everybody who was there?"

"I'd need to check. As I recall, we treated all the kids who were drugged as victims rather than suspects. Once a match was found with Floyd, we didn't bother to take any more samples."

"So, no DNA was taken from the Baxter boy?" asked Kat.

"I can't be sure, but I don't think so. I can check into it. Why? What are you thinking?"

"I'm thinking there's more to this than meets the eye. What if the pair of them were already in collusion at that stage?"

"Anything's possible, but Floyd only got out of prison a few weeks before the party, so I don't see what the relationship could be."

"It's just a hunch," said Kat. "Can you confirm we don't have the boy's DNA? Assuming that's the case, I'll see if we can't get a sample when he comes in."

"Good luck with that. I can't see his mother's lawyers agreeing to it without a fight."

## Friday 14th January 2033

Jason glanced at his watch. Five thirty-four in the afternoon. He pushed open the outer door of his mother's office and was relieved to see that it was empty. He padded across the thick carpet and put his ear to the door leading to her inner sanctum. She might well be working, but no sounds came from within. He knocked tentatively and waited for a reply with bated breath. Silence. He gripped the handle and twisted, then stuck his head through the gap. The lights were off. Good. He eased his way into the room and flicked on the light switch. It didn't bear thinking about what would happen if his mother caught him here, but if she came back unexpectedly, it would look far worse if he was skulking about in the dark.

His heart raced as he approached her desk and studied the wiring that led from the desktop through a hole to the system box below. There were two wires. One was the mains cable and the other the data cable. He removed the rucksack from his back and retrieved the padded envelope. From inside, he pulled out a unit the size of a matchbox, encased in bubble wrap. He peeled off the protective covering and examined the object. On each of the two long sides of the black plastic box were connectors, one male and one female. The gold pins glinted in the glare of the bright ceiling light. The device gave off an unpleasant, oily, industrial odour.

He felt around inside the envelope again. His fingers closed around a single folded piece of paper. The same pungent scent rose as he unfolded the sheet. The instructions were already familiar, but he read them again anyway. It all seemed simple enough. He moved the chair and wriggled underneath. The processing unit was a matt-black slab of plastic with buttons on the front and an array of connection points at the back. He tracked the chunky cable that linked to the monitor and detached the connector. He pressed it into the mating half of the small black box and made sure that it was secure, then pushed the remaining connector into the system box. A small green light illuminated on the side of the unit.

The device sat between the monitor and the processing unit. It would take a well-trained eye to spot it was there. Jason once again contemplated the wisdom of his actions. From what he understood, the gadget intercepted all signals that went to or from the monitor. That included not only what was displayed but also the screen sensors and the iris recognition camera. Once the signals had been recorded, they could be played back to allow somebody to log in and use the machine remotely. It was designed to remain dormant during the day, simply monitoring and capturing data. At night, when the office was empty, the wireless link would be activated to retrieve the stored information and, if required, to take control.

In effect, Jason was giving Floyd full access to his mother's computer. During their phone conversation the previous day, Floyd had argued that this was necessary so that he could determine the scope of the systems being used to secure the girl. It only required his mother to log in once, and Floyd would have the same level of access. The man had been vague about his plan to release Antimone, stating only that he needed to explore the system first. Not for the first time, Jason wondered whether Floyd intended to hold up his side of the bargain. Only time would tell.

He worried that if his mother discovered what he had done, it would cause irreparable damage to their relationship. That was a gamble he was prepared to take. He could have gone to the police, but there was definitely no way back from there. Even if he did so, there was the risk that his mother would hide Antimone away before they conducted their search and deny that she had ever survived. After all, Jason had no proof other than what he had seen with his own eyes. If the rescue attempt failed, informing the police was always a backup.

Jason stuffed the envelope and the paper back into his rucksack and returned the chair to its original position. He surveyed the room to make sure he had left no trace of his presence and headed to the door. Turning off the light, he pulled it shut behind him and crossed the floor of the outer office. He emerged into the corridor just as his mother approached from the lift.

She strode towards him with a frown on her face. "Hello, Jason. What are you doing here?"

"I came to see you, but you weren't in your office."

"If you'd called me, we could've arranged a time to meet."

"Oh, it wasn't that important."

"So, what did you want to talk about?"

"Um, I just wanted to apologise again for going to see Floyd behind your back. I know it was stupid, and I could have been hurt."

"Yes," said Rosalind, pursing her lips. "Just remember he's a convicted murderer. I suppose there's no harm done, but if he contacts you again, please let me know. Anyway, I've got some important things to finish off. We can talk more later."

"No problem. I'll see you at home. You are coming home tonight, aren't you?"

"Yes, I should be back in an hour or two."

"Okay," Jason said, "I'll get myself a takeaway."

Rosalind took a pace towards her office, then turned back to face him. "Oh, by the way, what were you doing at the railway station?"

"The railway station?"

"Yes, somebody mentioned that they saw you there this morning. Not planning another trip to Bedford, I hope."

"Um, no. I was supposed to meet a girl there—at the station, not Bedford. We were going to walk to school together, but she didn't show. She got the day wrong."

"Oh, a girlfriend?"

"Maybe, it's too early to say."

"Good," said Rosalind. "I'm glad you're moving on."

## Saturday 15th January 2033

The sound of a scraping chair brought Antimone to wakefulness. She opened one eye, then closed it again immediately, groaning at the bright light that seared her retina. Her head pounded with a pain that threatened to turn her brain to mush. She attempted to lift a hand to scratch her scalp, but something prevented it from moving. She tried again, but found she could only shift it a centimetre or two. Her eyes angled downwards. She immediately spotted the reason for her inability to move. A white plastic strap was wrapped around each wrist and attached to the bed frame. Antimone struggled for a moment before realising the futility of her actions.

"There's no point trying to get out of those." A woman's voice came from behind and to her left. "They're designed to hold far stronger than you."

Antimone craned her neck and gained an obstructed view of a nurse in a blue uniform through the bars of the headboard. The woman looked up from what appeared to be an electronic book reader.

"You caused quite a stir last night, young lady, going all superhero like that. You should have seen the shiner on that nurse, Emma what's her name—oh, I suppose you did. As far as I'm concerned, the silly cow got what was coming to her. She's a right lazy slacker, that one. Probably won't see her again for several weeks now, going off on sick leave and all that. Anyway—"

"How's the guard?" Antimone said, realising that she wouldn't get a word in edgeways without interrupting.

"Oh, a lot of blood, but no serious damage. He'll be off work for a week or two as well I should imagine."

"Good. Not that he'll be off work, but that there was no serious damage," she added hurriedly.

"I'm impressed by your ingenuity, young lady, but don't think about trying anything like that on with me." The woman's tone hardened. "There's a guard outside the door and another one patrolling the corridor. There's also another nurse in the monitor room keeping an eye on things. I only have to raise my voice and another half dozen guards will be down here in a flash. You never had a chance, you know. You can't make the lift move unless it scans your iris and finds you on the system."

"What's your name?" Antimone asked, knowing that the woman needed little encouragement to talk.

"You can call me Evie," the woman replied. "I'm going to be here for the next seven or eight hours. Plenty of overtime. I'll be able to afford a really good holiday this summer, I might even be tempted to go skiing if there was anywhere with snow in Europe anymore. I hear America's still okay, but it's a long way to go."

"I need to go to the loo."

"Right," Evie said. She rose to her feet and ambled across the room.

Now that Antimone could see her properly, she deduced that the woman was in her late thirties or early forties. Her brown hair was cut short and framed a face that looked like a five-year-old had assembled it. All the angles were wrong and everything was slightly out of proportion.

The nurse banged on the door with the flat of her hand. "Hey, Tony, open up. She needs to go to the toilet."

The lock beeped. A man's face peered through the glass window before he swung the door open and entered the room. His right hand rested on a half-metre long black stick tied to his belt. He wore a neatly pressed brown uniform and stood with his legs slightly apart, his eyes focused on the girl.

Evie loosened the straps on Antimone's wrists and helped her into the wheelchair. She escorted her to the small bathroom but made no attempt to leave.

"Can I have some privacy, please?" Antimone asked.

"Sorry, my dear. My instructions are to keep an eye on you at all times. After that stunt you pulled yesterday, they're not taking any chances."

Antimone shrugged and manoeuvred herself onto the toilet seat.

"It must be hard not being able to use your legs. I heard they've got this new treatment that can cure a fractured spine. People stuck in a wheelchair like yourself were walking around like a normal human being after a couple of weeks."

"I am a normal human being," Antimone said, frowning. "Now if you insist on watching, could I at least pee in silence?"

The nurse folded her arms. "I'm only making conversation,"

When Antimone had finished, she rinsed her face at the sink, then brushed her teeth.

"Back to bed for you, young lady," Evie said.

"Can't I stay in the wheelchair?"

"Dr Perrin said you were to be restrained all day. If you cooperate and behave, then they might let you sit in the chair, so you better start being nice to me."

Antimone groaned. "Can I see my son then?"

"The same applies. Not today. You need to earn the time."

"So, you're just going to leave me tied down all day with nothing to do?"

"You should have thought of that before hurting those people."

"Do you think it's right to hold me prisoner down here?" Antimone asked, scratching at one of the remaining scabs on her arm.

"I'm not paid to think about that sort of stuff. My only responsibility is to keep an eye on you. Now, back to the bed."

Once Antimone's wrists had been secured, the guard left the room and closed the door behind him. A deep despair descended upon her. Everything had gone so well at first, but the plan had been fatally flawed. Now her captors were prepared, and her chances of escape were even lower.

One thing was for sure, cure or no cure, if she got another chance, she would make it count.

## Saturday 15th January 2033

"Don't answer that." The lawyer leant forwards. "Mrs Atkins—"

"It's Ms Atkins, actually," Kat interrupted. "Look, we've got the boy entering the compound and breaking into the building. On top of that, he's clearly seen leaving with a known felon."

"What you've got is a fuzzy picture taken from several hundred feet up of somebody who seems to be wearing similar clothes to my client." The man sat back in his chair with a smug grin. "And if associating with a felon was a crime, my profession would vanish overnight."

"One can only hope," Kat retorted.

"So, at best you have circumstantial evidence in a case that's not even slightly in the public interest. You're not seriously telling me that you intend to prosecute, are you?"

"We haven't yet decided. If Jason were to cooperate and tell us how Mr Floyd got in contact with him, we might be prepared to be lenient."

The lawyer drummed his fingers on the table. "My client has already told you that he received a call on his mobile from Mr Floyd."

"We both know that's not true."

"And how would you know that, *Mrs* Atkins? I don't recall seeing an order to check my client's phone records. I hope you're not playing fast and loose with the law. It sounds like you might have need of my services yourself. I'd be happy to do a special deal."

Kat snorted. "If you were the last lawyer in the world, I'd still choose somebody else."

"Are we finished yet?" Rosalind asked. "Much as I enjoy listening to this banter, I've got a lot of work to do. My lawyer also charges by the minute, so that little exchange has probably cost me several hundred pounds."

"Well," Kat said, "if you're not going to provide any more information, Jason, I have no option but to put this case forward for prosecution."

A worried frown creased Jason's forehead. "What does that mean?"

"Let me deal with this," the lawyer said. "There's absolutely no chance that this would be taken to court. However, to save my client several months of stress, we might be prepared to accept a youth caution."

"Is that like a conviction?" Jason asked.

"No." The man turned sideways to address Jason. "You would have to admit the offence. It would be recorded on the Police National Computer, but it's not a conviction or a criminal record or anything like that."

"So, what would it mean, then?"

"Like I said, there would be a record. It might make it harder in the future to get a job working with children, for example, but at your age, I don't think it would have much impact."

"Would this remain confidential?" Rosalind asked. "I wouldn't want some hack digging this up and plastering it all over the Internet."

"Under the age of eighteen there are clear anonymity regulations," the lawyer said. "Even so, once it's out on the Internet it's very difficult to stop. My recommendation would be to let the police attempt to prosecute if they think they have a case. I strongly suspect it'll be too much bother and they'll just drop it."

"Just remember one thing," Kat said. "The crime that Daniel Floyd committed was particularly nasty. A young girl died as a result of it. I'm prepared to push very hard to go after anybody who's preventing us from catching this criminal."

"That sounds like a threat," the lawyer said. "I don't think we'll consider a caution after all."

"Take it how you like. I'm just stating my personal viewpoint."

The man rose to his feet. "I think we're done here."

"But—" Jason began.

"Don't worry about it," the lawyer interrupted. "Your mother pays my extortionate fees for my advice. I really think you should take it."

Jason took a sip of water. His hand trembled slightly as he lowered the plastic cup to the table.

"Actually, there is one other matter," Kat said, still sitting down.

The lawyer remained standing. "No, I think we've finished."

"I'd like to take a cheek swab."

"That's a new one on me." The lawyer grinned. "You need DNA to prosecute a trespass case? I thought you said your precious drone was all the evidence you needed."

"This isn't directly related to the breaking and entering. I was going over the case file for the incident at the birthday party and realised we didn't have any DNA on record from the people who were drugged. Would you mind giving me a sample, Jason? It's a simple procedure. Just a swab of the inside of your cheek."

"Well, if you were to drop all charges," the lawyer said, "we might—"

Rosalind rose from her chair. "No. I've heard enough. You can prosecute my son if you wish, but we'll fight you every step of the way. I've wasted enough time already this morning, and I have urgent business to attend to."

The lawyer looked gobsmacked. "Well if you're sure, Mrs Baxter."

"Come on, Jason, we're leaving," Rosalind said, heading for the door.

Kat leant back in her seat while the other three people traipsed out of the room. When they had gone, she withdrew a clear bag from her pocket and used it to pick up the plastic cup that Jason had taken a drink from. She poured the inch of water that remained in the bottom into one of the other cups, then sealed the bag.

Kat considered Rosalind Baxter's reaction. *Now I'm really curious.*

## Sunday 16th January 2033

A rhythmic chirping sound emanated from the corner of the room. At first, Jason couldn't identify the source of the noise. It seemed to come from the small blue rucksack. He unzipped the bag. The tone immediately became louder. He stuck his hand inside and closed his fingers around the smooth pebble shape of one of the phones he had bought to give to Antimone. The unit vibrated as he pulled it out and studied the display. An incoming call. He didn't recognise the number. He swept his hand from left to right in front of the screen and held it to his ear.

"Hello."

"Are you alone?" a male voice asked.

"Um, yes. Who is this?"

"Who the hell do you think, Sherlock? Given this number to a lot of people, have you?"

"Floyd," Jason said. "I thought we weren't going to call each other unless it was an emergency of some sort. What's happened?"

"Several things actually, but nothing to worry about immediately. The first thing is that somebody is watching you."

"Watching me?"

"That's what I said. Your mother's Head of Security has got a man tailing you. He's probably waiting outside right now—but don't look out of the window. They don't know we're onto them, so let's keep it that way."

Jason desperately wanted to draw back the curtains and attempt to locate the watcher, but he resisted the temptation. "How do you know that?"

"You're being particularly dense this morning. Didn't you get much sleep or something? Thanks to you, I've got access to your mother's computer. Several long-range shots of you were attached to emails. There are some of you talking to a woman. There's a close up of her handing something white over to you. Ring any bells?"

"That would be Rose. She passed a note to Antimone for me and then gave me her reply."

"Right, well they know she gave you something."

"Oh God. She was really worried about them finding out. I hope she's okay and hasn't been fired or anything."

"Hmm, I think I saw an email saying she'd resigned. Anyway, there were some more pictures of you entering what looks like a station."

"That would be when I retrieved the bug from the locker. Did they see me take the envelope?"

"No. The photos only show you going in."

"That explains how my mother knew I was there."

"What did you tell her?"

"I said I was meeting a girl, and we were going to walk to school together, but the girl got the days mixed up."

"There's hope for you yet," Floyd said.

"So, should I try to shake him next time I go out?"

"No, don't be stupid. Like I just told you, we don't want them knowing we're onto them. Just behave naturally. Anyway, the other thing I wanted to ask was whether you really want to go through with this."

"Why wouldn't I?"

"Once we start, there's no going back. You won't be able to return home. You'll be on the run like me, maybe from the police but also from your mother's people. From what I can tell, some of them are extremely dangerous. For instance, I was doing some research on the Head of Security, Anders Grolby. He was accused of killing civilians in Iraq before he worked for Ilithyia. From what I can tell, he only got off due to lack of witnesses."

"I'm more frightened of what my mother will do."

"So, you're ready to go up against her then?"

Jason remained silent for a moment. "Yes, I think so if it means Antimone will be safe."

"So why don't you just go to the police now and save us the bother?"

Jason sighed. "If my mother were to get wind of it, she would squirrel Antimone away somewhere they wouldn't find her and deny she ever survived. I can only talk to them when Antimone is out of there."

"On another subject, you weren't totally truthful when we last met, were you? You told me I wasn't the father of the child. You omitted to mention who the real father is."

"I was going to tell you, but the police arrived. I take it you know it was me. Anyway, I was drugged."

"Who drugged you?"

"I'm almost certain it was Dr Perrin's son, Max."

"Yeah, that stands to reason, judging by the emails I've read. Obviously, your mother has the same information, and I'm fairly sure she would be happy to use it if you pissed her off enough by doing something like, I don't know, stealing the one thing that she's counting on to make billions for her company.

You can do what you like when the girl's free, but you might end up facing some tough questions from the police. On the bright side, at least I'll be in the clear."

"Nobody's going to get hurt when we do this, are they?" Jason asked.

"Probably not, but you never know. She's heavily guarded, so we're going to have to do something fairly radical to get her out. It's going to be mostly down to you. If I show my face, I'll be arrested straight away."

"I'm ready."

"They can't suspect anything beforehand. You have to act totally normally. I'll pick you up after school tomorrow. That's when we'll do it, but we have to shake your watcher. Here's what's going to happen."

Floyd explained the plan to Jason.

When he had finished, Jason hesitated before speaking again. "Jesus. Are you sure that's going to work?"

"Who knows? I think it's the best chance we've got, but it's not without its risks."

"I don't know. It does sound horribly risky."

"Have you got a better idea?" Floyd said, the exasperation evident in his tone.

"No." Jason paused, then exhaled loudly. "Alright, I'll do it."

"Good. Take some spare clothes with you tomorrow, but you have to use the same bag as usual. You can't do anything out of the ordinary."

"My mother won't notice a thing. She's long gone by the time I leave for school."

"Yeah, but the guy who's tailing you might notice if you drag a suitcase behind you, though."

Despite the seriousness of the situation, Jason laughed. "Is that it then?"

It was Floyd's turn to hesitate. "There was one other thing I wanted to talk to you about, but it'll keep until tomorrow."

"Go on, tell me now."

"No, it can wait."

"So, tomorrow it is," Jason said.

"Yeah and remember to destroy the phone like I told you."

There was a click, and the line went silent. He glanced around the room at his belongings, attempting to imprint it all on his mind.

*What the hell have I got myself into?*

# PART THREE: EXTERMINATION

## Monday 17th January 2033

It took all of Jason's willpower to resist turning around and trying to spot the man who was surely following him. The weather was dank and blustery. Jason pulled the slate grey hoodie over his head. Even with the blue winter jacket, the wind still found a way inside the layers of clothing. It was still dark as he strode along the pavement, eyes forward. The small rucksack was bulging at the seams with the clothes he had bundled in earlier that morning. He had left some of his textbooks out, figuring that he would be unlikely to need them again if everything went according to plan. He would tell the teachers that he had forgotten to bring them to school.

He had barely slept a wink the previous night. The same thought kept bouncing around his head. *Was he doing the right thing?* One thing was for certain. His mother would be apoplectic with rage when she discovered what he had done. She claimed she was seeking a cure that would save countless lives, but what was her motivation? He strongly suspected that it was primarily the value it would add to the company, but if it ensured that women survived childbirth, was he wrong to intervene? Antimone's survival had provided a huge clue, but did that mean they could justify forcibly detaining her? Clearly, she didn't want to be there, or she wouldn't have asked for help.

He had retained the napkin, keeping it in one of the outer pockets of the jacket. He pulled it out as he walked and re-read his own words, and below them Antimone's reply.

GLAD YOU'RE ALIVE. ARE YOU OK? LOVE JASON

YOU HAVE TO GET US OUT OF HERE. ANTIMONE.

He had ended his own note 'Love Jason', but she had simply written her name. Was there any significance in that? Was she still suspicious of him? Maybe his mother had revealed his role in her rape, and she was just using him as a means to escape. It was impossible to tell from those few words. She had probably been in a rush, and there was no way to glean her feelings from something as simple as the way she had signed the note.

The other curious feature was the word, 'us'. That implied that Antimone wanted Jason to get somebody else out as well, but who could that be? Perhaps they were holding other women down there, and Antimone had befriended one of them. If that was the case, he was going to have to disappoint her. The plan would only enable him to get Antimone out. Anybody else would have to wait until the police arrived.

He returned the napkin to the pocket and put his head down into the biting wind that drove the fallen leaves before it. This would probably be the last time he made this walk. What would life be like after the escape attempt? His continued attendance at Oakington Manor would be out of the question, so he would have to find somewhere else to study if he wanted to continue his education. He struggled to get his head around the thought that he would be unable to stay in his mother's huge house. Would they put him into foster care? He was sixteen and old enough to get married, but he probably wouldn't be allowed to live by himself, even if he could afford the rent, which he certainly couldn't without a job.

And what would his relationship with Antimone be like? The fact that he had raped her, even if it was under the influence of mind-altering drugs, would be a huge barrier between them. Once the police were involved, it was sure to come out. Would she believe that he had not been a willing participant? How would he be able to prove he had been drugged and that Max Perrin was responsible? Again, there were too many imponderables.

On the positive side, Floyd would no longer be accused of a crime he hadn't committed. Not for the first time, Jason wondered whether the man really was a murderer. He was coarse and unrefined, but that was probably the result of spending all that time in jail. Underneath it all, he seemed decent. He had upheld his side of the bargain—or at least it seemed that he would do so—when it would have been easier to go to the police and present Jason as the rapist. Should he trust the man? At this point, there was little alternative.

The competing thoughts swirled through Jason's head as he trudged his way along the pavement.

Fifty metres behind, on the other side of the road, a man wearing a dark overcoat followed the boy.

## Monday 17th January 2033

Karen Atkins studied the report before her. She scrolled down the page, trying to penetrate the technical mumbo jumbo. She picked up the phone, read the name of the technician who had performed the analysis and said it aloud. After three iterations of the ring tone, a voice answered.

"Hello, analysis lab. Derek speaking."

"Hi, it's Kat. Can you come up here and explain this stuff you just sent me?"

The man replied affirmatively, and she replaced the handset in its cradle. She paced backwards and forwards, waiting for him to arrive. Less than a minute later, there was a tap at the door.

"Come in. Hi…" She had already forgotten his name. Her eyes strained to make out the text on his nametag as he pushed open the door. "Um… Derek. Thanks for coming up here."

"No problem," the man said. "What can I do for you?"

"This report. Can you talk me through it?"

"Sure. Terminal restriction fragment length polymorphism, or TRFLP, is a technique that exploits variations in homologous DNA sequences to detect similarities between the genetic makeups of individuals."

"In English, please."

"Oh…" Derek said. "Well, basically we run a test on bits of DNA—you know what that is right?—to see if somebody, a man, is a child's father."

Kat rolled her eyes. "I know what DNA is. So, you tested the sample obtained from Antimone Lessing's child and compared it to Jason Baxter's DNA? Is that right?"

"That's about the size of it."

"And it came back as a match. I thought we'd already identified Daniel Floyd as the father."

"Yes, we did."

"So how can both of them be the father?"

"Well, obviously they can't. The test looks for matching sequences of DNA. As you know, those sequences are passed from parent to child. That's how the technique works. However, that's also one of its weaknesses. There are bound to be genetic similarities between the father of a child and its grandfather. When the rape was reported, they took blood from the girl because they didn't want to risk damage to the foetus. The test they did has limited accuracy because they didn't analyse the baby's blood directly. Now we have blood taken from the child rather than its mother, we can be much more certain of the father's identity."

"So basically, what you're saying is that Jason Baxter is Paul Lessing's father, not Daniel Floyd?"

"Yes, that would be the obvious conclusion. Jason Baxter's DNA is a better match than Floyd's. It seems we've been looking for the wrong man."

"And Daniel Floyd is Jason Baxter's father, right?"

"Correct."

"Hmm. It does explain a lot," Kat said, "but it also raises quite a few questions. I checked Jason's birth certificate. It says his father was an anonymous donor. His mother was apparently undergoing fertility treatment at Ilithyia. According to her death certificate, she died in childbirth from a pulmonary embolism."

"So, Daniel Floyd got this woman pregnant. He was married at the time, wasn't he?"

"Yes. Floyd's wife disappeared eight months or so before Jason was born. If Floyd was carrying on with this woman, maybe that was his motive for killing the wife. I suspect that Rosalind Baxter already knows that her son is the rapist. They were out of the door faster than a rat up a drain pipe when I requested a DNA sample from the boy."

The technician seemed embarrassed and hesitated for a second before he spoke. "Um, I notice the form you filled in didn't have a proper case number. I'm guessing there's also no parental permission, so all of this is unofficial."

"Yeah, bloody politicians love putting roadblocks in our way, preventing us from doing our jobs properly, but they still expect us to get results. I'm going to drag him in again, and this time it's all going to be above board."

"How are you going to get the mother's permission?"

"I'll hold him for a day. If he doesn't talk, or the Baxter woman refuses to give her assent, I'll go and ask a judge. Given the serious nature of the offence, I'm sure it'll get signed off. Can we do a more detailed analysis of the baby's and Floyd's DNA and prove that Floyd isn't the father?"

"Yeah," the man said, "but it'll take a week or so. I'll get the paperwork raised for the full test today."

"Right. I'm going to be waiting for him when he comes home from school. Arresting her son for suspected rape should wipe the smugness off that arrogant cow's face."

## Monday 17th January 2033

The man wiped the condensation from the window and watched the stream of expensive vehicles entering the school driveway. Despite the heater being on full blast, his feet were still freezing. He placed the sports car magazine on the passenger seat and leant forwards. He examined the screen of his mobile phone and checked the position of the little green dot. For the time being, it remained somewhere inside the building. The first pupils emerged through the tall, black, wrought-iron gates and walked along the pavement. He planned to stay in the relative warmth of the vehicle for as long as possible.

Since leaving the army five years ago, he had drifted from job to job, working as a security guard and, for a brief spell, as a private investigator. Two years after entering civilian life he had been drinking with a group of friends in his local pub when he had run into an old acquaintance from his army days. The acquaintance worked at Ilithyia and had agreed to put in a good word for him with the Head of Security. After a short interview, Anders Grolby had offered him the job. Over the past two years, he had performed many tasks, not all of them strictly legal, but this had to be one of the strangest. Under normal circumstances, he would have considered spying on the owner's son as a seriously career limiting move, but his superior had assured him that he was following Rosalind Baxter's instructions.

The boy seemed to lead a very average life, and there had been few moments of interest. Most of the time was spent like this, waiting for him to either come out of his house or the school. There had been the incident in the car park when the woman had given the boy a note. Grolby had praised him for capturing the scene on film but had been less pleased when he had lost the subject for a minute or two at Northstowe train station. To make sure it didn't happen again, his boss had provided him with a micro transmitter, a small circular disc, no larger than the head of a nail. The small device was coated with an adhesive designed to bond to almost any surface. The previous day, the man had bumped into the boy on his way to school and had slipped the gadget into a pocket of the boy's winter jacket. The device's batteries held enough charge to track its location to within a few metres for the next ten days.

As he monitored the mobile phone's screen, the green dot moved. Finally, some action, even if it was just tracking a teenager on his way home from school. He set the Baxter house as the vehicle's destination so that when he arrived there after following on foot, the car would be ready and waiting, a refuge from the frigid winter afternoon. The map showed that his target was now less than fifty metres away. He returned the phone to his pocket and once more cleared the side window of condensation. The man recognised the blue jacket first. The boy emerged through the gates, the hoodie pulled over his head as it had been that morning. Unlike most of the other kids, he began the short journey home alone.

The man watched the boy in the rear-view mirror and waited. He didn't need to get too close because the tracker would tell him the target's location even if he lost direct sight of him. Opening the car door into the biting wind, he pulled the collar of his coat tight around his neck. He instructed the navigation system to follow the directions he had entered a minute earlier and slammed the door. The vehicle indicated and moved out. Ahead of him the boy turned left and passed around the corner out of view. The man increased his pace and hurried to catch up. He took the same turning as the boy down Huntingdon Lane and maintained the separation between them.

At the junction, the boy waited for a gap in the traffic and jogged across to the centre of the road where there was a narrow section of pavement. He stared to his left, studying the stream of vehicles, looking for the moment to complete the crossing. The man slowed down. He didn't want to end up standing next to the boy on the small paved area between the two busy lanes.

A car braked and indicated right. The boy darted across the remaining carriageway, then continued his brisk walk in the direction of home. The man speeded up again and followed the same route as far as the central section. The line of cars was continuous as commuters made their journeys home. The boy took a right down the next road, heading towards the railway station. The man wanted to get closer in case the subject went into the concourse again, but the traffic was too heavy to navigate.

"Come on, come on," he muttered under his breath. Eventually, a driver took pity on him, slowed and gestured for him to cross. The man gave a grateful wave and broke into a jog as he trailed his target. With a sigh of relief, he quickly spotted the blue coat and hoodie amongst the commuters streaming out of the station. The boy continued along the pavement, making no attempt to enter the glass and steel building.

At the T-junction, he headed left in the opposite direction to the majority of the traffic. The man relaxed slightly and kept the same pace as his quarry. The house was just over a half mile away down this road. As the boy progressed towards his destination, the properties increased in size. After three hundred metres, the buildings on the right gave way to open fields. The man gazed at the flat, featureless landscape, broken only by the occasional tree.

By now, most of the houses on the left would be classed as mansions. Closed gates and high fences screened the vast majority of them from the pavement. Not for the first time, the man wondered what people did for a living to afford to live here. Up ahead, the man spotted his white car parked at the kerb facing towards him, close to the entrance of the boy's house. Just beyond the gates was a stationary blue van.

As the boy bent down to type the access code into the electronic control box, the rear doors of the van burst open. Two men and a woman, all wearing dark uniforms, surged out. The boy whipped around in shock. The two men each took hold of an arm, and the woman pulled back his hoodie. She examined his face and seemed taken aback. She spoke a few words. He shrugged in response. The men released his arms, and he returned to the task of entering the gate's entry code.

The security man ripped off the glove to his right hand and rummaged in his jacket for the mobile phone. He inspected the map screen and confirmed that the green dot was located in front of the Baxter residence. He switched to the camera function and zoomed in to focus on the subject.

For several seconds he stared at the image before him.

The boy appeared to be approximately sixteen years of age and the same height and weight, but he was definitely not Jason Baxter.

## Monday 17th January 2033

Jason slid into the car seat, dropped the rucksack at his feet and loosened the scarf that obscured half his face. "Bloody hell, it's cold," he said, turning to face Daniel Floyd.

"Mm," Floyd replied.

"Hey, a manual," Jason said glancing around the interior of the vehicle. "It's a long time since I've been in one of these. What, so you have to turn the wheel and press the pedals yourself? Isn't that a bit dangerous?"

"Not as dangerous as what we're about to attempt. We might need to get away quickly, so I don't want to be travelling in a car that'll obey the speed limits and stop at every red light."

Jason's face became serious. "Are you sure this is going to work?"

"No. There are loads of things that could go wrong, but I think it's the best chance we have. If you don't want to go through with it, now's the time to say. Once we start, there's no going back."

"I've given it a lot of thought, and I've made up my mind. I can't let Antimone remain a captive. We have to get her out."

"Good." Floyd turned the key in the ignition. "I'd hate to think I wasted all that money. I called in a huge number of favours to get hold of the stuff."

"Where is the gear then?"

Floyd jerked a thumb backwards over his shoulder, indicating a green canvas bag on the back seat.

"Can I see them?" Jason asked.

"Let's wait until we get there. I'll take you through what to do when we're parked up. I want you to change into the clothes I've brought. They're in the other bag."

"You didn't mention that before. Why do I need to change?"

Floyd indicated and pulled out into the light traffic. "Think about it. If you just wander in through the main entrance dressed like that, somebody will probably recognise you. You are the boss's son, after all. However, if you're wearing the same gear as one of the doctors and a surgical mask too, the chances of you being recognised are much less."

"Good idea. Just make sure you don't crash this heap of junk while I've not got my seat belt on."

Floyd glanced across at Jason. "It's not a heap of junk. I bought it six months before... well, before they arrested me. It hasn't been used for over fifteen years, but it still started first time. That's German engineering for you. None of this cheap Brazilian rubbish that people are buying today."

"I'll take your word for it," Jason said, pulling the green designer sweater off over his head. "By the way, that suggestion of yours about swapping clothes with somebody else was a good one. I had to agree to let Brad keep the hoodie, though. He said he'd wait at the house for a couple of hours. I just hope my mum doesn't come home and find him there. He's probably already drinking her expensive wine. I assume it worked. Did you spot the watcher?"

"Yeah, he was driving a small white car. I didn't recognise the make. He sent the car ahead and followed on foot."

"I think I've seen it outside on the road a few times. I thought it belonged to the neighbours." Jason slipped into the pale green shirt and did up the buttons. "I'm going to stand out if I walk across the car park just wearing this thin top. I'll freeze my nuts off."

"Good point. Put the jacket on over the top. When you get in through the main entrance, put the surgical mask on and take the coat off. If anybody's watching, it'll look like you just nipped out for a spot of fresh air."

Jason took off his school trousers and wriggled into the green ones provided by Floyd. "They're a bit big," he said.

"I don't think anybody's going to stop you for wearing the wrong size trousers, do you?"

"Did you bring any shoes? I've only got my black school shoes."

"Jesus, it's not a bloody fashion show. Nobody's going to notice if your shoes don't go with the rest of your gear."

"Fine." Jason tied his shoelaces. "Do I look convincing?"

Floyd's eyes darted across, then back to the road. "Just like the genuine article, although I'm not sure I'd want you operating on me."

Jason refastened the seat belt. "What should I do with my school clothes?"

"Just throw them in the back."

Jason exhaled loudly as Floyd indicated left at the Ilithyia Biotechnology sign. "So, take me through the plan again."

Floyd went through the details as he navigated towards the car park. He manoeuvred the vehicle into a parking spot and applied the handbrake. He turned sideways to face Jason. "This is your last chance to pull out."

"No, I'm doing this. Show me how these things work."

Floyd stretched over into the back seat and grabbed the canvas bag. He pulled apart the handles and gingerly reached inside. "You have to treat these babies with a lot of respect." He explained how the devices worked and

212

handed the bag to Jason. Reaching behind the seat, he dragged out a portable computer. He pressed the power button and waited while the machine booted. Within seconds the display showed a login screen. "Good. Your mother's not logged in at the moment. Have you got everything you need?"

Jason nodded.

Floyd leant across, opened the glove box and pulled out a mobile phone. "Call me when you're inside. There's only one number programmed in, so you just need to press the green dial button. You'll probably have to hang up while you're getting the girl, but give me a call me when you're at the lift and ready to leave. I'll be waiting just outside with the car. Remember, put the surgical mask on as soon as you're through the main entrance. We don't want anyone recognising you. And try to look like you belong."

"Okay. Wish me luck." Jason pushed open the door. He stooped and leant inside. "By the way, what was it you wanted to talk to me about?"

"It's nothing to worry about. I'll tell you afterwards."

Jason shrugged. He slammed the door, turned towards the giant logo of the foetus and began walking.

## Monday 17th January 2033

Pale streaks of light fought through the angry-looking clouds at the horizon. Jason tightened the collar of the jacket around his neck. The icy wind cut through the thin material of his trousers, plucking at the seams like a witch's finger. His heart hammered in his chest as he strolled self-consciously towards the entrance. He kept his head down and avoided eye contact with the handful of people passing in the opposite direction.

A downward blast of warm air greeted him as he pushed through the rotating doors. He moved to a wall at the side of the main thoroughfare and shrugged his way out of the winter coat. He pulled the surgical mask up and over his mouth and nose. His eyes darted around the tiled entrance area, but nobody seemed to be paying him any attention. His finger trembled as he stabbed the green connect icon on the phone.

A voice responded before he heard the ring tone. "Yes."

"I'm inside and heading to the security door."

"Okay. I'm ready. Tell me when you're ten paces away."

Jason headed towards the double set of doors, holding the coat under his arm. Ahead of him, a man wearing a dark business suit waved a card at the reader and pushed his way through. He glanced back at Jason and held the door open. Jason showed him the mobile and shook his head. The man shrugged and continued on his way.

"I'm there," Jason said. He could have followed the man, but he wanted proof that Floyd could control the security system remotely. Two seconds later there was a barely audible click, and the light on the box changed colour from red to green.

"I'm through," he said. The corridor seemed quiet after the bustle of the reception area. "I'm on my way to the lift."

"Just wait a sec. I'll call the lift and let you know when it's about to arrive. Make sure you have the car to yourself." Several seconds of silence passed. "Right, it's on its way."

A ting announced the lift's arrival, and the doors slid apart. To Jason's relief, nobody was inside. "Right, I'm in."

"Okay, I'm enabling the lift panel. I'm not sure what you're going to see, but you want the basement level."

"Nothing's happening yet," Jason said. "Hang on, the panel's lit up, and there's a B on it."

"Go for it," Floyd said. "You better get your respirator on. Don't press the button until you're ready."

Jason pulled the cloth mask down around his neck. "I'm putting it on now. It's not going to be easy to speak to you with this thing on. I'll call when I need the lift again." Reaching into the canvas bag, he retrieved a device containing a face-sized clear panel with a stubby black cylinder protruding from the front. He slipped it over his head, the rubber moulding to the contours of his face. He put the phone in the breast pocket of his shirt and placed his hand inside the bag for a second time. This time, he withdrew a six-inch long, blue, cylindrical object. White Cyrillic writing curved around the circumference. A silver-coloured lever ran down the side and connected to a hinge on the top. A metal ring linked to a pin inserted through the mechanism. Jason depressed the lever, put his forefinger through the ring and pulled out the pin.

He took a deep breath and pressed the icon on the lift's control panel. The doors started to slide shut, but before they met, a green-booted foot appeared in the gap. The doors separated. A male doctor dressed in similar attire to Jason stepped inside.

## Monday 17th January 2033

Karen Atkins slammed the van door and stared at the illuminated building. "Let's see what you have to say this time," she said.

The man to her left turned to face her. "What did you say?"

"Oh, nothing. I'm just looking forward to Rosalind Baxter trying to talk her way out of this one."

Kat had managed to convince her superior to assign a couple of uniforms to assist her in arresting the boy. Her boss had not been pleased when he discovered how she had come across the evidence but had relented when she outlined the details of the case. He had even agreed to contact a judge who owed him a favour. Kat now held the authorisation to request a DNA sample whether the boy's mother assented or not.

It had come as a surprise when they had apprehended the wrong boy at the Baxter house. He had told them that Jason had asked him to swap jackets and wait in the house for a while before leaving. He claimed to have no knowledge of Jason's whereabouts or the reason for the bizarre arrangement. Judging by his confusion, he was as much in the dark about what was going on as Kat.

"Right, let's do this," Kat said, as a short beep signalled that the second man had locked the van. She strode towards the entrance to Ilithyia Biotechnology, the two policemen following three paces behind.

At the reception desk, the woman asked them what their visit was about. It was with some satisfaction that Kat announced they wished to discuss a serious police matter with the CEO. The woman placed the call, her eyes never leaving the three police officers. "If you'd like to wait here for a minute, somebody will be down to get you."

Kat paced backwards and forwards, sensing the receptionist's gaze flicking across to her at frequent intervals. She glanced at her watch and was about to approach the reception desk a second time when a small, narrow-faced man sidled up to her.

"Hello, I'm Julian Stefano," the man said, extending a hand. "I'm Mrs Baxter's personal assistant. Mrs Baxter is very busy. How can I help you?"

Kat grasped the man's sweaty palm and gave a perfunctory shake. "I don't think you recognise the seriousness of the situation. We're here to arrest her son."

Stefano did his best to hide the shock on his face. "I don't understand. Mrs Baxter's son?"

"That's what I just said. Now if you don't want to be arrested yourself for obstructing a police investigation, I suggest you either tell me where Jason Baxter is or take me to see his mother."

"Um… I have no idea where he is. Can you just wait a moment while I talk to Mrs Baxter?"

"I'm rapidly losing patience here. You better make it quick."

Stefano backed away, took out his phone and spoke into the handset in hushed tones. His eyes darted across to Kat several times during the conversation. He replaced the mobile in his breast pocket and retraced his steps. "Mrs Baxter will see you in the conference room. If you'd like to follow me."

He led the group through a door labelled 'Staff Only' and up a flight of stairs. He ushered them into an empty meeting room and hurried away. Three minutes later, Rosalind Baxter strode into the room, making no attempt to shake hands. She glared at the three police officers. "What's this all about? I thought we'd been over everything on Saturday."

"Mrs Baxter, we have a warrant for your son's arrest," Kat said.

"Not the trespassing thing again? My lawyers have assured me that there's zero chance of that ever going to court."

"No. This is about the rape of Antimone Lessing. Ironically, I believe the girl died at this very facility."

"What's that got to do with my son?"

"We've been re-examining the evidence and have concluded that your son was responsible. But I'm sure you already knew that. I also have a judge's order for a DNA sample."

"I don't know what you're talking about. You've been conducting a manhunt for Daniel Floyd for months."

"It appears we were mistaken," Kat said. "It seems that Daniel Floyd is your son's biological father. Would you care to explain?"

The blood drained from Rosalind's face. "That… that's confidential information."

"We can go into all that later. In the meantime, I want to know Jason's whereabouts."

"I have no idea. I assume he's at home."

"Apparently not. One of his school friends turned up wearing his clothes."

"Wearing his clothes? What do you mean?"

"We waited for your son to return—"

217

The ring tone from Rosalind's mobile interrupted Kat's words. Rosalind glanced at the display, then clicked the cancel button. "You were saying."

Kat grimaced, but before she could repeat her statement, the phone rang again.

"Excuse me," Rosalind said, "I need to take this." She left the meeting room and stood in the corridor. Her voice carried through the open door. "I'm very busy, Anders. I've got the police here asking about Jason … He what? … Another boy? … Well, where is he? … In that case, I suggest you find him as soon as possible."

Rosalind Baxter returned and faced the three seated police officers.

"I'm sorry, I have to go now. My assistant will show you out. I don't know where my son is. Please let me know when you locate him."

## Monday 17th January 2033

Jason turned his back to the doctor, but he could sense the man's eyes boring into his back. Prickles of perspiration formed on his forehead. The harsh sound of his breathing rushed in his ears. He heard the doors come together, and the floor sank away beneath him.

"You must be new here. I'm not sure we've met. I'm John Edwards."

Jason remained silent.

"I hope you don't mind me asking, but why do you have a full facemask on?"

Pressure pushed up through Jason's legs, and a ding signalled that the lift had reached the basement. An elongated swish accompanied the opening of the doors. The doctor stepped out, but when Jason risked a glance, the man was waiting for him. A bead of sweat rolled down Jason's temple and onto his cheek. He took a deep breath, turned to face the doctor and followed him into the corridor.

The man was studying Jason intently. His gaze settled on the blue canister in Jason's hand, then flicked down to the black lace-up shoes. Finally, he raised his eyes and focused on Jason's chest. "Why aren't you wearing ID? Are you authorised to be down here?"

Jason still didn't answer. Instead, he dropped the coat, tossed the cylinder a few feet away and strode after it.

"Hey", said the man. "Come—"

The object made a hissing sound, but there was no visible effect. For a moment, Jason worried that the gas grenade was not functioning correctly, but when he glanced behind him, the doctor was leaning against the wall with both hands, his head hanging down. Three seconds later, he had slumped to the ground, unconscious.

Jason rummaged in the canvas bag and withdrew a second blue cylinder. Holding the lever down, he yanked out the pin. He raced down the featureless white passageway and skidded to a halt where it angled to the right. Assuming Antimone hadn't been moved, they were detaining her in the room two doors down. However, when he had last seen her, a guard occupied a chair outside the doorway.

Jason edged his head around the corner. The guard was there, but rather than sitting in the chair, he was on his hands and knees. As Jason watched, the man coughed once, and his arms slid outwards. His head hit the floor with an audible thump. The sound of running feet echoed along the corridor from his right. Jason lobbed the second grenade ahead of him in the direction of the approaching footsteps. It bounced a couple of times, rolled and came to rest. A man wearing a brown uniform and holding a long black baton in his hand staggered forwards and collapsed.

Jason sprinted to the door the man had been guarding and peered through the small glass window. A woman in a blue nurse's uniform stood on the other side, staring at him in confusion. She partially obscured another figure lying on the bed. He pushed the door, but it refused to open. *Locked.* His eyes flashed over the smooth white surface. *No sign of a keyhole.* His gaze settled on a small box, a red light at its centre, mounted on the wall. *An electronic lock.* He strode to the prostrate guard and rolled the man onto his back. With trembling hands, he rummaged through the uniform pockets until his fingers closed around a credit-card sized piece of thin plastic.

Jason waved the card in front of the box. The light changed from red to green. He shoved, and the door opened inwards.

The nurse took a step backwards. "What are you—" She clutched at her throat and sank to one knee. Seconds later she toppled sideways.

Jason stood over the figure on the bed and stared down. For a moment he thought he had the wrong room. The pallid-faced girl with the layer of stubble on her scalp and the scabs covering her face looked nothing like the vivacious athlete he had known before. "What the hell have they done to you?"

Confusion washed over Antimone's face. "Ja—" she began. Her eyes rolled up in her head as she sagged backwards.

"Let's get you out of here," he said to the now unconscious girl.

Jason yanked off the white sheet covering his friend. She wore a thin blue patient gown. Now he could see that the scabs extended along both arms and legs, several of them still partially covered by plasters and dressings that were hanging half off. He placed his arms beneath her before realising that a pair of white straps bound her feet to the bed frame. Fumbling at the buckles, he released her legs then lifted her. He deposited her in the wheelchair and wrapped the sheet around her, tucking it in down the sides. Her head lolled to one side as he manoeuvred the chair to the door.

Jason pulled the door handle, but it didn't budge. He glanced at the small box to the side of the doorframe and spotted the red light shining at its centre. *The damned thing was locked again. Where had he put the card?* He tried first one pocket, then the other and sighed with relief as he grasped the thin plastic. He stuck his head into the corridor and surveyed left and right. Other than the two unconscious men, it was empty.

Jason grabbed the wheelchair handles and reversed out. At any second, he expected the blare of an alarm, but all he could hear was the rasping of his own breath. He swivelled the chair and propelled it forwards, only slowing to turn the corner. Sprinting past the unconscious doctor, he reached the lift and jabbed at the call button. The doors slid apart immediately. Retrieving the coat from where he had dumped it, he dropped it on Antimone's lap, then pushed her inside and snatched the mobile from his breast pocket. His finger prodded the green connect icon. He held the device to his ear and waited for an answer. Silence. In a mounting panic, he stared at the phone's screen. No signal.

"No, no, no," he said. "Not now."

He stepped outside the elevator. Still no signal. "Oh, crap."

"Hang on," he said aloud. He withdrew the key card from his pocket and waved it in front of the control panel. No effect. The only sign of activity was a bright red light emanating from the centre of the blank console. Finally, it dawned on him. "Damn. An iris scanner."

In despair, Jason returned the card to his pocket. *Come on, think.*

He exited the lift again and stared first one way, then the other down the corridor. His eyes settled on the comatose form of the doctor. *Of course!*

He rolled the man onto his back and grabbed him under the arms. Gasping from the effort, he dragged the man inside the elevator, surprised at how much he weighed. He hauled the man to a half standing position and heaved him towards the reader. When the man was in roughly the right spot, Jason held him around the chest with one arm and prised open an eyelid with the fingers of the other. No reaction.

*Maybe it was keyed to one eye only.* He adjusted his stance and swapped to the other eye. After what seemed like an age, the red light turned off, and a green G took its place. His finger prodded the letter. The panel now displayed an up arrow.

"At last," Jason said, lowering the unconscious doctor to the floor. The doors slid shut with a swish, and the lift surged upwards.

## Monday 17th January 2033

The lift doors slid apart. Jason expected a crowd of security guards to be waiting for him, but the corridor was empty. He removed the mask from his face and stuffed it into the bag. Next, he grabbed his phone and inspected the display. It was once again indicating a strong signal. He stabbed a finger at the green call button.

"Have you got her?" the voice at the other end asked without any preamble.

"Yeah. She's unconscious and in a wheelchair, but I think she's okay. I've got a key card, so I won't need you to do your thing. Where are you?"

"I'll bring the car as close to the entrance as I can get," Floyd said. "Let's get the hell out of here."

"See you in a sec." Jason pulled the doctor's card from his pocket and ran towards the security door. In his haste, Antimone's legs bumped into the sealed door. She gave a low moan, but her eyes remained closed. Jason waved the card at the small plastic box. The red light changed to green. Reaching forwards, he shoved the door open. A man wearing a pale blue shirt, yellow tie and black trousers stood on the other side, an access card in his hand. The man held the door for Jason as he propelled the wheelchair into the reception area. The man turned to stare as Jason hurried across the busy floor space.

Jason kept his eyes forward, but was aware of the glances he was receiving. He forced himself to slow down and tried to act as if he was simply taking a patient out for a breath of fresh air.

He was ten paces from the revolving door when a shout came from behind. "Hey you! Stop!"

Jason gave up all pretence of normality and sprinted the remaining distance. The front of the chair brushed against the leg of a woman who was chatting to a colleague to one side of the exit. She whirled around angrily. "Watch out, will you?"

Now all eyes were on him. Most people shrank back, but one man dressed in a thick, green, winter coat took a step forwards. The man reached out an arm, but Jason swatted it away and barrelled into the rotating chamber. He risked a glance behind him and was relieved to see that nobody had attempted to follow him inside the semi-circular compartment. It seemed like a lifetime before the gap opened onto the frigid January evening.

Jason snatched another hasty peek over his shoulder. A security guard had reached the glass panel and was pushing against it to make it turn faster. His actions had the opposite to the desired effect. The door juddered to a halt and stopped rotating altogether. The man glared at Jason and shouted something that was whisked away in the cold breeze. He removed his hands from the pane of glass, and the door lurched into movement again.

Jason surged ahead. He tipped the wheelchair back so that the small front wheels were in the air. The coat slipped off Antimone's lap and dropped to the ground, but he didn't try to retrieve it. A man and a woman who were heading to the building stopped to stare at the scene of a doctor propelling a patient at high speed towards the car park.

Another shout from behind. "Stop! Come back!"

Jason accelerated along the wide stretch of paving and spotted the blue vehicle parked at the side of the roundabout that led to the car parks and back to the main road. Floyd stood beside his car, hopping nervously from one foot to the other. Seeing Jason approach, he pulled the rear door open.

"Come on, hurry," Floyd shouted.

"I'm going as fast as I can." Jason skidded to a halt, one wheel of the chair bumping into the rear quarter of Floyd's car.

"Hey, watch that," Floyd said as he bent down and placed his hands below the unconscious girl's arms. "Give me a hand here."

"Piece of old crap," Jason muttered. He grabbed Antimone's legs and lifted. Floyd clambered across the back seat, dragging the girl with him. As soon as her legs were inside the vehicle, Jason slammed the door. He whirled to see the security guard advancing towards him, swishing his baton menacingly. The man jumped forwards and swung with all his power. Jason swayed backwards, the tip missing his chin by inches. Spotting that the man was off balance, Jason sought to nullify the weapon by enveloping him in a bear hug.

The man bucked and thrashed in an attempt to break free. Jason felt his grip weakening, and the guard released an arm. The man's elbow smashed into the side of Jason's head. Jason's vision turned grey as he staggered backwards. The man followed up with a vicious swing of the baton that caught Jason on the upper part of his arm. He fell to the ground and covered his head with his remaining good arm in anticipation of the blow that would end it.

A yell of rage erupted from a few feet away. Jason looked up to see Floyd flying through the air and crashing into the guard. The pair hit the pavement in a tumble of limbs. The baton bounced away. Jason sprang to his feet to retrieve it. He snatched it up and turned to face the two struggling men.

Floyd sat astride the guard, one hand pinning the other's throat. He drew his fist back and slammed it into the man's face.

"Leave..."

Another blow.

"... him..."

The crunch of knuckles against the soft cartilage of the nose.

"... alone."

Floyd cocked his fist again, but it was clear that his opponent had no fight left in him. Blood bubbled from his shattered nose and splattered the brown shirt of his uniform.

More shouts from the direction of the building.

Jason stared at the three men dressed in brown uniforms, sprinting towards them, batons drawn. "Come on. Leave him. We need to go."

Floyd clambered to his feet and faced the approaching guards. For a moment Jason thought Floyd would attack them too, but instead, he kicked the prostrate man in the ribs and headed back to the car.

"Does that collapse?" Floyd asked, gesturing to the wheelchair, his breath coming in huge gulps.

"I think so." Jason ran his eyes over the mechanism. "Here." He slid a lever across, and the chair concertinaed to half its original size.

"Toss it in," Floyd said, hurrying around the back of the vehicle and opening the boot. He slammed it closed and rushed to the driver's door.

Jason yanked the passenger door open and threw himself in beside Floyd. The engine roared into life, and the wheels scrabbled for purchase as Floyd released the clutch. The first of the guards made a grab for the rear door handle, but he was a second too late. The tyres screeched as the car surged forwards out of his reach.

Jason turned in his seat to see one of the men talking urgently into a phone and the other two tending to their injured colleague. He turned back to Floyd, a grin on his face. "That was close, but we did it."

"Yeah. I haven't had that much fun in ages, but it isn't over yet. We've still got to get to somewhere safe."

With that, Floyd gunned the two-litre diesel engine and raced towards the main road.

## Monday 17th January 2033

Rosalind Baxter held the phone to her ear. She spoke with a cold fury. "So, you're saying that the boy single-handedly waltzed into a high-security area, unlocked God knows how many supposedly secure doors and then casually made his way out with a girl who is worth billions of pounds to this company? What the hell do I pay you for, Anders?"

The voice on the other end began an explanation, but Rosalind cut him off. "I don't care about that now. Get the girl and my son back. Use whatever force you deem necessary. If you get the chance to get rid of Floyd that would go some way towards compensating for this cock-up. Oh, and one other thing. I want two armed men guarding her child, twenty-four hours a day. Do you think you can achieve that without messing it up?"

Grolby once again launched into a protracted apology, only to be cut off a second time. "Look, I don't want to hear it. Get the bloody girl back, and we'll talk then. You better have a good explanation for how they got past your systems."

Rosalind placed the phone on its cradle and rose to her feet. Grolby had grown complacent. For the first time, she contemplated the idea of removing him from his post. The problem was the man knew too much. Retirement would have to be of the permanent kind. She resolved to put out feelers, although such a matter would have to be handled delicately.

The situation with the girl was bad, but it could have been much worse. Luckily, the police had departed ten minutes before the boy—she no longer thought of him as her son—had performed his audacious rescue. It was clear that he had received help from somebody, and there was only one person she could think of who that might be: Floyd.

One thing in her favour was that they now had enough information to develop a cure without the girl. They had retrieved all the samples they required and understood to a large extent how she had survived. Yes, there was still work to do, but Perrin had assured her that the first trials were imminent. He even believed that the treatment would be effective on women who were already pregnant. They could trial it on patients who had given their permission without resorting to unwilling guinea pigs. At least two were due to give birth in the next two to three weeks.

Rosalind strode along the corridor and descended the stairs. Instead of heading to the reception area, she approached the lift that led to the basement. A security guard stood outside the sealed doors.

"Hello, Mrs Baxter," he said. "They're just confirming whether it's safe."

"Is Dr Perrin down there?"

"I believe so."

"In that case, I'm going down to see him. If it's not safe yet, get me the gear I need."

"I'll just check in," the man said, glancing nervously at Rosalind. He turned away and conducted a hurried conversation using a walkie-talkie. "They think it's cleared," he said after a moment, "but somebody will meet you with a mask when you get down."

The man stepped aside to allow Rosalind to enter the elevator. Seconds later she emerged into the white corridor. A guard wearing a gas mask held a spare one in his hand. "You'd probably be okay anyway," he said. "Most of the gas has dispersed, but it's best if you put this on just as a precaution."

Rosalind slipped the mask over her head. "Where's Dr Perrin?"

"He's in the emergency ward," the man replied, his voice coming through muffled.

Rosalind strode along the passageway, her breath sounding loud in her ears. She turned the corner and pushed through the swing doors into a room containing four beds, three of them occupied. Nigel Perrin leant over a patient and peered through the faceplate of his mask. He raised the heavily pregnant woman's eyelid and shone a torch in her eye, then directed the beam away. He repeated the process three more times. He turned to a nurse who stood beside him wearing the same gear and spoke a few words to her.

When he had finished, he glanced up and spotted Rosalind. "I hear Jason was behind this."

Rosalind strained to hear his muffled voice. "Yeah. We need to talk. Now."

"Pardon," Perrin said, turning his head sideways. "I didn't catch that."

In frustration, Rosalind tore off her mask and dropped it on the floor. She inhaled deeply, then exhaled. "See, no problem. I said we need to talk."

Perrin removed his own mask and cautiously sniffed the air.

"You're not going to smell anything," Rosalind said in exasperation. "The gas was colourless and odourless. Some Russian grenade they apparently use for special operations. God knows where they got it from."

"So, she's gone, but we probably don't really need her anymore. Have you heard anything from Grolby?"

"I spoke to him a few minutes ago. He's got his men looking for the car, but nothing yet."

"So, what did you want to discuss?"

Rosalind beckoned him to the corner, out of earshot of the other people in the room. "We've still got her son, but they might decide to go straight to the police. If that happens, they'll be here fairly soon, I would imagine."

Perrin frowned. "So, what do you want to do?"

"Well, we can't risk them finding these women, can we? They'd find out about the test subjects and that we kidnapped them. I think we'd both end up spending a long time behind bars."

Perrin's face paled. "What do you propose?"

Rosalind fixed him with a hard stare. "I suggest we transfer some of the patients from upstairs down to the basement."

Perrin pulled the pen from his front pocket and began clicking the tip in and out. "Their families know they're here. We can't just bring them down and do what we like to them."

"No, you misunderstand. I mean transfer them down here and treat them the same as we have been doing."

"How's that going to help?"

"Well, we'll have to move the existing patients out first."

Perrin hesitated for a few seconds before speaking. "When you say move them out…" A look of horror spread across his face as realisation dawned. "You mean kill them?"

"Exactly. They're going to die anyway. If the police raid the place, we're both looking at a long prison sentence. This way, there's no evidence."

Perrin stared at his feet. He returned the pen to his pocket. His rate of breathing accelerated. A muscle began twitching on his cheek. Slowly, he raised his eyes. "So, you propose to euthanise them and cremate the bodies, even though some are heavily pregnant?"

"Well we can't afford for the police to find them, can we? This is the only answer. Now that we're close to a cure, we don't need to perform illegal experiments anymore. We can easily obtain patients' approval to trial the new drug. They're not exactly going to say no when the alternative is certain death."

"But you just want to murder these women?" Perrin whispered.

"How many women have we already murdered over the years? Forty? Fifty?"

"We didn't murder them, well not directly."

"Oh, come on Nigel. What's the difference? If we hadn't made them pregnant, they wouldn't have died."

"It's not the same thing."

"Why? To all intents and purposes, we killed them. Why is this any different?"

"At least they had a chance. This is just plain murder."

Rosalind scoffed. "Had a chance? All the women we abducted and what percentage survived? Precisely zero. By making them pregnant we were effectively killing them even though it took nine months to play out. Now, do you want to spend the rest of your life in prison, or are you going to do what's necessary?"

Perrin placed his hands on his head. "I don't know," he muttered.

"Pull yourself together, Nigel. It's them or us. We need to move quickly. The police could be here any minute."

Perrin lowered his arms, an expression of resignation on his face. "Okay, I'll do it, but we have to get everybody out of here. We also need people we can trust to get them to the incinerator. There may only be four or five women down here at the moment, but somebody might raise the alarm with that many dead bodies all at the same time."

A thin smile brushed across Rosalind's lips. "I knew you'd see reason in the end. It's regrettable, but it's got to be done. We couldn't continue this vital work from behind bars." She turned to leave, then hesitated.

"Remember that what's at stake is the survival of the human race."

***

When Rosalind had left, Nigel Perrin glanced around the room to make sure nobody was watching him and picked up the telephone handset. He spoke a number and waited for the ring tone. A voice answered after two rings.

"Max, it's your father. I want you to pack an overnight bag and come here to Ilithyia. Just pack a change of clothes and pyjamas or something. Bring your toothbrush and any toiletries you might need. Can you pack a bag for me too? Nothing too big, though."

"… Look, I haven't got time to answer your questions now, but you have to understand that this is very important."

"… No. It's nothing to worry about. I'll explain it all when you get here. Will you please just do as I ask? Give me a call on my mobile when you arrive."

Perrin replaced the handset and once more checked that nobody was paying any attention to him.

## Monday 17th January 2033

The flat, featureless landscape flashed past the car window as they drove along the dual carriageway. The last tendrils of sunlight tinged the clouds at the horizon with an orange hue. After the initial rush of adrenaline, Jason's euphoria was wearing off. His eyes felt heavy-lidded as exhaustion crept up on him.

"How is she?" Floyd asked.

The words jolted Jason back to wakefulness. He loosened the seatbelt and twisted his neck to inspect the girl lying across the back seat. "She's still unconscious by the looks of it. Will she be alright?"

"She'll wake up with a headache, but there shouldn't be any lasting ill-effects—or at least that's what the guy told me."

"So where did you get those gas grenades from?"

Floyd glanced sideways. "When you've spent as long as I have in prison, you're going to make some contacts. He was just somebody who owed me a favour. I didn't ask where he got them, and he didn't tell me. Judging by the writing on them, I'd guess they were liberated from some Russian military armoury."

"Well, they were certainly effective." Jason lapsed into silence and stared sightlessly at the tarmac, lost in his own thoughts. By now his mother would know that he was responsible for freeing Antimone. He wondered what she was doing at that moment. No doubt she would be incandescent with rage. Before the rescue, he had been undecided about whether it was the right thing to do. His mother had presented a persuasive argument for studying the reasons behind Antimone's survival, but having seen the effects of the tests, he felt vindicated in his actions. Now he had crossed a line from which there was no coming back.

As he allowed his mind to wander, the memory of an earlier conversation rose to the surface. "You were going to tell me something. Before all this. What was it?"

Floyd said nothing.

At first, Jason thought he hadn't heard the question. He was about to repeat himself when Floyd indicated left, and the car slowed down. "Why are we stopping?"

Floyd pulled onto the hard shoulder, turned off the ignition and reached forwards to turn on the hazard lights. The whoosh of passing traffic seemed to intensity in the absence of the engine noise. He turned sideways in his seat to face Jason. "What did your mother tell you about your father?"

"He died. Of cancer."

"That's not true, Jason. She lied to you."

The car shook as a huge articulated lorry thundered past.

"Lied to me?" Jason said. "How do you know that?"

"Don't forget I've had access to her emails for the past few days. They tested your blood, didn't they?"

"Yeah, that was after they realised that it was me who... well, you know."

"You're right. They were checking whether there was something in your genetic makeup to explain how Antimone survived. But haven't you asked yourself why the police think I was the rapist?"

"Yeah, I thought it was a bit strange," Jason said. "My mother said it was because they were incompetent."

"Not that incompetent," Floyd said, letting the words hang.

"What are you saying? That you're my father?"

"Yes."

Jason gaped in shock. "My father? How did that happen?"

"You knew that my wife used to work for your mother, right? She was a researcher at Ilithyia. She was conducting research into infertility treatments before she died. This was all before the virus first broke out. She persuaded me to donate a sperm sample shortly after she joined the company, so I can only assume that somehow it was used to impregnate your biological mother."

"She told me my biological mother was a patient, and that she died in childbirth," Jason said. "A blood clot in the lungs or something. She never mentioned that she was responsible for making my real mother pregnant in the first place."

"It came as a shock to me too," Floyd said. "But think about it. If your mother was being given infertility treatments, it's entirely possible they would have used donated sperm, although I have to admit that I didn't realise that's how they were going to use mine. I thought it was just for experimental purposes."

"That explains why the police thought you were the rapist," Jason said. "We obviously share a lot of our DNA."

"Exactly."

"So, you're my Dad?"

"Yeah."

"And you've known for a day or two?"

"I wanted to tell you sooner, but you needed to be focused for this. That's why I waited until now."

Jason stared straight ahead and blew out his cheeks. The rhythmic tick-tock of the hazard lights was like a metronome accompanying his thoughts. After a few seconds, he turned and smiled shyly.

"Hi, Dad. It's good to finally meet you."

Floyd's relief was palpable. He grabbed Jason around the shoulders and pulled him in. "I'm proud to have you as my son."

Their hug was interrupted by a cough from the rear seat.

\*\*\*

Jason shifted sideways and stared behind him.

Antimone's eyelids fluttered open. "Where am I?"

"We got you out of there," Jason said. "You're in a car."

Antimone scanned the interior of the vehicle and raised herself to a sitting position. "Jason?"

"That's right."

Antimone's fingers rasped as they scratched the stubble on her scalp. "I... I don't remember."

"I had to knock everybody out, including you, otherwise we'd never have made it. Mr Floyd managed to get hold of some gas grenades and—"

The cogs in Antimone's addled brain crunched into gear. She shrank backwards. "Wait. Did you say Floyd?"

Floyd turned around in his seat. "Hello, Antimone."

Panic flooded her voice. "What's he doing here? He's the—"

"It's alright, Antimone," Jason said. "He's not the rapist. The police got it wrong."

Antimone shook her head rapidly from side to side. "No, no, no. He's a murderer. He made me pregnant."

Floyd frowned. "Actually, neither of those statements is true."

Antimone pushed herself sideways along the seat and shoved the door open. The blare of an air horn stopped her in her tracks as a three-section articulated lorry swept past, rocking the car in its wake.

"Antimone, stop," Jason shouted. "I can explain."

She stared into his eyes, her hand still on the door handle. A second or two later, her head jerked to the left. "Where's Paul?"

"Paul?" Jason and Floyd asked in unison.

"Yes, Paul, my son. Where is he?"

Jason hesitated before replying. "Um, Antimone, I'm really sorry, but he died two weeks ago, the day after he was born."

Her initial look of terror morphed into one of anger as she processed his words. "I saw him only yesterday. Why would you lie about something like that?"

It was Jason's turn to be confused. "But he died of a bacterial infection, didn't he? That's what my mother told me."

A hush fell, as if all the air had been sucked out of the interior of the vehicle.

Floyd broke the silence. "She's right, Jason. I saw some of your mother's emails about a baby. Now I think about it, they may have mentioned the name, Paul. That would explain a lot. She must have lied to you about that too."

"So, he's still alive? That means I'm a father."

"What the hell is going on here?" Antimone yelled. "What are you talking about?"

"It's a long story, Antimone. Mr Floyd—um, Daniel—didn't rape you. I'm Paul's father."

Antimone dragged herself across the seat and yanked at the handle on the passenger side. She flung the door open and toppled onto the verge. Jason opened his own door. The roar of the passing traffic was suddenly much louder outside the confines of the car.

Antimone clawed at the muddy grass as she dragged herself forwards. "Get away from me, you bastard," she shrieked.

"It's not what you think. I was drugged. We both were."

"Leave me alone."

"I—we—were set up. Just let me explain."

Antimone said something, but it was swept away in the roar of a passing lorry. Even though she was breathing hard, she now remained stationary.

Jason crouched down beside her. "It was Max. He put a date-rape drug in the drink at the party. It made us all extremely suggestible. Look, can we discuss this in the car?"

"Leave me alone."

"Antimone, I swear I was drugged. Why would I go to all the trouble of getting you out of there if I wanted to hurt you? I only discovered I was the father a few days ago when they did a blood test."

Antimone rested her head on her arms and sobbed.

"Antimone, can I help you back in?"

She raised her head and nodded silently.

"Can you give me a hand here?" Jason called to Floyd, who stood a few paces away, looking on anxiously. Between them, they lifted her and eased her through the open door. Jason knelt, facing Antimone over the back of his seat.

Mud streaked her face and the front of the patient gown. Her limbs trembled as she studied the two men with tear-filled eyes. Several seconds of silence passed before she spoke. "So, tell me what happened."

Jason shot a sideways glance at Floyd, then spoke. "Like I said, Max slipped something into the fruit punch. It was some sort of hypnotic drug. He told us to go to the ground floor bedroom. Then he raped you."

Antimone wrapped her arms around herself and shivered violently. "But you said you were the father."

"Yeah, he used protection. When he'd finished, he ordered me to… well, you know."

As she processed Jason's words, it all seemed horribly plausible. "Christ, is there anybody who hasn't had sex with me?"

"Well, me for a start," Floyd said. "I just had the misfortune to be in the wrong place at the wrong time. I saw you both come out of the bedroom. Neither of you looked in the least bit distressed. I thought you were just, um… getting to know each other a little better."

"What *were* you doing there?" Jason asked.

"I didn't murder my wife all those years ago. Eileen called me from work on the day she disappeared. She sounded upset and said she was coming home, but she wouldn't tell me what it was about. She never arrived. When the police questioned the Ilithyia people afterwards, they said she hadn't turned up at all that day. They found a record of the outgoing call, but your mother explained it away by saying that somebody phoned me to ask if I knew where my wife was."

"That still doesn't explain what you were doing at the house."

"I think your mother was involved somehow, Jason. The police never discovered anything at Ilithyia's offices. I was hoping to find some evidence at your house, maybe a diary with an entry like *'Murdered a member of staff today and framed her husband.'*"

"What? After all that time?"

"Well, I'd exhausted every other avenue so…"

"How do you know it was my mother?"

"Well, I don't know for sure. I suppose it could have been somebody else at Ilithyia. In any case, whoever it was must have planted Eileen's blood in the boot of my car. You can't imagine what it's like serving a sentence for the murder of your wife when you know some other bastard was responsible and got away with it. All these years later, I still find it hard to talk about."

"What about when you threatened me at the seaside?" Antimone asked.

"Yeah, sorry about that. Not my finest moment, I know. Look, I thought the pair of you had set me up. Remember, this is the second time I've been framed for a serious crime. My head was all over the place. I followed you from Northstowe. Then I saw you messing around and having fun while I was still a wanted man, hiding from the police. It all just got to me. All I can do is apologise."

"Well you scared the shit out of me," Antimone said, folding her arms. "You must be really proud of yourself."

"Like I said, I'm sorry. I did help to get you out of there, though."

"Yeah, thanks. Anyway, the bottom line is that woman still has my child. How are we going to get him back?"

"We could go to the police," Jason said.

"That's a big risk," Floyd said. "I suspect your mother's not going to just give him up. But if that's what you want to do."

"So, what do *you* propose?" Antimone asked.

"We have access to her computer. I suggest we try to find out what she's planning before we make our own plans. We might even discover where she's keeping the boy."

"*The boy,* as you call him," Antimone said, "has a name. It's Paul. Before we do anything, I want to call my parents and let them know I'm alive."

"I think you should wait until we know what Jason's mother is up to before doing that," Floyd said. "Telling them would be like talking to the police."

"Hmm. So where is this equipment then?"

"It's back at my squat in Huntingdon. We've hacked into her computer and can read anything that's stored on it, like emails and so on."

Antimone fastened her seat belt. "So, what are we waiting for? Let's find out what that evil witch is up to."

## Monday 17th January 2033

Jason, Antimone and Floyd sat around the tablet computer. The display showed a list of emails on the left side of the screen. The information was split into three columns: one for the title, another for the sender and the last for the time received. As they watched, the cursor moved to one titled 'Tim Belton reference request'. The sender was somebody named John James. The bold font indicated that the email had not yet been read. A second later, all the items in the list shuffled up one position.

"She just deleted it without reading it," Jason said.

"Who needs a reference anyway?" Floyd said. "You should try spending sixteen years in prison for murder. Then see how easy it is to get a job."

"When's she going to go home?" Antimone asked. Jason had lent her a chunky pale blue jumper which she wore over the thin hospital gown. On her feet was a borrowed pair of thick woollen socks. "How are we going to find out what she's planning if all we can do is watch her deleting emails without even reading them?"

"Patience," Floyd said. "She's got to stop at some point."

The three people fell silent as another five emails disappeared from the list without being opened.

The tablet rested atop an overturned plastic crate. An extension cable snaked away from a plug block into the adjacent room. The computer's power supply and a small fan heater occupied two of the four sockets. Antimone was in the wheelchair while Jason and Floyd leant against the pock-marked wall, sitting on the bare floorboards. A battery-driven camping lantern provided the illumination from its position on the floor in the centre of the room. At the side of the stark room was a sleeping bag resting on top of an airbed. A heavy brown blanket lay beside the opposite wall.

"So, have you found anything out about your wife?" Jason asked.

Floyd's eyes remained fixed on the screen. "I searched all over the network. There are files relating to other things at about the time my wife disappeared, but nothing directly relevant. There was one password-protected file on your mother's hard drive. It looked like it was last modified at around that time, but I wasn't able to open it."

"Sorry," Jason said, "I don't think I can help. You're talking, what, sixteen or seventeen years ago? I've no idea what my mother was into in those days. It could be pretty much anything. There are websites that list the most popular passwords, but I can't see my mother picking something that obvious."

"So, no suggestions?" Floyd asked, diverting his gaze from the tablet display to search Jason's face.

"What about her initials and her birthday or something?"

"It's worth a try. What's her—"

Floyd paused as a sudden movement on the screen caught his eye. The picture changed from that of an email program to what appeared to be a shiny, black surface. A hand entered the shot. The image jerked while the hidden person adjusted the camera angle. As the fingers moved out of the way, the picture stabilised, and Rosalind Baxter's face gained focus. A click came from the small speakers on the computer.

"Can they hear what I'm saying, Anders?" Rosalind asked a person who was standing out of the camera's line of vision.

Her eyes darted left and right then settled on a point at the centre of the screen. "Hello Jason, Antimone and Daniel. I assume you can all hear me. My Chief of Security, Mr Grolby, assures me that your little bug is picking up my voice and everything on the display. A very clever ploy, but I have to admit I'm disappointed in you, Jason. I'm assuming you're the one who put it in place. Don't bother answering by the way. I can't hear you.

"So, you managed to free your friend. First of all, I'm sure I don't need to remind you that she signed a contract when we agreed to treat her. She's now in breach of that contract, and I'll be seeking legal redress for the cost of her treatment."

"I don't believe this," Antimone said. "She's making out that I'm the one in the wrong."

Floyd waved a hand to shush Antimone.

"… generous offer to waive any legal action if she returns to the hospital immediately," Rosalind continued. "We're very close to a cure. The future of the human race depends on our ability to continue studying you, Antimone. You don't want to be responsible for the deaths of countless women who'll die in childbirth just because you couldn't handle a little discomfort, do you?

"I take it my son—my adopted son, that is—has told you that he is the father of your child, Antimone? Well, if he hasn't, welcome to the family."

A fleeting smile crossed her lips. She reached out her arms to somebody off-screen and accepted a small bundle, wrapped in a white blanket. "I guess I'm a grandmother now," Rosalind said, turning the bundle around to show the baby's face to the camera. She bounced the child gently up and down a couple of times. The baby opened one eye and yawned then settled back into a peaceful repose.

"Paul," Antimone said in a strangled voice.

"Don't worry, we're taking good care of him—for now," Rosalind said. Her arms extended to hand the child back. Her gaze focused back on the screen. "He's missing his mother, Antimone. So, here's what I'd like to propose.

"You—that's all of you by the way—come here to Ilithyia by nine o'clock tomorrow morning. Antimone, you'll be reunited with your son. You can call your parents and they can visit whenever they want. We'll continue to study you until we've developed a cure. We won't do any procedures without explaining them fully and obtaining your permission first, although I think we've already got all the data we need. When we start the first patient trials in a week or two, you'll be free to go home.

"I've decided to be generous and forgive your foolish actions, Jason. I was wrong to ask you to forget about your friend. I'm sure you'd much rather be at home than in some squalid hideout.

"Mr Floyd—Daniel—I'd be happy to show you the records we have available from the time of your wife's disappearance. I know you think my company had something to do with her death, but I can assure you that isn't the case. The police investigated very thoroughly sixteen years ago, and I'd be glad to let you see everything I showed them at the time.

"There is just one condition. If the police are involved, the whole deal's off. They'll only complicate matters. I'm sure we can sort this out like adults. If you want to discuss anything, Jason has my mobile number. If I don't hear anything, I expect to see you all tomorrow morning."

Rosalind gave a slight nod of the head. The screen flickered once then turned black.

## Monday 17th January 2033

Jason pulled the phone out of his pocket and turned on the screen. "It's still before seven. We've got more than twelve hours to make a decision, but I think we should just call the police." He placed the device on the floor beside him.

"I don't trust her," Floyd said. "It's all just a bit too easy. I mean, she could have let me see the files months ago. She's hardly going to show me anything incriminating, is she? And if she's so relaxed about allowing you to see your parents, Antimone, why didn't she let you see them in the first place?"

"I don't know," Antimone said. "She's still got my son. I don't want to do anything that puts him at risk. I vote for doing as she says."

"It all just seems too good to be true," Jason said. "I walk into her company, gas her security guards, and she's just going to brush it all under the carpet and take me back. I'm sorry, but I don't buy it."

"Maybe we can set up a message that goes to the police automatically if we don't stop it so that they know where we are if anything happens," Antimone said.

"Hmm, maybe," Floyd said. "The question is whether they would believe us, especially if we're not there in person to argue the case."

"Whatever we decide, I think we should all do it together," Jason said.

"I'm just nipping to the loo," Antimone said.

"Do you need a hand or anything?" Jason asked. He blushed as he realised the stupidity of his question.

"I think I can manage," Antimone said, a thin smile brushing her lips. "I have been doing this for four years, you know."

Jason turned back to the tablet. Floyd had closed the remote display application and was now staring at a password box. "You suggested your mother might have used her birthday or initials."

"You don't know how many characters then?"

"No, it could be any number," Floyd said.

"Well her birthday is the eighteenth of April, and she was forty-five two years ago so that makes her year of birth… um… nineteen eighty-six, I think. Her middle name is Susan."

Floyd typed in '180486rsb' and pressed the enter key. An 'Incorrect password' message appeared, and the password entry box cleared.

Floyd quickly tried several combinations, reversing the date, reversing her initials, swapping the order of the initials and the digits. "This is hopeless," he said.

"I've got another idea," Jason said. "I know my mother sometimes swaps letters for similar looking numbers and vice versa. Try changing the S for a five and the zero for an O, maybe even an L for the one."

Floyd rapidly entered several permutations of Rosalind Baxter's initials and birthday. "No, that's no good either." He leant back against the wall and sighed. "After a day like today, I could do with a stiff drink."

Jason frowned, then jerked forwards. "What did you just say?"

"I said I could do with a stiff drink. Why? Do you have one stashed away somewhere?"

"My mother's always going on about a particular make and vintage of red wine. It costs something like a quarter of a million pounds a bottle. Even the newer vintages cost several hundred quid."

"You'll have to narrow the field a bit for me," Floyd said. "Can you remember what it's called?"

"Chateau something or other," Jason said. "I remember it sounds like a woman's name."

Floyd opened a browser window and typed in 'Chateau expensive wine'. He scrolled down the list of results. "Lafite? Rothschild? They don't sound like women's names."

Jason shook his head. "No, that's not it."

"Mouton? Margaux?"

"That's it," Jason said. "Margaux. Try Chateau Margaux expensive wine."

"It says here that one of the most expensive vintages is seventeen eighty-seven. Apparently forty-five years ago, some bloke who owned a bottle took it with him to a restaurant. He didn't open it or anything, but a waiter knocked it off the table. His insurance company paid out about a quarter of a million dollars for it."

"That's the one," Jason said excitedly. "I remember my mother telling me the story. Try Chateau Margaux seventeen eighty-seven."

Floyd transferred back to the password screen and entered the letters. "No," he said. "That didn't work."

"Try capital letters and swap the words around."

Floyd tried several alternatives, his mood deflating with every failed attempt.

"Remove the Chateau part. So just Margaux followed by the date."

Floyd typed in Jason's suggestion and shook his head.

"Leave a space between Margaux and the numbers."

The password box disappeared. A list of files took its place.

"Bingo!" Floyd said. "Good guess. Let's see what's in here then." He opened the first file and scrolled down what appeared to be a report. "Just some test results by the looks of it."

He selected the next file. The scrollbar indicated he was about halfway through the contents when he stopped. "Hang on, what's this?"

He read the words on the screen, then moved the document down a page. "What's your birthday, Jason?"

"Tenth of April."

"What year?"

"Twenty sixteen."

"My God," Floyd said, his mouth dropping open in shock. In a frenzy, he opened several of the other documents and quickly scanned the contents while Jason looked over his shoulder. "This is staggering. It's far worse than I thought. We've got no choice but to go to the police now."

Jason's face was pale. He clasped his arms across his chest and shivered. "I can't believe she would do something like that."

"The evidence is here in black and white. When Antimone comes back, we'll all go to the police station and show them these documents."

"I just can't believe it."

"She's always been a bitch, but I never thought she was capable of anything like this."

"I thought I knew her. All this time—"

"I know it's a lot to take in. At least now we know the truth, even though it may be hard to swallow."

"It's just…" Jason's voice tailed away.

Both men sat in silence. Floyd continued to scroll through the documents. He closed the last one and glanced up from the screen. "Where the hell has that girl got to? I guess things take longer in a wheelchair, but even so."

"I'll go and check on her."

"Do you want to borrow the light?"

"No, it's alright. I think there's a torch on the phone." Jason felt in his pockets and realised the phone wasn't there. He cast his mind back and remembered putting it on the floor shortly after his mother disconnected the computer. It was no longer where he had left it. "Did you pick up the phone?"

"No."

"Shit. We might have a problem. The phone's gone, and I think Antimone took it." Jason rushed into the hallway, calling her name. No response. He opened the front door and stared both ways along the quiet street. Seconds later, he sensed Floyd's presence behind him.

"How much money did you put in it? Enough to get a taxi?" Jason asked.

"I think it was about a hundred quid. That's probably just about enough to get to Ilithyia."

"Well she's left, and there's only one place she could be going."

## Monday 17th January 2033

"So, you still don't know where they are?"

Grolby stared at a spot on the carpet. "My men are still looking, but as of this moment, no."

"Well, it's just not good enough," Rosalind said. "Floyd has been one step ahead of us the whole time. When this is all over, I'm going to need a full review of your security protocols."

"If I may say so, Mrs Baxter, our security against external attack was not at fault. The hardest thing to guard against is a breach from inside the company. By fitting the device to your computer, your son effectively gave Floyd the same access to our systems that you have."

"I never thought the boy would do anything like this, but even so, you're supposed to run a daily sweep for bugs. How did you miss it?"

"Well, Mrs Baxter, it uses a technology where it remains inactive for most of the time. It only starts to transmit when enabled remotely. When we did our sweep, it must have been in its dormant state. In this case, the best method of security would have been to prevent access in the first place."

Rosalind Baxter's eyes bored into Grolby's face. "So, you're saying it's my fault for allowing my son to get into my office?"

Grolby swallowed, but he raised his gaze and met hers. "Well… um… I'd strongly suggest that you keep your office door locked when you're not there. Rest assured that we'll perform a check on all other machines in the company just to make sure that no others have been compromised."

"I'd expect nothing less. So, do you know what data Floyd had access to?"

"Well he was logged on as you, so we've run a scan to see what files were accessed by your account from this machine when we know you weren't in this office. Clearly, he got into the security systems, which is how he managed to get your son into the basement."

"Yes. If that stupid cow hadn't brought him down there in the first place, none of this would've happened."

"Well, she's not going to be a problem in the future."

"It was a little public, though, wasn't it, Anders? Couldn't you have done something—I don't know—less dramatic? It'll only draw more attention from the police."

Grolby's jaw muscles twitched. "I try to vary my methods. The police are very good at picking up patterns. I remember warning you at the time that too many accidents in too short a space of time might make them suspicious. You told me to make it look a suicide, which is what I did."

"But you're the expert. It's not my job to do your thinking for you. Anyway, what else did Floyd get access to?"

"The majority of the folders he looked at were pretty old, dating from the time his wife worked here."

"That stands to reason. He's obviously obsessed with proving his innocence. There's nothing on the network for him to find. That was one of the first clean-up jobs you did as I recall. Was there anything else?"

"He could see all your emails."

Rosalind gave a short laugh. "Ninety percent of it's spam, anyway, and the rest is day-to-day drudgery. The only thing that might be awkward is the stuff about the girl and her child, but none of the emails mentioned either of them by name. Jason already knew most of it already. So, it doesn't look as though he found anything incriminating?"

Grolby hesitated before replying. "Well, there was one file that he transferred from your hard drive."

Rosalind frowned. "He transferred a file?"

"Yeah. He attached it to an email and then sent it to a disposable email address. Afterwards, he deleted the message from your email client, but it still shows up on the servers."

Rosalind's frown deepened. "What was the name of the file?"

Grolby consulted his mobile phone and read off the filename.

"The file's password protected, though," Rosalind said. "That should stop them seeing the contents, shouldn't it?"

Grolby returned the phone to his pocket. "That depends. If we're talking about a fifteen-year-old file then security standards have moved on a long way. Given enough processing power, it might be possible to crack the password."

Rosalind stared out of the window for a second or two, then turned back to her Head of Security, her face paler than before. "That file contains information that would be disastrous if it fell into the wrong hands. We've got to get it back."

"May I ask why you kept such sensitive information?"

"No, you may not," Rosalind snapped. "I want you to delete all records of that email from the server. I also want you to make sure it's gone from my computer."

"If you'll allow me," Grolby said, coming round the desk. "Would you mind logging in again?"

Rosalind swiped a hand in front of the screen and stared into the red eye of the scanner. When the welcome message was displayed, she stepped back to give Grolby access to the machine. She identified the location of the file and watched over his shoulder while he typed a sequence of commands.

"That's it. It's permanently deleted from this computer. It'll take a little longer to purge all record of it from the server. I'll do that from my office."

"No, I want you to do it now."

Grolby shrugged. "Okay, but I'll need to log on." He entered another set of commands and focused his gaze on the iris scanner. Next, he navigated his way through several layers of menu, muttering to himself as he did so. Finally, he swept his hand across the screen and turned back to Rosalind. "That's done too."

"All evidence of that file must be destroyed," she said. "If Floyd's got it, make sure you get hold of his computer and find out if he's saved copies anywhere else."

"You sound worried. Does it contain something I should know about?"

"Just remember who's in charge here. If what's in that file comes out and I go down for it, you're going down with me."

Grolby folded his arms. "The converse is also true."

The blood drained from Rosalind's face and gathered in two pink spots, one on either cheek. Her hands formed into fists, and her body trembled with rage. Grolby took a step backwards. The woman before him might be nearly a foot shorter in height, but the energy coiled inside her lent her the appearance of a dangerous wild animal.

Rosalind opened her mouth to speak, then closed it again. She took a deep breath, held it, then exhaled. "Yes... well. It seems our fates are intertwined. If you do your job properly, it won't come to that."

The colour slowly returned to her face. "Now I need you to do something down in the basement."

## Monday 17th January 2033

J ason held Floyd's phone in his hand. It was an identical model to the one that Floyd had given him earlier and that Antimone was now using to pay for a taxi.

"I'm calling the police," Jason said.

"Is it still nine, nine, nine?" Floyd asked, taking his eyes momentarily off the road and glancing sideways.

"Are you serious? What else would it be?"

"You've got to remember I've been out of circulation for sixteen years. There wouldn't be much point dialling nine, nine, nine from inside, even if you had access to a phone. I just wondered if they'd changed it to the American nine, one, one or some such nonsense."

Jason shook his head and tapped out the digits.

"Hello, emergency services. Which service do you require, fire, police or ambulance?"

"Police," Jason said.

"What is the nature of the emergency?" a woman's voice said.

Jason hadn't thought through what he was going to say. "Um… you've got to get the police to Ilithyia Biotechnology in Northstowe. My friend is going there. I think they're going to kill her and her baby."

"What's your name?"

"Jason Baxter. My mother runs Ilithyia."

"And your friend's name?"

"Antimone Lessing."

"How old is your friend?"

"Look, it doesn't matter. She's taking a taxi there now, and she's in serious danger."

"Okay. You said she had a baby. I assume that's somebody else's baby."

"No, it's her baby."

"So, you're saying she had a baby, and she's still alive."

"That's right."

"And your mother is the head of Ilithyia Biotechnology? What's her name?"

"Rosalind Baxter. Why are you asking me this?"

"You realise that making hoax calls is a serious offence for which you can be prosecuted, right?"

"For Christ's sake, this isn't a hoax call. My name is Jason Baxter, my mother is Rosalind Baxter. Actually, she's my foster mother. I think she's going to kill my friend."

Jason noticed that Floyd was gesticulating towards him. "Just a sec."

"Hang up," Floyd mouthed.

"What?" Jason said, frowning in confusion.

"Hang up," Floyd repeated, this time out loud.

"I'll call you back." Jason ended the call. "Why did you want me to hang up?"

"You should listen to yourself," Floyd said. "You tell them that your friend and her baby are in danger from your mother. No woman has survived childbirth for what, sixteen years, and yet your friend has a baby? I don't think I'd believe you."

"So, what do you suggest?"

"I think we need to take a different approach. They're never going to accept that Antimone is alive. If they bother to check the records, they'll find out that she reportedly died in childbirth two weeks ago. But they're still after me."

"How does that help?"

"Tell them that I'm at Ilithyia."

"If they didn't believe me the first time, what makes you think they'd buy that?"

"You've got a point. What if you mention the name of the policewoman who's after me? Can you remember her name?"

Jason racked his brains. "I've got it: Karen Atkins."

"I take it you don't know her number."

"No. I can call nine, nine, nine again and tell them I've got information for Karen Atkins on your whereabouts."

"It's worth a shot. Just try to remain calm and think about what you're saying."

Jason inhaled deeply and dialled again. This time, a man's voice answered, and he requested the police.

Before he could explain the situation, the responder said, "I've got a record of a call from this phone three minutes ago. It's been classified as a hoax. You do realise it's a criminal offence to waste the emergency services' time."

"This isn't a hoax. My name's Jason Baxter. I'm with a man named Daniel Floyd who's wanted by the police. We're on our way to Ilithyia Biotechnology in Northstowe."

"Daniel Floyd, you say?" asked the man, the suspicion evident in the tone of his voice. The sound of keys being tapped came down the line. "I'm showing an active arrest warrant for a man of that name. Why are you going to Ilithyia?"

"To confront my mother. Look, if you don't believe me, call Karen Atkins. She knows all about Mr Floyd. We're going to be there in..." He glanced across to the driver.

Floyd held up the fingers of both hands.

"... about ten minutes," Jason continued.

"I need to make some calls," said the man. "Will you be contactable on this number?"

"Yes, but we're not waiting outside. When we get there we're going in, so you better be quick."

"I strongly urge you to wait for the police to arrive. I'll try to contact Ms Atkins. Somebody will call you back shortly."

Jason stabbed the disconnect button. He turned to Floyd. "Do you think they believed me?"

## Monday 17th January 2033

Grolby entered the lift behind Rosalind. "What's this job?"

"I want you to move some things from the basement to the incinerator."

"What things and why do you need me to help?"

"You'll find out soon enough. I need somebody who I know won't blab."

"Okay, that sort of work. What about your assistant? Why can't he do it?"

"Stefano? I let him go home. Anyway, he doesn't know what's going on."

"I wouldn't be so sure," Grolby said, then lapsed into silence.

The lift doors slid apart. Rosalind strode down the corridor, the security chief trailing a couple of paces behind. She barged through the swing doors at the entry to the emergency ward and stopped to survey the three occupied beds. Grolby almost bumped into her.

A nurse sat at a desk to the side of the room. "Hello, Mrs Baxter. What can I do for you?"

"How are the patients?" Rosalind asked.

"At the moment they're all sedated. Dr Perrin was going to perform some tests."

"I see. Where is Dr Perrin?"

"He's in his office, I think."

Rosalind spun on her heel and retraced their route.

"Is there a problem?" Grolby asked, but Rosalind didn't reply.

She passed the lift and continued to the door labelled 'Chief Scientist'. She shoved it open without knocking. Nigel Perrin sat behind his desk, his head in his hands. Resting on the desk in front of him was an injection gun. He looked up at the sudden intrusion.

"I couldn't do it," he said in a monotone.

"For Christ's sake," Rosalind said. "I don't get it. You're happy to experiment on women we've dragged off the street, make them pregnant and watch them die when they give birth, but you haven't got the balls to do what needs to be done now?"

"Rosalind, be careful what you say," Perrin said, nodding at Grolby who stood awkwardly behind Rosalind.

"He's in this as deep as we are," she snapped, "as he reminded me a few minutes ago. So, you're just going to sit here feeling sorry for yourself?"

"The injection gun's loaded if you want to do it. I can't do this anymore."

"Can't do what anymore?"

"I'll help you develop the cure, but then I'm leaving. You won't need me after that. You'll have what you want. If you'd like to buy my shares at the current market price, you can have them. I've just had enough of all this."

"Jesus, Nigel. After all the years of effort and sacrifice, now of all times you want to quit?"

Perrin glared at Rosalind. "My mind's made up. I'll help you this one last time, and then that's it. No more."

"We've worked together for twenty years and finally, when we have the prize in our sights, you just want to walk away? If you see this through, we'll both be billionaires."

"Multi-millionaire or billionaire, what's the difference? I'm not like you. I want to spend time with my son. I want to be able to look him in the eye without feeling ashamed."

"Come on, Nigel. Pull yourself together."

"Sorry, Rosalind. I'm not going to change my mind."

The silence built between them. Finally, Rosalind sighed in resignation. "Okay, I see I'm not going to be able to convince you to stay. If that's your final decision, I accept the offer to buy your shares, as long as you agree to remain until the cure's developed. It'll take one or two days to raise the finance, but no more than a week. I hope you know what you're giving up."

"I'm going away for a few days with Max. It'll take that long to synthesize the latest treatment, anyway. I just need some time off from this place."

Rosalind looked thoughtful. "You *are* going to come back, aren't you? I can't do this alone, at least not at this critical juncture."

"Of course," Perrin said, nodding eagerly, "but I'm not going to inject those women. I couldn't live with myself if I did that."

"Okay, it's a deal. I'll clean up this situation. You spend a few days away, let's say no more than six. When you get back, we transfer the shares. That should give me enough time to get the money together. You stay on until we have a proven drug for the Orestes virus. How does that sound?"

"Good, good. It's a real weight off my mind."

"So, this is already loaded, is it?" she asked, reaching for the injection gun.

"Yes, everything's set up. Just press the trigger."

"Right. Come on, Anders, we've got some work to do."

Rosalind left the room clutching the medical instrument in her hand, Grolby trailing a few paces behind her.

They had reached as far as the lift doors when Grolby called from behind, "Mrs Baxter, can I have a word?"

Rosalind halted and spun around to face her Head of Security. "Yes, what is it?"

"Well… I've worked for you for many years. I've taken a lot of risks on your behalf and performed a large number of criminal activities. I want some of Dr Perrin's shares."

"You mean buy, right Anders?"

"The thing is, I don't have much spare cash at the moment. I want you to give me some—for free."

"Let's get this straight, Anders. You expect me to buy his shares, then just hand them over to you?"

Grolby lowered his eyes to the floor. He swallowed, then met Rosalind's gaze. "Yes. If what you say is true, and you do have a cure, the shares are going to increase massively in value. After what I've done for you, it's only fair that I benefit from that."

"You already have share options, Anders. You'll benefit like everybody else who works here."

"Yeah, but a few thousand shares isn't going to change my life. I'm sure you can afford to let me have more than that. Two hundred thousand more, for example."

Rosalind barked a short laugh. "You want me to buy two hundred thousand shares and just give them to you for nothing?"

Grolby frowned. "Didn't you just say that our fates were intertwined? If I understand correctly what you're planning, I'm about to become an accomplice to murder."

"Jesus, Anders, you're responsible for far more than five deaths, so don't play all innocent with me."

"All under your instruction, though, Mrs Baxter. I was only following orders."

Rosalind's eyes narrowed. "As you well know, that's no defence. I'll think about it."

A hard expression passed across Grolby's face. "Two hundred thousand shares, Mrs Baxter. I want your agreement now, or you're on your own."

Rosalind stared at him for a few seconds. "Okay, Mr Grolby, you have a deal."

## Monday 17th January 2033

Antimone pushed the door open. The autonomous taxi was stopped at the side of the entrance road, two hundred metres short of the Ilithyia building. That was as far as the credit on the phone would take her. The wheelchair was on the rear seat, and there was no way she could get it out by herself. She had suffered the same problem in reverse when she had left Floyd's hideout. Luckily, a passing resident who was out walking his dog had been kind enough to help her by collapsing the chair and stowing it in the back of the car.

She felt bad about leaving Jason and Floyd at the house. It was hard for her to trust them. For so long she had believed that Floyd was the rapist, but now it seemed he was totally innocent. It was weird to think that he was Paul's grandfather. As for Jason, she struggled to put her feelings into context. Had he really been unaware he was raping her? He was obviously racked with guilt and on balance, she believed his story. It was all too conceivable that Max Perrin was behind everything, and all because she had accidentally tripped him during athletics training. She shivered at the thought of him undressing her and pawing at her naked body.

As she imagined the sequence of events and Max's calculated act of revenge, a feeling of rage enveloped her. But for a fluke, what he had done would have resulted in her death. Her breathing came hard and fast as she envisioned herself plunging a knife into his chest. The only good thing to come out of all this was Paul. At the thought of her son, her sense of anger morphed into one of concern. That, after all, was the main reason she was here.

Rosalind Baxter had offered to reunite them and allow her parents to visit whenever they wanted. Antimone still didn't trust the Ilithyia staff, but once news of her survival was out, they would have no option but to honour their side of the deal. She felt a moral obligation to assist in any way she could to develop a cure. As Mrs Baxter had put it, surely a little discomfort was worth it to save the lives of countless women who would otherwise die in childbirth.

On the journey to Ilithyia, Antimone had tried to call her parents, but paying for the taxi had used up every last penny of credit on the phone. Floyd and Jason were sure to contact the police when they discovered she was missing, so even if the people at Ilithyia wanted to keep her presence a secret, that would no longer be possible. She had considered waiting for the following morning before going to Ilithyia, but the way Jason and Floyd had been talking, it seemed they were more likely to go to the police. There were clearly long-standing issues between Rosalind and both of the men. By coming alone, she hoped to take the tension out of the situation.

The problem, for now, was how to get the wheelchair from the boot. The headlights of a car approached from the opposite direction. Antimone waved to catch the driver's attention. The car slowed but then carried on past without stopping. For a moment she contemplated lowering herself to the ground and lying in the road. Cars would have to stop then, but what if they didn't? It would be ironic to be the first woman to survive childbirth in a generation and then die because either a human or computer driver didn't see her.

The glare of headlights approaching from behind lit up her vehicle. Once again, she waved her arms. The car drew up alongside, and the window wound down.

"Is there a problem? Are you alright?" the middle-aged male driver asked.

"My wheelchair's in the back, and I can't reach it. Could you do me a favour and help me get it out?"

The window closed, and the car continued forwards. Antimone was about to swear in frustration when she realised it had pulled in ahead, its hazard lights flashing. The door opened. A short man wearing a dark-coloured winter coat and blue jeans walked back towards her.

"I assume you're going to Ilithyia," the man said. "Why didn't you go as far as the entrance?"

Antimone felt the man's eyes studying her as she held up the mobile. "Out of credit. I'm supposed to meet my Dad inside, but there's no money left on the phone to call him."

"Hmm," the man said. He opened the rear door and retrieved the wheelchair.

"Just pull the two halves apart," Antimone said. The man did as instructed, and the chair locked into shape. He wheeled it beside the door. "Do you need help getting into it?" he asked.

"No, I can manage, thanks. Could you just hold it still while I move myself across?"

Antimone manoeuvred herself from the seat into the wheelchair.

"It's a bit cold to be out without a coat," the man said.

"I'll be alright," Antimone replied, shivering as the freezing night air cut through the oversized blue jumper. "It's not far." She noticed the man staring at the muddy stains on the hospital gown and pulled the hem down. "Thanks for your help." She propelled the wheelchair forwards without waiting for a

252

reply. Behind her, she heard the man shutting the door of the taxi. A moment later the man's car overtook her and then indicated right to turn into one of the car parks.

Antimone accelerated the chair, grateful for the exercise. No other vehicles passed her. She glanced behind and noticed that the taxi had departed. She received strange looks from a man and a woman walking in the opposite direction but reached the main entrance without further event. A curtain of warm air engulfed her as she negotiated her way through the rotating door.

The brightly lit area was relatively quiet. She approached the reception desk and waited for the receptionist to complete her conversation with a telephone caller.

"How can I help you?" the woman asked, peering down at Antimone from her raised seat with a bright smile.

"My name's Antimone Lessing. I'm a patient here. Could you call my doctors and let them know I'm back?"

"Lessing, you say. How do you spell that?"

Antimone spelled out her surname and waited while the woman tapped the information into her computer.

"I'm sorry, but I'm not showing any patient by that name unless you died two weeks ago." The woman gave a nervous laugh, then stared intently at the screen. "Oh, that's strange. Did you say your first name was Antimone?"

Antimone nodded. "That's me."

"They must have made an error entering the data. I do have a patient here with your name, but it says here that she died on the third of January and well... um... you're obviously not dead."

"No, I'm very much alive. Is there somebody you could call?"

"It also says your son... oh, never mind. That must be another mistake. It has Dr Perrin down as your main physician. I'll just see if he's available." The woman tapped the computer screen.

A second or two later she spoke again. "Yes, Dr Perrin. I've got an Antimone Lessing here for you. I think there's a mistake on the system. It says she's deceased but..."

"... Yes, she's here with me right now."

"... Okay, I'll ask her to wait."

The receptionist's smile had faded to be replaced by a slight frown. "Somebody will be here to fetch you in a moment if you'd just like to wait by the chairs over there."

Antimone felt the woman's eyes boring into her back as she wheeled herself to the waiting area.

## Monday 17th January 2033

Rosalind held the injection gun to the third patient's neck and pressed the trigger. A brief hiss signalled the end of the woman's life as the lethal drugs travelled along her veins towards the muscles of her heart and lungs where they interrupted the signals from her brain. Within seconds her breathing had stopped, followed a short while later by her heartbeat.

"There are two more in the single rooms," Rosalind said. "I want you to take these three up to the incinerator while I deal with the other two."

"I don't know how to work it," Grolby said.

"Never mind. I'll be done by the time you've got them up there. I'll show you what to do, or I'll do it myself."

Rosalind positioned the sheet over the woman's face. "You need to hurry. The police could be here at any minute." She bustled through the swing doors and headed down the corridor. Five minutes earlier she had instructed all the staff in the basement level to return to the main part of the hospital, so she knew she had the place to herself. She had also been to the control room and turned off all the cameras.

She held her identity card up to the electronic lock and entered the small room. A heavily pregnant woman lay unconscious on the bed. Without hesitation, Rosalind transferred the instrument to the woman's neck and squeezed the trigger. She loosened the sheet and covered the patient's head without checking for a pulse. She hurried on to the adjacent room. There she repeated the process.

Releasing the brakes on the hospital trolley, she pushed it to the door with its lifeless cargo. She swiped her card against the reader, pulled the door open and using one foot to keep it ajar, dragged the trolley towards her. Her hand caught the door frame, and she cursed, holding it to her mouth. She glanced at her watch. This was taking too long.

Returning to the task, she backed into the corridor and swung the trolley around. She propelled it to the lift at a half-run. She jabbed at the call button and waited impatiently for the doors to slide apart. When they did, Grolby emerged pushing an empty trolley.

"How many have you done?" she snapped.

"Two, so far. I left them in the incinerator room like you told me. I assume you didn't want me to leave the trolleys in there."

"That's fine. Get the last one from the emergency ward, then come back and bring up the one from room 202. I'll make a start on the ones that are already there."

Rosalind entered the elevator. She faced the scanner and selected the ground floor. A bead of sweat trickled down her temple. She flicked it off with her forefinger, then wiped it on the bed-sheet. The lift surged upwards, announcing its arrival with a ting. The doors parted. She hurried past several locked rooms. At this time of day, the facility was largely deserted except for the handful of staff that cared for the residential patients. She passed nobody else before reaching a door that bore a flame icon. She held her identity card to the reader, depressed the handle and dragged the trolley in behind her. A wave of heat hit her as she reversed into the room. A large yellow-coloured metal cabinet filled most of the floor space. Emerging from the top of the box was a circular pipe that led up into the ceiling. On the front were an open sliding door and a control panel containing a number of differently coloured lights and buttons. A small glass window occupied one side wall. Two human-sized bundles lay alongside the right side of the cabinet, each draped with a white sheet.

Without pausing, Rosalind shoved the trolley into the enclosure. The wheels rattled as they crossed the tracks for the runners onto a metal grid. The dead woman's left arm slipped from beneath the sheet, hanging loosely down the side. Ducking her head to prevent it from hitting the low ceiling, Rosalind followed and applied the brakes. She heaved the body onto the grid. Stepping over an outstretched leg, she released the brake and pushed the trolley out ahead of her.

She turned her attention to the two sheet-wrapped bodies. She grabbed a foot in each hand and strained backwards. The corpse was halfway into the combustion chamber when the door to the room opened. With a sigh of relief, she recognised the broad shoulders of Anders Grolby backing in.

"Give me a hand here, Anders," she said.

"What do you want me to do?"

"Take the arms. Help me get her in here."

Grolby parked the trolley beside the wall, then strode across and seized the corpse's arms. The work was much easier with two people, and soon they had deposited the second body alongside the first.

"How many can you put in here?" Grolby asked.

"It should deal with three easily enough. Let's do the one on your trolley, and then you can take it back down."

"Wouldn't this have been a simpler way to dispose of some of our problems, Mrs Baxter?"

"What makes you think it hasn't? Anyway, it's not always feasible. That's one of the reasons I need your special talents. That reminds me. You need to delete all record of our entry into this room from the servers."

Grolby shrugged. "Whatever you say."

He picked up the corpse and lifted it over his shoulder. He stooped at the entrance and heaved it on top of the other two. "I'll go and get the last one."

Rosalind grasped the lever on the sliding door and hauled it towards her. The metal panel slid sideways and sealed with a loud clank. The green button on the control panel illuminated. She depressed it for a moment, then released it. The green light went out, and a red one came on in its place. A roaring, whooshing sound filled the room. The wall glowed orange where the light from the flames penetrated the small window. The temperature in the room rose by several degrees, and Rosalind wiped her forearm across her forehead. Four minutes after she had pressed the button, the burners fell silent. A rhythmic ticking sound emanated from the combustion chamber as the super-heated metal slowly cooled.

Three minutes later, the outside door opened once more. Grolby backed in, pulling a trolley containing the final dead body.

"Well done, Anders," Rosalind said. "We need to wait for the red light to go out, and then we can load these last two. It needs a while until it's cool enough to open."

Several minutes passed as they waited in silence. Finally, the red lamp turned off. Rosalind took hold of the lever and shoved the door back. Despite the cooling-off period, a wave of heat flooded into the room.

"It's like working in hell," Grolby said.

"Yeah, better get used to it. Let's get these two in there. Then we can relax a bit."

Grolby put his arms beneath the body on the trolley and slung it over his shoulder. He took a couple of paces and heaved it into the metal box.

"I can manage this one," he said, bending down to pick up the last bundle. His foot straddled the tracks for the runners as he pitched it forwards.

"It needs to go further back," Rosalind said, glancing inside.

"You're the boss," Grolby replied, entering the chamber and grabbing the corpse by the arms. He hauled backwards until the dead woman was up against the rear wall.

"Is this far enough?"

"Absolutely."

Grolby's eyes widened in shock as the door panel slid along its runners. He took a pace forwards, but he was too slow. The sturdy mechanism slammed shut, trapping him inside.

The sound of fists banging on the thick metal walls of the combustion chamber sounded muted from the outside.

"I'm sorry, Anders, but you've become part of the problem," Rosalind said as she pressed the green button. "And this is the perfect solution."

At the same moment as she released the button, the main door to the room swung open.

## Monday 17th January 2033

Nigel Perrin surveyed the small room. He opened his mouth to speak, but the roar of the furnace drowned him out. He beckoned to Rosalind Baxter and moved into the corridor. His voice sounded loud in his own ears in the relative silence.

"I wondered if you'd be in here," he said. "I thought Anders was going to help you with that."

"Oh, he did, but Mr Grolby doesn't work here anymore. He's been fired."

Perrin picked up on Rosalind's slight smirk. "Fired? What do you mean? Oh, Christ, you didn't…"

"He made the mistake of overvaluing his own worth. He tried to blackmail me. If there's one thing I won't tolerate in my employees, it's disloyalty. Let's just say that he's probably feeling the heat a bit at the moment. Anyway, I'm sure you didn't come looking for me just to have a chat. What's going on?"

"It's the girl," Perrin said. "She's waiting in reception."

Rosalind frowned. "The Lessing girl? She's here now?"

"That's what the receptionist told me. Apparently, she asked for me."

"What about Floyd and the boy?"

"No sign of them yet. I couldn't get hold of Grolby, but I asked one of his men to escort her to one of the private rooms. She's refusing to go with him until she's seen her son. I ordered the security man to stay with her. What do you want to do?"

Rosalind closed her eyes for a second and inhaled deeply. She reopened them, her steely gaze boring into Perrin. "We don't need her anymore, do we?"

"No. I think we've got all the data we need. You're not going to—"

"Leave this to me, Nigel. I want you to get an injection gun."

"You're going to put her down like those other women?"

"If you'd let me finish," Rosalind snapped. "I want you to load it with sedative, something quick acting but with a short-term effect. I want to find out from her what Floyd and the boy are up to. I take it you did as I asked and kept test results relating to the girl on your own computer and off the network."

Perrin nodded.

"Good. I want you to bring your machine back here."

"You're going to destroy it?"

"Yes. If the police do come, we're going to need all the bargaining chips we can get. The more information is in our heads and the less there is written down, the stronger our position will be."

"But if the tests aren't successful, it could set us back months."

"I have every faith in you, Nigel. You're going away for a week. When you get back, we'll conduct the trials, and everything will work as expected. After that, you can retire and do what you want for the rest of your life."

Perrin remained silent. A moment later, the blood drained from his face as realisation dawned. "Hang on. It's all very well destroying the samples and test results, but anybody else could just analyse the girl again. That means you *are* going to… Oh God…"

Rosalind rested a hand on Perrin's shoulder. "You're right. The girl is the key to the cure. I'm sorry, Nigel, but she's got to go. You won't have to do anything. I'll deal with it all myself."

"Christ, Rosalind. She's only sixteen years old, the same age as our sons."

"I haven't got a son."

"You know what I mean: your adopted son. You're just going to put her down like an animal?"

"Look, Nigel. This is the only solution. Bring me your computer and any remaining test samples. Go away for a week with Max. When you come back, everything will have been sorted out. You can forget the whole thing ever happened."

"I don't know, Rosalind."

Rosalind's tone hardened. "Nigel, you *are* going to do this. Now get me an injection gun loaded with a sedative. After that, bring your machine here. Got that?"

Perrin nodded silently. His gaze lingered on Rosalind for a few seconds, then he turned away and headed down the corridor.

"And could you hurry, please?" Rosalind called to his back.

## Monday 17th January 2033

The unfamiliar ring tone made Jason jump. From the displayed number, he identified that the call originated from a mobile.

Jason stabbed a finger at the answer button. "Hello"

"This is Karen Atkins. To whom am I speaking?"

"It's Jason. Jason Baxter."

"Hello, Jason. I received a call from an emergency service operator telling me that you're with Daniel Floyd. Is that true?"

Movement from the driver's seat caught Jason's attention. Floyd was gesticulating at him and mouthing something. "Hang on a sec," he said into the phone. He placed his finger over the microphone hole and turned to Floyd. "What?"

"Put it on speaker," Floyd whispered.

Jason studied the display and tapped a button that displayed a loudspeaker icon. "Can you hear me?" he asked, holding the mobile in front of him.

"Yes, fine. So, are you with Daniel Floyd?"

"He's sitting beside me and can hear everything you're saying."

"Jason, Mr Floyd. The operator told me that you're on your way to Ilithyia. Why are you going there?"

"To smash my fist into that evil, murdering harpy's face," Floyd shouted.

"Who's face?" Kat asked. "Rosalind Baxter? Has something changed?"

"She didn't die after all," Jason said.

"I don't follow. Who didn't die?"

"Antimone Lessing," Jason replied.

Silence greeted his statement.

Jason plunged on. "I know it sounds impossible, but she gave birth and lived. My mother was holding her a prisoner at Ilithyia in an underground laboratory. They were studying her, trying to work out how she survived so they could develop a cure. We managed to break her out, but later on she sneaked away from us. We think she's on her way back there."

"Okay, slow down a bit," Kat said. "You're telling me that Antimone Lessing survived the birth of her child? So, both she and her baby are alive?"

"That's right."

"That's not what the records show. Can anybody else verify that?"

"Well, other than the people who work at Ilithyia, only us two," Jason replied.

"You said she sneaked away. Where were you when this happened?"

"We were at an abandoned property in Huntingdon. She said she was going to the loo. After a while, we went to check on her, but she'd gone. We think she used the credit on the phone to order a taxi. She's going to go back to Ilithyia for her son."

"That's not everything," Floyd said. "Rosalind Baxter murdered my wife. We were able to get a file off her computer. But that's not the worst of it. Wait until you hear the rest."

Floyd explained what they had learned from the encrypted files.

"Can you send me a copy?" Kat asked.

"Yeah, I think so," Floyd said. "Jason, get the tablet."

Jason leant into the back seat and grabbed the computer. He clicked the on button and waited for the machine to boot. "Okay. Give me your email address."

Kat reeled off a series of characters.

Jason read the sequence back to her, and she confirmed it was correct. "I'll type the password in the body of the email. Sending it now." He studied the progress bar until it reached one hundred percent. "Right. It's gone."

"I'll make sure we get a team to Ilithyia immediately," Kat said. "I want you to wait for them to arrive. Where are you at the moment?"

Floyd shook his head silently.

"Can you hear me?" Kat asked.

Floyd drew a finger across his throat.

Jason pressed the disconnect button. "Do you think she believed us?"

"It doesn't really matter at this stage. The police are going to Ilithyia, and that's what we wanted. The file should convince them we're telling the truth."

The phone rang again.

"Don't answer," Floyd said.

The sound of the ring tone drowned out a ping from the tablet computer.

Had they heard the announcement and checked the screen, they would have seen an automated email stating that the previously transmitted message had been rejected because the attachment was too large.

## Monday 17th January 2033

Rosalind glanced at her watch. *Where the hell was Perrin?* Her rising irritation dissipated when the door at the end of the corridor swung open. The white-coated doctor appeared, hurrying towards her. "Good. About time."

Perrin said nothing as he handed the injection gun over.

"Now fetch your computer and bring it back here. Then you can leave with your son."

Perrin turned and headed in the direction of the lift. Rosalind walked in the opposite direction and waved her security card at the reader before passing through the double doors that led to the reception area. Her eyes were immediately drawn to the girl sitting in the wheelchair and the guard standing a few paces away. Antimone's appearance wouldn't win any style awards. The thick woollen socks looked incongruous against the muddy hospital gown and the oversized blue jumper. The slack expression on her face sharpened at Rosalind's arrival.

"Where's my son?" Antimone asked without preamble.

A slight frown creased Rosalind's forehead. "We've been over this many times before, Antimone. We both know you don't have a son."

Antimone's mouth gaped in shock. "What? You agreed that I'd be able to see my son if I came back."

"It's very sad," Rosalind said, turning to the guard. "We've been treating her for months. She's obsessed with having a child, even though she knows that if she did, she'd die like all the others. I was worried this might happen."

"What the hell are you talking about?" Antimone shouted. "I gave birth to my son and survived. If you don't believe me, how do you think this happened?" She raised the heavy jumper, forced a finger through the thin material of the patient gown and ripped a gash above her abdomen. "How do you explain that then?"

The guard glanced at the livid scar and looked away. By now, several other people, including the receptionist, were watching from a distance.

"You're clearly very upset, Antimone," Rosalind said. "We've talked about this self-harm before. We both know that's one of the things we were treating you for. I see you've shaved off all your hair again. I thought we'd managed to beat this delusion, but I can see we were wrong. I'm afraid we're going to need to continue your treatment."

"Bring me my baby," Antimone screamed.

"The computer records did say she had a son," the receptionist said. She had left her desk and was standing two paces away. "Although—"

"Stay out of this," Rosalind snarled, turning to the woman in fury. "The records are wrong. Now can't you see I'm trying to help this poor girl?"

"I-I'm sorry."

"I'm going to have to sedate you," Rosalind said to Antimone, a thin smile playing on her lips. She held up the injection gun and took a pace forwards.

"No, no, no," shrieked Antimone, warding her off with both hands.

"Restrain her, please," Rosalind said addressing, the guard.

"Um… What do you–?"

"For Christ's sake, hold her down so I can give her a shot of sedative."

Antimone attempted to bat the man away. "Keep away from me, you bastard. She's got my son and…"

Rosalind darted forwards, held the nozzle against Antimone's neck and squeezed the trigger. A short hiss signalled that the device had fired. She sprang back out of range of Antimone's thrashing limbs.

"I want my baby," Antimone sobbed. Her arms slumped at her sides, and her head tilted backwards. "I want my…" Her voice tailed off into a whimper.

Rosalind stepped forwards and inspected Antimone's face. She raised an eyelid, then turned back to the small group of onlookers. "The show's over," she said. "I'm sorry you all had to witness that. She's a seriously disturbed young lady." She glared at the remaining two people who continued to stare at the unconscious girl. Eventually, they too moved away.

"Let's get her to a room," she said, turning to the guard. "Follow me."

She strode across the tiled floor towards the security doors.

## Monday 17th January 2033

"So, what's the plan?" Jason asked as the vehicle drew to a halt at the turning circle by the entrance to Ilithyia Biotechnology.

"We have to find out whether Antimone came here," Floyd replied, opening the car door. "If she did, we need to make sure that she and her son—your son—are safe. The police will arrive at any second. After what that murdering harpy's done, I don't trust her further than I can chuck her."

"You're right," Jason said, shoving his door open. "We can't afford to wait for them."

Side by side, they strode in the direction of the brightly illuminated steel and glass building. Ten paces short of the entrance, a security guard emerged through the revolving door.

"Hey, is that your car?" the man said. "You can't leave it there."

"Piss off," Floyd growled, barging past him.

"It'll get towed," the man called to his back, but the pair were already entering the circular glass entryway. The man spoke urgently into his walkie-talkie, then followed Jason and Floyd inside.

Jason inhaled the familiar faint medical aroma, his eyes taking in the polished tile floor and the curving reception desk. It was almost as if he was seeing the interior of the building for the first time, so much had changed over the past few days. He hurried to keep up with Floyd, who was marching towards the alarmed-looking receptionist. The woman tracked the bearded man as he approached and, despite being separated by the chrome and plastic surface, she took an inadvertent step backwards.

"Um... can I–?"

"Did a girl in a wheelchair come in here a few minutes ago?" Floyd asked. "Sixteen years old and wearing a blue jumper."

The look of surprise was all the answer he required.

"How long ago?" he asked.

"Um, about ten minutes," the woman replied.

"Where did she go?"

"I'm not sure I'm allowed—"

"Get Rosalind Baxter here now," Floyd said.

The receptionist's frightened gaze flicked to the security guard who had drawn his black baton. "Who shall I say is asking for her?"

"You can tell her that Daniel Floyd and her adopted son are here."

"You're going to have to leave or I'm going to call the police," said the guard from behind Floyd, clasping the black cylinder with his left hand. Droplets of sweat beaded his forehead.

Floyd whirled to face him. "The police? Good, but they're already on their way."

"Mr Floyd, um… Daniel. Look," Jason said. Four more guards were running towards them, the double doors swinging in their wake. Each of them held a baton and appeared ready to wield it if necessary.

"These two are leaving," said the first security guard as the others drew alongside him.

"I'm not going anywhere until I see Baxter," Floyd growled.

"Throw them out," the man said, grabbing Floyd by the arm.

"Get off me," Floyd yelled, shaking the man's grip loose. The other men surged forwards. A baton swished through the air, striking Floyd on the shoulder. He stumbled under the blow. Several hands grabbed his arms and despite his frantic struggles to break free, dragged him towards the revolving door. Realising that Jason proved less of a threat, a solitary guard grasped his upper arm and propelled him in the same direction.

Halfway to the exit, a loud female voice rang out. "Stop!"

All eyes turned to Rosalind Baxter, who was standing by the security doors. "I will not tolerate this sort of behaviour in my facility. That man's a convicted murderer. We're going to restrain them until the police arrive. Bring them over here."

The intensity of Floyd's struggle increased. "You fricking bitch," he screamed, spittle flying from his lips. "You're the murderer." Despite the overwhelming odds, he managed to free an arm and swung it, connecting with a guard's ear. The man staggered backwards, but a flurry of blows rained down on Floyd from the man's colleagues.

The fight didn't last long. A blow to the right temple dropped Floyd to his knees. Blood immediately welled up from the wound, splattering the floor around the struggling men. Several more strokes landed on his back and shoulders. Seconds later, Floyd slumped to the ground, barely conscious.

Two of the guards grabbed an arm each and hauled Floyd to his feet. Jason found himself similarly restrained. It had all happened so quickly that it was over before he could decide how to react.

Rosalind walked forwards to meet the approaching group. She beckoned the spare guard towards her and whispered something to him. The man nodded, then hurried away to the revolving door.

She moved to stand in front of Jason. Fury blazed in her eyes. "You betrayed my trust. I raised you as my son, and you did this to me."

Jason met her stare. "I know everything. You murdered my mother and you—"

The slap snapped his head to the side. The backhanded blow that followed it caught him equally by surprise. Jason tasted blood in his mouth.

"I want these two restrained and gagged. This boy needs to learn some respect. Follow me."

## Monday 17th January 2033

"Come on, Max," Nigel Perrin said. "We need to hurry."

"You keep me waiting about for more than an hour, and now, all of a sudden, we need to hurry," Max said petulantly. "Why the rush? I thought we were just going away for a few days."

"It's complicated," the boy's father replied as he exchanged the warm foyer for the frigid winter night.

The wheels of the small suitcase rumbled over the concrete paving slabs.

"Where are we going anyway?" Max asked, hurrying to keep up with his father. He still sported a black eye resulting from Jason's attack.

"I thought we might go to the coast," Perrin said, angling his head back to address his son.

"Why are we going during term time, though?"

"What do you mean? You've been off school for the last few days anyway, recovering. We don't spend enough time together. Work has been pretty intense recently. Now that there's a lull, I thought it would be a good time to get away."

The boy shrugged. "Whatever you say. You're the one who keeps telling me I need to take school more seriously."

The sound of sirens pierced the background hiss of traffic that drifted from the main road. Strobing blue lights cast a ghostly glow against the orange of the streetlamps.

"Shit," Perrin said, breaking into a run. The wail of the sirens grew louder.

"What's going on, Dad?" Max asked in consternation.

"That bloody woman's gone too far this time. She's out of control, and I'm not going to take a fall for her."

The wheels of the suitcase hit a crack between two paving stones and flipped it onto its back. Max stopped to right it. When he turned back, the first of three police cars blocked the way forwards, its bumper nudging up to the rear of the ancient silver vehicle with the broken passenger-side window. The siren tones from the different vehicles blended into a discordant wail until one by one they fell silent. At the same time, the intense blue flashing lights also turned off, leaving an imprint on Max's retina.

A mask of despair occupied Nigel Perrin's face. "No," he moaned. He hesitated for a moment, then came to a decision. "Quick, follow me."

"You're not in trouble with the police, are you Dad? I thought we were—"

"Just do as I say for once."

Max shook his head and grabbed the handle of the small suitcase. His father was running faster than he had ever seen him do before.

Perrin glanced behind. The gap between them had extended to ten metres. "For Christ's sake, leave that behind."

"But it's got all—"

"Just leave it!"

Max turned back to where a large group of policemen gathered beside the now silent police cars. He released the suitcase handle and broke into a sprint in the opposite direction. Despite the head start, he arrived at the revolving door at the entrance to the building a couple of paces ahead of his father. Both men barrelled into the same compartment. Max shoved against the glass. Sensing the pressure being applied against it, the mechanism braked and halted.

"Let it go," Perrin said, jerking his head around to check on the progress of the policemen. "You can't make it go any faster." One of the men was crouched by the abandoned suitcase, talking into a radio. The rest were jogging towards them and would be at the door in a matter of seconds.

With agonising slowness, the glass panels lurched back into movement. As soon as the gap was wide enough, Max slipped through into the stuffy warmth of the foyer. Perrin emerged and sprinted across the tiled floor, drawing several bemused glances from the small number of onlookers. He reached the sealed double doors and fumbled in his pocket for his identity card.

"Where are we going?" Max asked.

Perrin said nothing as the red light changed to green. The locking mechanism released. He barged through two steps ahead of his son. The doors swung back into position and locked with an audible click.

"Dad, I asked where we're going."

Perrin halted at a door labelled with a large flame logo. Panting for breath, he turned to face Max.

"God knows why, but I'm going to try to warn that madwoman."

## Monday 17th January 2033

Rosalind Baxter glanced at the phone's display. That was the second time in a minute that reception had tried to get hold of her. It could mean only one thing. The police had arrived. There was still time. She had allowed the guards to go home early. Now that the fugitives were accounted for, their services were no longer required. Nobody knew where she was apart from Nigel Perrin, and he had departed ten minutes ago.

It wouldn't take long to dispose of the evidence, and then what? The police might have their suspicions, but they wouldn't be able to prove anything. There might be some awkward questions to answer, but she had no doubts that any prospect of criminal prosecutions would soon be swept under the carpet when she delivered a cure.

She placed the tablet computer on the metallic grid of the combustion chamber floor. She smiled at her good fortune. Not only had the email been blocked because the attachment was too large, but Floyd and Jason had been foolish enough to leave the machine in the car. The security guard had found it on the back seat after breaking the rear window.

Rosalind straightened up and looked down at the girl. She was still unconscious, facing the sliding door. Her head lolled to one side in the wheelchair. It was probably for the best. She would only struggle if she realised what was about to happen to her.

It would be a tight squeeze, but all three adults would fit in. She retraced her steps to the main part of the room. Floyd sat in one wheelchair, the right side of his face caked in blood from the gash in his temple. She had strapped his arms and legs to the frame of the chair with plastic ties. His eyes were closed, and his breathing sounded wet and shallow.

Beside him sat Jason, similarly restrained in a wheelchair. In contrast to his father, he was clearly conscious. His terrified eyes darted about the room as he struggled against his restraints. A cloth gag tied across his mouth prevented him from speaking.

"It's ironic that you should all be in wheelchairs," Rosalind said as she directed Jason's chair towards the heavy door of the furnace. He tried to speak through the gag as the wheels rattled across the thick metal grating. She positioned him to Antimone's left.

"You only have yourself to blame," she said. "If you'd done as I asked, you wouldn't be in this situation. I'm sorry it's come to this, but you know too much."

Jason attempted to talk again, but the gag turned his words into muffled grunts.

"You're trying to tell me that you told the police the whole story, right?" Rosalind said. "The thing is, that's *all* it is without proof, a story, and the evidence is lying there on the floor beside you."

She paused as if listening to him. "Oh, you sent an email to the police containing that encrypted file? Yes, I know. Unfortunately, it was too big and their server bounced it. Maybe you should've checked that they received it before storming in to rescue your helpless little cripple. After all that money I spent on your education, who'd have thought that you weren't even capable of sending a simple email? Still, I suppose it's partially down to your genetics. Anyway, much as I'm enjoying this little chat, I still have work to do."

Rosalind's footsteps echoed in the cramped metallic box as she strode across the gridded floor. She grabbed Floyd's wheelchair by the handles and swung it around so that it was facing the furnace. An electronic beep came from behind her.

Rosalind turned her head to the source of the noise and saw Nigel Perrin standing in the door frame beside his son.

## Monday 17th January 2033

"Nigel, why are you here? I thought you'd left?"

Perrin entered the room, his gaze focused on the injured man in the wheelchair. "The police have arrived." His eyes rose to meet Rosalind's and then dropped once more to her captive. "What are you doing?"

"What does it look like, Nigel? I'm disposing of the evidence."

"Is he dead?"

"No, not yet."

"Jesus, Rosalind. You're going to incinerate him while he's still alive?"

"I'm right out of sedative shots, so unless you have something suitable in your pocket, yes, that's the plan. I'm sure it'll be very quick."

Perrin swallowed hard but remained silent. The focus of his attention wandered to the open incinerator chamber. He took two tentative steps forward, trying to pick out details from the dim interior. He squinted and angled his head forwards as he attempted to make sense of what he was seeing.

Gasping with shock, he stepped backwards. "The girl and—that's not your son, is it?"

"No, he's not my son," Rosalind said, a frown creasing her forehead. "He's somebody who lived in my house for sixteen years and then betrayed me."

"Christ, Rosalind, you're mad. You're going to kill your own son?"

"I just told you, he's not my son. You don't get it, do you? He knows everything. He and Floyd hacked into my computer and downloaded a file containing all the details going right back to the beginning. He tried to send it to the police. If he wasn't so incompetent, they would have all the proof they need to put both of us away for the rest of our lives. I'm not going to let that happen. This work is too important for anybody or anything to stop it."

Perrin reached into his pocket for a pen and began absent-mindedly clicking the tip in and out. "So, you plan to incinerate three more people to cover it up?"

"Oh, come on, Nigel. How many have we already incinerated today? And how many women died because you deliberately made them pregnant?"

"What's she saying, Dad?"

Perrin had forgotten that his son was standing beside him. "Look, Max, it's complicated. Sometimes you have to—"

"Actually, it's quite simple really," Rosalind interrupted. "Your father abducted women off the street and impregnated them so he could use them as guinea pigs for our tests. Why else do you think he had those drugs in his office that you then stole and put into the drink at the party?"

Max turned to face his father. "Is it true, Dad?"

Perrin hung his head, then looked up and met his son's stare. "Yes, it's true. The women we took were drug addicts and prostitutes. They had a very low life expectancy, anyway. At least this way, they were doing something useful with their lives. I know it's not right, but we were trying to save the human race. Somebody had to make the sacrifice, so why not choose those who valued their own lives so little?"

A wintry smile flashed across Rosalind's face. "While you two have your debate about the morals of the situation, I've got a job to finish here. That is unless you both want to spend a long time in jail. Don't forget that Jason knows what you did too, Max. He probably also told Antimone."

She turned away from the father and son and propelled the wheelchair towards the dark interior of the chamber. She positioned it in front of Jason's chair.

"Goodbye Jason," she said. His head rested on his chest so she couldn't see his face.

As she spun around to leave, a voice called out from behind her.

"Now!"

## Monday 17th January 2033

The gag bit into the corners of Jason's mouth and obstructed his breathing. He inhaled loudly through his nose. His mother was talking to somebody. The sound of voices carried into the dimly lit chamber, but he couldn't make out the individual words. A droplet of sweat trickled down his chest as he struggled to free his hands. The tie-wraps were far stronger than the thin plastic suggested, and all he succeeded in doing was deepening the welts that already ran around both wrists.

Jason forced himself to relax. There had to be a way out of this. He glanced to his left. Antimone was still unconscious, her head lolling backwards, but unlike him, she wasn't bound. If only he could wake her, she might be able to release them.

He focused his attention on the gag. He contorted his face, trying to loosen it enough to get the knot out of his mouth. His frustration grew as the material resisted all his attempts. He slumped back in the chair and groaned in despair. Tendrils of panic teased away at the edges of his mind and threatened to overwhelm him. His mother apparently planned to burn them alive. Would she really go through with it? How much pain would he feel? How long would it last?

An idea occurred to him. He strained against the tie at his wrist and pushed his elbow forwards as far as it would go. At the same time, he angled his head downwards so that his chin was touching his shoulder. It felt as if the joint was about to dislocate as he tried to dislodge the gag, but he did manage to shift it down a millimetre or two. He attacked the task with renewed vigour. After a few more seconds, the damp material rolled down and hung loosely around his neck.

He turned to face the unconscious girl. "Antimone," he whispered.

No response.

"Antimone," this time a little louder. "Wake up."

A slight movement of her head. "Come on, for Christ's sake wake up."

Antimone's eyes fluttered. A dribble of saliva ran down from the corner of her mouth. She moaned as her head lolled to the side.

"Antimone, if you want to live you have to wake up."

A single cough. Heavy lids blinked open as she stared uncomprehendingly at her surroundings. "Where am I?" Her voice came out as a low rasp.

"Thank God. We haven't got long. We need to get out of here."

"Where are we? What's going on?"

"I don't want to frighten you, but my mother's got us in an incinerator. She's talking to somebody. If we don't do something, we're going to die. Is there any way you can loosen these tie-wraps?"

Antimone's frightened eyes darted around the interior of the chamber. "An incinerator?"

"Come on, the clock's ticking. My hands and feet are tied down so I can't move."

Shock tinged Antimone's words. "She's going to burn us alive?"

"Yes, unless we can free ourselves somehow."

Antimone moved her wheelchair forwards a short distance and peered down at the black plastic bands binding Jason's arms and legs to the chair. "I don't know. These are impossible to break without a cutter of some sort. You know, a knife or scissors." Her head jerked from left to right as she surveyed her surroundings. "I can't see anything in here that we could use."

Jason racked his brains, but his thoughts kept returning to the flames that could turn them to ash at any second. "Come on, Antimone. Think."

"I can't see anything in here that would do the job."

"She's talking to somebody outside. Maybe they can help us."

Antimone cocked her head to listen. "That sounds like Dr Perrin. He's in this as deep as she is. He was the main doctor who was investigating why I survived. We certainly can't trust him."

"So, we're dead then?"

Antimone's thoughts turned to her son. He would grow up without a mother—if they let him grow up at all. She couldn't allow that to happen. "If I can get her on the floor, it should even things up a bit."

"How are you going to do that?"

"I'm going to have to knock her over first."

"How do we know she's even going to come back in here?"

Antimone frowned. "We don't, but Floyd's not here. I assume he arrived with you."

"Yeah, she grabbed him at the same time as me, but what's that got to do with it? He was unconscious when I last saw him. He's certainly not going to be in any condition to help us."

"Whatever condition he's in, she's going to want to dispose of him just like us. He knows too much. So, somebody is going to have to come inside."

Jason struggled against the ties again. With mounting desperation, he tried to bounce the wheelchair forwards.

"Keep it down," Antimone hissed. "We don't want her being prepared."

"I can't believe she's really going to do this. Maybe she's just trying to scare us."

"She's certainly doing that. I'm not prepared to gamble that it's a bluff, though."

"You don't know her like I do. I've lived with her for sixteen years. She wouldn't do that to me."

Antimone's tone hardened. "Listen, Jason, there's something you've got to understand. That psychotic bitch out there—don't think of her as your mother—is going to kill us both unless we stop her. I've seen what she can do. She's more than capable of putting us down."

Jason swallowed hard. "Okay, so what's the plan?"

"I pretend I'm still unconscious. I need you to tell me when to move."

Jason did his best to hide the quaver in his voice. "I'll shout when it's time."

## Monday 17th January 2033

The wheelchair surged ahead under Antimone's powerful strokes. The plan might have worked had her right wheel not clashed with the chair in which Daniel Floyd was restrained. As it was, the contact soaked up some of her forward momentum and threw her off course. Instead of striking Rosalind full on, the footrests caught her with a glancing blow. It was sufficient to knock the woman off her feet but not powerful enough to incapacitate her. The wheelchair slewed to the left and came to a halt, straddling the runners which guided the furnace door.

It took Antimone's eyes a moment to adjust to the bright illumination from the ceiling lights. The collision had winded her, and she struggled to recover her bearings. The wheel of her chair was jammed up against the wall of the incineration chamber. Nigel and Max Perrin stood side by side, staring in shock at the scene before them. Rosalind Baxter knelt on all fours, blood splattering the floor from a gash to her forehead.

Antimone tried frantically to release the trapped wheel, but the chair refused to budge. "Max, Dr Perrin, you've got to help us."

Father and son remained silent and motionless. Rosalind slowly rose to her feet and fixed Antimone with a hate-filled stare. Blood trickled from the wound to her head. She brushed a hand over her face, leaving a streak of crimson across her cheeks like an elaborate war-paint. Her voice shook with fury when she spoke. "You stupid little…"

Rosalind limped towards the immobile wheelchair and glared at Antimone. When she was a pace away, she halted, her face distorted in a grimace of rage. She lifted her leg, drew it back and stamped it into Antimone's knees.

Even though she felt no direct pain, Antimone cried out at the shock of the blow. The wheelchair lurched backwards a few inches. Rosalind moved closer and lashed out for a second time. The wheel broke free, and the chair rolled back a short distance before tipping on its side. Antimone used her arms to break her fall but found herself lying on the metal grating, her legs entangled in the wheelchair's struts.

Rosalind surveyed the three prisoners, her eyes picking them out one at a time. She inhaled deeply, then turned her back and hobbled to the sliding door. She grasped the handle and pulled it towards her. The door rattled as it ran along the runners and closed halfway. She took two paces to the right and reached for the handle again. The door slammed shut with a metallic clang.

She extended a finger to the green button. A beep from behind made her hesitate. She craned her neck and watched as Karen Atkins led a group of six men wearing dark coloured uniforms into the room.

"Mrs Baxter and Dr Perrin, you're both under arrest."

## Monday 17th January 2033

Rosalind turned to face the group of policemen. "What are we under arrest for?"

"Where do I start?" Karen Atkins said. "Why don't we go back sixteen years or so?"

"You've got no proof."

"So, you know what I'm talking about? Good. Well, let me tell you what I know. Seventeen or eighteen years ago you started doing research on an artificial virus, creating its DNA from scratch. Somebody had the bright idea of mixing it with the flu virus to create a pathogen that would spread more easily. One of your researchers at the time, an Eileen Floyd—that's Daniel's wife—threatened to become a whistle-blower and stop what she regarded as dangerous research. To keep her quiet, you kidnapped her. Did I mention she was pregnant with Jason at the time?"

"So, you worked out who the boy's real mother was?"

"Yes, when we discovered that Daniel Floyd was Jason's biological father, it didn't take much effort to determine who his mother was."

"Well done," Rosalind said, clapping slowly. "It's only taken you sixteen years. And who says our police are slow on the uptake?"

"So, you framed her husband, Daniel, for her murder," Kat continued. "He didn't even know she was pregnant. You held onto her for eight months and used her as a test subject. She was the first victim of the Orestes virus. She didn't know you had infected her and nearly escaped. By the time you recaptured her, she had infected a number of other people. After that, it didn't take long for the virus to spread across the world. I still don't understand why you adopted Jason. I can only assume it was because you wanted to continue studying him."

For the first time since the police had arrived, Perrin spoke. "It was an accident. We never meant to release it. If that woman hadn't—"

"Shut up, Nigel," Rosalind snapped. "They've got nothing."

Kat ploughed on. "So, once that happened, hundreds of thousands of women died in childbirth, and the world desperately began looking for a cure. But you had a head start, didn't you? As the creators, you knew its exact genetic makeup and had already developed anti-virals for the laboratory-generated version. It was only a short step from there to developing the drug that propelled Ilithyia Biotechnology to the forefront of medical science and turned you both into multi-millionaires."

Perrin fiddled with the collar of his shirt. "We were only trying to rectify our—"

"Pure supposition," Rosalind said, talking over him.

"But that's where it started to go wrong. The virus mutated, and the treatment became ineffective. Now you were in the same boat as all the other medical companies, desperately trying to come up with something that would actually work. It was the flu part of the virus that mutated. Ironically, that's what Eileen Floyd tried to warn you about in the first place. Fast forward sixteen years or so. The number of women who have died because of your actions is now in the millions, and your son gets Antimone Lessing pregnant while he's under the influence of some nasty drug that also originated from this facility. She doesn't know she's pregnant until it's too late for an abortion. By sheer coincidence, she ends up giving birth here and somehow survives. I understand her child survived too despite you writing a death certificate claiming that he died from a biological infection."

Rosalind folded her arms. "I had nothing to do with any death certificate. You won't find my name on it."

"So now you have the clue you need. You fake Antimone's death, making it look as if she died like all the other women. You study her in your basement laboratory, out of sight of any medical ethics committees. The only problem is that your son likes this girl and discovers you're holding her prisoner. He breaks her out, but then you grab her again. Luckily for us, he told me the whole thing. How did I do? Is that about right?"

"Very clever," Rosalind said. "A very good story, but with no proof whatsoever. Have you got any witnesses? Where's the evidence?"

"Oh, I'm sure if we dig deep enough, we'll find something. So where are you keeping them?"

"Who?"

"You know exactly who I mean, Mrs Baxter: Jason, Daniel Floyd, Antimone Lessing and her son, Paul."

"I have no idea."

"Well, that's strange because we have several eyewitnesses who saw you talking to the three adults no more than half an hour ago. What about you, Dr Perrin? You're heavily implicated in all this. What have you got to say for yourself?"

Perrin swallowed loudly. "Um… I don't know." He stared hard at the floor.

"The thing is, if one of you were to talk to me, we'd look very favourably on that. I can't guarantee you wouldn't serve any time, but your sentence would probably be much more lenient."

Perrin raised his head sharply and returned Kat's gaze. He turned briefly to Rosalind and back to Kat again. He licked his lips. "Um… if we had a cure, would that help to reduce the sentence too?"

"Yes, I'm sure a judge would show leniency for something like that," Kat said.

"Okay, I'll tell you everything. Sorry, Rosalind, but I can't live with this any longer."

"Don't say anything, Nigel," Rosalind growled. "They don't have any evidence."

"No, I've made my mind up."

Rosalind moved so quickly that it caught everybody else in the room by surprise. She lunged forwards and snatched up the pen poking from the front pocket of Perrin's jacket. She drew it back and jabbed the point into his eye. Perrin screamed and held both hands to the protruding cylinder, blood pouring through his fingers. But she wasn't finished yet. She formed her hand into a fist and slammed it into his face, driving the pen deep into his brain.

Nigel Perrin collapsed to the floor, his body convulsing. His son knelt over him. "Dad! Dad!" he yelled.

The policemen surged forwards, but Rosalind had already returned to her position by the control box.

"If anybody moves, I push this," she screamed. A silence fell over the room, broken only by Max Perrin's sobs. "I mean it. There are three people inside this incinerator. I'm the only one you're going to be making a deal with now."

One of the men took a step forward.

"I warned you," Rosalind said.

Then she pressed the green button.

## Monday 17th January 2033

A ll eyes in the room focused on Rosalind. Even Max Perrin looked up from the prostrate body of his father.

"If I take my finger off this button, the furnace will start up. Once that happens, there's no stopping it until it completes its cycle."

"What do you want, Mrs Baxter?" Kat asked.

"Let me see. My arm's already starting to get a bit tired by the way. I want an amnesty for all previous crimes. My lawyers will have to check it over to make sure there are no loopholes. In return, I will complete the development of a cure for the Orestes virus, but I must be free to run my company how I see fit. I'm happy to make any deal conditional on the release of a treatment. Oh, and the people inside this furnace get to live."

"You're responsible for more deaths than any other person in living memory, and you just want us to sweep it all under the carpet? You're out of your mind."

"Well, I don't expect *you* to have the authority to make such a deal," Rosalind said, a thin smile lifting the corners of her mouth. "I'm guessing it'll have to go as high as the Prime Minister. Andrew Jacobs is a friend—well, maybe not a friend—but certainly an acquaintance of mine. I suggest you call him right away. I'm not sure how much longer my arm will hold up."

"I'll see what I can do," Kat said.

"You do that. Incidentally, I want all your colleagues to place their radios and mobile phones on the ground. I can't have you hatching some plot behind my back. I also want your phone on speaker so that I can hear what's being said. And don't mention where we are. Just so you know, if they try to cut off the power, this facility has a backup generator. If the lights so much as flicker, I'll release this button. Just tell them that I'll produce a cure if they agree to my terms. Otherwise, I'll destroy all the research and the girl too."

"You heard her." Kat turned to the six uniformed men. "Put your phones and radios on the floor."

"When you've done that, sit with your back to the wall over there," Rosalind said. She glanced down at Max, still crouched over his dead father.

"You," she said, pointing at the nearest policeman. "I assume you're carrying handcuffs or something like that."

The man nodded.

"Right, I want you to restrain the boy. I don't trust him not to do something stupid."

Max stared up at her as he struggled to comprehend the meaning of her words. When they finally sank in, a look of hatred filled his face. "You murdering bitch," he screamed. He tried to stand up but slipped in his father's blood.

The policeman lunged forwards, enveloping Max in a bear hug.

"Help him," Kat snapped.

Two other men joined the struggle. Within seconds they had cuffed Max's hands behind his back. Still struggling against his captors, Max raised his head from the floor. Blood streaked one cheek. "I'll kill you for this," he yelled.

"Restrain his feet too," Rosalind said, "then put him against the wall with the rest of you."

The three men lifted the writhing boy and carried him to join their colleagues.

"I'll kill you," Max sobbed, mucus and tears mingling with the smears of blood.

## Monday 17th January 2033

The beep from the electronic lock ratcheted up the tension that had enveloped the room. It had been ninety minutes since Kat had made the first of several phone calls. Standing apart from the seated policemen were two men wearing business suits but no tie, deep in discussion with each other. They were Rosalind's lawyers and had arrived half an hour earlier. They didn't seem happy about the situation and, at that exact point in time, were discussing the downside if Rosalind failed to deliver on her side of the bargain.

The door opened slowly. Two dark-suited men stood framed in the doorway. They held identical poses, right arm folded across the chest, right hand hidden inside the black jacket. Their eyes swept the room for any sign of imminent danger. When their inspection was complete, they stepped into the room leaving enough of a gap between them for Andrew Jacobs to walk through.

The Prime Minister glanced at the seated police officers. His eyes widened in shock as they focused on the dead body of Nigel Perrin. With a conscious effort, he directed his attention to Rosalind Baxter.

"About time, Andrew," she said. "I was beginning to think you weren't going to come."

"I'm a busy man, Mrs Baxter."

"So that's how it's going to be, is it? Well, Prime Minister, we seem to have a situation here. My terms are simple: an amnesty for any past crimes and freedom to run my company as I see fit. In return, I will provide you with a treatment for the Orestes virus."

"Yes, Mrs Baxter, my people told me about your proposal. I understand that you were responsible for creating the virus in the first place."

"It has been suggested that might be the case, but you're not going to get me to admit to anything unless you sign the amnesty. Just so you know, my arm is getting extremely tired."

"And you have three people trapped inside the incinerator chamber. I'm assuming that if you release that button, it turns on."

"That's right, Andrew, and if that happens, all our research and the only person to survive childbirth in fifteen years go up in flames."

"Your son's in there too, I hear."

A look of anger flitted across Rosalind's face. "He's not my son. I adopted him. Then he… well, never mind. Are you going to sign the documents, or are you going to consign those three people and thousands of women to a needless and painful death?"

"We don't negotiate with terrorists, Mrs Baxter."

"Is that a no then? I'll be sure to mention that you declined my offer when I go to trial. I'm sure that will play well with the electorate. Even your good looks won't get you out of that one."

Andrew Jacobs focused his gaze on Perrin's dead body. He sighed deeply and slowly raised his eyes to meet Rosalind's belligerent stare. He hesitated for a moment as he considered his options. Finally, he came to a decision. "On this occasion, I might be prepared to make an exception. However, any deal we make will be conditional on you delivering a working treatment."

"I've already offered that, Prime Minister."

"You will be placed under house arrest until such time as we have independent proof of the efficacy of any drugs your company produces. After that point, we can't allow you to remain as the CEO. You'll sell the company, and you'll donate ninety percent of the proceeds to childcare charities. That's my final offer."

"You want me to give away ninety percent of the company I've devoted the last twenty years of my life to?"

"I would've thought that was far preferable to spending the rest of your life in jail, Mrs Baxter, and I can assure you that prison wouldn't be a pleasant experience once the details of your exploits got out."

"And there would be a media ban on any news relating to Ilithyia's involvement in the creation of the Orestes virus?" Rosalind's gaze centred on the seated form of Max Perrin.

"Yes, although we don't have jurisdiction over the international press."

"If I agree, I think it would be in your interests to keep it out of the newsfeeds too. You and your party's ratings would certainly suffer if this deal ever became public knowledge."

"Yes, Mrs Baxter. Mutually assured destruction is the technical term, I believe."

Rosalind frowned and stared at the floor for a couple of seconds. Then she raised her head. "Alright, Andrew, I accept your terms. Get them written up and pass them by my lawyers. I'd like you and your men to remain here until everything's signed."

"Don't worry. I have no intention of leaving until this is resolved."

"Oh, and by the way, my finger is getting really fatigued. I'm sure you can see the need for expediency."

## Seven months later

Rosalind Baxter reached forwards and held the stem of the wineglass between her fingers. The ruby coloured liquid clung to the edges as she swirled the contents and inhaled the earthy aroma. She tilted the glass back and allowed the liquid to brush against her lips. Room temperature, just as it should be. She sipped a small amount and rolled it around the inside of her mouth. With a sigh of satisfaction, she returned the glass to the place mat.

Rosalind picked up the bottle and inspected the label: Chateau Margaux, Premier Grand Cru Classe, 1975. Not the finest vintage but pretty damned good all the same and at over five hundred pounds a bottle, certainly not cheap. Not that money was an issue. Her bank account balance hovered somewhere between nine and ten digits now that the sale of Ilithyia had finally gone through. It wasn't as much as she had once dreamed of, but it was more than enough to last the rest of her life in considerable comfort. Even after donating ninety percent of the proceeds to charity, the remaining ten percent amounted to over eight hundred million pounds. If she drank a bottle of this vintage every day, it would still take over several thousand years to exhaust the funds she had amassed.

She hadn't seen Jason in months. He had collected his things accompanied by a social worker a couple of days after the incident in the incinerator room. She heard he was living with the Lessing family and that both he and Antimone were now attending a state school. Antimone's mother was looking after the child while the teenagers were at school. If Rosalind was honest with herself, she missed the company of another human being in the house, but she felt no remorse for her actions towards her adopted son. He had brought everything on himself when he chose the disabled girl in preference to the woman who had given him everything over the last sixteen years.

She leant back in the armchair and allowed the strains of Beethoven's violin concerto in D major to wash over her. Her enjoyment was disturbed by the banging of a door on the other side of the house. She rose to her feet and stared out through the darkness at the well-tended garden, faintly illuminated by the glow from the lights inside. A summer storm was due to build in strength that night, peaking at some point in the early hours of the morning. She closed the window and returned to her chair.

The door banged again. Rosalind gave a tut of exasperation. Another window must be open somewhere. She stood up once again and padded in her bare feet into the hall. The sound came from upstairs. Now that she thought about it, she remembered leaving the bedroom window ajar. She marched up the stairs and opened the door to check. Sure enough, the curtains were billowing in the stiff breeze. She strode across the room and pulled the latch shut without bothering to turn on the light.

Rosalind retraced her steps and sat once more. She grabbed the remote control and set the playback to the start of the second movement. The melancholy tone of the violins matched her mood exactly. She took a sip of the wine and closed her eyes, holding the glass in her hand. The notes seemed to resonate in her chest as they blended into one another. She swallowed another mouthful and started humming the melody.

"Hello, Mrs Baxter."

Rosalind jerked forwards, sloshing the remaining quarter of the contents on her cream-coloured trousers. "Jesus, Max, what the hell are you doing here? I thought you'd be in prison or youth detention."

Max smirked. "You say that after everything you've done. You're really quite something, aren't you? They can't prosecute me without the whole ugly story coming out, and that would jeopardise your little arrangement, wouldn't it? Anyway, I thought we needed to have a little chat."

Something cold ran down Rosalind's spine. "I'm calling the police." She placed the now empty glass on the mat and pushed off the chair.

"I don't think so. Sit down."

Rosalind found herself sitting down again. "What? I don't—"

"That drug I took from my Dad's office. I kept some. I thought it might come in useful again once I'd seen how effective it was."

"But—"

"Yes, Mrs Baxter, while you were upstairs, I poured some—rather a lot, in fact—into your wine. Ironic, isn't it, that you should fall victim to the same drug that you used to kidnap all those other women?"

Rosalind stared at the empty glass. Her head spun, and she experienced a strong sensation of watching herself from a distance. She tried to speak, but her mouth refused to work. A deepening panic built up inside. Try as she might, she was powerless to move. Whatever was coming next couldn't be good.

"You murdered my father in front of me. Now it's payback time."

"I... I..."

"No. Don't talk. I want you to listen. You rammed a pen into my father's eye. And then you shoved it all the way into his brain. That wasn't a very nice thing to do, was it?"

Rosalind lifted her eyes, trying to focus on his face.

Max reached into his pocket and pulled out a pen. "This is identical to the one you killed my father with." He clicked the end three times in quick succession. "My father used to buy them in bulk, that's how I know it's the same."

He took a step closer and handed the writing implement to Rosalind. "Here, take this."

She reached out and grasped it between her fingers.

"Make sure the tip is sticking out."

Rosalind's eyes seemed to move of their own volition. Her gaze pinpointed on the tiny circle of blue ink.

"Now I want you to listen carefully. You're going to push the pen into your right eye, and you're going to do it very slowly. You're only going to stop when I tell you to. Is that understood? By the way, you may scream if you want."

Rosalind's hand shook as she moved it closer to her face. "N-N-No"

"Yes, you're going to do this, Mrs Baxter, I want you to feel what my father felt before he died."

The tip quivered as it approached her eyeball.

"Do it!" Max yelled.

The point touched. Eyelashes fluttered up and down in a blur of movement.

"Do it!"

Rosalind pushed the tip through the surface of her eye. The tendons in her neck stretched tight. A howl of agony erupted from her mouth. When she had exhausted her breath, she drew in a deep, shuddering lungful of air and screamed again.

Max watched impassively as the pen penetrated millimetre by millimetre, every tiny movement followed by an ear-splitting shriek.

"That's far enough."

Rosalind's trembling fingers relaxed their grip a fraction.

"I could kill you right now, but I want you to suffer. You're going to wait until the music ends. When that happens, you're going to push it in as far as it will go. In the meantime, you're going to think about all the terrible things you've done in your life. Do you understand?"

Max raised his voice. "Do you understand?"

Blood, snot, and tears mingled together and dribbled down Rosalind's face. Her breathing came in short pants, each breath accompanied by a moan of torment. Her head moved in an almost imperceptible nod.

"Remember when the music ends, the pen has to go all the way in."

Her good eye focused on the panel showing the time remaining on the album.

When she forced her gaze upwards again, he was gone.

*The story continues in Termination: The Boy Who Died*

# Author's Notes

Dear Reader,

I hope you enjoyed reading this book. If you did, I would be extremely grateful if you tell your friends and leave a review on Amazon, Goodreads or preferably both. Reviews are an important factor in helping to sell books and are especially important for independent authors. I pay particular attention to all comments and use them to try to make my books better.

If you would like to keep up to date with future books, please sign up to the mailing list at www.rjne.uk.

I would like to express my gratitude to my early reviewers and readers, including Tony C, Tim, Fergus, Brian, Caroline, Juliette and members of my Facebook launch team. Special mentions go to Ross for his continual encouragement and advice (sorry, there are still no pink spaceships in the book!), Alex for her editorial work, Marika for her many useful suggestions, Tony M for the early manuscript mark-up and Sowmya and Mark P for their last-minute feedback on ways to improve the story. All the above gave their time freely to help me with this book, and their efforts are greatly appreciated.

Thanks also to Hampton Lamoureux for the cover design. He has designed the covers for all the books in this series, and I'm in awe of his talents.

My wife, Judith, and daughter, Emily, also deserve a mention for their patience during the writing process. I think both are heartily sick of our discussions about the Decimation world, but I couldn't do it without their support. I would also like to thank the members of the Facebook One Stop Fiction Authors Resource Group (OSFARG for short) and in particular Kathryn Bax for the stream of interesting and useful writing advice, including information on how to set up a launch team.

Several of the above told me they would have preferred a particular character to get his/her just desserts. You may be pleased to discover that a sequel is imminent in the form of Termination: The Boy Who Died.

Although the story takes place fifteen years in the future, many of the technologies I describe are in development now. Advances in flexible display screens are regularly in the news as are self-driving cars. The problem of how to stop pedestrians or other road users from taking advantage of a computer driver is something I have given a lot of thought to. Using the car's cameras to identify perpetrators is fairly obvious but is unfortunately easily thwarted. The phone touch screen technology I describe is already available from a company called Ultrahaptics. Smart watches seem to be all the rage but maybe not yet with the capability of detecting a pregnancy. I'm not aware of anybody designing a Marilyn skirt or a T-shirt that displays the wearer's internal organs, so these are my gifts to the world!

The possibility of a pandemic is all too real as evidenced by the recent Covid-19 outbreak. When combined with the threat of antimicrobial resistance, the future begins to look like a scary place. Fortunately, there are no viruses I know of that cause the symptoms I portray.

If you enjoyed this book you might also like to try some of my other novels including, The Rage, The Colour of the Soul or Assassin's Web.

As I mentioned earlier, the story continues in Termination: The Boy Who Died. More information can be found on my website at www.rjne.uk.

Thanks for reading.

Richard T. Burke
March 2021

To read the author's blog and to see news of upcoming books, please visit www.rjne.uk or follow him on Twitter @RTBurkeAuthor or Facebook (https://www.facebook.com/RichardTBurkeAuthor).

Printed in Great Britain
by Amazon